KILL HIM, AGAIN

Center Point
Large Print

**This Large Print Book carries the
Seal of Approval of N.A.V.H.**

KILL HIM, AGAIN

W. R. Garwood

CENTER POINT LARGE PRINT
THORNDIKE, MAINE

This Center Point Large Print edition
is published in the year 2022 by arrangement with
Golden West Inc.

Originally published in the US by Bath Street Press.

The text of this Large Print edition is unabridged.
In other aspects, this book may vary
from the original edition.
Printed in the United States of America
on permanent paper sourced using
environmentally responsible foresting methods.
Set in 16-point Times New Roman type.

ISBN 978-1-63808-324-5 (hardcover)
ISBN 978-1-63808-328-3 (paperback)

The Library of Congress has cataloged this record
under Library of Congress Control Number: 2022930370

To
Bob and Greg
who heard the tale
many times before.
Our trails will cross
again, old pards.

KILL HIM, AGAIN

1   Billy Meets an Angel

He didn't seem like a man on the run.

He looked more like a kid, riding down a dusty mesa road that mild New Mexican night of July 14, 1881.

But he was a wanted man—wanted mighty bad by Sheriff Pat Garrett of Lincoln County.

And he was still on the same old troubled trail that had led him into that bloody feud, the Territorial papers called The Lincoln County War.

And his troubles hadn't shrunk away any in the past year.

It was now two months-and-a-half since he'd broken out of Pat's jail up at Lincoln—fifteen days ahead of the Santa Fe Hangman, and he still wasn't ready to leave the Territory.

Now as he rode back toward the crumbling hamlet of Fort Sumner from a fiesta, with Celsa Gutierrez, his side-kick Barlow and Barlow's girl Margarita, vagrant mesa winds tossed Celsa's amber hair about.

The buckskin outfit covering the curves of Celsa's swelling breasts and rounded thighs was tinted tawny white by the gleaming "Peso" moon—but The Kid could only think of that other girl back at the dance.

9

She'd arrived at *Doña* Luna's *bailé* at *Puerto del Luna* after the festivities began—a small, slender, young lady in a plain black dress, with a pin of silver at her throat and a silver comb in her dark, upswept hair. She was followed about by a stiff-necked, young Mexican all duded up in fancy, gold-laced pants and gold-encrusted jacket.

The Kid hadn't heard who she might be. He'd been too busy swinging Celsa and the other girls around the dance floor. But the young Mexican had pointed him out to the girl. Billy caught some of the fellow's lingo, ". . . outlaw from Lincoln . . . killed twenty-one . . . wanted by . . ."

He saw that she was watching him, and that her eyes kept moving back to him, as though she couldn't have enough of staring at such a *lobo*.

They were plumb beautiful—those jet black eyes. Her face, framed by smoothly coiffed black hair, was that of a she-angel he'd once seen painted over an altar at Albuquerque. That straight nose, those gently slanted cheekbones and firmly rounded chin—was all angel. But no angel ever had a mouth half so inviting.

Si—The Kid had done his share of looking also. She was an angel right enough, but an angel too high for a kid on the dodge.

As the evening had swung along, Barlow got himself half-soused from a bottle he'd concealed outside the ranch house.

That wasn't good. Old *Doña* Luna only allowed Billy to her *fiestas* because of the fighting he'd done back in '78 for her husband, the lately deceased *Don* Estaban—and old Cattle King John Chisum.

Near to midnight as he nudged Barlow back toward the house, fretfully followed by the girls, figures were silhouetted against the orange rectangle of the open doorway.

Doña Luna came out with the young Mexican "heel fly"—and the girl in black. "*Señor* Bonny. *Señor* Barlow." The old lady was short with them. "May I present *Señor* Francisco Sandoval, and his sister, *Señorita* Esmeralda Sandoval. They are in the Territory from El Paso del Norte, staying for the time with the Chisum family."

Billy bowed from the waist, the way he recalled *caballeros* below the border behaving. Barlow nodded as Celsa and Margarita stared at the moon.

"I had a wish to meet Billy The Kid. It will, perhaps, be something to tell my grandchildren, someday." The girl's eyes flashed in a face as sedate as the old *Doña*'s. Her brother seemed irked with the ceremony.

Up close, the girl was pretty as a painted dream. Billy was thankful that the light was so poor that she couldn't see the blood heating the tan of his face.

Doña Luna turned away after the introduction,

to see the Sandovals into a conveyance, hitched to a darkened corner of the building.

Others were now emerging into the moonlight. The fiddles were fading into whispers. The fiesta was over.

"*Billeto* . . . now the *bailé* is finished—and we've got to ride all the way back to Sumner. Barlow ought to be shot." Celsa fumed while The Kid went around to the corral at the back.

The Sandoval buggy creaked past, as he came up with the mounts, yellow wheels glinting in the lamplight. Young Sandoval held the reins, ignoring The Kid, but the girl, Esmeralda, glancing out, waved a pale hand to him.

He raised his *sombrero*, watching the buggy blend into the night. "Esmeralda, goodbye. Happy flights among the rest of the angels," he grinned to himself.

On the ten mile ride homewards, Margarita scolded as Celsa and Billy laughed. Her words flew about Barlow's ears. "*Inconstante*! *Perfidio* . . . *boyaro* . . . act like *Billeto*? Same size . . . face almost . . . his nice . . . but yours . . . always out of sorts!"

Margarita was right. It was downright odd-like, how close he and Barlow looked. Almost like spittin' twins. That was one of the things drawing them together when they rode for the old Mule Shoe Ranch in '79—the year after the Lincoln County troubles burned out.

Jogging along toward Sumner, Barlow nipped away at a small flask and glumly cursed his girl and her chattering.

"Whyn't you gentle down?" The Kid rode up beside him. "All that *aguardiente* you got on the outside of has shriveled your head to about the size of a piñon nut."

"Don't go wet nursin' at me, Kid. I'm most old as you and a hell of a lot better lookin'."

"Maybe, but not as smart." Billy reached over and punched Barlow's shoulder. "Bobby Bee, I'm just tryin' to keep you in one piece. Ain't we been friends since I run into you in Arizona?"

"I know that, don't I?" Barlow grumbled, slapping at his horse's head with the reins. "What'd you think I come over here to hook up with you fer? Fer a feller, like you, on th' dodge, y'can use all th' friends you can git. And I'm sure a better friend of your'n than such folks as Jesse Evans."

"Yeah, I know," Billy answered. Just for a moment the mild breeze, sliding down from the foothills onto the mesa, seemed to grow colder as the moon wandered behind a stray cloud. Jesse still might be jailed in Texas—but you never knew.

2 And Near Becomes One

As they rode past the first of the small adobe huts that marked the western edge of the rambling settlement of Fort Sumner, a shadowy figure darted into their path.

"*Alto*! *Alto*!" The man threw up a hand. "*Compañeros . . . mucho peligro*! They say Pat— Pat Garrett and riders have been out to Saval Guiterez'." It was Jesus Silva, one of The Kid's friends.

"Sure it was Garrett? Who's with him?" Billy ground out.

The stocky shadow of Silva swayed back and forth on the moon-washed ground. He was upset, wringing his hands. "God knows for sure. But your neck ain't worth *dos reales* if you should run into him." Silva tugged at The Kid's bridle. "Pile off, *amigo*, until we see if he's still around."

"Why—he's dusted back toward Lincoln by now. Pat don't ever tackle anyone past dark." It was big talk, but The Kid felt uneasy. That long-legged Mick was never going to drag him back any Goddam rope—never—no sir!

"That's th' stuff." Barlow sniggered and leaned over to paw at Celsa. She gave him a shove and pulled her pony up by The Kid.

"Let's stop," she pleaded, "who knows what that gringo's up to?"

"Oh ho, that's fine talk about your own brother-in-law, ain't it?" Billy chided her. "Pat must be lookin' for me to come back to his hoosegow. Well, *gracias*, Jesus, I reckon we'll stop by for supper." It wouldn't hurt to be careful, even though Garrett had no jurisdiction in this county—he was Sheriff of Lincoln County only.

They swung down and tied the horses to the splintered hedge before Silva's hut.

Billy lingered after the others went in, peering up the empty street of the old abandoned military post. It was late to be about in the sleepy hamlet, and as far as he could see, nothing moved.

Within the adobe, Barlow was demanding that Silva's wife, a tall Indian woman with a bad eye, cook them up a meal.

"*Si*—it would taste pretty fine. That's a good stretch from Luna's and the ladies could stay to supper," The Kid agreed.

But the girls protested that they should be home, or their folks would come looking. And if that *lobo* of a Garrett were about, he might come snooping close. No, it was better if they left.

Billy saw they were too upset for more funning. It showed him the trouble he could fetch down on the little community if he really stayed holed up around Sumner.

It wasn't that the whole village, oldster and

kid alike, wouldn't fight tooth and nail for him. They didn't like Garrett—even if he had married Celsa's sister a couple of years back. They remembered the Lincoln County War and the gang who'd put Pat into office afterward— old John Chisum and those crooked lawyers of the Santa Fe bunch. Both were bad tastes in the mouths of all Spanish-Americans hereabouts.

Billy went out with Celsa to help her mount the little paint pony. The white rose at her temple was a hazy star in the dusky red-gold of her hair, and her lips were close to his—close and clinging as he bade her *"buenos noches."*

When he helped her friend, Margarita, up into the saddle, that little flirt leaned against him, whispering, "be cautious *Billeto*, for our sakes."

Barlow was too busy with Silva's wine to come outside.

After the girls turned down the side lane that ran past the peach orchards of Sumner, and were gone in the night, Billy returned to the adobe. His nose wrinkled with anticipation at the rich, spice-red odors of the bubbling chili where it chuckled in a black pot over the fire.

Barlow hulked in the doorway, knife in one hand, bottle in the other. "This old she wolf," he mumbled, jerking a thumb at Silva's woman, "she'll fry up fresh beef if we fetch it from Maxwell's."

The Kid shook his head and yanked off his

16

worn *sombrero*. "Best stick close. Don't go a'paradin' around lookin' for trouble. Maybe not Garrett—but somebody's been around."

"T'ain't no trouble. No one's lookin' fer me. It's just a piece up to Pete Maxwell's and he's always got a fresh beef hung out on his gallery. Fact is I seed one there this mornin'."

"OK," Billy grinned. "Guess old high-pockets, if it was him, is out to Guiterez' ten miles off, or just plain gone. No one around here'd give him room to lay his backside anyhow."

Silva was so agitated that his hands shook, slopping wine from his cracked glass. "*Diablo* take them!" He chewed at the ends of his sparse, grey mustache, round face shining with sweat. "I told you, *Billeto*, you should go down into the old country." He wiped his damp palms on the knees of dirty, brown canvas trousers. "For weeks and weeks—Holy *Santa Clara*, we all been hammering away at your mule head. And you piddle away the summer with fiestas, Monte games and these empty-headed little sluts."

"Who'd have thought old Pat would have gumption enough to come sniffing down this way? Ain't even his baliwick . . . out of his own county." Billy rubbed his chin with his hand and winked at Barlow, who leaned against the doorway in a half-stupor.

"Go along and get your beef," said The Kid. "I can taste it now. In the mornin' we just might take

17

a little jaunt down to th' *República de Méjico*."

"I'll nose around a mite and be back with th' grub." Barlow was gone into the moonlight with his knife.

Billy was settled down by the fireplace, digging into his big, earthen pot of flaming hot chili—when a gunshot ripped the night quiet. There was another! The racket of the explosions was shattering.

"*Madre de Dios*. Holy Saints . . . ah the devils . . ." Silva and his woman were cowering in the kitchen's corner.

The Kid flung open the door, caution forgotten, and ran up the sandy street, dashing through Pete Maxwell's back gateway.

His eyes caught slight motion along the ghost-white slashes of the picket fence. Pulling his Colt, he thumbed two shots at the blurs. Bright spurts stabbed out into the moonlight.

The shadows fired back—guns booming. A bullet ripped through his left cheek, punching out a tooth. Yellow flashes spat at him again. The strangers were in force, shooting to kill.

With jaw and mouth spouting blood, Billy started back over the fence and took a slug through the left shoulder. Spun by the sledgehammer shock—he landed beyond the fence on his face. Staggering up in a daze, he emptied his pistol at the house as another bullet seared his scalp.

The black and silver world was a swirl of bloody sparks as he stumbled onto the gallery of the adobe behind Maxwell's.

A fat, shapeless woman wavered like drifting smoke as she tugged him into her room.

When he came to himself, the woman, old Deluveña, Maxwell's Indian serving woman, was packing his wounds with hot beef tallow to stop the blood flow. Her broad, dark face was creased with fright and hatred as she murmured curses upon "those gringos" at Maxwell's.

When she bound his head and shoulder with strips of cloth torn from her bed sheet, he muttered a request that his .44 be reloaded with shells from his waist belt.

The hut door opened and closed quickly as Celsa entered. The tiny, orange finger of the room's sole candle revealed a pair of emerald eyes ablaze with anxiety. "*Billeto*! Don't move. For the love of *Dios* don't make a sound, crazy one."

"Got to get out—can't wait for them to trap me in here . . ." He was up teetering on legs that seemed forty rods long. His head rang and throbbed as he struggled to speak. "Got to— Celsa. Can't wait in here." He lurched toward the door.

Both women threw themselves in his path. "*Escuhar salvajez*! Listen, wildness! Garrett— that was him! He's killed poor Barlow. Barlow lies upon the porch of Maxwell's. And he's just as dead as Maxwell's beeve—and they're passing him off for you—at least Pat is, and his two deputies, who are strangers, never having seen you—they agree with Pat. And that coward Pete, he says nothing at all." Celsa ran a trembling hand through disordered, flaming hair.

"Me?" he mumbled—jaw all afire. "Me? Why Garrett wouldn't be dumb enough to pull that. What's keepin' him over there?"

"Those shots of yours—Garrett thinks the village has him surrounded. He fears our people—for what he's done . . . and is afraid to come from the house, with his men, before daylight." She pushed and half supported him back to the rough bed.

He sagged back down, head swimming and pounding. Those wounds made him weak as a day-old calf. "Well . . . let'm call Barlow . . . Th' Kid. Wait till tomorrow . . . and he'll find out who . . ." Everything began dwindling away again.

At three in the morning, Old Deluveña, who'd slipped out, returned to her alley hut with The Kid's horse. A tall Mexican, wrapped in a serape, against night chill, sat astride a second horse beside the adobe. The two women guided Billy through the door. No sound came from the deathly silent house of Pete Maxwell.

"Here's Frank Lobato, come to ride with you

to his sheep camp to the south of Sumner. We've packed your saddle bags, your gun is loaded, and you must leave." Celsa spoke with soft urgency.

Still dazed, he recalled something of the fight and asked—"where's Barlow . . . where'm I goin'?"

"Here, climb up, *Billeto*." The man swung down and helped boost The Kid aboard his mount. He draped another serape over The Kid's shoulders.

"Barlow's lying stiff dead over there—with half the women of Sumner holding a wake *over your remains,*" Celsa whispered. "Garrett and his men are still barricaded in that fat Pete Maxwell's room. They think Pat killed The Kid."

3   But Escapes

Scrambling up over a rise in the barren mesa, two miles from his Pecos sheep camp, Juan Chivari halted for a breather.

Born seventy years before in Mexico's Chihuahua Provence, he was long used to the silent fury of the mid-day sun. But the vast, scorching glare of the fiery New Mexican noon was only partly responsible for his woeful expression. Juan's main concern was the loss of a prime lamb, strayed or seized by some predator while he lay sleeping off his whiskey head.

He peered among the mustard yellow Apache plume and the verdantly green rabbit brush, wiping at his aching forehead, and cursing the red-haired gringo who'd stopped at his campfire the previous night.

All was at *la siesta* in the heated, crystal light, except a pair of eddying, slowly circling dark flecks—buzzards riding the towering air currents above some dying or dead thing.

And while Juan stared dull-eyed at the drifting motes, wondering if they might not be circling his lost lamb, one scavenger began an awkward down-thrust spiral—while its companion veered away.

The distant crack of a gun came to him like the sound of a broken twig.

Someone behind those rolling ridges was picking off those feathered undertakers—and at a good height too.

Juan stood unmoving as the echo crumbled into whispers among rock and shrub. "He's good, that one," he marveled. Perhaps it was his *compadre* of last night. He hesitated, but no further sign or sound came to him through the heat-filled hush.

That red-headed stranger had been a generous gringo. He and Juan emptied one of the fellow's *bottelas* under the July stars. And he was wild, with eyes—crazy green like *El Tigre*. Upon awakening, Juan had been most gratified to find his windpipe whole and the gringo departed.

"Yet, he might have been pitched from his horse—if he had the big head, like me." Wiping his face on his soiled sleeve, Juan began to trudge forward.

He arrived at the tawny rim of the last rise in the course of five minutes. The dead buzzard lay off to his left, one wing caught upright by the stiff leaf of a yellow-tinted blazing star. Its back and breast were torn by the bullet, and drops of bright blood stained the yellow petals. Ants were already marching up and down the ruffled, jet feathers.

He turned away from the carrion and shambling to the crest of the hillock—froze in midstep.

A man lay beside a clump of creosote bush, pistol pointed straight at Juan.

"*Madre di Dios*! I mean no harm, *Señor*." Juan's brown fingers fanned out trembling over his hat. It wasn't the red-headed man, but another stranger—and bad hurt by the looks.

The stranger raised up on an elbow. His face was so swathed in blood-stained bandage that the herdsman could not be sure of his expression, until the man motioned with his six-gun. "*No temeroso*, *amigo*. (Don't be afraid, friend)."

"*Con mucho gusto*, *Señor*. You have lost your horse?"

The gringo, he was young, sat up and slid the .44 back into its weathered brown holster. He seemed about middle sized. His hair was brown and his eyes—pain-filled, yet piercing, were a blue-hazel, nearly grey. When he smiled at Juan, his large, almost prominent teeth flashed with whiteness.

"Guess I musta pitched off some time yester-day. After I left a sheep camp." He shook his head as if to clear it—"Anyway, when I came to a while back and saw those buzzards linin' up for th' fiesta—I threw a shot at one . . . and when you showed up just now—reckon I was ready for you, too."

"*Si, Señor*, that you were."

Juan approached and held out a wrinkled, brown hand. "Come with me, *Señor*, if you wish. My camp is only a mile back toward the river.

24

You need the water. *Nombre Dios*, the sun will fry the bullets in your *pistola*."

Gathering himself up from the rocky ground, the stranger took a step toward Juan—and fell, unconscious, into the bushes.

Though Juan was not large, he was raw-boned and hardy. Within moments, the pistol was transferred to his own belt, and the young stranger draped over his powerful shoulders.

He started back with his burden. The path campward seemed more rocky underfoot than before. And the sun, how it raged and broiled. Juan's head felt bad. He commenced to belabor that merry gringo of the past night, but found he needed his breath for the job at hand.

It was an endlessly long journey but at last Juan came to the beginning of the flat rangeland. Filled with coarse grasses, it ran two miles down to the winding Pecos. His camp was halfway to that rusty, red river.

When, at last, he arrived puffing and blown before his patched, green tent—the flock was already strung out on its way to the river. His two dogs, a black-and-brown mongrel, named *Canción*, or Song, for its mournful baying, and *Blanco*, a white cur with a touch of scotch border collie, were guarding a flank each of the slowly moving woolies.

Juan hunched into the tent, which lay in the flat patch of shade thrown by a gambel oak, and dropped the Gringo upon a rude cot. He opened the man's shirt and felt his chest. The stranger was breathing—but most slowly. He had a bad shoulder wound, and gunshots on scalp and jaw. The bandages were grimy but still tight. Juan feared to change them. The wounds could break open, and the old herdsman needed to watch his flock until they returned from the river. He could ill afford to lose more.

"Poor friend, small wonder you were so tipsy." Juan pulled off the young man's boots. He seemed to be a stockman from his garb of checkered grey shirt, black vest and dusty blue denim pants.

Juan unbuckled the man's half-filled cartridge belt and lay it beside his head, together with the pistol, a short-barreled, single-action .44 Colt, with pearl-handled grips.

The Gringo was pale—pale as his bandages. He murmured indistinctly, and now and then trembled. Juan covered him with a blanket. He moistened a bandana with some water from his canteen and placed it to the man's grey lips. There was little else he could do.

The old shepherd crawled back out of the tent and poured himself a stiff jolt from the remnants of a bottle that had escaped his drinking bout. If the wounded man came to himself, Juan would save a bit.

"*Dios*, mercy, I needed that." He glanced at the

sun. It journeyed toward the west and the time stood at near two o'clock. By now the flock was at the watering spot in the Pecos shallows.

"Nobody near but me and old *Señor Muerte* (Mister Death)," Juan mused aloud. "And he could fetch away the young Gringo before supper." He took another nip. *"La via esta duro, amigos* (the road is hard, friends).""

4 He Plans

At the first there was no such thing as time. There were dim stretches of awareness followed by blank emptiness.

He passed slowly through many periods of light and darkness—an endless string of days threaded together with slowly strengthening alertness—a rosary of days. At the start, some were scarlet with pain, others dull and burning yellow with fever, later they faded to the cooler olive-greens of simple peace. Now for the past week they had been bright, crisp blue, blue as the early mornings over the mesa.

"How long I been here, *anciano hombre*?" Billy asked—the first day up, as he sat hunkered on a log in front of the tent.

The old shepherd turned from cooking the evening meal of mutton and beans, raising four fingers, "*Cuatro semanas*. Yesterday was the tenth of August—the *Fiesta of San Lorenzo*." He smiled widely showing crooked teeth. "You been Juan's guest twenty-eight days now." He jerked his head with a wry twist. "And, you know, there was many a time I figured you'd up and leave without paying your lodging—but *Gracias á Dios*, you're ready for another game of monte after the meal."

"Twenty-eight days, that's a good spell to stay put in one place." The Kid shrugged, then winced and rubbed his shoulder. *"Ayer pertenecer los pasado*, (yesterday belongs to the past)."

"Supper's ready, *Señor*." Juan never asked Billy his name, and The Kid, not wanting to involve Juan in his troubles, never gave his name—so it was just *Señor* and Juan.

"*Si*, it's a good while since I fetched you back all full of holes—*Señor*," Juan mouthed around a gob of beans. "The *Pejar Haja*, that pesky stick-leaf called blazing star, it has finished blooming, and over there," he waved his spoon at a tall clump of thorn-filled bushes crowning a slight hillock behind the camp, "the *Gata Garra*—the old wait-a-minute bush, its yellow flowers have only a few more days to live." He shook his grizzled head. "Everything changes."

The Kid scraped his tin plate clean and swallowed the last of his bitter, black coffee. *Blanco* and *Canción* sat licking paws and chops outside the crimson rim of the fire circle, waiting their portions. The dusky mesa beyond was thick-dotted with grey heaps of drowsing sheep.

"*Si*, Juan old *amigo*, everything changes. That's *evidente*." Billy nodded toward the west where the sun's last red pennants unraveled away into tattered streaks beyond the Pecos and the distant purple smears of the foothills along the horizon.

"Everything changes," he went on, "and I figure

on making some changes, myself, over that way." The Kid jerked a thumb in the direction of the village of Tularosa. A plan had been forming in his mind for the past few days. He'd ciphered out a scheme, but it would take a pair of Cattle Kings to make the game pay off.

One King, Paddy Coghlan, was in the little settlement of Tularosa, a good day's ride to the southwest. The other—old Uncle John Chisum, lived over to the southeast. "Ever been to El Paso, Juan?" Was she still at the Chisum's? Probably long-gone back to Texas.

Beef would certain taste good after all this mutton and beans. Pat Garrett stopped him eating that last chunk of Pete Maxwell's beef. Could he keep him away from Uncle John Chisum's?

"Get the cards, Juan and we'll see if you're as lucky as ever."

They played for a spell while Billy mulled things over. "Juan, you've up and won again— *feliz* as ever," and Billy winked at the lop-eared *Blanco*. "Juan, you've got to get me a horse."

"I'm going to move camp soon, *Señor*, and I got to go to Roswell for supplies. If you watch the layout, I'll see about a horse for you tomorrow. There's generally some for sale down there."

"Here." Billy fished up a couple of gold pieces, just about all he had left in the world. "Tell 'em to throw in a center-fire saddle with a Winchester and scabbard to boot." He spat into the dying fire.

"If anyone gets nosey—tell 'em it's for a new hand over to Chisum's by the name of Sandoval." He'd remembered the name, after all.

Juan left next morning before first light and returned at sundown—arriving so softly out of the growing mauve-tinted twilight that The Kid's pistol was out before he recognized the old man.

The herdsman led a little black mare with four white stocking feet. She carried a bag of provisions slung over the saddle. *Blanco* and *Canción* serenaded her with fervor. But when the mare lowered her head and kicked *Blanco* out of the way, both dogs retreated among the safety of the sheep.

Billy looked at the mare while they ate supper, and liked what he saw. She was a trim, sturdy piece of horseflesh. "Why didn't you ride her, old *caballerango*? It's a long haul from Roswell."

"No, *Señor*, that's too fine a beast for an old sheep dog like me." Juan beamed at The Kid. His purchase had been appreciated.

In the earliest dawn-gleaming, Billy saddled and bridled the little mare. He'd already decided to call her Angel, despite her fire. Taking a cup of coffee from the shepherd, he drained it. "*Mucho gracias*, old friend." He pumped the wrinkled hand that the blinking Juan shoved out. "This is *adiós*—but I've got a lot to repay."

"You more than paid, *Señor*." Juan wiped his mustache with a bony finger. "Ain't you growed

31

a mustache like mine? And ain't you let me win at *La Monte* every night since you could sit up and deal for yourself? It takes *un poco* monte thrower to do that!"

Angel, loose-reined, lowered her head at the circling dogs and started across the dew-wet mesa. Billy looked back and waved his hat at the old man.

He was astride a fine horse and the sun-bird was rising out of its nest of golden feathers. His wounds felt pretty well healed, and it was time to be going. Tularosa could be made by dark if they up and hustled.

"Go it, Angel." He slapped her with the reins and she leaped ahead. "Go it—stretch yourself. Let's see you fly a little."

5   He Visits a King

The sun was igniting the giant granite mountain face of Old Baldy with the false fires of evening when Billy reined in.

Below, the velvety green valley of the Tularosa wound between craggy, twisted rock masses like a curving strip of brilliant mosses.

He was still wobbly in the saddle. "Two days, Angel," he spoke to the little black mare. "That storm back in the Sierra Blancas put the *kibosh* on a one-day jaunt. But we're here in one piece— and down there is the gent we want."

The village of Tularosa, on the west bank of the winding river Tularosa, was well-named. Marshy green sedge skirted the water, thickly spread with the tule reeds and cat-tails, waving in the evening breezes. Billy knew the *rosas*, the roses, and tule reeds, were thinning out with late summer, but he could see patches of red and white blossom still clinging to the sides of the shady adobes.

A town of reeds and roses, ruled by the King of Rum and Rangeland—Paddy Coghlan.

"Hup!" Billy clucked to the horse, and she ambled down the foothill trail, carefully setting white stocking feet among the gravel and smaller boulders, coming down to the sandy, main road that ran toward Mescalerra and Lincoln.

He rode north a short piece and taking a side-trail, crossed the rippling river's brown shallows into the town.

Doves were calling among the cottonwoods. From down the valley the La Luz mission's bells answered sleepy bird song with their faint, golden chimings.

Herdsmen and farmers were coming into the settlement from their small plots of land. Tularosa housewives made their graceful way up the street, water jugs balanced on glistening, dark heads.

Billy urged Angel into a trot toward the rambling, green-fronted building that was the combination saloon and store of the King of Tularosa. He slowly swung down and tied the horse at the hitching rack among a scattering of cow ponies and cavalry mounts, the latter bearing regulation government saddles and brands.

Looking through the bat-wing doors, he was in time to see Paddy Coghlan, in the full regalia of a successful merchant-prince with plug hat and claw-hammer coat, moving toward the rear entrance. Customers shouted and clapped Coghlan on the back as he passed them.

No doubt about it—Paddy was a good business-man, and he was known to be pretty open-handed about credit—at times. Just the man The Kid needed to see.

Swinging off the porch, Billy stalked to the

building's side and was waiting when the tall, burly Coghlan strode past.

"Got a light for a tired traveler?" Billy pulled a battered cigar (Juan's parting gift) from his vest and teetered it between his teeth as he stepped into Coghlan's path.

"Here you be cowboy." Coghlan scratched a match on his boot. It sputtered blue. As he raised the tiny flame, its light twinkled across The Kid's face.

"*Gracias*!" Billy grinned at the gaping King, sucking the thin fire streak into the tip of his stogie.

"Howly—what th' divil?" Coghlan's beard rested upon his chest. "Sure—you look . . ."

"Like th' divil? I know but gettin' better." Billy chuckled at the King's amazement. "Garrett's six-shooter slugs are bound to make you puny—that is, if you take an over-dose."

"Kid . . . you're Billy! And you ain't dead a bit!" Coghlan staggered against a nearby cotton-wood and wiped his face with a bandana.

"Where you goin' in such a big rip? If you're late for supper, *Madama* will take your scalp." Billy referred to a fact, common in Tularosa, Lincoln, Fort Sumner and other parts of the Territory. Paddy's wife was the *Queen,* and she ruled the big man as completely as he ruled his own empire.

"Well, yes—I'm late—but Kid?" Coghlan

straightened and placed his hand on Billy's shoulder. "How come you're here? Thought you was six feet under pushing up the cactus.

"Don't know how it happened . . . but I know Garrett," Coghlan continued after a deep breath. "His deputies have been making it damned hot around this part of the County." Seeing Billy was uncommunicative, he lowered his voice. "They was here a week back, letting on they was looking for rustled beef—getting damned nosey about brands and bills of sale."

"Hell Paddy, you ain't been playin' it dumb?" Billy poked a finger into Coghlan's ample midriff. "You got plenty stock of your own to take care of beef contracts."

"Yeah, but Garrett's getting a mighty big head since he up and killed—since he says he got you. Fact, says he's gonna clean up the County with a new broom."

Billy gave a short laugh. "New broom? We'll see who raises th' most dust." He glanced down at his soiled clothing. "Pretty dusty myself, and not too spry lookin'—what with these tore up duds."

"Come on back to the store." Coghlan led The Kid up the empty alley. Billy followed, gun ready. It was quiet and peaceful in the gentle dusk, but things had looked almighty peaceful back at Fort Sumner.

Coghlan's general store was connected with his

saloon and wagon-yard. They paused on the back step while Paddy unlocked the door. Coghlan closed and locked it before scratching a match on the rough plaster of the wall.

Shelves, bulging with canned goods, blankets, yard-goods, hardware, clothing, saddles and ammunition, sprang into sight in the yellow arc of the coal-oil lamp. Up toward the front of the store, several glass cases reflected the lamp in curved brilliance from sides and tops.

"Pick out what you need." Paddy waved a thick hand at the rich stock of merchandise.

"This'll sure put me in your debt. I ain't got two *pesos* to clink at the minute." Billy hauled down a pair of blue Levi's that looked his fit along with a red, checkered shirt. "But I got a good idea how I can pay you back . . . and then some."

Coghlan placed the lamp down on a cracked case, filled with plug tobacco and cigars. He rubbed his scrubby, close-trimmed brown beard.

They stood looking each other in the eye. With a grunt, Paddy walked behind the tobacco case and picked out a couple of clear Havanas from a gilt box.

"Here," Coghlan growled, "get rid of that saloon Short-Six you're smudging up the air with and try a gent's cigar." He noticed Billy's hand resting lightly on the butt of his Colt. "Not that a gent can't smoke whatever he's a mind to."

"Thanks." Billy took the proffered stogie, and,

with a smile, lit it up at the lamp's top, drawing in a big lung-full and letting it out with a sigh.

"You got a *mucho cantidad* a'working under that beat-up old war bonnet." Coghlan squinted past the pale blue threads of smoke. "Here," he selected a low-crowned, grey Stetson from the shelf. "Might as well go the limit—though my ould grandma back in Ireland said never to do business with any man that smiled like a Kilkenny Cat."

Retrieving the lamp, Paddy jabbed his cigar toward a partitioned space at the room's corner. "C'mon back. Between Chisum, Garrett, that sneaking little range detective of a Charlie Siringo, and my wife—divil if I don't need some relaxing." He peered at Billy. "Maybe you'll be able to explain all this hocus-pocus, dead-or-alive business. You know, don't you, that just be being alive, you're making liars out of some mighty dangerous men?"

The Kid watched Coghlan open the door of a large, black, iron safe. Paddy drew forth a leather-bound account book and a dusty bottle. "Wolgenmuth," he grunted, jerking his head at a painting on the safe door, depicting a hunting scene on a pine covered hill.

"My partner and bookkeeper, Morris Wolgenmuth, damn nigh cries every time he sees that pitcher. His home country is in the Black Forest." Coghlan settled back in his cane-back chair.

"Imagine anyone homesick for such a hell of a looking spot. Now, County Antrim, where I hail from—that's the beauty spot of the ould sod."

"Antrim." Billy grinned. "Sounds familiar."

"Yeah, Antrim, Bonney—and what other monikers have you used?"

"Oh, McCarty—and Roberts, th' name I was born with. Bonney's my aunt's family name. She married an old hard-rock miner called Antrim. I took th' name when I was just a yearlin' livin' with them over at Silver City—but that's a long, old trail. Let's talk, you and me, about other things with more profit to 'em!"

The Havanas were glowing stubs and the lamp chimney dark with soot before they arrived at the end of their dickering. The bottle was half-empty, but Billy knew that Paddy was just as shrewd as ever.

Billy's glass was still full, as he rarely touched anything much stronger than beer. He wanted to be able to move in an instant without whiskey fumes slowing him down.

Yes, Paddy was a shrewd trader, and sharp. Hadn't he run cattle, and not always his own—and kept stores and saloons all the way from Texas to Tularosa? And each time he moved, he'd bettered himself. Billy heard that Coghlan had picked up every open town lot in Tularosa as far back as 1874 and branching out into the Three Rivers Valley, got himself all sorts of water holes and streams by hook or crook—but that took money to grab money and Paddy could never seem to grab enough. That was why he'd wangled a beef contract for the army post at Fort Stanton and the Mescalero Apache Reservation.

Now the authorities—and Garrett were starting to look cross-eyed at the King's source of beef supply.

"All right," Coghlan agreed, "if you think you can get away with that many, go ahead. I sure can use them. I got a shipment due at Fort Stanton, and another at the Reservation by the first of the month." He tipped the bottle once more and corked it. "To be damned honest, I was just about pulling out me beard, figuring how to meet them deadlines." He handed The Kid some coins. "Here's an advance—forty dollars in gold."

"I want you to know that a hundred head will just about put me even with Chisum." The Kid tossed his cigar stub on the floor, grinding it out with the heel of his boot. "I told old Uncle John that I'd collect one way or th' other for all that back pay he never got around to let go of. And I guess he owes me a little extra."

Coghlan put the account book and bottle back in the safe.

Billy gathered up his bundle of clothing and selected extra ammunition, a pair of blankets, canteen, coffee-pot, and a small skillet, as well as a slicker and a pair of powerful field glasses.

"Never can tell when I might want a look at th' moon," he grinned.

Outside in the alley, Coghlan paused, "You got everything all set? You drive Chisum's stock to my Three Rivers Ranch anytime after tomorrow. Wolgenmuth's got to go up there with a relation that's been visiting. So he'll be on hand to tally the count—and pay you off." He offered Billy another stogie but The Kid refused. He felt too full of smoke as it was.

"This Dutchman of yours don't know me and that's th' way to work it," he said. "None of you'll get mixed up with what just might happen to a certain Pat. Just tell Dutchy to bring th' money."

"You didn't say why you want all this cash. Get-away gold?"

"Nope, *get him* gold!"

"Get? You're not going to try for Garrett, are you? Howly Saints, Kid. Don't go and do any-thing so crazy. You must have been handed your life on a platter as it was, with Garrett plugging the wrong man." Paddy puffed strenuously on his cigar until its shifting glow twisted his features into a burly devil's face.

"There's plenty of sun-grinners around here or on down toward th' border that'd shoot their grandma's eye out for th' price." Billy hitched his gun belt. "We'll let Chisum's money pay off one of those bush-whackers for th' job. Sort of poetic justice, like they say in th' books, eh?"

41

"There'll be hell for breakfast around these parts. Remember, I don't know a thing," Paddy rumbled. They walked down the alley and around the corner. Coghlan pulled out his watch and struck another light. "Howly Mother. Me wife'll skin me. It's past ten-thirty."

"O.K. Your stock'll be at th' ranch come Monday night."

"As I told you, Kid—pick your own men. Like as not, you can get some right in th' saloon." He scratched his bristly beard. "Fact is, there's some Texans in there now. Fresh in from the Big Bend. Maybe on the dodge. But go on in, with that long-horn mustache nobody will know you anyway."

They shook hands and Billy watched the King of Tularosa hurry homeward to the hot tongue of his Queen—and a cold supper. He turned and walked over to a rickety, two-story hotel, sandwiched between a private adobe and the town blacksmith shop.

After registering in as W. Roberts, The Kid went to his dingy, second floor room, deposited his supplies and changed into the fresh clothing. Locking the door, he came back down and crossed the empty street to Paddy's saloon.

Angel nickered at him from the hitching rail. He untied the little, black mare, led her down to the wagonyard and instructed the hired hand to rub her down and give her the best feed and stall.

When The Kid returned to the saloon, he found it still busy, although the hour was late. Through rifts of smoke, he saw the usual groups of Mexicans in colorful shirts and wide denim trousers, playing at Monte. Several poker games involving ranch hands were in progress along the walls.

There was also a scattering of blue-uniformed, black troopers from Fort Stanton still at the bar. These seemed less interested in games of chance than they were in the faded charms of a pair of, still curvesome, Mexican women. That pair of dubious beauties, garbed in bright skirts and blouses, wandered among the tables, singing softly and plucking away at battered guitars.

The bartender, Stay With 'Em Brown, a fair-haired man with a walrus mustache, hobbled around a wooden leg dispensing liquid cheer. He was the only person in the room The Kid recognized. Brown, a former horse wrangler at the Frying Pan Ranch near Tascosa, Texas, won his name but lost a leg by staying with a horse that rolled upon him.

Billy elbowed a space at the bar. "Whatcha have?" The bartender wiped up a fleck of beer in front of The Kid, watching him with a mildly puzzled expression.

"Glass of beer—and a little information."

"Yeah." Brown sat a slopping glass before Billy

and leaned over the bar with his change. "Ain't I seed you in these parts afore?"

"Maybe—but I'm askin' questions. Where's these Texans who got in here today?" Billy ran a thumb over his mustache and looked narrowly at Brown.

Brown took a couple of swipes at the bar-top with his rag, and nodded toward a table in the back of the room. Three hard-cases were hunched over a bottle, staring back at Billy. "That's the bunch, but I'd be keerful. They ain't none too friendly 'cept with Rosa and Yucca Annie—an' I guess that's 'cause they been out of touch with womenfolk for a spell."

"*Gracias.*" Billy took a sip of brackish beer, studying a gaudy looking woman in lavender tights, smirking out at the room from a beer poster.

Brown stumped down the bar to cater to the thirsts of a trio of Fort Stanton troopers, who were demanding bracers for their ride back to the post. He returned to Billy. "I got it. You used to come over to Tascosa about the time they was missin' stock at the Frying Pan and L and S ranches, couple years back." He leaned forward confidentially, not noticing the careless attitude of Billy's hand near his pearl-handled colt. "Don't go by the name of Charlie Siringo, do you? I heered he was down this way working with Pat Garrett and giving old man Coghlan fits."

Billy winked slowly at Brown and let his hand

drift away from his pistol. This gent had him pegged for one of the stock detectives working through the country for the larger ranchers. "Just keep it under your hat." He turned and walked to the rear of the bar room.

The three Texans, still looking him over, were roughly dressed and carried six-shooters slung low. One was fairly clean-cut, with a pleasantly sleepy expression. The others were grim and clamp-mouthed.

The Kid came right to the point, explaining he needed several hands for a week's work picking up stray stock.

"And who's payin' fer ridin' th' circle?" This from the sleepy Texan. The other two sat staring at Billy with sullen expressions.

"Me," The Kid answered. "I'm reppin' for a certain *hombre* who's got to get up a bunch of beef to Fort Stanton, pronto."

They bent their heads in discussion. The cantina girls, circling like hesitant moths, were weaving along the rear wall, when the smaller of the two, Yucca Annie, brushed the arm of the darkest Texan.

"Goddam, get away you Greasers," he ground out, jerking his chair back so suddenly that it tipped over a whiskey bottle. "Spill my liquor will you?" He fetched the frightened girl a belt on the side of the head with a big, grimy fist.

Things happened fast. The girl hit the floor in

45

a flurry of petticoats and olive-tinted thighs. The Texan followed her to the rough planks an instant later, head cracked by The Kid's pistol barrel— while the remaining pair found themselves staring into the unwavering black muzzle of Billy's six-gun.

"He had that coming, the big calamity!" The one-legged barkeep was beside The Kid, covering the trio with a Winchester carbine. "You sure filled your hand in a hurry," he said to The Kid. "Hey, you two," he ordered the downed Texan's friends, "git that big noise out'a here before he's put to bed with a pick and shovel."

Billy holstered his pistol and helped the bedraggled saloon girl to her feet. "To pay for your *guitarra, Señorita.*" He pressed a five-dollar gold piece into her hand, shoving the splintered musical instrument with his toe.

She took the money, dropped it between her breasts and smiled.

The two cowboys picked up their friend by his loose-sprawled arms and legs, lugging him out the back door into the alley. Billy followed.

"Well?" He inquired of the procession as it wended its silent way up the sandy alley to the darkened wagonyard.

"Deal me in," the sleepy Texan answered from the foot of the small cortege. The puncher at the head, grunted a sullen refusal.

"*Bueno,*" Billy replied to the first man. "Meet

me at th' saloon soon as you settle down Prince Charmin'." The droop-eyed cowhand snickered as his companion swore under his breath.

The black cavalrymen were in front of Paddy's saloon, mounting up when Billy got back. "Pretty healthy lookin' soldier boys," The Kid mused to himself. "Well, Uncle John's beef will keep 'em fat and sassy."

"*Pardona, Señor,*" a low voice at his elbow made him wheel around. "I am Frank Fega." A small, thin Mexican-American was shoving a plump, jovial native ahead of himself into the yellow light of the open cantina door. "An' this is Jose Tafalla. The little girl you aided was his cousin."

"*Es non importante,*" Billy shrugged, grinning back at them. "We got to keep these *Tejanos* cut to size, heh?"

The smaller Mexican edged closer, pushing the fat man toward The Kid. "We were at the next table, playing La Monte." He raised one shoulder. "One could not help but overhear your talk with the *Tejanos*—we will ride for you when you wish; we and one other, a Felipe Chavez, who lives close by and can be counted on not to talk." Both Mexicans smiled at each other.

"*Gracias, amigos.*" Billy took them each by the hand. "Let's go back into th' cantina, we'll soon have a fourth rider. Come on and we'll make some pow-wow over th' *bottela.*"

47

6 "South Spring Ranch"

Shortly after daybreak, when the mists rolled up from the valley, and the sun slanting its red lances among the river reeds, brought new life to the tightly folded roses along brown adobe walls, The Kid rode north in the direction of Lincoln and Sumner.

His *vaquerós*, three Mexicans and the Texan, were to meet him at Black Springs, near the forks of the Padilla and Salt rivers on the evening of the third day.

The first day took him up through the windy passes of the White Mountains—the Sierra Blancas. Skirting the Mescalero Apache Reservation, he crossed the high plains, with the cobalt blue Pajarita Peak on his right.

At sundown the jutting purple of the Capitan Range lofted before him. He rode up into the first foothills of the mountains and unsaddled Angel in a small clearing in the thick stands of ponderosa pine.

He shook out a mixture of oats and corn, purchased at the Tularosa wagon-yard, feeding the mare in a woven grass morral, or nosebag, before cooking his evening meal.

Next morning, Billy roused up in his blanket at first light. All was peaceful and unmoving save for a small herd of mule-deer, threading daintily along the green slopes to drink at a chuckling, twisting mountain branch of the Padilla.

Angel stamped her white-stockinged feet and nickered at them, but they merely stared at her with large, luminous eyes as they went their quiet way.

"It's all right, Angel. Let 'em take their turn. Everything comes to them that waits," he grinned to himself. "Like somethin's comin' to Chisum and Garrett."

Lincoln was already twenty miles to the west when Billy struck out over the swelling brown mesas toward Fort Sumner. The arching sky was full of majestically moving clouds, piled into high, white vast steps, climbing ever up into the blue of the zenith.

All about him stretched yellow-centered, golden crown beard—the notch-petaled sunflower of the mesa. They swept off on either side, swung in behind and advanced in front, until it seemed to the drowsy Kid that he rode through an endless field of golden coins.

With the fresh mountain breezes far away and blazing daylight shimmering overhead, he splashed through the dark-ochre shallows of the Padilla, fifteen miles from Roswell, proceeding on a dead line into the northeast and Fort Sumner.

An hour past noon, he halted in the relative coolness of a juniper thicket. While Angel

49

munched at bunch grass, The Kid chewed down a piece of jerky supplied by Coghlan.

In the stillness, the hot mesa wind, languidly pushing through the yellowish-green branches, brought him the pungently tart odor of juniper, the distant cry of a circling hawk and the nearer, brittle yapping of a hunting coyote.

Angel tossed her head and snuffed at the warm sheets of air. Billy leaning against the trunk of a large tree, glanced at the little black mare and noticed her ears were lying back. Her eyes rolled. "*Quen es, Angelina*? You can't smell old Juan's *Blanca* away over here?" He stepped to the edge of the grove.

Not two-hundred yards to the north, and crossing at a slow trot, were five horsemen. He went back to the horse and pulled his field glasses from the saddle bag. "Angel." He gently stroked the mare's nose. "Don't make a sound. Just be *tranquilo*—a fine lady."

He felt the hairs on his neck prickle as he leveled the glasses on the riders. "It's a good thing to have an appetite—sometimes," he muttered. "That's Siringo's lawdogs. They could have jumped me before I knew what was goin' on."

The glasses brought the jogging riders into sharp focus. The little, wiry, round-shouldered man, riding a small bay, was Charley Siringo, the cattle detective. No doubt of that. Billy recalled him from Tascosa days, soon after the Lincoln County trouble. They'd been on friendly terms then, but that was before such big cattlemen as Chisum had put Siringo on their payroll.

Billy didn't recognize the others, but they were all loaded for bear; two Colts apiece and a saddle-gun on every horse.

"Headin' straight for Sumner, or I'm a mavericker," Billy informed the mesa winds. "That settles th' hash! They're probably runnin' down a line on Coghlan." He tightened Angel's saddle. "We're goin' in th' opposite direction, *Angeleo Mio*. Things are a might healthier back south—down around Chisum's range. We'll see Celsa some other time."

About five o'clock he hit the Fort Sumner road below the little cluster of adobes that was Chaves, and rode on south toward Roswell. The dusty track was empty except for an occasional farm cart or wood cutter. These traveled homeward while the descending sun pierced the steep marble-like cloud masses—firing them into tall pillars of orange flame.

Such folk as he met, greeted the rider of the handsome black horse with *"buenos tarde"*—never suspecting him to be the very one some had recently burned candles for in their small churches.

The light flattened, losing brilliance with the approach of evening. The mountain rims to the west burned purple, and along the roadside, yellow patches of wild zinnias paled, then blended into the thickening dusk.

Roswell lay quiet in the twilight hush when The Kid passed through. There were not many people abroad during the supper hour and Billy was skirting along South Spring River when the last gleams of day showed him to be within pistol shot of old John Chisum's South Spring Ranch.

He reined up, and listened. There was nothing to hear but the clink and jingle of Angel's bit and the rhythm of her deep, steady breathing. He swung down and tied the horse to a small scrub tree near the ranch-house fence.

The stock Uncle John was about to donate, unknowingly, to the "Pat Garrett fund" was off to the east, but Billy wanted to smell out the ground at the ranch. He wasn't going to be caught napping on this one.

He went under the lowest strand of the barbed wire with practiced ease and ghosted up to the adobe and log bunkhouse. Only two punchers were inside, both noisily intent upon winning a checker game. A dog barked, one shrill yelp, up at the rambling main building. Before it could get down to business, a stern female voice from the kitchen quashed its efforts.

Colt in hand, Billy drifted by the back of the ranch house, ears straining, eyes searching the velvety blackness. Nearing a side window, he inched forward carefully to the lamp-lit window. Peering along the side of the frame—he came close to dropping his gun.

The face he couldn't put from his mind was there—and only inches from his own. Miss Sandoval sat at a small table opposite Sallie Chisum, Uncle John's niece.

For a moment—so long that it seemed to stretch forever—he froze, mind in a turmoil. And as he waited, Sallie got up from the table and went through the kitchen door with a dish.

Billy hesitated no longer. Glancing around in the darkness, he tapped on the glass with a finger.

The girl's startled gaze swung toward the window. And as she saw him her lovely mouth opened. Arising hastily, she hurried out of the room.

The Kid stayed by the side of the house, gun in hand, ready for just about anything.

"Billy." Her soft voice came to him in the dark as she moved like a shadow. "You—you're Billy?" She neared him in the patch of light and he gently took her arm and tugged her back into the shielding gloom. He felt her tremble at his touch.

He uncocked his Colt and holstered it. "*Señorita* Sandoval. I . . ." He swallowed down a sudden dryness, like heat thirst but different.

"You—were killed. They all said this . . . on that night we met at Luna's." She paused in an effort to continue. "You—weren't killed. I knew it! I felt it somehow. I told the Chisums so. *Señor* John smiled, and I hated him. But Sallie, she wept with me."

"Yes, Miss Sallie knows me from away back."

"And my brother, we had a terrible fight. He said you were—a—common outlaw and that—," she forced out the words, "that folks' stock . . . would be safer."

"You believed that?"

"Oh, no! And now here you are. I don't understand yet—but I'm thankful." He felt brilliant eyes seeking every feature of his face as she went on. "I knew you the moment I looked out the window. I knew you in spite of that mustache, and the scar on your cheek . . . oh yes, I knew you!"

She glanced back into the dining room. "Sallie will be seeking for me." She placed a hand on his. Her fingers were smooth, but they clasped his with surprising firmness. "We'll meet again, somehow, before I leave?"

"You're goin'?"

"Yes." Now both her hands clung to his. "I don't know why but I kept putting off my parents in El Paso—kept making excuses to stay here. My brother left two weeks past and now I must go at the end of this week."

"I'll find out some way to meet you." It was hard for him to believe that this lovely, high-toned, young lady would be interested in any such hand-to-mouth, on-the-dodge saddle tramp as himself. "Do you really want to see me again?"

"Oh, yes!" Her slender body was tightly against him. He didn't know who had made the first move, and it didn't matter, for he held a figure more richly-rounded than he'd dreamed possible.

"You really came to see me," she said, stating a fact that seemed to give her pleasure.

"Yes. And to collect the rest of my back pay from Uncle John." The words were out before he realized what he'd said.

She tensed away from him. "Collect your back pay? How?" Suddenly she tore herself from his arms. "Don't tell me—I know! You're going to take more of *Señor* Chisum's cattle."

She was gone from his arms and out of his sight.

He backed off, Colt in hand, and slipped away to the fence. He crawled under the wire and untied the mare. So far there had been no alarm. Maybe she hadn't told—yet!

Tomorrow night he must meet his men.

The following day, came the raid on Chisum's herd—no matter what turned up.

7   Malo Sonar

The Kid reached Black Springs late in the night. He'd thought of making camp at the Pot Hole Springs or Devil's Cave along the way, but kept riding—fed up with women and world.

He'd pushed Angel through the sultry August darkness, stopping every so often to rest the mare, but determined to keep on to the rendezvous site. A pointed, battered moon hung low in the west—like the horns of some half-visible, giant storm-steer, lowering over the jagged barricade of the mountains. Heat lightning rippled its ghostly glare among the sullenly luminous billows of the cloud cliffs as they slowly moved along with the ominous majesty of a heaven-high landslide.

Billy dismounted twenty yards from the rocky lip of the springs, near a grove of mixed piñon and juniper. He was feverish and wrung out. His half-healed wounds were paining and his head rocked on his shoulders light as wind-blown cottonwood tassel.

He refilled his canteen and then led Angel to the cool, bubbling basin of the springs. The little mare drank slowly, lifting her head and shaking dripping water beads from her nostrils. Her ears twitched and she rolled her eyes at him—mirroring his restlessness.

"Drink all you want, *Angelo mio*." He patted

her glistening, sweat-dampened flank. "You're th' only lady *muy simpático* with me." He laughed dryly. "And just about th' only Angel that won't flare up and fly away."

Guiding the horse back into the protection of the grove, he unsaddled and rubbed her down until she was gentled. He shook out some corn into the woven grass morral. Rolling himself up in his blanket, under a juniper, he slowly sank downward into restless slumber—

—And he was a real kid again—not more than sixteen, sitting a shabby, cracked saddle, aboard a boney, old white horse. A young, red-haired beanpole rode by his side on a thin, buckskin pony.

They went racking down a narrow, winding road between high, brush-covered foothills, leaving the crazy jumble of raw, yellow-pine cubes and oblongs that were the stamp mills, saloons, shabby stores and rickety shacks of Silver City, New Mexico Territory.

"Jesse," he reached out and poked at the young'un beside him. "Just because we're goin' off from town together, don't mean you gotta stick with me."

Red-headed Jesse Evans, dressed in hand-me-down cowboy clothes, and rusty cowhide boots, narrowed his green eyes as he pulled off the stained, narrow-brim hat he'd lifted from a careless peddler. "Always stick to you—Billy.

Could never lose me if'n you tried. We been pals since you come to town with your folks a long piece back."

Billy rubbed sweating palms on his blue-striped shirt and glanced down at the stirrups, where his feet rested in their lace-up brogans. He meant to get a real outfit like the one Jesse'd stolen, and pretty soon. "Yeah, it's been you and me, Jesse—a long while all right."

"An' now we're goin' to be honest-to-God cowboys!" Jesse laughed a high, sharp yelp and his green eyes blazed. "I guess you had th' right to slice that big blabber-mouth ox of a black-smith with your toad-sticker for carryin' on about your family in th' saloon. Didn't do more'n let a little of his hot air out anyways. But no jail house'll ever get you! And now we'll see th' world and someday . . . ." He hit the patient pony a larrup with his hat. "Hi-yup, you bastard!"

Down the trail the two horses went racking, heading for old Mexico and—

—the foreman of the Jingle Bob Ranch squirted an amber dart of brown spittle at a creeping horn-toad. "Wait a minute. I'll call Evans out. See if'n he knows yuh." He turned from where Billy sat a rangy, wild-looking roan. "You're pretty young. Cain't take on every punk of a grub-line rider 'at shows up." He bellowed at the log bunkhouse— "Hey Evans! C'mon out an' look a'here!"

A fiery head poked out the door and—Jesse

Evans bounded down the steps at a jump. "Gawddam! Look here! A long ways from Silver City. Two years, hey Billy?" He grabbed at The Kid's leg, nearly yanking him from the saddle. The roan reared. The foreman fell back and Evans tumbled in a heap.

"Hey lookit that." Jesse sat on the sandy ground and slammed a fist into the dirt. "Ever see anyone stick that tight to a bronc?"

The mount, fresh from a wild-horse remuda in Mesilla, kicked a hole in the sky, exploding all four feet off the ground. Billy was shaken and tossed again and again like a dice in a cup—but he held on and at last gradually calmed the horse down to a quivering halt.

"That's 'nuff for the likes of me," the foreman grinned. "If you know this kid, and he can ride like that—I reckon Uncle John Chisum's got another hand on th' payroll and—

—Glad to have you with us, Billy." John Tunstall, resplendent in a bottle-green coat and dawn-pink riding breeches, stood before him, hand on hip. Tunstall's handsome, florid face, with its dapper, blond mustache and long sideburns, beamed with good-will. "I've had my eyes on you for some time, in Lincoln and on the range. You've seemed the most alert, really posh rider at Mister Chisum's ranch."

"Posh?" Billy grinned back at this young Englishman, newly arrived in the Territory and openly intent on building up a spread to compete with the cattle king Chisum.

"Sorry, I meant to say *espléndido*. The very best! That's the Britisher in me, Billy." Tunstall laughed and held out his hand. "Shake on it, son. We'll get along. You probably can teach me a thing or two about our cattle business. And never fear about your forthcoming pay from Mister Chisum. He's honest and won't fail to settle up when he can. Things have been hard on him since this trouble started between McSween and I, and Murphy and Dolan."

Tunstall referred to his backing of a young lawyer named Alexander McSween, both in the running of a store in Lincoln and in open political opposition to the powerful Murphy-Dolan group. It was common gossip that Murphy and his side-kick Dolan were bank-rolled by a powerful bunch in Santa Fe.

"Chisum's torn between backing Murphy and Dolan and staying on good terms with the rest," Tunstall concluded with a smile.

Billy dug a toe into the sand. He already worshipped this handsome young Englishman.

"You're still a youngster, Billy," Tunstall chuckled, "but I can tell you'll be faithful all the way."—

—back from Lincoln Billy had felt that something was dead wrong. For months he'd been afraid of Mister Tunstall running into some of

Sheriff Brady's regulators. They were in and out of Lincoln more and more on Murphy and Dolan's dirty business. And he'd heard that Jesse Evans was now riding with them. Evans, shrewd and cautious, had stuck with Chisum after Billy left.

As he rode up over the crest of the hill leading to Tunstall's ranch, he saw someone lying in the middle of the crooked, weed-rimmed road. It was a long piece off, but his heart cracked apart at the sight of those long legs, in riding boots and dusty pink breeches. "Come on," he shouted to the two riders with him, "those Goddam devils finally got Mister Tunstall. We got—

—to get out of here tonight—*pronto*!" Billy called to his men above the crackling roar of the falling, burning timbers in the McSween house at Lincoln.

McSween, Tunstall's friend and bitter foe of Murphy, Dolan and Uncle John Chisum, was dead on his face in the flame swept street. His outflung hand still clutched the Bible he'd carried from the besieged home.

Bloody firelight flooded the main room of the thick adobe where Billy, Tom O'Folliard, Jim French, Ygenio Salazar and several other loyal Tunstall-McSween men crouched at the windows with leveled Winchesters and Sharps. For five days, since July 17 of this year 1878 they'd swapped shot for shot with the combined forces of Sheriff Peppin, the slain Sheriff Brady's successor.

The whole Murphy-Dolan crowd were wild as hawks at the open backing of the Santa Fe politicians. They were out to kill off every Tunstall-McSween man, without mercy. And with the McSween home burning over their heads, fired by Jack Long, while the U.S. Troopers from Ft. Stanton stood by and looked the other way— there was nothing for it but to get out to fight another day.

The fire's orange claws slashed nearer to the defender's blistering faces. Red sparks spun about their heads like maddened hornets.

Billy ran from window to window, slapping the men on their backs—doing a jig to cheer them up. "Load your belts. Six shells in every pistol. Fill the rifles' magazines," he shouted. "Comes th' first break in th' firin'—we go through th' door and hit for th' river."

He beat out a spark gnawing at his sleeve. "Think th' gate to th' right of th' yard's best bet. We go single file, and fast. No jammin' up!" The fire gaining strength roared like a furious beast, gorging the room with thick, fuming, acrid smoke.

"All right," Billy yelled, "let's go! To hell with Murphy and every stinkin' Ring man from here to Santa Fe!" He kicked open the back door and the group burst into the smoky night. Their guns spat their own fire as they lashed out at the horde of ambushers along the adobe walls.

Billy fired his Winchester carbine from the hip as he ran. Some of his men folded up in sprawling bundles, but he dashed on yelling, "Come and get us, you bastards—you can't hit—

—th' broadside of a barn, Garrett. No wonder you went busted."

Pat Garrett, gangling ex–buffalo hunter, holstered his smoking Colt. "You win again, Kid." Garrett went up and kicked an unpunctured, empty bean can into the Fort Sumner irrigation ditch. "C'mon, let's us go up to Rosita's to play a little Monte."

Billy stood looking at the riddled can he'd been firing on. "When're you goin' to get an honest job again, Pat, and stop tryin' to clean me at cards? You ain't bucked at anyone but me since you lit here from th' Texas Panhandle moren' three months past."

"Well," Garrett drawled in his best Tennessee coon-hunter brogue, chewing at the ends of his droopy mustache. "I figger to git even with you someday, if I keep on your tracks, Kid." He wrapped a long arm about Billy's shoulders. "I'll git an honest job about as soon as you do." He laughed. "And you'd smell a lot more honest, yerself, if'n you laid off folks like that Jesse Evans."

Billy glowered at the tall Garrett. "Listen, Big

63

Casino, Jesse's my friend. He may be pretty wild and, maybe, he did jump on th' other side of th' fence in this county ruckus. But he's still a friend."

"Kid, you're lettin' loyalty dim your thinkin'. Evans is nothin' but a rustlin' killer, and you damn well know it!" Garrett's Irish was up. "It may a been before my time but there's plenty of talk he murdered that Tunstall."

Billy felt cold in spite of the bright sun and yanked away from Pat Garrett's clutch—

—It was cold. Mighty cold. But it was December 22, 1880. He tugged the blanket tighter around him as he crouched by the paneless window in the shack at Tivan Arroyo (Stinking Springs), six miles due east of Sumner.

Garrett and his posse had jumped The Kid and his men just before daylight. From time to time flying lead ripped into the scarred adobe walls. The posse's first shots had dropped one of the horses across the empty doorway of the big adobe.

"Good thing we got horse meat," Dave Rudabaugh, Billy's roughneck rider turned his square, hard face from squinting down the bead of his Winchester rifle. "That's all we got for our Christmas stockin'."

Garrett's voice came to them through gaps in the firing. Its drawling irony made the cold even more unendurable. "Here's a hot fire and some

64

good hot Arbuckle, Kid. Whyn't you'n your pards come out to dig in?"

"Goddam that Pat," The Kid grinned through blue lips. "If I could get his Irish coconut in my sights, I'd give him hot fire."

A gasping whimper arose near Billy's feet where his friend Charlie Bowdrie, another ex–Chisum hand, lay dying. Pat was getting to be a better shot.

Rudabaugh, his face bleak with contained rage, tugged the dying Bowdrie up on his feet and crammed a six-shooter into the limp fist. "Go out and get someone before you kick off, Charlie!" He slewed the tottering man around the dead horse and thrust him out through the doorless opening.

Billy dropped his empty saddle-gun and blanket, making a grab for Bowdrie, but jumped backwards as a bullet spat adobe grit into his chilled face.

It was too late, and he turned away shrugging. "Go get 'em, Charlie. Take as many with you as you can."

Garrett's men ceased their fusilade of shots as Bowdrie came stumbling forward, Colt dangling loosely in his hand. He dropped in his tracks before he reached them.

"Well," Billy stared around the barn-like room, "we might as well follow Charlie. We're down to th' last cartridge."

Rudabaugh glared. "This is sure gonna be a sweet Christmas."

Without looking at each other, the four, Billy, Rudabaugh, Pickett and Wilson, walked to the doorway and flung out their empty weapons. Stamping their feet on the frozen ground, they filed down the snow-covered path toward Garrett's leveled gun.

"Who'd thought you'd be givin' me this kind of a present, Pat?" Billy grinned as Garrett slipped a pair of wrist chains on and locked them tight. They were heavy and freezing cold.

"You had to go and start up a war that was plumb finished, Billy," Garrett drawled. "Recall I told you about bein' too damned loyal? Now you've gone and made it plenty hot for yourself."—

—It sure was hot, Billy thought. But it would get cooler when the sun had burned up over the peak of this makeshift jail, on the top floor of the Lincoln County Court House, and began to slant for the steep, brush-spattered hills behind Lincoln.

But wasn't it hot now?

"Sure is hot today, Bell." Billy spoke to J.W. "Long" Bell, Garrett's jail guard. The long-jawed deputy was propped against the fly-spotted wall in a broken-runged chair, wide-brimmed hat down over his eyes, and his mouth gaping—

despite the buzzing flies that circled in and out the open windows.

The window, nearest Billy, overlooked the little dirt road that snaked through shambling Lincoln, past Murphy's store and the ruins of McSween's house—where they'd battled in the flames months gone by.

That same road stretched past Tunstall's store and grave, as it now ran past Billy's prison—where he was held like a mad dog. Chained for sticking to the losing side of a fight.

"Jerusalem, it's hot." The Kid attempted to raise his manacled arms high enough to pluck the sweat-soaked shirt from his body. The leg shackles, that picketed him to a six-foot area of the room, rattled and clanked.

"Hey, Bell! You best wake up." The other guard, Bob Ollinger, came out of the hallway from the gun room, polishing the stock of a shotgun. "This kid'll jump you one of these days—you keep on dozin' all th' time." His broad, pock-marked face twisted in a disagreeable smile.

"Oh, Kid's all right. It's just too damn hot to think straight. Ain't it, Kid?" Bell pushed up his hat, letting his chair thump on the floor.

"Well, I'm goin' over to eat at th' Dutchman's." Ollinger stalked back into the hall, long, yellow hair hanging damp and limp down his back. "So don't you go and let that tricky cuss pull anythin'. If he does, blast him plumb center." He growled over his shoulder at Billy. "Think it's hot now, Kid? It'll be *mucho* hotter n'this, where you're goin' in just fifteen days!"

Billy grinned slightly and stretched as far as he was able toward the open window. There was very little breeze. It was hot.

With Ollinger across the street, Billy suggested a game of cards and presently they were sitting huddled over a big, wooden soap box, playing at Monte. Bell had unchained The Kid's leg irons but left his wrists shackled together.

The lanky guard won hand after hand. Billy had never played so badly. He appeared disgusted. His customary smile faded. He began slapping each card down on the box. Suddenly one flew wide of the mark.

"Easy, Kid. Ain't no use gettin' riled 'cause I got a winnin' streak for a change." And Bell, leaning over to scoop up the errant pasteboard—straightened up to the breath-choking sight of Billy The Kid with a Colt .44 in his fist.

"*Gracias*, Bell! Appreciate your help—just like I appreciate your gun." Billy flourished Bell's own six-shooter under the eyes of the startled guard. It was a big chance—but he'd taken it, grabbing Bell's pistol from the holster as the jailer bent down.

Billy became all business. "O.K., Bell! Toss th' keys!" His voice leaped to a shout as Bell dived headlong for the hallway. "Hold it—I ain't kiddin'!"

Billy fired twice, trying to halt Bell. The explosions slammed through the sleepy summer heat. Both shots were purposely wide of their target. But Bell threw up his hands, stumbled and bounced down the stairwell. One of the slugs, striking the wall under his arm, had ricocheted through his body, killing him instantly.

"Poor bastard! Well, I told'm to halt," and Billy, hobbling fast to the window, stared out. There came Ollinger at the lope, fringes rippling on his buckskin shirt, stringy, yellow hair a'flutter around his beefy, Indian-like features.

"Bell got The Kid! Plugged th' dirty bugger," he bellowed as he ran, six-shooter at the ready.

Billy spun back, slipping on the rough planking in his frantic haste to get Ollinger's shiny, double-barreled shotgun from the rack across the hall. The past week had been a windy bluster of Bob Ollinger's brags—brags of how he'd cut down a young fugitive on the Pecos—brags of how that spindling young'un ran like a "scared chicken" before Ollinger pulled down and blew him to shreds. And how many times was it that Ollinger had patted that glistening murder weapon, promising to plant all twenty-four buckshot between Billy's shoulder blades? Plenty!

The Kid was at the front window, with Ollinger's cocked and loaded shotgun, pointed downwards—waiting when the big man puffed into the front yard of the Court House.

"Hey, Bob," Billy yelled down. Ollinger, hesitating between the gate posts, seemed about to turn back. "Look up here," The Kid commanded. "Use that gun or—."

Ollinger, stung into action, whipped out his Colt to fire—and took both barrels from his own shotgun—full in the chest—

—the crash of the discharges jolted Billy as wind shatters a drifting smoke column. He was empty, ghost-bodied in the chilly moonlight that swirled around and through him. Everything wavered and bobbed as he crouched under a Fort Sumner cottonwood, desperately trying for a sure shot at the shifting shadows before him.

His eyes sharpened and he knew the faces of his enemies.

There was dead Sheriff Brady, blood caked in a splotch on the middle of his woolen shirt. There was Bell, sighting a rifle at him, with his long, bony face creased with rage. There came a shotgun poking around the corner of an adobe, and the broad, evil smile of Bob Ollinger leered as he sighted with the very gun that Billy had used on him.

All the dead were there. There was fat Hindman, and black browed Joe Grant, and all the others who'd gone down in fair fights before The Kid's gun or the weapons of his men.

With murderous grimaces, these corpses slowly surrounded him with leveled pistols and long guns. "Don't," he tried to shout, "don't—too many of you. Can't keep fightin' you!"

More shadows swarmed out into the cold moonlight, and he trembled to see Celsa there, and Juana of long ago, and the tavern keeper's daughter from Anton Chico. None of the women spoke, but all lifted pistols, so heavy that little Juana needed both slender hands to hoist her big, glinting six-gun.

"No! No!" he was screaming at them in a voice that was soundless. He fell to his knees in the silvery dust, teeth clattering. It was so horribly cold. "No! No! Pat, stop them!" But the tall, gaunt form of Garrett shrugged skeleton shoulders, fading back into the chilly shadows.

Dead and living drew nearer, linked by the bonds of their hatred. Billy saw Esmeralda, her face a smooth mask, as she stood before the entire phantom posse. Her beautiful, red mouth opened, as her narrow hand pointed toward him. All the guns roared out their thunderous message of death.

He rose, tried to run—but his legs were paralyzed with cold and numbing fear. Bullets smashed through his body. Blood streamed forth in thin, red ribbons that swayed and rippled around him in the pallid night.

The crashes of the impacts continually battered

him. He tried to call out, but fell backward, weeping. "No! No! Not you—not you." Faces spun around him and—

—a face was close to his. Peering down at him. Someone was shaking him by the shoulder.

"*Señor*, you're all right then, eh?" Billy saw, through sleep-swollen lids, the thin, mustached face of the little Mexican, Frank Fega, who was to meet him at the Springs.

"Hunnh? You're here? You're here already?" His mind was still only half-functioning. The thudding of horses' hooves shook the earth as he rolled out from his blanket. "What're you doin' here so soon?" The Kid gaped at the red bow of the sun, slowly arching above the dark tree line.

Over in the grove, Angel whinnied at the approaching riders.

"We come early, *Señor*." Fega waved toward the dismounting Texan and the others. "Someone back in Tularosa they tipped the play to that little, foxy-face Charlie Siringo. He's out with a bunch trying to cut trail before we grab beef from somebody like *Señor* Uncle John Chisum."

"Ah," said Billy, standing on shaking legs, rubbing at his eyes. "Y'know what we're up to?"

"*Si, Señor*," Fega smiled. "We know. But we'll go along."

"*Bueno*," Billy grinned. "We'll get there before they do—and if not, why maybe we'll burn some little powder."

8 Chisum's Beef

Billy and his men made a quick breakfast over a small, smokeless fire and mounted up. "You've come a hard piece," he said. "But we're gonna push on just as hard to keep ahead of snoopers like Siringo."

"I don't mind some exercise," the Texan drawled. He pulled his Winchester carbine from his saddle-boot and looked over the lever action. He was alert now, grey eyes glittering. The Mexicans carefully inspected their own weapons.

"All right," Billy said. He rode Angel up from the depression surrounding the springs and took a long survey of the horizon with his field glasses. Nothing was stirring.

"Come on, Frank, Felipe and Jose." He glanced at the cowboy. "What'd you say your name was—Texas?" He sensed something about this one. Reminded him of the redhead down in that Texas jail—Jesse Evans! The same wild look about the eyes Jesse used to get when things were ready to pop. He wished, for a moment, that Jesse would come riding over the hills. Could he use him? Well, you bet!

"Your name?" he repeated.

"O'Day—like I said. Tom O'Day."

"Well, your peepers are sure wide open this

mornin', O'Day," he grinned. "Peep O'Day suits you. Just keep 'em wide open until we gather up that beef."

He led the group out at an easy trot. Wouldn't do to wear down the mounts by running them—unless they had to spur them up.

An hour later they crossed the shallow Padilla, its placid, brown surface broken into yellowed flakes by the splashing legs of their horses.

"Those clouds," Fega pointed at the sky as they rested their mounts on the far bank of the Padilla, "they could fetch up the Devil's Grandmother of a rain."

Billy thrust up his hat brim with a thumb and studied the weather. Thunderheads of the previous night were herding close-packed overhead, their opalescent bulks yellowish-black with wind and rain. "Let's keep right on. This'll give us some help. A wet trail's right easy to track."

The Mexicans and O'Day looked at The Kid, but said nothing.

It was a full twenty miles from the Padilla bends to the north range of Chisum's Jingle Bob—but they were crossing the rocky waste of the Devil's Ribs, northwest of Roswell, just after noontime. The air was now heavy with impending storm, as though great weights were bulking over the dusty land and all things upon it.

O'Day's face, strained and sallow by the amber of the storm gleam, was that of a man long sickened with fever. And the Mexicans were as blanched as the rock and stone their horses trotted across.

"You're sure th' most unhealthy lookin' bunch I've spotted in a long time," The Kid observed, "but that's all right. You got th' same color I've seen on men before they put up a hell of a scrap."

"You ain't no lily yourself," O'Day drawled.

"*Si*," Billy answered, "you're right, there."

"You see some troubles before, *Señor*?" fat Jose asked.

"Oh, a few scrapes," Billy replied. "But look out—there's part of th' herd. No cowhands around that I see."

Below on the barren tableland, wide expanses of grazing space ran unbroken by hill or mountain. Smooth, undulating waves of grassy plain flowed eastward toward the dusky, blue horizon that was Texas.

Close to three hundred head of cattle were bunched up, moving slowly east in the direction of a large, brush-filled hollow, several acres across. The animals' dun-colored backs merged with the tawny-olive of the deep, dry grasses, but their jostling, shifting horns sparkled with strange lights.

"Hey," O'Day yelled, "come on, if those critters get into that scrub this weather, you'll need giant powder and crow-bars to prize 'em out!"

"Whoa up!" Billy barked. "*Mucho lento*!

This ain't Texas, and we ain't aimin' for no stampedes!"

He sent the Mexicans toward the herd's north flank with instructions to turn it. "Cut out about seventy-five or so," he shouted. "Peep and I'll start another bunch due east toward th' Panhandle, then I'll swing back and join up."

Dust Devils began to dance their small, whining circles. The horses' manes tossed and twitched in the growing breeze. Scattered drops exploded like tiny bullets along the rocky ground as Tafalla, Chavez and Fega rode down the slope.

The storm broke while the trio loped toward the main herd. Lightning arched pink, quicksilver spears at the bending grasses; and the rushing winds brought the sting of rain.

"Come on, O'Day," The Kid called, "now's th' time to make those tracks!"

"I drive decoys east leavin' a plain trail for a posse to foller?" O'Day's lips formed words in the downpour. "Slick! Well, I'll do it but I want myself a bigger cut."

"You'll get your share, don't worry." Billy slapped the mare forward into the storm. They drove headlong over the incline, hooves throwing sparks and stones. The herd racked on toward the brushy bottoms like a thousand-headed animal seeking its den.

The Kid, glancing back over his shoulder, saw a horseback figure, outlined by storm-flash on the hill rim—but it vanished in a tattered sheet of rain.

"Well," he thought, "too late to stop now. Whoever that was better watch out when th' herd turns to come rippin' up th' ridge."

Frank, Felipe and Jose were down on the edge of the restless cattle mass, guiding them with high-pitched yells and flourishes of arms and serapes. Their pistol explosions were swallowed in the nearly continuous cannonades of thunder.

Billy and Peep galloped through the rain in time to head another bunch of cattle from the brush. But the excited Mexicans failed to stop a good half of the herd from wheeling back into the scrub.

"Let 'em go," Billy motioned them off. "We've got enough to give Uncle John th' six day weeps." He rode up shouting, "Take 'em up th' slopes and point straight northwest for Three Rivers Range."

"You follow soon, *Señor*?" the plump Tafalla inquired as the silent Chavez cocked a curious eye and Fega grinned wetly.

"Soon as O'Day and me get that bunch over there headed toward Tascosa. I want plenty of sign showin' out that way."

The cattle were eager to move. The incessant crackle of the lightning was a great whip of sound, lashing over their backs.

Billy and O'Day drove the smaller group past

scattered, rain-drenched thickets as the Mexicans urged the larger part of the herd up and across the rocky slopes.

The storm was slowly shifting eastward and the frenzied bellowing of the Coghlan-bound herd welled up as the rain-filled wind subsided. Billy turned in his saddle, staring back into the last of the lancing gusts. "Keep 'em movin', Peep," he called. "I'm goin' up th' ridge to give them *corridas* a hand before they fumble th' whole kaboodle."

O'Day responded with a wave of his wet *sombrero* as he pushed the decoy herd along.

As Billy and Angel cantered up the rocky slope, a dozen head of cattle came plunging diagonally back down the incline. And a rider, astride a pinto, raced to keep ahead of the frantic beasts.

It was Esmeralda Sandoval, black hair, wet with rain, streaming back over her shoulders.

Even as Billy spurred his mare forward, the girl's horse stumbled. She made a desperate effort to stay in the saddle, grabbing at the saddle-horn.

The Kid instantly flung Angel in the path of the steers. "Hi-Yoop! Back there—Turn you sons ...," he yelped with Apache-like fury. "Turn! Turn out!" The beeves wheeled clumsily, grazing the slipping, side-stepping black mare, to go by with a clatter, heads low in a wild-eyed bunch.

The impact of a steer's horn and flank threw

Angel sideways, feet rattling on stone and boulder. The Kid fought her head up, but she went over in a jarring heap onto her left side. Billy's leg was pinned between crushing horseflesh and rock.

"Billy! Oh Billy!" The girl had reined in and was running across the slippery rock surface to him, lovely features glistening with rain. "Are you hurt—badly?" She knelt beside him, raven-black hair falling across his outstretched hand.

His eyes narrowed with pain as he looked up at her. "No doubt about it . . . at all."

"Oh, you are hurt!" She clasped hands tightly together, tears sparkling at the edge of down-swept, velvety lashes. Her red mouth was an anguished scarlet mark on her pale face.

"*Pardone*! No! I'm all right." He smiled tightly. "I meant . . . you're more beautiful when you're scared . . . than when you're mad." He ground his teeth at the mare's dead weight. Angel, still stunned, bled from a wounded shoulder. Billy leaned an elbow on the wet ground and yanked his trapped leg. "Can't move," he grunted, "g'me a hand."

Esmeralda was tugging at The Kid's knee when hoof clatter swelled beyond the ridge. "More cattle?" she gasped.

"No—horseman." Billy reached for his pistol—but it wasn't in its holster. "How many Chisum's men followed you?"

She watched the ridge. "No one knew. I told no one."

A rider broke over the skyline. "It's all right," Billy relaxed. "That's one of mine."

Jose Tafalla reined up in a spray of wet pebbles. "Hey, *Señor*! I chase the runaways, and here you are." His unshaven, double chin creased in a porcine smile. "That's good luck for me."

"What's the matter with you? *Comedraja*," the girl snapped. "Get off and help here!" She rose and ran toward the big Mexican, clenching her fists. "Stupid, fat-bellied *borrico*!"

Billy pulled at his boot. "Easy, Esmeralda. Where'd you learn such alley Spanish? Jose's gonna help."

"That's right—*si*!" Tafalla drew out his long-barreled six-shooter. "And it's myself I'm gonna help to these reward money Sheriff Pat Garrett's been tryin' to collect." He shook a thick, hairy finger. "You thought I didn't know you—Beely Keed?" A chuckle bubbled deep in his fat throat. "*Si*, I knew you. That mustacho don't fool one who's fought against you at Seven Rivers Canyon an' Chisum's South Spring just four years back."

"No wonder I didn't spot you," Billy grinned thinly. "Your gang shot at long range, then ran for it." He gave a desperate tug and his stiffened leg came free.

"Hold it, *Señor* Keed—right there!" Tafalla tight-reined his horse, pointing his Colt at them.

"What are you trying to do?" Esmeralda pushed back her tangled hair and threw herself against Billy. "You can't—," and she wrapped her arms about him. He could feel her warmth, in that moment, pressing through their sodden clothing, her softly-rounded breasts against his shoulder. The faint odor of flowers from her hair came to him over the smell of wet earth and sweaty horseflesh.

"You're th' vinegaroon who tipped Siringo," Billy ground out. "Well, don't hurt this girl or—."

"Or, what, *Señor* Keed?" Jose leered. "You shouldn't ought to make threats—no dead man can do such." He cocked the heavy, single-action Colt. "But you're right. I told one of those drunk Texans at Coghlan's bar to pass word to Siringo—told him where we headed, but didn't say Beely Keed, *por Dios*, no! I want your five-hundred dead-money dollars myself. That's good business, no?"

"Get away Esmeralda—he wants me." Billy attempted to push the girl's supple body from him, but she clung with the tender strength of a stubborn child.

"That's all right, *Señorita*. Ladies first," Tafalla snorted. "You gotta go anyway. Can't have witness, and I'll say Keed done it."

Billy shoved the girl hard and made a grab for his saddle-gun. She tumbled, cat-like, onto her knees and catching up a handful of wet gravel, flung it full into the face of Tafalla.

The Mexican threw out his arms—and began to slide sideways from his horse. Off down the slopes a gun cracked in the quiet.

Tafalla lay stretched on his back, spread-eagled, cocked six-gun still in one brown paw, a red, round hole punched into the middle of his forehead. His blood-spattered hat lay by his boots.

The Kid stumbled over and pulled Esmeralda to her feet. He clasped her trembling body to his. "That's O'Day down there." He raised his free hand to the distant figure. The man waved back, stowed away the rifle in its boot and turned his horse back in the direction of the slowly ambling decoy herd.

It had been a great shot, better even than that of the old rattler Buckshot Roberts, when he'd put a bullet through poor Dick Brewer from three-hundred yards back at Blazer's Mill in '78.

Billy retrieved Tafalla's soiled, silver-laced hat and dropped it on the mutilated face. "You'll have to leave word at the ranch that someone got a rustler up here. They'll get him proper burial."

The girl clung to him in silence. Behind them there came a scrambling and they looked around to see Angel pawing herself upright, to stand with downhung head.

"Your pretty horse is going to live," she smiled faintly.

"Some angels got a lot of sand," Billy grinned to her. "Yeah, she probably was knocked out on th' rocks." He limped over and ran his hand down the mare's trembling legs. "Don't think she broke any bones, but that horn gash'll lay her up for a spell." He brushed pebbles and grit from the horse's flanks. Angel pushed her nose against The Kid.

"You called her—Angel?"

"Name seemed to fit her," Billy shrugged.

Overhead, leaden clouds were edging ponderously in again, threatening rain storms.

"We got to move out of here, *ahora*. Someone from Chisum's bound to ride over this way, lookin' for you—but you can't wait 'em out in another duck-drownder."

He took her by the arm and led her to the little brown-and-white pinto. Smooth flesh beneath the white, silken shirt was cool to his touch, warmth gone. Her face was drawn.

"Come on," he gave her a hand-up into the saddle. She sat astride, reins held loosely. Her dampened, black riding-skirt, rumpled up above beautifully tooled, brown-leather boots, disclosed a glimpse of a smoothly curving calf. "*Gracias*," she murmured, red mouth downcurved with sudden fatigue.

Billy hunted among the wet rocks, found his pistol and came back to Tafalla. He pulled the .44 from the Mexican's clenched fist and shoved it into his own belt. "Won't be needin' this. There's no bounty huntin' in Hell."

The girl swayed in her saddle, head bent nearly to the pinto's mane. She straightened and pressed a hand over her eyes. "I'm sorry—I've never seen a man killed—life taken so swiftly."

The Kid swung his aching leg over the Mexican's roan and settled into the wide, brass-riveted saddle. With Angel's reins in his left hand, he asked, "Can you ride?"

She nodded wordlessly. Both looked past the dead man, where he lay with extended arms. Beyond, along the range floor, the runaway cattle were entering the brushy scrub. Farther off, O'Day and his false trail-herd were distant brown dots strung along the plain.

"The birds—they are out again." The girl indicated a section of the rocky soil, covered with sparse vegetation, now all ablaze with thousands of water-drop suns. A mottled-brown road-runner darted around a small bush, cocking its head to peer at them with sharply inquisitive eyes. And high above in the now darkening sky, piñon jays circled a thinning rift of gold.

"*Si*, but not for long." Billy gestured toward the northwest, where more rainclouds were gathering. "Fega and Chavez are crowding that beef at a smart clip. They're real trumps—top hands to move that much on the hoof. If they don't get much storm, the critters will go along *todo correcto* for a spell. But we got to beat those clouds ourselves."

They rode north into the barren uplands.

9   Esmeralda's Heart

Billy and the Sandoval girl rode into the Devil's Cave as a storm, more vicious than the last, roared down over the barren, rock-filled mesa.

The high-arched cave opening was in the smallest of the upthrusting, red-banded rock formations, collectively called the Devil's Ribs. These rose, in sharp waves, to heights of one-hundred or more feet, three miles west of the northern limits of old John Chisum's Jingle Bob Range. Ancient people of the mesas had made use of this particular cave in the distant past. Their fire smoke still streaked the vaulted ceiling.

Outside the wide cave-mouth the rain was now a grey, rushing blur. Within, the dusky, echoing quiet was full of the clink and clatter of stamping horses.

Billy helped Esmeralda from the saddle, taking advantage of the moment to hold her soft, slender body in his arms.

He felt her tremble. "It's O.K., Angel."

She smiled. "Angel? Why do you call me the name of your pretty, black horse?"

"Well," he grinned, thrilled by her voice and nearness. "You're really the first—Angel." He gave her a bear-hug and heard her breath exhale from the pressure. She clung to him, long lashes brushing his cheek. The perfume of her hair fetched memories of old rose gardens in villages below the border. "Angel," he whispered, "that's th' name I gave you th' night we met at Portales."

She shivered, again, in his arms. "That terrible night—that *terriblemente* night." She gave a nervous, half-stifled laugh. "I didn't mean that it was terrible—because of you. I meant terrible for what they did to you—that Pat Garrett! And what they still do to you—now."

He released her and turned toward the cave mouth. "You're cold," he said, looking out at the downpour. "It's gonna keep up for a spell." He kicked around the rocky floor and turned up spare pieces of brushwood from more recent fires. He carried the chunks and branches to a spot near the entrance, arranged a pile, lighting it with a match.

She approached the growing orange flame and held a hand over the heat. "Billy—don't let them do any more to you—don't let . . ." She bit her red, lower lip. Her eyes flashed in the firelight. "Don't let them push you into more trouble." Looking straight at him, her smooth chin tightened. "Sallie Chisum's told me about you— that you were always polite and cheerful with her from the first day you rode into Chisum's ranch. You were only sixteen then, weren't you? She still has the Indian tobacco pouch you gave her."

Esmeralda's eyes softened. "Sallie still weeps

for the boy who rode into that awful Lincoln County trouble. She thinks you're dead, and it tore my heart not to let her know."

"Yeah," The Kid went over to Angel and inspected the horse's flank in the growing fire-light, "guess I was pretty green when I first showed up to Chisum's." He clenched his jaw. "But I learned fast."

"Yes, you were a boy who grew up too fast." She held both hands to the crackling blaze. "And you're still traveling too fast." She looked at him, her face reflecting his own tenseness. "You'll have to stop some day—and I think I know how you can do it."

Billy grinned to himself. This little lady could surely do her share of thinking. He said nothing, patting the mare's nose. The black's wound was clotting up some. He slipped his canteen off the saddle-horn and wetting his red neckerchief, cleaned the edges of the gash.

"You know how I plan to stop runnin'? And how I'm gonna keep th' Territory from bustin' my neck?" he inquired ironically. "I'm just gonna up and stay dead. That's how!"

"No, I don't like that." She ran her fingers through her damp hair and bending, spread it in a dark fan to the fire warmth. "I mean you're going to receive money—probably quite a lot for those cattle you're taking."

"*Pozo*?" He pulled the dead Mexican's pistol

from his own belt and thrust it into the saddle bag.

She lifted one slim finger, exactly like a teacher expounding a lesson. "You take that cattle money and hire a very good, a very smart lawyer. I know of one. He handles my father's business at El Paso—a *Señor* Ortiz. He'll prove most of your troubles were forced on you." She dropped her hand. "Even John Chisum has said, and I heard him, that you weren't half so bad as some folks had painted you—that you chose the losing side, the wrong side, the side without sufficient influence." Her mouth was tender as she spoke. "But I—I'm very glad that you fought for those who needed you most. I couldn't have cared, if . . ."

"But I'm helpin' myself to Chisum beef." He broke in bitterly. "And how bad does that make me?"

"I found you had rights in that, also. At first I was upset to think you'd take *Señor* Chisum's cattle, but Sallie, herself, admitted that when you went against *Señor* Chisum's powerful friends during the Lincoln County trouble—he would not pay your back wages. And . . ."

But he took her back into his arms, holding a hand over her lovely mouth. "*Quieto*—don't get yourself so riled."

He felt a more subtle warmth now than fireglow and sensed she felt it also. "Esmeralda?" he whispered.

"What?" She looked at him from under her long lashes and he kissed her. She turned in his grasp, tried to pull away—for only a moment. Her arms tightened about his neck and her vibrant mouth was eager and glowing against his. Her pliant body pressed against him until it was as though fire and responding closeness were fusing them into one.

She wriggled free of his arms to stand before the roaring blaze, doing up her hair in the elegant manner, and fastening it with a silver comb, fashioned like a harp.

"Really," her expression and voice were aloof. "I don't know what to think. I give you my best advice and concern, and yet all you wish to do is paw at me—a Sandoval, whose ancestor was one of the ancient *Señor* Cortez' officers. You attempt to handle me like some common woman of the cantinas."

Her eyes, crinkling ever so slightly at the corners, belied her proud words and haughty expression. "Besides," she sniffed, "that big gun and belt of yours has nearly sawed me in two."

He unbuckled his pistol belt, untying the holster's leg string and hung it on the roan's saddle. Beyond the cave-mouth, the grey water curtain was patched with bits of sun—but it still descended with hissing force as thunder mumbled and muttered.

"Here," he took her hand. "Sit by th' fire and get

good and dry before that rain lets up. You've got to get back to Chisum's and take Angel along." He gently seated her upon the dry, sandy floor of the cave. Fire color rose and fell upon her sweet face and delicately curved figure, painting them with orange and red. For a moment she relaxed, with hands clasped over knees, staring into the glowing heart of the flame.

Watching her, he remembered other campfires, and suddenly realized that he'd never sat at one so comforting.

"Billy," she spoke softly. When he looked up from poking at the fire, she kissed him.

Murky, blue, cave shadows were reaching toward the paling fire as The Kid held her in his arms, thinking how child-like, yet so completely womanly she was. He tossed his hat aside and gently tipping up her head, kissed her responding mouth, faintly aromatic eyelids, delicious curve of cheekbone, smooth chin and the pale, olive beauty of her throat.

"Does my mustacho bother much?" He grinned down at her. "You know, you're th' first lady I've kissed since I raised it."

She lifted a hand, as rosy-pink and slender as those of the pink plaster saints all-in-a-row along the mission wall at Las Luz. One slim finger lingered on the newly-healed scar tissue of his left cheek. "Perhaps the first lady you have kissed recently—but not the first you've kissed,

91

seguramente?" She lay back, resting her head on his shoulder. "I've been kissed before, also. I'm not so unworldly as you might believe. General Cortinas, with his big mustachoes, he kissed me upon the face when I was only ten. He's the one the Texas Rangers call *bandido*—the way some call you names, because you fought for what you felt to be right."

The horses moved restlessly and shook their bridles. Smoke from the ebbing fire silently indicated the passing time—and brought him the thought that Siringo's hunters might come this way. But they must not find him with her. He couldn't allow her to be harmed by name or weapon. The image of fat Jose pointing his murderous pistol at her, threatening her lovely life, brought a chill to him.

Somewhere off beyond the Backbone's ridges two men were trying to keep all those cattle bunched together and headed for Three Rivers. Billy made an effort to rise, to get under way, but felt sleek, black hair against his cheek. She was looking at him with eyes large and filled with a light not found in fire-embers.

"So, you love me," she murmured.

He bent to kiss her again, filled with a strange yet pleasant feeling. And something told him, "that's what it is—*amor*, passion—love!"

"Yes," he whispered, "yes."

She moved happily in his arms, and her

rumpled skirt, turned to allow the fading heat to dry its rain-dampness, disclosed dimpled knee and pale, fire-tinted thigh. Her white blouse was open at the neck, and he gently placed his hand beneath its surface to caress her.

This was not the sort of women with which he was familiar. Never had he known such a girl. "Never," he thought, "has a woman really known me or loved me in this way."

Her arms were smooth around his neck. She was smoothness—like velvet breeze at dusk—fine and rich as flour-gold. Her breath in his ear—the soft rustle of the beautiful aspen leaf, hesitant and trembling.

He kissed the tender woman-curves of her, seen only by the caressing red glance of the fire, and his own half-closed eyes—and heard her voice repeating softly, urgently, "Be kind, Billy—oh, be kind."

This was the answer to hundreds of lonely trails. This was the final answer to all half-realized loves and half-forgotten hates. This was haven to which wild horse raced and stallion plunged and kicked in wind-swept surging—and song began that wasn't really song—more a voice lifted up, ever up, steadily as gilded bell at Las Trampas was struck by silver clapper until growing, ringing resonance spread around and through him, driving wildness before—to burst in golden completeness.

"The rain stops," she spoke quietly, and raising herself, straightened blouse and skirt. She kissed his scarred cheek. "This is a most wonderful thing. I could stay—oh, I could stay, but I think you should go before someone comes to hurt you." The fire was an ashy bed of dulling embers, smothered by engulfing gloom and the wash of daylight streaming in.

They trod out the last fire-sparks and led the horses into the brilliant sheen of afternoon. Clouds were thin, grey wisps fleeing to the east through a tall, blue sky. The sun drank in the moisture on rock and sand.

The Kid pulled the saddle from the Mexican's horse and transferred it to the black, taking his own gear for the roan. Now he was all haste—fearful that Siringo's or Chisum's men might appear over the slopes to find her with him.

He tightened Esmeralda's saddle and helped her up. "Get ridin' for Chisum's now, Angel. Take my mare with you. Have 'em doctor her right off. I'll get her when I can."

"Will you come back before I leave?"

"I'll be back soon as I can—don't worry. If I get strapped for time, don't worry. I'll come down to El Paso. Just wait for me. I'll find you. They'll come down and find Tafalla." He rode up beside her. "*Adiós amado.* You're *mi verdadero pasión.*"

"*Adiós mi solomente hombre.* I'll wait even in

94

El Paso. The cattle money will allow *Señor* Ortiz to start legal proceedings." She reached out and grasped his hand, smooth fingers closing over his rough palm. "Have faith—we'll find the way." Her eyes fell as she released him. "If you wish it."

"*Yo deseo!*" He took her face in both hands, turning it to the blue sky, and kissed her. "I wish it—*mucho!*"

Heading the roan north, he rode fast into the rocky expanse, following the Coghlan-bound herd, never looking back. He couldn't trust himself to see that small, proud figure riding out of his life—if only for a short while.

10   Kate's Eyes

The Kid's normally buoyant spirits were unaffected by dismal weather and hard work. When he rejoined Fega and Chavez, he broke the news of Tafalla's treachery and death with characteristic cheerfulness.

Stunned into silence, Fega recovered within the hour with a shrug and the inevitable "*quién sabe?*" The silent Chavez continued with the work in hand.

One unseasonable storm after another swept down upon the trio, and the first night was spent in a dreary and wet camp a bare fifteen miles from the Chisum Range. There had been no sign of pursuit—so far.

Despite bad weather, they moved so swiftly that they were herding the rustled Jingle Bob stock onto the north section of Coghlan's Three Rivers Ranch on the second afternoon of the drive.

The blue distances of the San Andreas were aglow with declining sun and the shining immensity of Old Baldy reared its heights scant miles to the north when they herded past the willows that lined the smallest of the Three Rivers—the Frio.

They rode near scattered brown adobe *casitas*, tucked into green gardens along the river—the houses of Coghlan's laborers and ranch hands. "That's th' ranch house, *Tres Rios*, near those trees past th' orchard," Billy indicated a good half acre of peach trees, their foliage spangled with yellowing fruit.

"*Señor* Paddy *cierto* has one fine layout," Fega marveled with a wag of his head. Chavez grinned silently.

Two large, rough-timbered corrals stretched in elongated ovals beside several low-crowned, white barns. Mexicans working about the buildings glanced at the incoming cattle and their drovers with incurious eyes as they casually opened the near corral gate.

"They seen this before," Billy yelled at his riders. "Keep pilin' 'em into th' *pluma*. I'll ride on up to th' house."

Before he could spur-up the roan to press through the thronging beef, toward the cottonwood-shaded ranch headquarters, a small springwagon came jouncing toward them. A little, wide-shouldered man teetered on the edge of the wagon seat, sawing away at the reins.

"Hey, you fellers! You make plenty damn noise mit dem cows." He pulled the fat, brown mare to a halt and stood up, bristling, black brows bent in a fierce scowl. "Why'd ya come so early yet? Everyone sees this big herd coming here!" His voice was rasping and raucous as a mountain jay.

The cattle, ambling into the wide corral, were

subdued from the rough terrain and repeated storms—all fire and wild spirit pounded from them. But the small, burly fellow, who Billy took to be Wolgenmuth, Coghlan's right-hand man, hopped about in jay-like agitation, waving his fists at the last bunch of steers.

"Somebody givin' you trouble, Mister Wolgenmuth?" The Kid grinned down from the roan.

"Trouble? Mein Gott, trouble you say?" Wolgenmuth halted his nervous dance steps, pawed in the pockets of his green, checkered coat, produced a bandana and mopped his broad forehead. "Up there at the house is *Madama*—Paddy Coghlan's wife. She insists to come up here mit us undt wait for Paddy. Undt she complains to me about the noise undt dust from your *verdampt* cows. Undt asking me questions she should get by Paddy."

The Kid laughed at the fuming little "Dutchman" and turned his horse back to his drovers, who with a pair of ranch hands, were doing a handy job of prodding the last of the beeves into their corral.

"Button 'em up." Billy swung down from the roan and tied him to the corral rail. He walked back to Wolgenmuth, rubbing the small of his back. All this heavy work wasn't agreeing too well with a recent "invalid" but he had to keep going. "Ready to start th' tally?"

"Gott, ja!" Wolgenmuth dug around in the

wagonbed and clawed up a yellow, rawhide book. "The sooner I get this crazy business over, undt get them cattles off here into that mountain range, the better." He kept twisting his thick neck as though expecting to see the Law come pounding hell for leather to arrest him. "Coghlan's losing his mind, what mit Herr Garrett and Siringo both liable to ride in at any time."

They went down to the narrow fence that connected the two large corrals. Fega, Chavez and several hangers-on followed.

"I make it close on one-hundred head," stated The Kid.

"Ve vill see—ve vill see," Wolgenmuth grunted. He took out a stubby pencil, opened the ledger and traced his way down a page with a stumpy finger. "Ja, I have it—Roberts, Mister W. Roberts. That's you?"

"It'll do."

"Ja, undt it says forty dollars advance payment made, ah—six days ago?"

"Time skedaddles."

"Ja." Wolgenmuth made a painful grimace, his attempt at a smile. "Undt ve made these *verdampt* cows skedaddles through here undt out to the mountain range. Where maybe Garrett don't see." He grunted his way to the top rail of the corral and with a nod to the assembled ranch hands reopened the ledger.

The men armed themselves with long, stout

poles, which lay on the ground nearby. While two swung open the double gates between the pens, the rest ran to the front and rear of the herd and began poking the animals through the narrow stretch into the empty corral.

The bawling cattle plunged and reared their way through the gates with Billy, Wolgenmuth, Fega and Chavez keeping individual count; Wolgenmuth with his chewed lead pencil, Billy with nicks cut from the top rail with his pocket knife, and Frank and Jose upon their thumbs and fingers.

The sun was a bleary red smear behind the ragged mountain tops by the time the last beeve was prodded into the north corral.

"I make it vun-hundred undt vun," Wolgenmuth clapped the ledger shut and clambered awkwardly down to continue twisting his neck at the skyline.

"Me, I get one hundred and five," The Kid ran a finger over the edge of his mustache. "I reckon you was about as interested in th' scenery as th' cows." He rattled the knife blade along a row of twenty-one nicks—one for each five cows, and sliced off a long sliver.

"And I, *Señor* Wilgenmoot," Fega grinned evilly, hacking at the corral post, with the blade of a wicked-looking knife, plucked from his boot top. "I also make it *uno centésimo cinco*!"

Chavez, glowering silently behind Fega, nodded in agreement.

Wolgenmuth glared at the slowly circling stock and rubbed at his bristly chin. "*Ach tueffelhundts*, it could possibly be so. Vun hundred undt fife at fife dollars a head."

The Kid bit down on his sliver. "One hundred and five at eight dollars a head." He hitched up his gunbelt.

"*Por Dios barba*! Eight dollars." Fega echoed Billy and tugged away at his thick, black mustache.

Chavez quietly loosened his six-gun in its holster as the clustered *Tres Rios* Mexicans grinned behind their hands.

"Really! Uncle Morris, why don't you pay these men?" a female voice broke in behind the debaters.

Billy turned to see a blonde girl, standing with hands on curving hips. Her deep, blue eyes were appraising—but her wide, full, red mouth was warm and friendly. She was dressed in, what Billy took to be, some sort of riding outfit. The tight-fitting scarlet of the cloth swept down from trim shoulders, over swelling breasts to a narrow waist, flaring out sensuously across hip lines. Hair as yellow rich as the desert marigold was piled upon her shapely head.

Billy and his two *compadres* doffed their sombreros. The Kid felt dusty and worn.

Wolgenmuth stared at the girl and back to Billy. He lifted his arms over his head, palms up to the crimson sky—as if to hold back the night. "All right! Vy not?" He jerked a thumb at the grey-bearded Mexican who'd bossed the steer corralling. "Rafael will see dot you eat. Come to the house later undt ve'll settle up."

The stocky, little man turned away and clambered into the springwagon, beckoning the girl to join him. She swung up gracefully, neat ankles, in white boots, flashing from under the scarlet skirt. As an afterthought Wolgenmuth nodded at the girl. "Mine Niece, Katerine Castle, from Boston in the State of Massachusetts. Her father, mine brother-in-law, has himself a ranch up in Vyoming. She goes tomorrow to Santa Fe to meet him."

The girl rested a hand on the iron-railing of the wagon seat, smiling at Billy.

"Billy Bon—, Roberts, Miss," The Kid stumbled over his name. "And these are my right- and left-hand bowers, Frank and Felipe."

Fega swept the sand with his dusty *sombrero* as Chavez followed suit.

She turned to Wolgenmuth, speaking to him in a low voice.

He scowled before baring his teeth in his painful smile. "Kate vants you Mister Roberts, should come up to have the meal mit us." He clucked at the horse.

"No thanks—we'll be fine with the hands here." Billy clapped his headgear back on.

The wagon rolled along toward the grove of trees and stopped. "Both you and your friends are to come, Mister Roberts," the girl's clear voice commanded. Wolgenmuth slapped the reins over the horse and left Billy by the corral.

"*Señor* Roberts?" The old, silver-bearded Mexican, Rafael tapped The Kid's elbow.

"*Si?*"

The old man glanced at his fellows as they made off for their huts. "I heard the little black *Señor* say he fears to see Sheriff Garrett come with his men." He pulled at his beard and closed an eye. "These Siringo may come—but not Garrett."

"Why not Garrett?"

"*Porqué*, he is gone to Santa Fe for the rest of these month. This I heard from my cousin, Siquio Sanchez, who lives at Lincoln."

Billy knew Sanchez mighty well. And he was glad Sanchez' relative didn't know The Kid. "*Grácias*. That's mighty interestin'." He slapped the reins in his hand. "Why didn't you tell Wolgenmuth?"

"Oh no, he's a man who needs worry. He wouldn't be happy unless he could *cuidado*, fret all these times." Rafael took over the horse from Billy. "That's how it goes with most *Anglos*. You see that. I can tell." He rubbed the roan's neck with a wrinkled, brown hand. "I will take care of your mounts."

Billy grinned, "*Grácias*, again. But don't you figure I'm *Anglo*?"

"Well—you are not all *Anglo*—not these cold-blooded man of *El Norte*. Not you." The old man tapped his own chest. "You seem to me more like another *amigo* who thought of Mexicans as real *Americanos*, not *sucio* strangers. *Si*, you're much like that poor one—Billy Keed." He sighed and started off toward the barns with the horses.

"*Si*," and Billy and Chavez raised their hats in honor of the departed. "Let's get in to supper," The Kid said.

They washed up in the kitchen and walked into the dining room from a long hallway. The room was bright with yellow candlelight.

Mrs. Coghlan, a thin, nervous little lady, past middle age, dressed in black, sat at the head of the large table. The blonde Kate was at the *Madama*'s right. Morris Wolgenmuth sat glooming at his plate on her left. Three places were set for Billy and his men at the foot of the table.

"Stop right there—you!" Mrs. Coghlan waved a fork at them, her long-lipped, Irish Biddy face screwed-up with distaste. "Mister Coghlan and I don't hold with any firearms in our houses. You all march right out and hang them on that hall rack." Her small, watery-green eyes glinted in a sallow face.

"Poor Paddy," Billy whispered to Fega. "Sorry, Missus," he got up. "I guess we just ain't got our society manners unpacked from our bed rolls." He winked at Kate, who raised blue eyes to the ceiling. "C'mon Frank and Felipe, let's shed our hardware."

They unbuckled their gunbelts out in the hall and hung the guns on the prongs of an elk head. "Mum's th' word," and Billy slipped his .44 under his shirt, stuffing the short-barreled six-gun down into his waist band, leaving vest unbuttoned.

The Queen of Tularosa and Three Rivers sat a fine table but they'd scarcely begun to pay homage to her beef roast, when a horseman clattered up to the front of the ranch house.

"That could be Mister Coghlan," the *Madama* peered up, "or Mister Peppin, but neither are due back before tomorrow night."

Billy felt the comfortable bulge of the pistol in his shirt. He didn't mind Paddy but he wasn't anxious to bump into old "Dad" Peppin, sheriff before Garrett—back during the Lincoln War.

"I go look—could be *Herr* Peppin, back from Fort Stanton about dose beef we got to deliffer." Wolgenmuth cast a regretful eye at his plate and waddled out into the hallway.

Muffled voices rolled down the hall and Wolgenmuth was back in the room, blinking and grimacing in the candlelight. Behind him, swaggered—Peep O'Day, filthy with trail-dust and Colt in hand.

"Young man," the *Madama* squealed in high-pitched indignation, "you march out and put that firearm in the hall! I don't allow—," she stabbed her imperious fork at the Texan.

"Sorry, M'am! I like my gun where she is," O'Day broke in sharply, staring at Billy, who sat with fingers on shirt front. "Sorry, Missy," he nodded at Kate, where she'd half-risen from the table, her red mouth a circle of crimson surprise.

"Y'made good time, Peep," Billy broke in, waiting to see just what O'Day's play was. He sensed it meant trouble. This crazy Texan was sure like Jesse Evans—always going off half-cocked.

"Yeah, that damned dummy herd's half way to Tascosa—but I didn't see hide nor horn of any— ah, nobody."

"Young man, you git out of here with that gun! I said Mister Coghlan and I don't allow firearms in this house. Why can't you cooperate like those?" The *Madama* pointed her tell-tale fork at Billy and his men.

"Thanks for tellin' me, old lady. Got a little quick business here—pleasure to know everyone's clean." O'Day jabbed the Colt into Wolgenmuth's padded ribs hard enough to make him grunt. "How much did that beef fetch, Dutchy?"

Wolgenmuth made visibly frantic mental calculations. "Eight hundred undt forty dollars!"

"O.K., trot that out to th' penny. Just about

enough to get me a long ways off." O'Day poked the quivering Wolgenmuth. "Where'd ya keep it?"

Wolgenmuth dumbly motioned toward the hall. O'Day hurled him through the doorway, slammed and bolted the door from the other side, before Billy could rip the pistol from his shirt.

"You've got some rough fellows working for you." The girl Kate stared white-faced at The Kid.

"He's fired right now!" Billy scrambled for the door leading into the kitchen but it was locked. O'Day could move fast for a sleepy-looking *Tejano*.

Footsteps thudded down the hall. A gun exploded beyond the heavy oak door and splinters screamed into the room with the bullet.

"Get down!" Billy dodged around the table and grabbed the Castle girl by the shoulder as he went by. An outer door crashed. They heard shouting and the sound of a horse, running fast away from the ranch house.

"You're squeezing me—just a little too hard."

The Kid looked into two large, blue eyes, fringed with dark lashes—and came to himself. "Sorry," he grinned, releasing her.

"This west of yours is still awfully wild, isn't it?" She smiled.

"Yeah, pretty frisky sometimes."

"Morris!" the *Madama* shrilled from behind

her big wooden chair. "Morris, is everything all right?"

The bolt creaked in the hall door and it opened slowly. Wolgenmuth tottered in. "*Ach Gott*! *Dot tueffel* took all money in de safe!"

Billy felt hot blood climbing into his face. "He got all—th' money—all that steer money?"

Wolgenmuth plopped into his chair, nodding weakly. Kate opened the little man's collar, fanning him with her napkin.

Billy ran through the hall and out the front door, followed by Tafalla and Chavez. The August night was black as O'Day's heart. He'd play the devil trailing a madman like that in such pitch when he couldn't see the gun in his own hand.

"Well," The Kid mused, "I owed Peep plenty for knockin' that murderin' Tafalla off our necks—but didn't think it'd cost th' bundle."

"What now, *Señor*?" Fega and Chavez were beside him.

"Ain't sure." Billy absently spun the cylinder of his Colt. "We're out of money, so there's no rush to get back th' way I come." He thought about his Angel from El Paso. What could he offer her now?

"Mister Roberts, could you come back in?" Behind them, Kate stood in the doorway, her trimly rounded figure blocking out the com-plaining *Madama*. "We'd like to talk to you about escorting me to Santa Fe."

108

"Well," Billy mused, "this might work out." His mind quickly turned back to the old Mexican's information concerning Pat Garrett in Santa Fe. Maybe right soon Garrett would find himself in the middle of The Kid's gun-sights.

11   Three Queens

Billy said farewell to the faithful Fega and Chavez following a night spent in the Three Rivers bunkhouse. He had just about enough extra cash to pay them their well-earned wages.

When The Kid took up the reins of Paddy Coghlan's elegant fringe-topped surrey, at mid-morning, the blonde Kate, decked-out in a green traveling outfit, sat beside him.

On the spur-of-the-moment, the *Madama* decided on a shopping trip to Santa Fe, and went along—to keep her eye on things. Morris Wolgenmuth hunched despondently beside her on the rear seat. He would drive the surrey back to the ranch from the state station at Carizozo, twelve miles to the north.

The stage, a four-seated Concord, boiled in half an hour after the jaded pair of bays pulled the surrey up to the ramshackle adobe stage stop.

The terrain from Carizozo over to Socorro was a full fifty miles of lava beds and seemingly endless stretches of barren country, shouldered on both sides by the Dark Mountains, the Oscuras.

The pitching, plunging stage, jammed with shabby Mexican herdsmen and grimy placer miners from White Oaks, was a noisy, windy container of alkali dust—allowing little communication between the frosty *Madama*, wide-eyed Kate and Billy.

The haste with which their dusty-bearded driver lashed his sweat-lathered mules toward Socorro was underscored with anxious shouts from over-armed stock tenders at swing stations: "Seen any Apaches? . . . Heard Nana and his band of devils jumped th' Ninth Cavalry! . . . Seen any smoke out that way?"

It was long past sundown when The Kid, with the thin Mrs. Coghlan at his left shoulder and the rounded sveltness of the girl on his right, saw the stage was rocking down into the Rio bottoms. Scattered lights speckled the blue murkiness of Socorro. The team pounded along side lanes to turn into the town's main street and halt before the wooden-verandahed Grand Central Hotel.

Billy herded Kate and the *Madama* back to the hotel an hour later, after a passable supper of over-fried steak and eggs at the French Restaurant. He registered them for an upstairs double-room, taking the spot across the hall for himself.

When the women settled down for the night, he was able to get over to Spiegelberg's clothing store and pick up a black Stetson and a new brown, sack suit. This outlay put a hole in the rest of the money left from paying off his drovers— but he couldn't land in Santa Fe looking like a saddle tramp.

Before he turned in, he tried on his new suit and rigged up a shoulder holster to hang the Colt under his loosely fitted coat. The belt, minus its cartridges, slung over his right shoulder and notched-up, with the holster tied down with a length of twine under his left armpit—was a trick taught him by Dave Rudabaugh. Or was it Jesse Evans? He wondered about both those hard cases.

Dave, he'd heard, was on the dodge again—and Jesse was supposed to be in a Texas pen—but you never knew about long-riders.

At sunrise, Billy and the women were on the platform when the two coaches and engine of the up-train from Deming for Albuquerque, Santa Fe and Las Vegas clanked past the new brick station, chuffing out pillars of dusky red smoke and shreds of pink steam.

They took seats in the forward part of the first coach, trying to make themselves comfortable against another long ride.

The coaches swarmed with silver miners and freighters from the Socorro mines, all pro-fanely bored with the town's forty-four saloons and on their way to make a weekend along Albuquerque's red-light line.

An apprehensive *Madama*, in her rusty-brown traveling dress, shrank back into her seat like a bright-eyed mesa moth burrowing at a pine bough. And Kate sat, scarlet-faced, staring out at the smoke-shrouded sheds and buildings that jerked by with increasing speed. These were shortly followed by rolling hills, river banks and plateaus as the train headed north.

When the *Madama* kept up her twisting and fuming, in obvious distress at being close-confined with so many dangerous hard-cases, The Kid casually opened his coat, disclosing the pistol in its holster. He grinned to see how the brief sight of that Peace-Maker gentled the fussy Mrs. Coghlan.

With the *Madama* quieted, he turned his attention to the most boisterous miners and promoted a thumbed-up pack of cards from the conductor. By the time the adobes and more modern brick buildings of Albuquerque glided up beside the coach windows, Billy's nigh-honest game had stilled much of the uproar and lightened the miners by the sum of eighty-five dollars.

The miles clicked away and noon arrived to disclose the only food available, tamales and enchiladas. These doubtful viands were toted through the cars by a plump, out-of-breath Mexican in a none-too-clean white coat.

Billy ate his share but Kate and the *Madama* merely nibbled at their portions. Kate soon gave it over and began to glance at both the Santa Fe New Mexican and the Las Vegas Optic newspapers, abandoned by some of the more literate Socorro miners.

"It says here," Kate reported, "that Sheriff Garrett is at Santa Fe, and that he told a newspaperman that Billy The Kid was really terrorizing folks at Fort Sumner. The man asked Garrett, 'It's said by some people that The Kid was cowardly and never gave a man a chance.' And Garrett said, 'No, he was game. I saw him give a man one once.' Do you believe that Mister Roberts?" There was something in her voice that gave Billy a start.

He looked over at the *Madama*, who was searching the Optic for nuggets of social news, wedged in among patent medicine and liquor ads. "Well—I guess you'd say that he gave anybody a chance that deserved it."

"But do you think Sheriff Garrett gave him what he deserved, shooting in the dark without any warning?" Kate twisted the paper in her well-kept hands. Her eyes seemed to be carefully examining The Kid from head to foot.

"He deserved just what he got!" the *Madama* snapped from behind her wrinkled paper. "Mister Coghlan says the sooner this Territory gets settled down and all the hooligans and Indians get run off or killed, the better it'll be for business," she sniffed, "and for our chances for Statehood."

"Well, Paddy," Billy thought, "that's somethin' you never told me. And what about all your rustled stock and other crooked shenanigans."

"Right you are, m'am," he conceded out loud,

brushing enchilada crumbs from his new coat sleeve. "New Mexico's bustin' at th' seams to be a state and no one will be gladder than folks like me when things quiet down."

"They'll get those Apaches, do you think?" Kate bent across to hand him the paper and Billy could scent the perfume on her—different from the rose garden of Esmeralda's hair, probably like those lilacs he heard grew back east. The neck of her green dress was low, and as she leaned back past him, he couldn't but help see the cleft between her firm, full breasts.

"They'll get 'em." He rolled the paper and swatted at a fly on the window. The *Madama* twitched behind her social news at the whack. "They'll get 'em and pen 'em up, like all wild things in th' way of business—I mean progress."

"This Billy The Kid? You're a ranchman, yourself. Did you ever come across him?" Kate's blue eyes sparkled with interest.

"Oh—he really wasn't much, like any cowhand—did see him once or twice, at a distance."

"Was he—?" Her question was lost in the wailing blast of the engine's whistle, signaling its approach to the switch-back station at Galesto Junction.

The rolling, grassy plain was gone and brushy, carved hills hulked around them, steeper with each mile the train climbed toward Santa Fe.

Wary of Kate's seemingly sudden interest

in "The Kid"—Billy feigned slumber against the coach window. The huffing train rounded a steeper grade. Twisted piñon pine boughs brushed the sides of the green and yellow coaches. The whistle again echoed flatly off among the craggy, brownish rock-faces.

The train clicked on and on, over the always curving roadbed, until The Kid's pose of sleep gradually came close to actuality. The corner of his drowsy vision caught bits and pieces of the onflowing landscape. The hills swelled into foothills, passed on to expand into bluffs and tableland—at last to become the eight mountain ranges rimming the Santa Fe Valley. The women across from Billy were vague hazes of color—

Things sure had a way of working out funny, he reasoned sleepily. Here he'd tried to play two Kings—Chisum and Coghlan, against that Jack of Spades—Garrett, only to have the Joker—Peep O'Day deal him the Deuce. The game wasn't over yet. Right now he held two Queens. The Black Queen of Clubs—*Madama* Coghlan, and the young blonde Queen of Diamonds—Kate Castle. But the only Queen he wanted was the Queen of Hearts—Esmeralda.

And the game wasn't over—not yet.

12   Santa Fe

"Santa Fe! Santa Fe!"

Billy jerked up in his seat, half-awake, gun in hand.

"Santa Fe! Santa Fe! Everybody out." The Conductor was bawling away as if everybody in the coach had been struck stone-deaf during the trip. "Santa Fe!"

"We're here." Kate was in the aisle beside Billy's seat, reaching for her black leather, telescope traveling bag on the wall rack. The *Madama* was fussing away at her purse and peeking out the window at the slowly drifting station platform.

"Put that gun up, before someone sees it." Kate's hand was cool on his flushed forehead.

"*Lo siento*—sorry," he muttered, slipping the .44 back into its shoulder holster. He got up and peered through the soot-speckled plate glass. Knots of Spanish-Americans, in red-slashed yellow serapes and wide hats, sat a'top boxes and barrels, along with blue-uniformed troopers from Fort Marcy. A scattering of miners and cowpunchers joined in gawking at the few passengers descending from the coaches.

"There's Father over there," Kate waved to a tall, thin person, wearing a white mustache and imperial. The man, dressed in a light *sombrero* and black broadcloth suit, was elbowing his way toward them.

Billy thought her father had a worried look about the eyes—but that probably came from the sudden sight of the *Madama*.

The Kid helped the girl and Mrs. Coghlan down the coach steps to the rough plank flooring. The engine hissed and coughed behind them. Its big stack, panting out an occasional spark, filled the air about the platform with the odors of burnt grease and cinders.

"Now here's our girl, and Mrs. Coghlan." Kate's parent removed his wide-brimmed hat, shook the *Madama*'s thin hand and gave Kate a kiss. He looked inquiringly at Billy, who stood a few feet off with his hands in his pockets.

"That's Mister Roberts, Father. He very kindly escorted us up from the ranch. He fetched a bunch of beef to Three Rivers the other day, and lost all his money to some robber, who took it from Uncle Morris the same night along with the ranch money, and . . ." Kate's words spilled end over end, blue eyes flashing.

Castle held up his cigar to stop the onrush and turned to The Kid. "That's too bad, Mister Roberts, but I'm glad to meet you. Thanks for being so kind as to come along with our ladies." He held out a hand to Billy's proferred grip. His eyes were cross-hatched with fine lines, nice eyes like Kate's but vaguely anxious.

The handshake wasn't too hearty. Billy became certain that this man had more on his mind than the *Madama*'s fidgeting and sniffing. "It's a pleasure to help, Mister Castle."

"I suppose Morris Wolgenmuth reported this robbery?"

"I instructed him to do it myself," the *Madama* cut in. "Let's not stand around here in the sun with all these loafers." She turned to Billy. "Thank you, young man. You get in touch with Mister Wolgenmuth, or see Mister Coghlan in Tularosa to check with him about your affairs." She tugged Kate's elbow. "Let's be going. It's hot out here, and we should get to the hotel and freshen up." Like a fussy old brown hen, she shooed father and daughter ahead of her toward the waiting line of hacks that carried fares to the business district.

Billy stood looking at the mountain ranges guarding Santa Fe. The nearer, rounded foothills were great brown and green walls, shimmering with scattered thickets of aspen that ran down to the orchards and small farms along the city's suburbs. The flat adobe buildings of the town, itself, stretched in uneven rows from one curve of the valley to the other as if some giant had given up an unsuccessful attempt with building blocks.

The towering sand-yellow cathedral of St. Francis dominated the other buildings about the

119

city's plaza. And up on the hills to the northeast, Fort Marcy's earthworks were fringed with tiny, white wooden walls. A fluttering red dot flying from an all but invisible pole was the American flag.

Yeah, it was the same old Santa Fe—all right.

The Kid shifted his gaze to the station itself. Ah, he remembered it, *maldito pozo*! Wasn't more than five months back he'd been taken from that station and shoved aboard a train headed down to Mesillia—and Lincoln—and death!

They'd hauled him out of that stinking hole of a jail over on Palace Avenue with that big devil of a Bob Ollinger for a guard. They weren't taking any chances either. Didn't old Tom Catron, the King-Pin of the whole dirty Santa Fe Ring send his own law partner, W. T. Thornton, down to see there'd be no slip-ups at the trial? They sorely need a goat for the Lincoln County troubles. And weren't about to let Billy The Goat get away.

"Billy," a girl's voice cut through bitter memory. It was Kate. How'd she know his name?—oh yes, he'd introduced himself as Billy Roberts down at Three Rivers.

"Billy," she looked curiously at him. "Are you in any kind of trouble? You were looking so strange when I came back here just now—and you pulled out that big gun so fast on the train."

"Kate?" He stared at her. "Oh, no! There's no bother." He smiled slowly. "But you better not let the *Madama* have to round you up again. She certain makes everybody walk th' chalk."

Her face was pink with sun-heat, and something else. "I . . . wanted to tell you we're leaving, Father and I, tonight on the six o'clock train. He's got to go back north to our new ranch and I'm going with him." She wrinkled her perfect nose. "I don't care too much for your New Mexico. It's just too wild—but maybe I'll like Father's Wyoming."

"Katherine!" The *Madama*'s shrill war-whoop echoed from the hack.

"Here's my new address up there in Rock Springs—if you should want to write." She shoved a folded note into his hand and retraced her steps through the thinning crowd to the waiting hack.

Billy waved and moved off along the splintered boards. He was suddenly tired. Was it the train jaunt or this place, Santa Fe? Maybe it was a hell of a dumb thing to do—coming up here. What if he ran into someone who knew him, in spite of his mustache and new duds?

"Hey, Chief! Seed any Apaches down th' line?" A big, beery loafer, with a broken nose slanting to the left, and patched checkered pants perilously held up with one red suspender, lurched off the line of barrels and jostled along beside The Kid.

Billy looked him over, grinning slightly. "Just one thin old buck and him hidin' in th' shade of a telegraph pole, tryin' to cool off." He brushed on past.

Halfway down the platform steps, he was nearly bowled over from behind. With one motion he dodged the broken-nosed loafer's rush and pulled the Colt.

The fellow's face blanched as he fell back in a desperate effort to escape that rattle-snake quick gun. "Hey now, Mister—hey!" He backed further off, with gaping jaw, sweat popping out on his shallow forehead. "Hey—wait!" Three of his shabby friends huddled behind him, staring wildly.

The Kid dug down and fished up a two-dollar piece. "Here!" He tossed the coin to the trembling vagrant. "No harm done, but you come nigh seein' th' elephant. Have a couple on me, with your pards." He winked at the crestfallen toughs and started on uptown, waving aside the hackmen.

He cursed under his breath. He'd been so careful as to buy new clothes and hide his pistol—but this fool had made him tip the hand.

He might as well have come into Santa Fe with a card pinned on his coat reading: "Gunman—Danger!"

13 Two Chances

The Kid walked into the lobby of the Exchange Hotel, the old La Fonda, at the corner of Lincoln and Palace streets. A few patrons drowsed over their newspapers.

A small, thin, desk clerk bobbed a bald head at The Kid and whipped the register around. "Stranger in Santa Fe?"

"Passin' through."

"Bet you could be interested to know you're in a famous place?"

"Might." Billy glanced down the list of names, but didn't find the Castles. He signed in as "W. Roberts, Socorro, New Mexico."

"Well, right over there," the clerk pointed through the open doorway to the empty floor of the adjoining barroom, "that's where, twelve years ago, Captain Rynerson killed the Chief Justice of our Territory."

"Knew there's some reason for no justice around here!"

"Ha, eh? ya crackin' jokes? Well, I bet you heard of Rynerson!"

"Yeah, I heard of that sidewinder." The Kid was too frazzled out to strike up a pow-wow with this busybody.

"Best not talk that way, Mister." The clerk ran

123

a finger up and down pink suspenders and looked around the lobby. "Captain Rynerson's District Attorney now and a tough man to buck."

"I heard that too." Billy picked up his key and went along the long, narrow hallway to his room at the far end of the ground floor. He locked the door behind him and lay down on the iron bedstead. He thought about Esmeralda, and how he first met her. It seemed as long ago as the fight at Blazer's Mill or the time he met Governor Lew Wallace—and time gradually ceased, in slumber.

Shadows were thick in the room when he roused. He sat on the edge of his bed, pulling on his boots while the sound of distant music buzzed on his window. At first he'd thought it was a blue-bottle fly bumbling along the panes.

Brushing his hair in front of the wall mirror, he squinted through the gloom at himself. He sure looked different from the fellow they'd chained up in the jail down the street, back in the spring. With these scars and new mustache, he looked different enough to walk right up to Pat Garrett and get away with letting him have it good.

He wondered where Garrett was at this very minute. In town somewhere. His neck tingled at the thought.

The same clerk was behind the lobby desk and as gabby as ever. "Heerd our band, eh?" He snapped his suspenders. "Well, sir you got to get up pretty early to find a better brass band than the Twenty-Second Infantry Band." He wagged his shiny head. "Too bad you got out here late, but there's a good half-hour left if you want to get on down to the Plaza."

"Might do that," and Billy walked out of the lobby into the street. The night was gathering in soft waves of dusk. A star sprang out as brilliant and brassy as the band's high-flying cornet.

He sauntered down the boardwalk, half-hoping to see Kate, but he remembered she and her father were on the north-bound cars for Wyoming. That was pretty sounding—Wyoming!

He was barely inside the picket-fenced Plaza grounds, threading his way among Mexicans in gaudy blankets and the Anglo citizenry of the city, when he heard that name.

It was a name that halted both step and breath. The soldier-musicians, in the low, six-sided, wooden bandstand, were tuning-up for the last set, with instruments that sparkled and flashed in the dying gleams of light—but that name—it came clearly to his ears—"Garrett!"

He listened and peered at the indistinct mob of figures, milling about the grassy Plaza, ". . . our hats off to you . . . been told before, I suppose, Captain Garrett," came the voices of several women.

And then—he saw him!

Pat Garrett, himself, tall and stooping, unmistakably silhouetted against the lighter gloom, ambled toward The Kid. A woman hung to each of Garrett's elbows. Several well-dressed men followed. "Tell us, was he a good shot?"

"Well," Pat's coon-hunter drawl was forced and slow, "about as good as they come, I'd say."

"But—you were just a little bit better," a woman marveled at the big, gangling lawman. His dim reply was muffled by the outcrash of the band, playing "Marching Through Georgia."

The Kid stepped aside and pulled the Colt .44 from his shoulder holster. It was a moment he'd chewed over until he could taste it.

He brought the pistol up to waist level, undetected in the dark. The murderous leaden ball behind the Colt's vengeful snout waited for hammer-snap to drive it through the unsuspecting Garrett's middle in a blast of smoke and fire.

Billy's finger tightened. He thought, "this is the way you got Barlow—when you were shooting to cold-cock The Kid! Now it's damned different. Now—you big baboon, it's your turn!"

But his hand shifted, ever so slightly, lining up on Garrett's long legs. "Be a cripple, Garrett," he whispered to himself. "Take . . ." And as his finger squeezed down, the damned fools with Pat crowded around again, thick as flies on a sugar teat. They stood not twenty feet off, listening to that blatting band wallop out "The Girl I Left Behind Me."

The women pulled this way and that, as they

pointed out someone or other to Garrett and the other men folk. Billy half-raised the Colt again—but slowly uncocked it and stuffed it back in its holster under his coat.

"Why," he thought sullenly, "did I go and do that?" But he already knew. Gettin' smart! The kiss of *Señora Fortuna* was still bright and shiny on his forehead—and he realized it.

With Garrett cut down, there'd be no way out. He didn't have a mount or any escape figured out. It would have been plain suicide, and that was why he held off.

Gettin' smart—at last.

He turned away from the still-unsuspecting Pat and his admiring throng. There would be plenty of time later. Garrett would be around somewhere when he was ready for him.

Billy went across San Francisco Street and dined at a small restaurant on Don Gasper Street. He was hungry. The keyed-up feeling gave him an appetite. He saw nobody he recognized in the low-roofed beanery. The few customers, mainly cowhands and miners, kept noses to plates as they polished off their victuals.

Once out of the place, he looked over the night. The sky was crisp, blue and complete with hundreds of crystalline stars. Over to the east, the rising moon blazed its mellow fire, rolling up like a golden peso. In the Plaza, two blocks off, the band was playing a final number, its echoes ringing away into the foothills. The crowd was already drifting toward homes and saloons.

Garrett was probably on his way—but he would see him later.

The gas-lights of Santa Fe, newly installed in the spring, were yellow blobs of brilliance. People appeared for an instant and then were gone as they passed the flame of the man-made moons.

When he paused at the corner of Galisto and Water Street, he thought he noticed a figure down at the next corner, dodging out of the rays of the street lights.

The Kid turned and proceeded along the boardwalk, listening for the sound of footsteps. That was what he'd done ever since Lew Wallace had kow-towed to the Santa Fe Ring—listened for someone following.

He'd been careless once—stopped listening the night Garrett made his murderous play at Fort Sumner. But never again!

He recrossed the dusty roadway and melted into the shadows near an ancient, gnarled cottonwood. Off through the night, sounds broke out as sharply pointed as thorns on the great Joshua trees—series of yells from cantinas—wooden crack-banging of shutters set swinging by sudden swoops of wind sliding down from the encircling mountains. There came the sudden screeching cawing of some muddled rooster, who upon opening his golden-circled-bead-like eye, mistook the vast moonface for coming day. And there sounded muffled tramplings of the Army Band, marching route-step up the heights to the fort—bits and fragments of night-talk from the thinning crowds—and tap-tap-tap—of boot heels across the street, just out of sight.

It seemed someone was interested in him, and his visit to Santa Fe. And he was just as curious, lingering along to see what this fellow was up to. He didn't wait long. The man angled over the street at exactly the spot The Kid crossed, and strolled up toward the cottonwood.

Billy eased around the other side of the huge trunk and pulled his Colt—and waited, motionless.

The seedy-looking stranger stopped, peering down the street. As he tossed his cigarette into the road and started on again, he froze to the unmistakable, metallic, double click of Billy's cocking Colt.

"All right," Billy ground out, "speak your piece!"

The man, still thrown into high relief by the street light, swallowed loudly enough to be heard. Keeping his hands carefully in sight, he cautiously offered, "Well, Mister, all I know is I was told to give you this note from some gent. I ain't armed," he added in hasty afterthought.

"His name sure wouldn't be Garrett?" Billy's

voice was low and wary. He kept the pistol pointed level with the man's belt buckle.

"No sir, not Captain Garrett. This is from a real big bull moose, leastwise I was told so by the gent that give'd it to me."

Billy's neck tingled, again. Someone recognized him, after all.

"This'un said to give the note to the young feller in the dark Stetson. Said he was a friend of yours, personal. Said it was just a friendly note. Got a five-spot for catchin' up with you—must'a been pretty urgent."

"Seems so." The Kid reached his left hand for a white bit of paper the man held out gingerly. "All right, Mister Errand Man, dust out of here. Only next time be careful who you creep up on."

With a sigh, the man hustled off into the darkness—lost in the night.

As Billy reentered the lobby of his hotel, five minutes later, unopened note still in his pocket, he passed two men, sitting near the door. He pegged them for merchants in their rusty-black suits.

They glanced at him and turned back to their checker board.

The overfriendly clerk was eating supper in the barroom, and his disinterested replacement, behind the desk, merely nodded as he gave Billy the key.

Inside his room, The Kid lighted the brass lamp

130

without locking the door. Came a sharp rap at the door as he reread the two lines on the folded piece of paper.

Turning, gun in hand—and those ten words stampeding through his mind: "Once dead, stay dead! Leave town or die by dawn."—he heard the slightest rustle at the window facing the alley.

He hit the floor on his hands and knees, sliding into a corner by the bed. The slamming blast of a hand-gun boomed out from the window as his door shattered inward. For an instant, the man in the doorway stood with upraised pistol, squinting into the dim light. With a thud, he crashed face down. It was one of the checker players.

"Die by dawn? Their time table's out of kilter," Billy clipped as he scrambled up. He leaped the sprawled figure and flattened himself beside the window, Colt ready. Footsteps echoed up the alley, as vibrant quiet hummed in the room.

Billy beat out a small, curling thread of orange flame that was licking its way up the dingy drape. "Through th' curtains. That's what threw him off—couldn't see for sure and plugged his own man when he bulled in th' door."

Shouts and footfalls filled the hall. Both desk clerks rushed through the splintered doorway, followed by a fat bartender and the other checker player. The Kid noted that this man was breathing pretty briskly, as if he'd run in off the street—or up an alley.

The corpse at their feet was "resurrecting." The shot from the window had only furrowed an inch or so of hair and the tip of a left ear. Blood trickled down the man's neck.

"Which of you lobos wants to tell me what sort of a shootin' gallery you got here?" Billy grinned tightly at the shaking clerks while his .44 covered the growing crowd at the door.

"All right, *todo correcto*! Sainted Luke and Lazarus, can't any you Anglos ever keep peace around town?" A very bulky Mexican with a squint eye came shoving his way through the craning group.

"Hi, Deputy Salazar, nothin' much doin' I guess," the bald-headed clerk chattered, "sorta mistake, kinder think. You see—this gent—."

"Ah! *Cerrar arriba*, less noise, *Señor* Greenberg." The Deputy bustled on into the room, little black eyes snapping in rolls of brown flesh. "You there, *Señor*," he ordered Billy, "put up that there *pistola*! We don't allow firearms in our streets."

"*Esta non calle, Señor* Deputy," Billy replied with a smile as he holstered the gun under his coat. He was sure no one would try anything with this policeman around, but he was wary for what might happen.

"*Si*, it ain't no street in here. You talk pretty good Mex," the Deputy nodded at The Kid. He turned to the uneasy checker player and his glassy-eyed friend. "You there, *Señor*! Get your

pal to the doc's before he spoils all these carpets."
He looked over at The Kid. "I'm sorry, *Señor*, but
I gotta take you three down to the *calabozo* for
questions—after they patch up that one."

"You're runnin' in who? For doin' what?" Billy
pulled a puzzled expression as he yanked at his
mustache. He'd decided to play the green ranch
hand in the bit town. This Salazar was a stranger.
He hadn't been around Santa Fe in any official
capacity when Billy and the Lincoln County boys
were stuck in jail in the spring. Shouldn't be
any trouble with him—if Garrett didn't enter the
picture. Billy made up his mind to pull down on
the Mexican if he tried to disarm him.

As they stepped out of the hotel onto the
veranda, a tall, craggy-faced man took Salazar
by the arm and whispered to him. The Deputy
listened quietly for a moment and then shrugged.
"All right, *Señor*," he spoke to Billy. "This gent
vouches for you one-hundred percent." He went
on down the steps, shoving the other two ahead.

The big man, who looked like a cowman, in
spite of his store clothes, flung open his sack coat.
"No guns, and no tricks, Mister," he grunted.
"There's someone couple blocks off who'd like
some words with you, providin' y'don't want to
go on down to jail with those." He stepped back
and stared at The Kid. He seemed to be trying to
place him.

"Lead on, McDuff." Billy followed the man

off the porch. "Just stay out ahead and keep your hands quiet." He was going to find out what this was about. But he was ready to shoot or run. It was up to "them."

14 The Ring

Ten minutes walk away from the Exchange Hotel brought Billy and his big, burly guide deep into Santa Fe's Mexican quarter. The man turned in at a house enclosed with a vine-wrapped wall. There were no street lights at this end of town, but the moon, now high in the heavens, lit the small courtyard with a clear, pale light.

Billy had a momentary, uneasy feeling. The scene called up that too-recent moonlit night in Fort Sumner. He could spot nothing out of the way but his gun was cocked and ready as they went up to the adobe cottage's door.

"Hold on a minute." The big man beat his red fist twice on the iron-studded oak. He placed an ear to the planks and listened. "O.K. G'wan in."

"Stand off. Don't make sudden moves or you could live to regret it—maybe!" Billy lifted the latch, kicking the heavy door open with the toe of his boot. It swung in, revealing a room lit by two, dim wall-lamps.

A man, in shirt sleeves, sat at a table in the small room's center, with folded hands in plain sight. It looked all right—except for one thing. The stranger's head was covered with a black bag, with eyeholes and a slit for a mouth—like the sack an executioner yanks down on the head of a condemned man.

"Close the door." The muffled voice was pleasant.

Billy pushed the door shut behind him and stood with gun pointed at the masked figure.

"Sit down," the man indicated a chair across from him.

The Kid hooked it with his foot, pulling sideways to the wall so it angled to both man and door.

"Bullhead will guard the house. We can discuss matters in peace." The grim head tilted toward Billy. "I believe a little peace wouldn't come amiss with you, eh?"

"What'd'ya want?" Billy sat down with cocked six-shooter lying by his right hand as he kept an ear cocked for any movement outside. He looked the masked figure over narrowly. There wasn't much to see; a plain but expensive-looking white shirt, string tie and dark pantaloons stuffed into mighty fancy, red-tooled boots, half-hidden in shadow. A coat and hat, both plain and dark, hung on pegs near a bolted door at the back of the room.

The masked man looked at The Kid and drummed long, white fingers on the table's surface. "It isn't what I want, to turn your question around. It's what you want!" He bent forward. "What do you want here in Santa Fe—

Mister Roberts, alias Billy Bonney, alias Henry Antrim, alias The Kid?"

Billy gripped the .44, staring from door to mask.

"Don't be disturbed. I could have had you disposed of on the way here, if I'd wished it done." The voice was low and steely now, not pleasant, but still calm. Eyes glittered behind the mask.

"Like you tried back at th' hotel?" Billy tensed.

"Someone else ordered that. It's not the way I do things. And that's why you're here now, talking to me."

"Who else knows I'm here?"

"Catron, Rynerson and I."

"What about those two quick-draw artists your bunch turned loose on me at th' Exchange?"

"Those fools were told you were a political enemy—that's all."

"Your brand of politics seems mighty deadly."

"Politics is the greatest game in the world." The masked man clenched his white hands. "With words, only words—we divide and rule. Men with ambition and brains are enabled to move mountains. It's been done before and will be done again—the greatest game in the world."

"Damned dirty game!"

"Possibly—but a game that has paid very well here for some years." The man thumped a pale fist on the table top. "But—you are evading the question. Why are you here in Santa Fe instead of gone to Mexico?"

"Just decided to pay a visit." Billy placed the gun back on the table. "And look up an old friend."

"And very nearly found him tonight, in the Plaza. But that's all over! We take care of our own. You can't kill Garrett or anyone else here."

"All right," The Kid smiled bleakly. "You'll tip Garrett I'm around, so I'll have to hit th' trail." He pulled off his Stetson and placed it on the table beside his Colt. "I've told you what I was after. And now—what's your game?"

"My game is to save the life of a dead man—yours!"

"And how're you gonna do that?"

"Garrett was foolish enough to think he'd got you that night. Hysteria, perhaps. We know those Mexicans down at Fort Sumner took the body of the boy killed there and held a hasty funeral. The corpse wasn't above ground long enough for anyone to get a good look at it, killed at midnight and buried before noon. So—the coroner's report is so much moonbeams."

The man chuckled dryly, as he continued. "Garrett told his deputies he'd shot you and they took him at his word—none, including his man Poe, we discovered, had ever seen you face to face. So, whether Garrett believes it now, we're not certain. But he's openly gone on record as killing The Kid, and it would embarrass him, even politically ruin him, and others if the truth were told now."

"Embarrass others—such as th' Santa Fe Ring?" Billy spat out the words like a bad taste.

"I dislike your title for, what is, a highly developed and very private operation. You make it sound like a common gang of black-legs. However, there's no reason not to be honest with you. You're a dead man anyway you look at it. You can never come back—with two airtight murder charges plus a conviction hanging over you. Hanging is a very apt phrase."

"Old Sheriff Brady and 'Buckshot' Roberts?" The Kid's throat tightened with anger. "At least ten others fired at Brady when he was killed, and I was too far away from Blazer's Mill to see Charlie Bowdrie plug old 'Buckshot'—but your dirty gang of lawyers saw to it that I got th' axe for both killin's."

"That's beside the point now. You've obviously slipped out of the whole thing with the Devil's own luck, and here you are!"

"Yeah, and here I stay!" He was stalling to see what this masked hypocrite was up to.

"But you won't—and that's the very crux of our meeting. You're to give up this vendetta and leave New Mexico or . . ." The faceless man slowly placed a long, thin hand on his own scrawny neck. "This Territory is headed for

Statehood and we intend to be at the reins when that happens. Tweed, Gould and others back East have been skimming off the cream—but we'll take care of our own section. And wc don't propose to have such 'Robert the Bruce's' as you fighting lost causes!"

The man in the mask waved a skinny finger slowly at The Kid. "Your efforts could call unwelcome attention to us. You've got to realize, Bonney or Roberts—or Kid—you're an anachronism. You are attempting to carry on a blood feud that's five years past."

"Gettin' even for Tunstall, Brewer, McSween, Bowdrie, Barlow and th' others ain't no lost cause, far as I'm concerned." Billy stood up with gun in hand. "I might be able to let th' right folks know what's goin' on with your crooked shenanigans."

"True, but you've been convicted and the hangman's still waiting. I just don't see that you have enough protection to come in and appeal."

"Someone feels I can," Billy replied, thinking of Esmeralda.

"Foolish, but as I've said, you're dead, or will be shortly—if you don't cooperate." As the man rose to face The Kid, Billy got a good look at the only bright and cheerful thing about him—those red-stitched boots.

The masked man held out an envelope. "Listen carefully. Here's what you're to do. There'll be a passenger train running south tomorrow at two p.m., take this! There's enough money to get you out of the Territory. If you ever come back, it's your death. Simple as that."

The front door creaked open and Billy spun to cover it. The big guard stood waiting, hands to sides. The Kid looked back at the table—but the masked man had slipped out the, now unlocked, back door, with coat and hat.

"Let's *vamoose*, Pard. The party's over," and Bullhead jerked a thumb at the front gate.

"*Grácias*, but I'll find my own way, *paro*." Billy dug the Colt into the man's bulky middle and shoved him out of the way. He was bitterly tired of anyone connected with the Ring.

He trudged up one dusty, moonlit street after another until he emerged from Burro Alley onto Palace Street. His dodging route left his scowling guard far behind.

The capital was shuttered up for the night but several cantinas were still doing business. Songs and shouts echoed along the deserted streets from behind closed doors.

As he lingered on a corner near the White Bull Saloon, he tore open the envelope. It contained two-hundred dollars in fifties. With the seventy contributed by the boisterous Socorro miners and the remnants of Wolgenmuth's travel money, The Kid possessed three hundred. It would get him a far piece—if he decided to go.

15 Partida

Billy crossed the street and stood on the corner of Palace, opposite the saloon. He debated returning to his hotel but another thought came to him. Who was the masked man? He was a high-up—but it wasn't old Tom Catron, U.S. District Attorney, and acknowledged head of the Ring. The Kid had seen him before at a distance. And it couldn't be the hairy-pawed Rynerson. That one had shambled into the Santa Fe Jail last spring to sneer at Billy and "the outlaws."

On a hunch, he walked back over to the cantina. "Beer," he responded to the barkeep. With slopping glass in hand, he studied the dozen or so customers along the mahogany. They were mostly businessmen in plain dark suits along with some ranchers and miners in rougher garb. All wore undecorated boots and gaiters.

He finished his drink and walked out to find the red boots in the third saloon. The man stood at the far end of the bar talking to none other than the gorilla-like Rynerson. Billy lingered at the street end of the bar, watching the pair.

Rynerson was fuming to his companion about something. He smacked a thick hand down on the bar-top and wagged his heavy head at the thin-faced man in the fancy boots. Billy guessed

District Attorney W. L. Rynerson was furious because his own hired killers had fumbled their job. And Red-Boots had kept them from another attempt—for the present.

The Kid began to get edgy with his position in the room. Garrett could amble in, or the man in the red boots might glance down the bar at any moment and see him. And there was no telling what Rynerson's reaction could be. The Kid eased back through the swinging-doors, to wait in the night.

He didn't wait long. The moon a'top the Cathedral was just rolling off to the north when Rynerson emerged from the bat-wings and stood swiping away at his long, Viking mustache. The spindly, white-faced owner of the gaudy foot-wear followed. They stood, talking in low tones. Rynerson appeared to be calmed by the other's speech, and presently walked off down toward the Plaza. White-Face headed along Cathedral Street in the direction of the river, Rio Santa Fe.

The man in the red boots was nearly to a motionless hack at the end of the block, when Billy, panther-footing behind, dug the Colt into his back. "*Presa sobre!*" The Kid's collar was turned up and his hat turned down.

The startled hackman lashed at his drowsing plug and clattered off, yelling: "Hold up! Hold up at Water and Cathedral."

The man on the end of Billy's gun remained

calm. "Haven't much money, my friend, and I'd advise you to clear away before that driver brings help."

"*Non entender*," Billy's voice was muffled behind his hand. "*Moverse!*" He shoved the Ring Chieftain ahead of him into a nearby alley. That noisy driver could fetch trouble before he found out who this fellow was.

At the alley entrance, the man twisted away, flashing a derringer from his belt. Billy hit him over the head with the Colt's barrel and he dropped like a gut-shot wolf.

As The Kid bent over to search him, he heard the thudding of feet. That hackman had sure got busy. Billy ripped a billfold from the fallen man's coat pocket and tore it open. It held papers and a slim, leather notebook. There was a good wad of greenbacks as well.

"Over there by the alley! Could be a Mex. Heered him throwin' Spanish." A bullet clipped chips from the corner of the building and shrilled into the night.

The Kid saw half-a-dozen men running at him. Another pistol cracked with a spurt of fire. The slug keened overhead.

He hurled the wallet and money into the downed man's face and darted through the dim alley, pausing midway to fire at his pursuers' feet. The shadowy bunch scattered along the walls as the booming shot kicked up dirt and stones.

Before they could rally, Billy was around the corner, running toward the Rio Santa Fe. When the straggling line broke out from the buildings, he was halfway over the arched plank bridge that extended Gaspar Street across the moon-rippled river.

He dashed down the incline of the bridge and along a winding road paralleling the water. Vaulting over a low adobe wall, he footed it across a small garden and came near tripping over a young couple who sat "sparking" in a rose arbor.

"*Perdón ambos*," he called, scrambling the far wall into the next yard.

Taking a breather in the shadows, he heard men shouting and the tramping of feet. Presently, it seemed, they were gone on down the road. He got his wind back and pushed through a creaking iron gate into the next yard.

A dog bayed from the house as The Kid came bursting through the bushes. Shutters flew open but there was no further movement as he jogged across the yard and clawed his way over the end wall, fully expecting a load of bird-shot.

When he emerged onto the next narrow street all was still. A whistle quavered in the quiet night. He was near the train yards.

He holstered the gun and pulled the black, leather notebook and papers from his pocket. One of the sheets was a telegram flimsy. He stood behind a cottonwood and scratched a match on his boot heel.

The telegram was addressed to a Mr. E. A. Fiske, National Bank of Santa Fe, New Mexico Territory and had been sent from Socorro on the previous day—August 20, 1881.

The message was right to the point: "Billy Kid heading Santa Fe. Not killed as reported. Watch Garrett." The signature made Billy burn his finger—"Coghlan."

"Well," he thought, "you never knew about friends—or enemies. Old *Madama* told th' truth out of school when she said Paddy wanted th' Territory cleaned up. Hand-in-hand with th' Ring. That was th' only way that Vinegaroon could stay out of th' pen. And him lettin' on to be leery of Siringo and Garrett. A hell of a King! But who had got th' word to him? Was it Wolgenmuth, or th' *Madama*—or Kate? I can't believe the girl knew—but whoever it was, the King knew what to do."

He struck another light and thumbed through the small book. It listed many large sums of money taken in and paid out through the National Bank of Santa Fe. The figures and entries proved that the Ring fattened itself on stolen cattle, sold at sky-high prices to Government Indian Agencies, as well as from falsified land deals and crooked shakedowns.

It was all in black and white. There was also a

list of what seemed to be aliases or cypher names of Ring Members: T. B. Catron was Grapes; Major Godfroy, Indian Agent at the Mescalero Reservation was Hampton; W. L. Rynerson's handle was Oyster; and E. Fiske of the National Bank of Santa Fe, owner of the book, was Terror.

There were more names and notations, but the match burned out. The Kid grinned tightly. Here was enough gunpowder to blow the entire filthy tribe, including Garrett, into the Federal Pen. And Fiske had been the man in the mask. No wonder he could pass out two-hundred dollars at a crack for hush money. Billy hoped the bastard woke up with a real headache.

Hearing a noise in the next block, he thrust telegram, book and papers into his coat and dodged along the walls. It was the group returning from the river road.

He worked his way toward the depot, keeping in the deep shadow of the houses. Footsteps rattled close behind—but it was only tree branches tossed in the rising wind. The moon sank over the jagged, black mountains and the smell of piñon pine smoke from a hundred chimneys swirled pungently through the Santa Fe night.

That engine whistled again, loud in the lonesome stillness. Black plumes threaded up beyond scattered sheds and buildings.

There came the thud-thud-thud of more running feet, and a gun barked. He darted across a lane and between warehouses, fronting on the Santa Fe Railroad tracks. Those devils were certain persistent.

He waited behind a pile of crates and barrels with his .44 at the ready. Two men puffed up and began poking along the platform. One was the fat Deputy, Salazar. Now the bacon was really burned. Fiske must have come to himself and whooped for real law. Billy wasn't about to swap lead with them and bring down that other bunch. They must be circling, trying to pin him from both directions.

The freight engine began to hiss and chuff its way toward The Kid's platform. Its big headlight blazed along steel-bright rails.

"There he goes!" And the two officers fired a shot apiece down the tracks, where, pushed by rising wind, several large tumbleweeds bounced out of the darkness into the headlight's path.

"Hey," a hoarse voice whispered in Billy's ear. A hulking figure squatted behind the next barrel. "Don't go a'usin' that there shootin'-iron on me," the man grumbled. "I knowed you'd git into a fix, throwin' down on folks." He held up his empty hands. The train was almost upon them, and the light of its passage turned the gloom into sudden day.

Billy recognized the broken-nosed loafer of early afternoon. The fellow made a sign for caution, and gestured in the direction of the closed railway station. The rush and clank of the passing boxcars jumbled his words.

"What?" Billy mouthed at him.

". . . Git goin'. Got a shack . . . depot. Saw you talkin' . . . at th' saloon . . . follered you. Figger . . . you somethin'." He motioned and began crawling away.

The Kid holstered his gun and was kneeling to follow—when the man dived at Billy's feet, knocking him into a pile of crates.

"Help! Hey you, Salazar! Down here, I got'm!"

The Kid wriggled loose from the man's bear-hug and kicked him in the head. Salazar and the other officer were running toward Billy.

An empty boxcar rattled past, open door gaping black. Another and another of the string of empties flashed by. The green light on the caboose sped toward him. Billy bounded up and dived headfirst into the last car's open door.

He left a pair of Santa Fe's finest, waving guns and fists at the sardonically winking red and green lights on the dwindling caboose. He also left a pain-filled vagrant, discovering his bent nose to be permanently tilted from one cheek to the other.

"Well," Billy mused, "I've left Santa Fe in more style." But a boxcar still beat a passenger car, if you had to be all chained-up to travel—the way he'd left town last Spring. He knocked the dust from hands and knees. He was better off

149

this trip, with a good stake and a hole card that could crack the Santa Fe Ring apart like a rotten stick. He was free and his gun was handy—and he meant to keep it that way.

He reached out and pulled the door shut, as the train picked up speed.

16   Las Vegas

An hour before daylight, the freight lay on the siding at Las Vegas, New Mexico Territory. Billy's new, twenty-dollar brown suit had failed to keep out the night chill of the mountains. He was drowsy and cold.

False moonlight of palest dawn streaked the east when The Kid cautiously slid open the box-car door. He climbed stiffly down and walked over the rough ties toward the Old Town section.

He passed vague shacks and sheds, coming to a row of adobe huts. White fluffs of smoke were already feathering upward from the chimneys, as mistresses of the hearths stirred ashes and tossed on fresh piñon branches. His breath, like the smoke, curled into the still air.

He paused, listening by the huts, watching for whatever might be moving at this early hour. He went along searching—hunting for a place to hole up before daylight.

As sure as the Queen of Spades was black, the Ring would have the telegraph humming with his description—though they'd not name him as The Kid. Every track town would be tipped off *pronto*.

What appeared to be a livery barn loomed out of the opaque pre-dawn to his left. He crossed a vacant lot to reach it. Subdued tramplings of horses came from inside the barn. No one was about so far, but his luck couldn't hold.

Billy's thirst was big and hot in his throat. A sudden collision with the cold metal of a horse trough brought him to a halt. Scooping the frigid water in his hands, he drank deeply and removed his hat to wash cinders and soot from his face.

Searching along the rough, splintery back of the building, he found a loose board. Prying it up with a bit of effort, he slipped into the warm, hay-scented darkness of the barn's interior.

A horse nickered at him. He patted its soft, velvet nose, thinking of Dandy Dock, the little race-horse he'd sold to Doctor Hoyt down in Tascosa and all his other mounts, but particularly of that little black mare, Angel. Maybe he'd get back to her some time—and his other Angel.

Clambering up the wooden ladder, The Kid burrowed deeply into the sweet smelling hay of the loft.

Billy awoke late in the afternoon. He looked through a large knothole near his head and saw that shadows ran long from the west. He could spy out the town cathedral's orange bulk, the rusty streak of a factory chimney and several adobe houses.

Near one of the houses, a woman in a quilted skirt and a red blouse worked at baking in her outdoor oven. From the distance it was hard to tell but he guessed she baked tortillas. He watched her until he was certain he could smell the cooking cakes. He grew so hungry he was forced to look away, but he couldn't ignore that knothole for long.

Beyond the adobes, near the river and the new town part of Las Vegas, pigeons about the cathedral tower flamed up in a flash of sun-stained wings. Bells were clanging out for evening services. It was Sunday—but what a hell of a way to spend it. By morning he'd have to take his chances across the Galinas River—over there in New Town.

When soft-colored dusk spread, the yawning stable-hand, who'd appeared in mid-afternoon to feed and water the animals, sat on a wooden bucket below the mow, smoked two corn-husk cigarettes and locked the barn for the night.

Billy waited until deep dark, before coming down the ladder. He went through the loose board, drank his fill at the tank and made his way back to the loft.

He was wolfish with hunger when he roused up in the morning. The sun looked to be about nine o'clock. The same stable-hand was in front of the barn arguing with some loafer. Billy slipped down and squeezed out through the back.

Dusting off his clothes, as well as he could, he passed between scattered shacks and barns and came to the iron framed Galinas River bridge.

Two small Mexican boys were fishing the swift mountain stream from the near bank.

"Lots of bites?" He stopped to watch them.

"No, *Señor*." The boys turned from their intent scrutiny of the crinkling brown water to look at him. "Our father will give us the nickel, if we catch enough."

"He likes fish?"

"No, *Señor*, he trades them at the market for whiskey."

Billy dug down and handed them each a silver dollar. "Give your father one; tell him you sold a big batch to a mighty hungry man." He winked at their glowing faces. "Keep th' other for yourself—goobers and rock-candy, maybe?"

The boys were gone on the dead run, fishing poles abandoned.

He crossed the bridge into town. There could be eyes watching—eyes that knew exactly who he was, but that was a risk he'd have to take, until he got out of this country. "It's pretty near hell to be so popular," he grinned to himself through tight lips, and shifted the gun under his armpit.

Being very hungry, he walked into the first beanery he came to, and ate his way through two orders of steak and eggs. Several town-people and cattlemen looked him over as they lingered over their cups of coffee. He felt grubby and downright tramp-like, despite his store-bought suit.

He paid his bill, rubbing his chin and felt the bristles. "Time to get cleaned up—then clear out," he thought. Those incurious eyes were making him jumpy.

Across the sleepy street, a small unpainted barber shop stood beside an overpainted saloon. Billy walked in and settled down in the single chair. He kept on his coat to hide the gun.

"The works—*completo*," he instructed the Mexican barber, and sank back to relax under the skillful, brown fingers.

"*Pardon, Señor*," the barber was gently shaking him out of his doze. "I am finish, and you are all set."

Cursing wryly to himself for drifting off, The Kid sat up and looked sharply at the broad, good-natured face looming over him like a pale, brown moon.

"That's a new cut on your head. I was gentle as I could be." The barber's round eyes rolled anxiously. "You should ought to be ver' cautious, carrying around the gun under your coats here in town. They don't like firearms in these limits— *porqué*, no!"

Billy got stiffly out of the chair, feeling the Colt still bulking under his arm. "*Grácias*! I'm leavin' town about now." He flipped a five-dollar gold piece into the man's coffee-colored palm. "New ordinance?"

"*Si*, since that *Señor* Rudabaugh was our

marshal. He had small regard for any gunmens but himself. Funny, though," the barber scratched his own thick thatch, "they had these Rudabaugh, *Señor* Beely Kid and some other mens locked in our *calabozo* back last winter for some such gun troubles. I see them!" He chuckled and brushed The Kid's dusty coat.

"Yeah, I heard about that." Billy clapped his Stetson on and winced at the still tender scar a'top his scalp. It could have been a nigh thing. This fellow had come to the hoosegow to barber up the prisoners when he, The Kid, had been held there before being taken down to Santa Fe. He now recognized the barber—but it just went to show how talk of a man's death could throw smoke in everyone's eyes.

The Kid made for the door of the shop, fingering his mustache.

"They tossed a red-headed cowboy into our Las Vegas jail these last week. Tryin' to shoot up these town." The barber seemed determined to amuse and educate his customer all the way to the middle of the street. "And they jus' let him out these mornin'. Somebody says it was someone down at Santa Fe telegraphed up his fine moneys. *Mucho priesa* an hour back, he leaves. I, myself, see him ride out on his big horse, kicking sand and dust in a cloud."

"Nice to have friends," Billy answered over his shoulder. The memory of that rat-ridden hole up the block brought on the damp sweat.

It was the second jail in this part of the Territory that he was determined to miss. And he now wanted to be gone from this place. And gone *muy pronto*!

17   The Man in the Pines

Billy entered the bright-red Romero Mercantile store, next to the Adams Express Company and spent forty dollars on supplies.

"Lessee," the clerk toted up the bill. "That's a Winchester carbine with saddle-scabbard, saddle bags with these here provisions, canteen, skillet and java-pot, slicker, two blankets and ammunition fer th' rifle—along with *sombrero*, Levi's, shirt—th' works. That does it! Orta keep you goin' fer a spell."

Billy paid up and gathered his bundles. He was beginning to dread running into someone who could recognize him from the past winter—like that Mexican barber. He had to admit the Santa Fe Ring had shaken his belief in his own sunny star—just a bit.

"On my way to see a pardner down in Texas," was his farewell to the clerk. Might as well lay down a crooked trail.

That trail took him north on the Mora Road toward the little settlement of Buena Vista. Riding a twenty-dollar bay, purchased from the stable-hand at the barn in Old Town, where he'd shucked the store suit and got into his riding gear, he turned off in a shallow valley and pushed into the wilds of the northwest.

Las Vegas was now two hours behind, but The

158

Kid kept the bay moving at a fast clip. He had a feeling that someone could be on his tracks. Time and again he pulled in to slow the horse as he looked back at the last ridge.

There was nothing in sight. Ahead the vaulting hills were beginning to climb in more gradual waves to form rolling, brush-flecked tablelands. The sun was low in the west over the Sangre De Cristos.

The wind came whistling downward from the mountains to whisper about his ears. At this height the air cooled off rapidly. It was time to start looking for a camp-site.

He eased up on his mount as they skirted the slopes of the bulking foothills. Trees were thickening in his path and he threaded his way among oak and yellow pine.

He was riding down a long sweeping expanse toward a river, he thought to be a branch of the Pecos, when a rider emerged from a clump of pine not more than forty yards away.

It was so unexpected a sight that The Kid's hand was only halfway to his saddle-gun when he saw the man was covering him with a Winchester Rifle.

And more unexpectedly—that voice—calling him by name!

"Hold up there, Billy!" There was no mistaking the rollicking hail of Jesse Evans.

The Kid reined-in. "Jesse!" He kept his hands

in sight. "Jesse, what in the devil're you up to? Where'd you pop from?"

Billy's horse cropped scrub grass as Evans rode his black mare forward at a walk, Winchester at the ready. The Kid could see the smile on Jesse. It stretched from ear-to-ear across a stubble of week-old whiskers. Looked like Jesse'd been anxious to see him. No time out for a shave.

"Well, Kid, how'n hell are you?" Evans halted twenty feet away and slightly lowered the rifle. It was enough!

Billy had swept the cocked Colt out of its holster in one motion before Evans could bring the Winchester back up. "Put it away, Jesse!" Billy smiled coldly at Evans. "I'll set this down to a case of nerves. Surprised to find me alive and kickin' ain't you?"

Evans squinted green eyes at The Kid from under his ginger-colored eyebrows and rolled a chew in his cheek. "Yeah, guess that's about it." He shoved the Winchester back down into a scuffed saddle-boot.

Billy noticed that Evans looked worn and seedy. The saddle-gun seemed to be his only weapon.

Evans responded to the glance Billy threw at his lack of armament. "Lost my hogleg back a ways. Bought this rifle from a trader just a spell ago."

Billy kept his six-gun on Evans. "Life's full of

160

surprises, Jesse. What're you doin' way up here? Heard you was in th' jug back in Texas—guest at Huntsville, wasn't it?"

"You heard right." Jesse scrubbed a broken-nailed thumb across his wiry chin stubble. "Fact is, I tried to write you last fall. Don't know if you ever got it." He spat his quid out and scratched his chest. "Those damned long-horn Rangers to Fort Davis probably short-stopped the note."

"Never got it." Billy kept the Colt on a line with Evans's belt buckle. "I was in some hot water myself back about then."

Around them, the shadows spread out from the tree groves and flowed thin and blue down the slopes. A breeze lilted and pressed among the juniper and aspen. In the pause, Jesse wiped at his forehead. His eyes flickered at The Kid and away.

"Hell, Kid, thought you was somebody on my tail just now." He scratched again and tugged his weathered *sombrero* down over his long red hair. "I bin on th' dodge so long I forget how to act half-human. Seems a long time since we worked Chisum's Ranch." He wiped his mouth with the back of his hand. "Ain't got no liquor on you? Could sure stand a belt."

Something jingled in Billy's head, like two bottles clanked together. He recalled the wild rider of Old Juan's story—the "crazy-eyed" hombre that the old shepherd caroused with the night before he'd found the shot-up Kid.

He remembered the Las Vegas barber's tale of the red-headed cowboy, jailed for carrying firearms, and how that redhead rode out of town in such a big rip.

And he looked thoughtfully at Jesse.

"Jesse, let's make camp and hold a little reunion." The Kid holstered the Colt back on his hip. "That piñon grove over there looks right *bueno*. I got no drinkin' liquor, but I can feed you up right handy."

They rode toward the trees as the mountain winds whispered among the shrubs and branches of the grove.

After a supper of bacon, tortillas and coffee, the two sat and grinned at each other across the crackling warmth of a piñon fire.

He filled Evans in on his own twisting, turning trail since that night at Fort Sumner, leaving out Esmeralda and the events at Santa Fe.

"Well," Jesse spat into the red eye of the fire, and watched it wink. "Well, I guess I saved your life for sure by keepin' that old Greaser up half th' night. Sure felt like celebratin'—just four days out of Huntsville Pen. That liquor tasted *mucho bueno*—and I had to lay up for a few hours, ridin' like hell to get away from any trailers. Could'a been noisy if'n they'd caught up." He spat again. "And you sure have made a hell of a racket, yourself, lately." He rose and tugged at his saddle bag, covered all the while by Billy's watchful eyes.

"Here." Jesse held out a small, yellow, paper-covered book. "Take a squint at that."

Billy took the thin little book and glanced at the cover: "The Authentic Life of Billy The Kid. By Pat Garrett."

"Yeah, I got that in La . . . back a ways." Evans sank against the trunk of a pine. Billy saw the fire glitter in his eyes.

"You read this here stuff?" It sort of tickled The Kid in spite of himself. The book, as he thumbed through it, contained four or five pictures, crudely done woodcuts—one of them, Pat Garrett, the hero, leveling a hand-gun about the size of a small cannon at "Billy The Kid." The pictured Billy toted a butcher knife in his hand and looked like a wild Indian with the blind staggers. Poor Barlow!

"Hell of a thing, ain't it?" Evans snickered. But he didn't sound amused.

"You got this? They're peddlin' them in Las Vegas?"

"Well—yeah I got it there. They said it had just come in from th' print shops back east. Had to have somethin' to look at whiles . . . well, they had me in th' jug there for goin' heeled on th' streets. Hell of a thing."

"Read it all?" Billy didn't know what to think

about the little book. It gave him a crawling feeling, like being full of grey-backs or looking at a reward poster. "You read this here thing in jail?"

Evans leaned farther out of the light, seeming uncomfortable with growing fire warmth. He shrugged against the tree trunk, settling his back into a more comfortable spot. "I read it there, some."

"And read it some more out here—eh?" Billy's neck was cold in spite of the blistering heat. His neck tingled, and not with mountain winds. "You had time to lay around out here . . . waitin' for . . ."

The Winchester, suddenly in Evans's hands, boomed deafeningly in the trees. The bullet clipped a lock of The Kid's hair. The book fell into the fire, flaring with an orange snarl.

Billy dived, rolling over on his side, almost under the hooves of Jesse's black mare and hurled the flaming mass of paper into Evans's face as the rifle slammed again.

The slug went wild but The Kid's shot didn't.

Jesse fell headfirst into the fire.

Billy dropped his Colt and tugged Evans out of the mass of white-hot coals, burning his hands. Jesse was mortally hit. While The Kid ripped at Evans's shirt in frantic effort to get at the chest wound, Jesse rolled his green cat's eyes and gasped, "Hell of a reunion."

The Kid brushed the last sparks from Jesse's hair, but he was already dead.

"Why, Jesse?" But Billy already knew for damned certain—

The Ring!

After covering Jesse up with his saddle blanket, he'd sunk down into exhausted slumber, rising in earliest light to do what he had to.

He was through burying Evans by the time of full daylight. He placed the last boulder on the grave, fifty feet away from the campfire in a pine grove, and looked at his hands. They were raw and blistered from the fire and clawing in the rocky soil.

Now he squatted over the rekindled fire and boiled up some coffee while the sun's gold poured through the trees and washed away the last of the dank night shadows. He felt no need for food.

Slowly going over the few effects taken from Evans's body, Billy found little of interest, except a sheet of paper. Jesse'd had no money, dying stone-broke. Probably expecting pay from the Ring—at some other place.

He stared at the thumbed and much folded paper map, drawn with crude detail and saw it was a trail running from New Mexico northward into Wyoming. It was a trail skirting towns and larger settlements—a trail he'd heard of but never ridden. The Outlaw Trail.

Where Jesse had obtained the map was hard to say, but Billy saw Evans had made plans to ride far and secretly. Now he, The Kid, would make good use of it.

He saddled, rolled his camp gear with his sore hands and stood holding Jesse's Winchester. He was coldly furious with himself—but what could he have done?

Jesse'd had him in his sights when he first rode down into the groves, but somehow Evans hadn't been able to pull the trigger. That was the difference between Jesse Evans and Pat Garrett, in fact, the difference between a real man and those sneaking Ring devils. But Ring money had obviously got looking better and better to Jesse when he faced The Kid across the campfire.

And now Evans was dead—as dead as the Lawyer Chapman that Jesse had shot down in the Lincoln County War.

"Damn th' whole bunch!" Billy hurled the spare Winchester off into the brush and mounted up.

18 Outlaw Trail

For two weeks following Jesse's death, The Kid rode on a northwesterly route, using a crude map taken from Evans's pocket.

The afternoon of the first day's flight from that fatal pine grove came to a halt when he paused to turn Evans's black mare into the unguarded back pasture of a small horse ranch in the Turkey Mountains. He just hadn't been able to loose Jesse's mount to shift for itself.

The fourth day found him replenishing his dusty gunny sack with supplies at Durango, Colorado. He rode on out of that mountain-rimmed town before nightfall. The place was too near the telegraph—and the Santa Fe Ring.

Week's end saw the twisted green juniper and piñon pine of Colorado give way to the grey sage and scattered willow groves of Utah. It was a long spell since he'd shaken the sand of New Mexico from his boots—but now he intended to make a good job of it. On up the line lay Wyoming—a long piece from Santa Fe, and a lot farther from El Paso.

He crossed the coffee-brown Dirty Devil River at Hanksville, Utah, being ferried across by a silent old boatman for a dollar, and passed to the west of that upthrust bulk of badland plateau—Robbers Roost.

He traveled the furtive route of the lonely and hunted, the Outlaw Trail—the route of the long rider. Water hole by water hole and canyon cave by cave, he camped and made his way along that trail.

And now that trail led him out of the arid wastelands east of Vernal, Utah into a red and orange labyrinth of rock that reared up into one sandstone cliff after another. The map told him he was near the second of the great stopovers on the outlaw route—Brown's Park.

Lying on the borders of Utah, Colorado and Wyoming, Brown's Park, one of the great holes, or valleys, of the West, stretched its verdant length for thirty miles behind its guardian cliffs.

With his back to the declining sun, Billy rode down a steep, boulder-studded trail that eventually came out at the base of a towering canyon. Overhead, the sun still stained the high, sandstone walls but the brawling, plunging mountain stream The Kid followed was wrapped in mauve half-light.

Shadows mingled with rising river mist. In another hour it would be sundown and The Kid wanted to be out of the canyon maze before dark. He prodded his horse along the gravel strewn edge of the little river seeking an exit.

As he rounded a wide swinging curve of the rock, the walls fell back and he was riding out of the canyon's dark confines into a wide, hazy-green world. He was beyond the cliffs and Brown's Park opened its secrets to him.

Here the sunlight still glowed with a softer, more mellow beam.

Dismounted, he was tightening the saddle cinch when he noticed a rickety flatboat inching its way across the dun surface of the wide river that the canyon stream flowed into.

He waited for the boat to ground itself on the willow fringed shoreline.

"See you comin' 'long th' crick and come over to tote you, if'n youse so inclined." The boatman, a thin, young, light-skinned negro smiled at Billy through a face full of black freckles.

"I'd be so inclined," Billy grinned back and led his mount down the soft, boggy bank into the battered craft. He was glad to talk to a human again. He'd been on the trail for a week without seeing a soul. "Let's get across, Speck."

The boatman landed him on the opposite shore of the river, he called the Green. Off to their right, a log ranch house sprawled among a poplar grove. "Mistuh Crouse's place," Speck volunteered, "but don' plan on stoppin' by. He daid drunk agin and threatenin' to carve out my livuh."

"All folks hereabouts that mean?" Billy swung back into the saddle and tossed a coin to the man.

"Nope, suh," he shook his bushy head, "heap o' folks pass this way at times, but we don' ask questions. Mistuh Crouse's good 'nuff when he ain't confused." He pointed down the valley. "Two or three places down theah, ten or fifteen mile. Hoys and Bassetts. They sometime puts up folks—an' don' ask riddles neitha."

The light was thinning, flattening out. Back of the cliffs, the sun was sinking into a flaming bed.

Nodding to the young boatman, Billy rode off down a faint wagon track, past the log ranch buildings. The thought of that drink-sodden rancher within brought back that night at Fort Sumner. It was never far from his thoughts. Redeye had killed Bobby Barlow as surely as Garrett's gun. And damned foolishness had nearly got himself.

There'd been no sign of pursuit since he left Jesse's grave—a grave that had come pretty nigh being his own. Camping along the hidden trail had begun to ease the edgy feeling he'd had over trackers, but he'd ignored the fact that other hired killers might know the same route.

As he rode past a small stand of poplars, he turned in his saddle and looked back at the sunset and the river's glittering surface. All was as calm as the silently flowing river—but the old hunted feeling began to return with the coming of night.

19   Brown's Park

A gunshot, cracking the silvery bowl of morning, wrenched The Kid from a deep slumber. Another explosion came echoing from the direction of Green River crossing two miles up the valley.

Billy pulled on his boots and stomped up. There were no more shots. "Probably tryin' to rouse the flatboat to tote him across," he muttered.

Day brightened. Billy finished his cup of coffee, put out the small fire he'd kindled near his blankets and stowed the pot and cup in his gunny sack. He had already shaved and washed in the small, cold stream that wound through the valley floor to meet the Green.

He wasn't anxious to meet any stranger crossing the river after him. Could be some owl-hoot coming in to hole up. Just the same, The Kid saddled and rode in the direction of the ranches that the black boatman had pointed out the past evening.

He passed a small ranch to his left, but kept on. The place was too open, in its thin grove of oak and cottonwood. It was early and he felt comfortable riding down the pleasant, still green valley—rimmed to the east and west by reddish-brown sandstone ranges. He planned dropping in on the next place he came to—in time for a bite.

It made him feel like a grub line rider, again, bumming handouts but now he had plenty of scratch to pay for his food.

Jogging along, about ten o'clock, The Kid came over a slight rise and saw a log ranch house a mile off, half hidden in a golden grove of aspen. The hills surrounding it on three sides folded up into tall walls of sandstone, enclosing the southern end of the valley.

He looked back and then ahead at the apparent dead-end. All seemed peaceful and still.

Nearing the buildings, he rode between stubble-filled fields. Golden petaled fire wheels bordering the recently harvested land, dipped in a sudden wind that swept along the rough wagon road. And he saw, in that instant, a small girl in buckskin suit, dabbling among the stones and stubble—and the spotted, green loops of a rattler, coiling within a foot of her back.

He drew and fired as the reptile blurred its horny tail. The child, apparently about five, sprang up, staring at him.

"You sure scared me, Mister," she piped, ignoring the quivering snake. "You can take me back to the house," she commanded as she approached the head of his horse, dusting off her hands on the bead-work skirt.

The Kid swung down and lifted the calm, little girl up onto his saddle. He took the reins, and kicking the snake out of the road, led the bay down the track. "That your place?"

"Yessir," she bobbed her red-gold hair. "That's Bassett Ranch and I'm Ann."

"Queen Ann?" he smiled at the sturdy little figure in the saddle.

"Not a queen, just Ann—but the Ute injuns call me Princess." She poked a small, dirty finger at her blue and red bead-work. "They made me this."

"*Bello*—beautiful for sure. Who's that?" Billy nodded toward a stocky, little man in shirt sleeves, who stood in the middle of the track, peering at them from under his hand. The man's long, red whiskers flared out in the wind that ruffled the fire wheels. Behind him, the aspens turned and tossed their golden fans.

"That's Mister Basset, my Pa." She waved at the man, who advanced toward them. "He musta heard you shoot the snake."

"Welcome," the little man shouted in a high voice. "See you found yourself a young lady." He shook a finger at Ann. "Anna, your mother and I just will have to keep you in the corral, I presume."

Billy looked the man over as he strode beside the horse into the shadows of the trees surrounding the ranch house. Another transplanted Easterner, he figured. The whole west seemed to be filling up with them.

"Just passin' through, Mister Bassett. Thought your little Indian could stand a lift."

"He kilt a big snake that was going to bite me, too, Pa," she shrilled, taking an excited swipe at The Kid's shoulder and knocking his hat over his eyes.

"Easy there, Anna, here's your mother." Bassett tugged his ginger-colored beard and lifted the child down. "Come on up to the house." He didn't inquire about The Kid's sudden appearance in this lost valley.

As he sat at the Bassetts' table, The Kid downed his third cup of coffee and grinned at the efforts of Bassett's pleasant looking wife to completely stuff him with food. "Couldn't eat another bite if they paid me in gold, M'am, even if it's about the best eatin' beef I ever tasted."

"We couldn't begin to repay you—for what you did." She smoothed her neat, checked apron. "We've been out here since Anna was born. Have you ever been East?"

"Might be headin' that way, sometime," Billy replied, pushing back his chair and winking at Ann, who was trying to poke the cartridges from his gunbelt.

"We thought you might be going that way, seeing you were heading for the Rock Springs trail," Bassett broke in, returning from the cabin's other room with a letter in his hand. "If you might be going out through Irish Canyon, you could be on the way east to Rock Springs. That's where we get our mail. Mrs. Bassett's sending off to the mail order house for a few dozen things."

Billy noticed that Bassett hadn't come out and asked him his plans. This was one Easterner who appeared to keep his nose out of folks' business. He'd have to, to survive in this wilderness valley.

"Rock Springs?" The name brought back a pair of deep-blue eyes—Kate's! Why did he think of her, when— Most likely because Rock Springs, Wyoming was a lot nearer than El Paso, Texas. "Rock Springs. Lot of ranches around there?"

"It's the shipping point on the Union Pacific. And there are several good sized spreads nearby," Bassett answered, stroking his heavy beard and staring out a small side window.

Billy stood up and plucked his hat from its peg by the door. He'd also heard the drumming beat of a hard-pressed horse, coming down the valley.

"Hold on a moment," Bassett lifted his hand and stepped out the kitchen door.

Billy waited by the wall with his hand on his gun. It was probably just a friend of the Bassett family—but in an almighty hurry. He grinned reassuringly at Mrs. Bassett, who stood by the window twisting her apron in her reddened fingers. She smiled faintly as she turned back to the cracked glass.

"It could be that drunken Charley Crouse,

from up the valley," she volunteered. "He often comes down to see my Herb. And always in a big hurry." She hovered in front of her child like a mother hen.

The Kid felt a jolt of pity for such folks. They weren't cut out for this sort of life. But it wasn't up to him to tell them what to do. There were plenty of folks from good families coming out to this wild land—like these Bassetts, and the McSweens, Mister Chapman and Mister Tunstall—but a lot of them died of the country.

"It's all right." Herb Bassett's startled face bobbed in front of Billy's leveled Colt. "It's a . . . he's gone on down toward the Little Snake River. I sent him off that way."

The Kid jammed his pistol back in its holster, staring past Bassett's shoulder. He caught a glimpse of a black horse and rider loping out of sight beyond the low, rough log barn south of the ranch house.

"No," Bassett removed his square-rimmed glasses and wiped them on his shabby vest as he answered Billy's unspoken question, "never laid eyes on him before, but we get quite a few riders passing through from time to time." He replaced his glasses and cleared his throat. "Said he was after a horse thief and wanted to know if any strangers recently showed up. I told him nobody. Your horse is around back—where he couldn't see it. I sent the fellow off—but you don't have much time. He could be back from the river in less than an hour."

"Give me your letter." Billy picked it up from the kitchen table and tucked it into his vest. "I'll see it gets mailed at Rock Springs." He tugged little Ann's curls and slipped a ten-dollar gold piece under his coffee cup on the table. These folks could sure use it.

Five minutes later, he was cantering up the slope that led to the Rock Springs trail, due east of the Bassett place. Within half an hour he was well on his way through the canyon. But the glimpse of that rider on the black horse kept returning to him.

The man had been large and bulky in the saddle—but what would a big bucko like Bull-head be doing way up here from Santa Fe—and hunting for a horse thief?

"Horse thief, hell!" He spurred the bay into a gallop as the rocky cliff faces spread away and the trail ran open over rolling brushlands northeast into Wyoming.

20 Kate's Castle

Rock Springs, Wyoming wasn't much. Surrounded by the rocky-faced hills that gave the place its name, it was just a haphazard collection of shacks, sheds and buildings, strung along a curve of the U.P. tracks.

As Billy rode down its one street, he tabulated the total town at: one store, two eating houses, four saloons, one hotel, one livery stable and one depot—complete with sprawling cattle pens.

He posted the Bassetts' letter at the store and got directions to Castle's Double-K Ranch.

Coming out on the rickety, wooden porch to mount up, he watched a pair of noisy punchers go dashing by on horseback, riddling the late September morning with shouts and shots.

"Some U-Cross boys a'lettin' off steam," the store-keeper chuckled. "They got their beeves off on th' cars last week and been takin' life as she comes ever since."

The Kid followed those riders out a well-defined road, winding up from town onto sage-brush flats to the north. Here rangeland stretched as far as the eye could see. Off along the smoky line of the horizon, dim smears of another ridge of the Rockies loomed with cloud-like vagueness—the land of the Yellowstone—and Hole in the Wall.

Picket-pin ground squirrels reared up along the road, watching his approach, only to dive away into patches of dusty golden ragwort, chattering in disgust. White-crowned sparrows whirled about in flocks, adding their trilling whistles to the picket-pins' clamor.

"Everyone's wild and woolly this morning." The Kid clucked his bay into a trot. The air was crisp and cool. Ahead, the land slanted down into a gently rolling valley, bisected along its length by a willow-fringed stream.

Billy rode down toward the river bottom at a slow walk. He pulled the Winchester carbine from its boot and threw a shell into the chamber as he caught sight of movement along the willows' cross-slashed shadows.

A faint breeze, spangling the green and yellow foliage, covered the sound of his approach, and he was within twenty feet of the two punchers before they realized he was there.

A thin, brown-mustached young fellow in a checked blue shirt and furry, black chaps, doubled over his horse's mane with high-pitched laughter. His companion knelt, whooping with lusty shouts, on the edge of the little river's bank. He was batting a broad-brimmed Stetson at a beautiful, blonde girl, who stood nearly waist-deep in the swirling water, with her back turned away from them.

The Kid's shot in the air brought the black-chapped cowhand upright and stiffened the riverside jokester into a kneeling statue.

"Hold it, boys," Billy ground out, the smile on his face cold and thin. "Hold 'er right there! I kinda think th' lady don't hanker for your admirin'—from th' ways she's givin' you th' cold shoulder."

He sent a Winchester slug slamming into the river bank, spattering dark mud into the eyes of the cowboy making a play for his pistol. He fell on his face in the muck while the mustached puncher on horseback elevated two rigid hands.

The blonde girl, who twisted her head around at the shots, was Kate Castle.

Her blue eyes widened and her cheeks were flushed, as much in apparent dismay at the sight of The Kid as at the sudden exposure of her rounded, water-beaded figure.

"All right you!" Billy waved the smoking carbine at the mounted man, "pile off. Join your friend on th' ground—and on your face!"

Kate turned back, facing across the stream where a small pinto grazed on the far bank. "Billy—ah, Mister Roberts," her voice was level, almost amused. "I never expected to see you here—or have you see me, this way. What shall I do now?" She looked back at him over her smooth shoulder and patted a hand at her tangled mop of golden hair, again displaying a brief glimpse of a rounded, swelling breast.

Billy glanced aside at the two punchers, but they were heads-down in the river sand. "Wade over to your horse, Miss," he ordered. "I'll take care of these coyotes."

As soon as Kate had gained the bank and disappeared into the underbrush, he dismounted and poked the men up with his Winchester.

Within three minutes, the pair rode off minus guns and pants.

"They'll be waitin' for you, if you come back this way—after your blood cools," The Kid called after the glowering pair. He wrapped the two gunbelts and weapons in the men's pants and wedged them into a wide bole of a water-twisted willow.

Swinging back into his saddle, he watched the pantsless punchers galloping along the stream for a long moment, but they were on their way and it didn't appear they'd be back.

He rode out into the glittering water and edged along over the muck and pebble bottom onto the opposite bank.

Kate Castle guided her mount from the willow thicket, now clothed in a brilliant blue riding outfit, her yellow hair streaming out under a neat grey, curl-brimmed *sombrero*. Her cheeks held a high color and her mouth was vivid with a flashing smile.

"Billy! How are you? How did you find me . . . how?" Her words tumbled and tripped out, matching the swirling, tumbling stream in their swiftness. Unabashed at her recent experience, her blue eyes glistened with excitement.

"Miss Kate," he reined in beside her and took her hand. It was warm and firm. "I was on th' way out to your place—to look up some friends, I guess you'd say—." He grinned into her face, "But I never thought we'd bump into each other—like . . ."

"What'd you do with those U-Cross men? They really weren't doing anything. They just rode up when I was taking a dip." She grasped his hand in both of hers. "But whatever you did, you better come along." She looked down the stream. "They're pretty wild—and could come back. It's only four miles over the hills to our place."

"They won't be back for a spell." And he told the laughing girl how he'd parted the punchers from their pants and pistols.

"Good," she beamed and laughed again. And that sounded *bueno* to The Kid. He hadn't heard a woman laugh for weeks. He let the girl's hand go and followed her up the trail that led away from the river toward higher ground.

The morning was now alive with clouds and sunshine. They galloped along, herding the swiftly flowing shadows of the sheep-woolly clouds over the wind-rippled grass-ocean. This was the high-wide country of Wyoming, and it was beautiful to The Kid—mighty nigh as beautiful as the laughing, carefree girl, riding at his side.

All too soon the land dipped and Billy saw the white-painted buildings of the Double-K Ranch stretching to his right in a shallow, pleasant valley. Beyond the ranch itself, a quarter of a mile off, another of the mountain-fed rivers curved away out of sight with its yellow sandbars and green willows.

The Castles had quite a spread. The Kid saw this as he dismounted to give Kate a hand down. Painted bunkhouses and sheds stood sentinel-like behind a large, two-story, frame house that loomed above them in the prairie hollow. A gingerbread trim emphasized its castle-like appearance.

Several well-fed ranch hands perched on the corral rail, clambered slowly down and took the horses, leading them to the nearest barn.

"Daddy modeled this place after Marquis de More's over in Dakota," Kate proudly announced to the gaping Kid.

"Those foreigners generally can run a payin' business," Billy replied, thinking of John Tunstall. But it seemed to The Kid that the paying here had been done by Castle. What stock Billy noticed on the ride in were pretty scruffy for such fine grass. And the buildings, though newly built, were already weathering and had a run-down look.

21   Shots in the Dark

Billy saw little of Kate for the next week. The day after his arrival the foreman put him to work riding the line camps bordering the Castle Range. His job, though run-of-the-mill, was welcome for the freedom and solitude it afforded.

He rode a full eighty miles, leisurely making the rounds of the ten line camps during the following five days. He was to check on the condition of the shacks and dugouts and ready them for the coming of bad weather, and their lonely inhabitance by the "Buck Nuns," or line camp riders.

He packed along a gunny sack of nails, a claw hammer and a hand axe. He re-hung doors on bent hinges, batted shingles into place and swamped out the old dirt and rubbish that often earned these places the odorous title of "boar's nests."

Each evening he unrolled his blanket and slept in empty bunks or dented and shaky iron bedsteads, lulled to sleep by cheerful chuckling blazes in repaired fireplaces or basked in the bright glow of little, cast-iron, three-legged wood burners.

There was some tinned food on the shelves and he pieced out these windfalls with a sizeable chunk of sowbelly that he carried in his slicker along with coffee and a small coffee-pot. Water came from the many little mountain streams meandering in crooked aimlessness from the direction of the ever-present, cloud-like Big Horns to the northwest—part of the Yellowstone Range.

With nothing to do at night, he thumbed in a tattered mail order catalogue, the first he'd ever laid eyes upon. He'd picked this up in the second line shack. The variety of items from corsets to hay rakes were a source of amusement and instruction. And it held thoughts of Kate, and The Angel, at a distance—especially if he kept out of the corset sections.

His other reading matter was the little black book. By now he was familiar with each shady deal of that bunch in Santa Fe. It was all there, the noble deeds of those dirty black-legs—Grapes, Oyster and Terror. For the present it was "Kid on the dodge"—but *justo esperar*!

Some time during each day he rode out into the great, grassy wastes, searching for Double-K stock, and several times he found some strays from the neighboring ranches. These he drove back in the direction of their own range.

He was often caught in downpours of sudden fall rain but his sowbelly slicker kept him dry.

For the most part, his tour of the line was nearly as monotonous and lonely as his recent trip up the outlaw route. Only once did he see a rider and that horseman passed beyond the Double-K range—never answering The Kid's hail. Billy saw the man didn't want to hold any palaver and let him disappear into the vastness of the cloud-brushed distance.

At the end of the week, The Kid had patched, cleaned and ship-shaped the last line shack and headed back early in the afternoon toward the ranch, eager to see Kate.

He'd successfully kept away most thoughts of her, but now, though he pictured the eyes and voice of Esmeralda—running over each gesture and word, like a young'un says his ABC's, Kate grew sharper in his mind.

Riding to the curve of the river, a minor branch of the Snake, he found the water up a bit from recent rains, but had no trouble in fording across near a grove of sun-bleached cottonwoods—and came in sight of the ranch buildings up the valley.

He unsaddled and cleaned up in time for supper.

After feeding with the dozen hands in the long, log dining hall, he had just mounted the corral rail, with some of the punchers, when another ranch hand came rattling toward them in a buckboard, bringing supplies and mail from Rock Springs.

Michigan Slim, the stocky young cowpoke in a high crowned hat and light-grey california pants, unloaded his cargo, placing aside a small bundle of papers and envelopes for the ranch house.

"Here Michigan, I'll take th' mail up to th' house." Billy hopped down and held out his hand.

"Not much," the man grunted. "Don't mind doin' it myself." He grinned lopsidedly. "Ya seem to be thick enough now with our Cattle Queen, she . . ." He stopped short, staring at Billy's hand, where it rested casually on his gun butt. "Aw, I don't mind. G'wan take th' stuff."

The Kid went up the path toward the house as Michigan Slim held a pow-wow behind, ". . . think that drifter's a bad un I do . . ."

"Don't know, seems ready to do his share, and smile," came the voice of Old Jake, the foreman.

"Could be—but he smiles at th' dumbest times . . ."

Out of earshot, Billy glanced through the bundle as he neared the front porch. He'd bullied the fat puncher, but it couldn't be helped. He had a hunch about that mail.

There were several periodicals: Godey's Ladies Book, copies of the Cheyenne paper, Atlantic Monthly for September 1881, the Yellowstone Journal and two envelopes. One was postmarked September 15th from Kansas City and the other—from Santa Fe.

The Kansas City letter was addressed to Miss Kate Castle, Double-K Ranch, Rock Springs, Wyoming Territory, and the other to—Granville Castle, same address.

187

Billy was still staring at the handwriting on the Santa Fe letter when Kate came out on the verandah.

"Here's the mail," Billy looked over his shoulder at the punchers down at the bunkhouse—"Kate."

The girl, smiling her welcome, stepped down and took the bundle. She seemed about to speak, but catching sight of Slim and the others, perched on the railing, inspecting sky, top of the house and their own dirty fingernails, she turned back silently.

Billy sauntered down to the bunkhouse. If that was the way it was going to be—well *bien*! He was glad Kate had sense. A week here, or two, and if everything was *quieto*, he'd think hard about trailing back down to Texas.

The Double-K punchers, including Michigan Slim, kept their debates confined to such bothersome stock ailments as Screw Worm and Lump Jaw—with side excursions into the "poorness of the ranch grub" and the rigors expected of the coming winter. Nothing was remarked on the Cattle Queen, or silent greeting of The Kid. The look that Billy had given Michigan when he returned to the bunkhouse was enough.

Billy sat in a corner near the oil lamp, cautiously studying the Ring Book, taking no part in the talk. Somehow, though he was naturally easy going and convivial, he didn't want to visit.

From the conversation, he could see that all hands, including Jake, the foreman, weren't overly sold on work, though the old fellow would probably show more ambition with a different crew. They seemed about the poorest excuse for cowhands that he'd seen in a long spell. John Chisum wouldn't have scratched his head very much for an excuse to cut their pay—*desaliño*!

It was apparent that Kate's daddy wasn't making a go of it with this crowd. And that was another of their complaints—no pay for two months, and no money in sight.

If he, The Kid, had his way he'd fire out every one and bring in some real cattlemen, like the ones in New Mexico. They might raise some hell down there but thcy knew how to work.

As Billy thumbed over the pages of the note-book, the close-cramped writing suddenly hit him between the eyes—the same hand as on the letter from Santa Fe that he'd just turned over to Kate. None other than old Terror himself, Fiske of the National Bank of Santa Fe, and paymaster of the Ring.

Why was that *mofeta* writing Mister Castle?

Before he could worry over the matter, the bunkhouse door opened and Castle's Chinese house cook shuffled in, bearing a large tray in his amber paws with his black rope of a pig-tail bringing up the rear.

The wind-baggers broke up to surround the three dried apple pies.

The cook sidled over to The Kid, wagging his head like a polite clock pendulum.

"Wantee look see me?" Billy stuck the little book under his belt, next to his shirt.

"No sir. Miss Castle would talk with you as soon as you come up to the house."

Billy followed the Oriental outside. The air was cooler but felt heavily of storm. Down the valley along the river, the cottonwood leaves were twinkling in the wind, catching the last russet rays of sun in blood red sparks.

She was waiting for him just inside the front door. Several lamps threw a soft light over an interior that was anything but castle-like. Once The Kid stepped over the oaken threshold, he could see most of the gingerbread elegance was on the outside. A hall of plain, white-painted timber traveled the length of the house, with two or more large rooms leading off each side. At the hall's end, a crude railing ran up massive, hewn steps to the upper story. Beyond the stairs was a door leading into the kitchens, and servants' quarters.

The Kid looked around for the "celestial" but he'd vanished into the yellow lamp glow. Only Kate stood before him—in a flowing, thinly-made gown of soft blue—almost as blue as her eyes. But what made The Kid swallow twice, was the fact that when the girl moved back into the light to admit him, he could see—nearly as much—as the day he came upon her in the river.

"Billy." She held out her hand. "I'm glad you got back all right. I wondered about you all the time you were out on our range."

"Was really mighty restful," he winked and took her hand. And before he could do more than give it a polite shake—she was in his arms—in his arms and he was holding much more than one slender hand.

"Let's go into the living room," she whispered, turning up her fragrant mouth to him again. "I've got so much to ask you—and, I might catch cold here in this draft—I was just coming from my bath."

The living room, with its great stone fireplace, topped with a moon-faced Seth Thomas clock, and crossed hunting rifles, hung on deer antlers, was barely discernable in the pale light of the one lamp standing on the stone mantle. All else was shadowy and vague except—Kate.

The girl settled close to Billy on the worn, horsehair sofa, her softness against his thigh.

"Daddy'll be back tomorrow. The letter was from him."

"*Bueno*. He's in Santa Fe?" The Kid watched her narrowly in the dim, bland haze of the lamp. Her face changed, ever so slightly.

"No." She stiffened. "No, that was a letter from

one of Daddy's business partners. Daddy's due to arrive from Kansas City."

"Wind's comin' up." It was all he could think to say. Kate was bothered by his question, for certain.

The wind was rising. Outside in the thick, spreading dark, its gusts wrestled the gingerbread-work of the house and rattled the frames of the windows and doors. It whistled through the cracks and crevices of the warped wooden walls. What would winter be like in such a place, in this wide-open land?

"What was that?" Kate turned. Her golden head was close to his as she stared out the nearest window, eyes shaded by her hand. The robe fell open—and Billy could see firm young curves, as far as her slender waist.

"What? The wind?" He couldn't see or hear anything but the girl.

"No, the men down at the bunkhouse—I thought I heard some noise. Could they be fighting?"

"Probably a row over the last hunk of pie." Those saddle tramps from Slim to Old Jake couldn't get up enough spunk to do any damage.

"No." Kate seemed to notice her robe. With a swift side-look from under her velvety lashes, she pulled it tightly about her. The curves became more noticeable than ever. "I'm afraid they might be getting angry about wages. You must have heard them. That's why Daddy went to Kansas City. His friends in Santa Fe—couldn't, or wouldn't help. He's trying to get a mortgage, or a loan."

"Miss Kate. You asked me once, if I was in trouble—now I'm askin'. D'you need—money?" He looked around the room. For all its size, it was poorly furnished. All the Castle money must have gone into stocking the range and putting up buildings. The big clock, hunkering on the mantle, looked chipped and dented. Even the furniture had seen better days. Certainly a come-down for top-shelf Easterners. But they'd probably weather the trouble and make a go of it—if the old man had the quiet firmness of Kate.

"Miss Kate?" He repeated his question.

"Well, yes. Daddy wasn't able to get much— but he hopes to collect some outstanding notes before long—a few weeks or so." She caught his hand and again that erratic robe parted—this time from her shoulders. Her firm, richly-rounded breasts jutted out at him. Lamplight kissed her smoothness—an instant before The Kid.

"Billy. Oh, we must—we . . ." Her mouth, soft and red, fed the hot fire, blazing through him. "Billy, come from the window. We'll be seen." She tugged away, and holding the robe together with one hand, led him across the room and through a door at the end of the hallway. "I want—you to see the rest . . . of the place . . ."

"What's this?" But he knew. A bedroom. Hers. A small, neat, crystal lamp flickered on a large, dark wood bureau, rcflecting a cluttered collection of perfume bottles, glass pots and jars—women's beauty ammunition. "Here—come here," he muttered with suddenly thick tongue and dry lips, as he grabbed at her.

She came unresisting into his arms, and her robe opened—this time completely.

"Hurry, oh hurry!" Her fingers were prying and pulling at his shirt and belt. "Hurry," she whispered as he stroked her smoothness and sat down beside her on the creaking edge of the big, brass bedstead.

"Wait, let me get this weapon off." He unbuckled the gunbelt, thinking, surprisingly enough, of the last time he'd shed it for such a reason. Esmeralda—she and he, but . . . ! Now this was different. Kate was here and he—but Esmeralda was different. That was love. Kate was here and waiting for him. And he couldn't keep from her—couldn't if he wanted to.

As he placed the gunbelt next to his hat on the bureau, between a pair of green scent bottles, he saw the two letters.

"Blow out the lamp, Billy. Please!" Her voice was soft, womanly urgent. "Hurry, blow it out!"

He puffed the small flame into darkness and was reaching for her when he heard voices down toward the bunkhouse—and a shot. "What in th' hell?"

She was beside him, her bare arms about his shoulder, still clinging and fondling at him. "Oh—not now! Not when we're here—and—oh." The girl, whimpering under her breath, pressed closer to him, her fingers busy again at his clothing. "Don't mind them. You said they were probably at some foolishness." She clutched him as he swung up from the bed.

"Maybe those X-Bar boys. Maybe?" He buckled his gun on and stepped to the window.

"Come outa there Bonney! We know you're in there." Outside in the hush, the wind picked up voices, tossing them against the weather-bleached walls of Kate's castle.

"Bonney?" Kate sat up and spoke through the shadows. "Who're they looking for? That's not the sheriff, nor our boys."

"Nope." Billy knew who it was. No one but that big, hulking, bloodhound of a Bullhead from Santa Fe. He'd stuck to the trail. The Kid reached for his hat on the edge of the bureau, and his fingers brushed the two envelopes. He stuffed them into his pocket—on a swift hunch.

"Who's out there? Oh, Billy, who's out there?" She padded, naked beside him. "Oh!" She flinched back as lightning's blue flash lit the room.

Billy cursed Bullhead when his eyes took in

195

that rounded beauty—what a time! "Kate! I'm gonna leave. That *hombre* out there could get excited and shoot up th' place."

"Who is . . . ?"

"Never mind, just some trouble followed me here. It'll turn out right." He reached in his pocket and pulled out his wallet.

"That man's looking for Bonney," her voice was low, puzzled. "We don't have anyone by that name."

Feet were running toward the house, lost in thunder that shivered beams and rafters. "Here," he reached out in the darkness, feeling for her. "Here, take this. Settle up with your saddle hawks. Pay me later." He gave a short laugh. "I won't be needin' much."

"Miss Castle! There's a posse of men. They seek horse thieves." The Chinese cook was pounding on the bedroom door.

"Wait! I'll send them packing." Kate went out, wrapped in her robe.

But Billy didn't wait. He flung up the back window. Slinging a leg over the sill, he dropped to the ground. A clap of thunder split the gusting night sky. Blue light outlined a wild-eyed Bullhead, coming around the corner of the house, rifle at the ready.

In that instant, both fired. The Winchester slug blew glass from Kate's window. Billy couldn't see where his six-shooter's slug hit.

He headed for the bunkhouse and corrals. Before he was halfway, another bolt of hell-fire ripped the sky to yellow ribbons. He saw a black knot of figures circling the Castle house. Some lifted weapons as the night swung back into place.

A man near the bunkhouse took a snap shot at the running Kid. The bullet hummed past his shoulder. Billy angled toward the corral. In the next flash, he glimpsed a white horse tied off by itself. The rain came down in dark sheets as he untied the mount and vaulted into the wet saddle. He hadn't taken time to get his sowbelly slicker.

Turning the horse, he headed at a fast gallop along the valley road toward the river. Behind in the almost continuous storm flashes, he saw men swarming down from the big house and mounting up. One, he thought, could be that X-Bar puncher he'd treed at the creek last week. They were all after his scalp at once. Bullets hissed overhead and slapped into the water-soaked ground, as he lashed the horse toward the dark grove of cottonwoods at the ford.

He was at the rushing water's edge before the nearest rider was within a quarter of a mile. The river was up strongly from the rain. The ford was way under, but he'd have to chance it.

Billy let the white mare get her wind, watching the storm-painted riders approaching. As the first of their shots sputtered out between thunder crashes, he stuffed his Colt between his shirt and pants for safekeeping and found the Ring Book ready to fall from his belt.

Jamming the book back, he plunged the mount into the surging current—as near the shallows as he could remember them.

Next moment he was thrown from the horse by the shocking force of the waters. Sputtering and choking in the muddy violence of the flood, he managed to hold onto the reins and make a grab at the saddle-horn.

The raging river spun them downstream and out of sight of the riders on the bank, within a water-rushing moment. Gasping and swallowing water, Billy let the mare have her head, struggling to keep her turned into the current.

Over and around they went. The horse neighed wildly, threshing her hooves within inches of the floundering Kid. But she straightened out and began to swim strongly.

The saddle-horn, rolling out of Billy's grasp, caught him against the temple, and frigid numbness swept him along with the current— but his head cleared, and he was clutching the saddle-girth when his feet stumbled and dragged on gravel bottom.

They were across.

22 Hole In The Wall

Bullhead's white horse, with Billy hanging to its tail, clambered out of the rushing river a full five miles below the ford—both exhausted from the battering current.

The night wind still prowled among the scrub along the river bank. The Kid, minus his hat, wound a bandana onto his head. Without a dry match, he walked up and down the bank for hours, trying to get warm enough to sleep. The horse was tied to the projecting roots of an overturned cottonwood.

When the sun began to burn away the night mists, Billy was crouched in a hollow made by the wind-topped tree. He dozed and shivered until the sun was high enough to pour down its warmth in earnest.

Unsaddling the mare, he pulled bunches of grass and rubbed her down. There was a half-full bag of grain tied to the saddle. He shook out enough for a feed. He owed her plenty. If the animal had lost her head, it was anybody's guess what would have happened.

As he settled back in the hollow to doze again, he spotted an old friend, his *sombrero*, water-logged and snagged halfway out on a sandbar of the receding river. Though he was nearly dry, he waded back out and retrieved his lid.

Drying in the glaring sun and sheltered from the sharp northern winds, he roused about noon to saddle up. All was quiet beyond the river bank. Mountain breezes plucked at the grass with transparent fingers. It was just The Kid and his mount in all the wide circle of windswept vastness.

There was no sign of Bullhead or the X-Bar punchers, but he couldn't go back to Castle Ranch.

He rode north fifteen miles, searching until he found a comparatively shallow crossing within a mile of the northernmost line shack on the Double-K range.

That night in the snug line camp dugout, he went over his personal effects, sitting near the red, crackling fire. The little leather book was water-stained but legible—but the two letters from Kate's room were faded and nearly undecipherable. The note from Mister Castle was completely gone except for a few words. But Fiske—"Terror" of the Ring used better ink. Billy could make out several lines: ". . . You will agree . . . man is apprehended . . . a danger to each . . . must seize the . . . before the fellow . . . tries . . . any means to put him and his . . ."

There wasn't any need to read between such lines. The Ring was deadly determined to get the book back. Bullhead's one-man posse was evidence of that determination.

He wondered if Kate knew about the Ring—but only the letter from her father was open. The Santa Fe note was sealed—or had been until Billy ripped it apart.

Before he turned in for the night, he cleaned his Colt, wiped all the ammunition, and re-studied the water-spotted map of the outlaw route. By the rough pen tracing, he saw he was three days hard ride from the last leg of the Outlaw Trail—Hole In The Wall.

The three days stretched into five, due to the wildness of the country and The Kid's unfamiliarity with the terrain. The first day took him out through the white, glaring bleakness of the Alkali Flats. He was dry as a horn toad before day's end brought him to the blue circle of Picket Lake, high in the reaches of the Continental Divide.

Next day he crossed the shallow Sweetwater, north of Split Rock. He was camped for the night, on the banks of Dry Creek, when the cold brilliance of the North Star flared up above the black horizon.

Journeying for two long and lonesome days, he made do with the odds and ends of canned goods, taken from the last line shack along with a pair of snowshoe rabbits, the latter potted in a juniper thicket on the cloud-shadowed slopes of the eastern side of the Divide.

Descending from one plateau to another, he

saw the distant purplish red smudge of the Little Rockies, and the Big Horns, swell up from the earth—the badlands and site of the Hole In The Wall.

The fourth night was unusually cold for the season. Billy built a roaring blaze of dried brushwood and basked by the shelter of an upthrust rock formation, a mile down from the wide Powder River. For several hours, until the fire died away, he lay with his Winchester, listening, but all was still.

After breakfasting on the remnants of the canned goods, and his last grains of coffee, The Kid rode along a wide loop of the brown, swirling Powder. On both sides, the badlands reached up, sharp-toothed and filled with gaping gorges and blind box-canyons. The map didn't tell him how to get through this broken land, but he reasoned that if he could cross the Powder he'd be only half-a-day's ride from the Hole.

Stripping down to his skin, he bundled his clothes and boots, and wrapping his six-gun in the middle, lashed the package to the saddle. He gingerly eased the horse into the broad stream, swimming along beside. Fear of that last river was still on him.

The current, while swift, wasn't too much for the mare and they made the crossing in good shape. But The Kid was mighty relieved to be on dry land. You couldn't buck *La Fortuna* too often.

The country northward became rougher by the mile and Billy rode through some of the most desolate land he'd ever seen. Nothing but thin grass, sagebrush and rock—mostly rock.

The winds, coming down from the Big Horns, were blowing sand and grit into his face along with spurts of rain. The day, blue at dawn, was making up into storm weather. He pulled the bandana up over his nose and pushed on into the dust clouds, squinting at the looming, red-rock cliffs that grew ever steeper on his left.

Several times he reined in to study the nearly smooth, red sandstone bulwarks of the Red Wall.

About nightfall, though it was hard for The Kid to tell if the darkness sweeping in was sundown, or another storm, he halted by a narrow crack-line crevice opposite another loop of the Powder that crooked off among the sage flats.

He dismounted and walked to the opening. It wasn't much of a hole, if Hole it was. The broken gash in the towering cliff was only wide enough for a horse and rider.

Leading the mare, he was picking his way among small chunks of sandstone and sagebrush when he came upon a man. This stranger was sitting against a spur of the wall, rifle leaning against his side, and head tipped back—sound asleep in spite of the lightly falling rain.

The Kid pulled his Colt and poked the pistol in the sleeper's ear.

"Hey! Goddam, whut's up?" The man, a long, thin, lantern-jawed hard-case, in ragged puncher's clothes and a battered *sombrero*, awoke with a hiccup. He stumbled up, kicking over his sleeping syrup—a nearly empty bottle of Old Crow. "Hey, ease off on that hammer, Pard! I was just huntin' along here."

"Me too, and I found it."

"Whut?"

"The Hole! Hand over your rifle, until we go and meet th' rest. More of you 'hunters' around?"

"You dammed betcha. And Flat Nose George, heered of him? Well, he won't take too kindly, throwin' down on one of his bunch." The man passed over the Winchester rifle and under The Kid's direction stumbled along the trail through the Hole, followed by Billy on horseback.

The rain and wind seemed locked out by the sheer, red sandstone cliffs, vaulting above them into the dusky, lowering clouds.

Twenty yards beyond the crevice, the walls opened at a right angle and The Kid was in the Hole itself. The stillness was what he noticed most, complete, almost oppressive quiet, as though something waited out in the narrow valley.

Half a mile to the north, where the walls curved in a broad sweep a branch of the Powder cut through the valley, and by its fringe of cottonwoods stood Hole In The Wall Ranch. There, the grumbling, cursing guide led Billy.

The rain-fat, ragged clouds had surged over the cliff barriers, at last, ripping their grey hides on the heights. Water fell in a steadily increasing downpour. Billy found himself wishing for that old sowbelly slicker.

They pulled up in front of several cabins, a rough pole-barn and corral, filled with a bunch of beautiful, sturdy horseflesh.

"Yuh best let me hail and tell 'em we got a visitor," the footsore sentry growled at The Kid, looking around for reinforcements.

"Go on—tell 'em Th' Kid—Texas Kid's outside and gettin' wet."

"Yeah. Hey in there! You, hey!" The man, wiping water from his eyes with his forearm, pounded on the stout, wooden door of the larger cabin. "Open up Godammit, it's rainin' to beat hell!"

The door cracked open slightly and a rifle inched out—snake-like. Its deadly black eye watched The Kid as he dismounted, Colt in holster and Winchester pointed at the wet ground.

Billy felt as soaked as if he were in the river again. Watching that unwavering rifle muzzle, he failed to hear the approach—noiseless in the rain, of two men. A pair of guns were jammed into his back, and his Colt plucked from its holster. They also relieved him of the Winchester.

"Ha! Got'em. Bring 'im in. I tole th' side-winder he'd fetch trouble comin' uninvited." His ex-prisoner chortled and darted into the cabin ahead of Billy and his two guards.

The Kid was shoved forward across the stone slab doorstep, and the door slammed behind him. As his eyes became accustomed to the interior, he saw a group of men standing near the cabin's fireplace. And as his two captors moved around to face him, he saw one was Peep O'Day.

It was O'Day, in spite of two weeks' growth of beard, looking two years older and ten years wiser. O'Day's blue eyes watched him closely from under drooping lids, a lopsided smile peeking through his whiskers. "Well now. I don't say this is any sight fer sore eyes, but welcome to th' Hole—Texas Kid."

In the milling, muttering crowd, Peep went at explaining his connection—and their business deal in New Mexico. But The Kid didn't notice O'Day mentioning how the firm had been dissolved.

"Hell, yuh say this feller's A-One?" Billy's guide grabbed a bottle from a plank table near the door and downed a jolt. "He up and . . ."

"Yeah, we see. Got the drop on you at the Wall. Flat Nose ain't gonna like that much, Cully." Peep laughed as he thumbed Billy to a seat by the fire.

The Kid put out his hand to the scrubby-bearded, round-shouldered puncher who held his six-gun. "Could you oblige me—unnh?"

"Phoenix's th' handle—Texas Kid, and we'll wait til Curry gets himself back."

"You sure come a hell of a ways huntin' me," O'Day spoke in a low voice, as the others went back to their card game.

"Ain't quite right, Peep. I just come up th' same trail as you."

"Musta got into a bind, heh?"

"Some, but you can help me out. Square me with your pards here. I'd like to hole up for a spell." Billy leaned forward. "I figure you own me more'n that."

"Hey Cully, think Flat Nose is comin' and he'll be raisin' hell about no guard out," a young roly-poly cowhand snickered from the poker game.

Cully arose snarling and stalked out the door. The rain was letting up its drumming drive on the roof. Presently the pound of a horse galloping, mingled with the rain-drip.

The door opened slowly and a man entered followed by the glowering Cully. The newcomer batted water from a high-crowned *sombrero*, and pulled off a yellow fishskin slicker. He wasn't a large man, scarcely taller than The Kid.

His broad face was mild—but his coal-black eyes were as mean as a poisoned rattler. A broken nose hooked down over a black, walrus

207

mustache—Flat Nose George. "What're ya doin' ridin' into th' Hole and pullin' down on my men? Ya a damn lawdog?" The voice was flat and husky-quiet. Like the rumbling growl of a lobo wolf. This was more than a hard-case. This was a killer.

"Sorta on th' long haul, you'd say." The Kid stuck out his hand. "These gents relieved me of my weapon and I'd appreciate it back. Peep'll vouch for me."

"Yeah?" Curry's deep, black eyes swept the grinning O'Day, and Peep stopped grinning. Flat Nose turned away from Billy's outstretched hand, ordering the hefty young puncher, he addressed as Matt, to rustle his tail and get grub on.

Billy sank back on his chunk of upturned firewood and waited for supper. At least he'd get something from that frying pan. Frying pan—for certain! Out of the frying pan and into the fire would be more like it. He sat still, looking at his Colt in Phoenix's belt, and listening to Curry and his crew discussing an upcoming bank raid.

After supper, Curry, O'Day, Phoenix, Cully and the grinning youngster, variously addressed as Matt Warner and Ras Lewis, sat around the sandstone fireplace, with The Kid.

Billy's horse had been fed and turned into the corral.

Peep, keeping his eyes off The Kid, kept up a drawling discourse on horses, especially his paint pony that he'd raced over at some shindig at Buffalo, Wyoming Territory, the nearest town to the Hole.

Curry, morose and quiet, began to warm up with each tip of his bottle. Going over to a smaller table in the corner, he presently began to trace out a map route with Phoenix and Cully. Shortly he beckoned to O'Day and Warner, ignoring Billy. Their voices rose and fell until The Kid began to nod.

Making an effort to rouse himself, he looked around the cabin, staring at the two cracked lamps, the chinked log wall, the rough floor and crude bunks and chairs.

There was little to relieve the monotony of the barren interior except a poster advertising a three-ring circus, playing Cheyenne on May 6 and 7, 1879. A large-busted lady in faded lavender tights dangled by a well-filled leg from a trapeze as highlight of the bill. The Kid grinned to himself. She sort of looked like that frisky Kate. Some amateur artist had added, or expanded certain portions of the lady's anatomy.

Curry cast his flat glance over at Billy. "Watcha want, Texas Kid?"

"Just lookin' for somethin' to pass th' time," Billy answered as he noticed a couple of battered books stuck up on a rafter.

"Them's Big Nosed George Parrott's," Phoenix offered. "He left 'em here just before they grabbed him in Laramie for th' U.P. job. George couldn't read—just liked pitchers." He bent back over the table with the rest of the hard-cases, arguing the finer points of a hold-up.

Billy took the books and sat down by the fire. Outside, the wind keened and murmured around the chimney. It had the sound of winter in it. And let's see, it was the end of September already. He felt restless. This raid Curry was cooking up—he didn't want any part of it.

The book, minus a cover, was the Farmer's Almanac for 1877. The other volume had a green cover with a little yellow jackass on it. "Bill Nye and Boomerang." There were some funny pictures in it. Yeah, books were funny. He remembered the one he'd given to Charley Siringo down on the LX Ranch in Tascosa the fall of '78. And now even he, The Kid, was in a book. It wasn't much of a book—full of lies cooked up by that old drunk Ash Upson, and sworn to as gospel by Garrett, but that book had saved his neck back in the pine grove outside Las Vegas, when Jesse'd tried to gun him. Yeah, funny!

Charley had given him a meerschaum cigar holder, and where'd that gone? He'd bet Siringo would have been glad to swap that book back. It was just a bunch of buffalo-chips about society folks back East by some duffer named Howells.

He stared at the pages of the book before him, hearing the whisper of the wind and the buzz of voices across the cabin—thinking of Siringo and New Mexico Territory where he'd grown up on trouble.

He dipped into the Nye book, trying to get his mind on something pleasant, for a change.

Soon he had made his way through such short pieces as "The Fragrant Mormon" and was chuckling toward the end of "Killing Off The James Boys."—

"Hardly a summer zephyr stirs the waving grass that does not bear upon its wings the dying groans of the James Boys. James Boys have died in Texas and in Minnesota, in New England and on the Pacific Coast. They've yielded up the ghost whenever they had a leisure moment— Let's ignore the death of every plug who claims to be a James Boy, unless he identifies himself. If we succeed in standing them off while they live, we can afford to control our grief and silently battle our emotions when they are still in death— Until we know we are snorting and bellowing over the correct corpses."

Funny, and here he was stuck with a bunch of saddle tramps who were out to take up where Jesse James left off, and even funnier, if the folks with Garrett who identified Bobby Barlow as The Kid could read this—well—it might get them thinking a mite. He chuckled wryly again.

The meeting in the corner broke up at last. Curry folded his maps. "Let's turn in. And you,

Texas Kid, if you're as good as O'Day says, we can use you tomorrow. So bunk over there in the corner." His eyes glittered in the firelight. "And you, O'Day, watch him." He stalked out into the wind-filled night to the other cabin.

Billy turned back to the fire with the book, but Cully yanked it from his hand. "Texas Kid, you need lotsa sleep if you're gonna ride th' long trail with us. Turn in!" He tossed the book back onto the rafter and leaned against the rough wall, dirty-nailed hand near a Winchester that hung on a pair of whittled pegs.

"O.K. It's a good night for shut-eye," Billy winked at Peep. He felt the blood burning in his neck. He'd like to take the butt end of the rifle to that big *borracho*. That's what Esmeralda would have called him. He sat on the bunk and a desire filled him to see her lovely face—those soft black eyes—and to touch her warm sweetness, and hear her voice.

He must have been *loco* to get riled up over that crazy Kate. It was Esmeralda all the time. He knew it, now, and had known it all the time since he first laid eyes on her.

He'd be damned if these *lobos* were going to ring him in on more trouble. He tugged off his boots and pants and bedded down. "Peep, what's your play in this?"

"You shut up, Texas Kid, and you too, Peep. We're gonna be out early so button up." The

212

gruff voice of Cully grumbled at them from the shadows.

Billy could see a weapon glint in his hands. He rolled over. There'd be *mañana*, and then he'd call these jaspers—Flat Nose with his mean eyes, Peep and the rest—just as soon as he could get his hands on a gun.

Outside, the wind raised a pallid voice over the shaggy roof of the Hole In The Wall Ranch, and descended to poke phantom fingers in the ashes of the hearth. Its voice sang a twisting, uneasy song over the great Red Wall, over the ice toothed ridges of the Powder and the Big Horns. Custer and the bones of his men lay out there—and the bones of a million slaughtered buffalo—and over it all the winds of the Yellowstone churned and bubbled, and cried. He thought of Kate and her rich, smooth curves—and of The Angel—and of tomorrow.

23 Out of the Hole

"Who's out to th' gap?" Curry glowered at the assembled gang where they sat at the plank table, wolfing down a breakfast of beef and flapjacks, cooked up by Peep.

"I think it were Phoenix's turn," Peep offered turning from the fire, "but I guess it weren't. He's here now."

The lantern-jawed Phoenix came bursting in the door, buckling on his pistol belt. He still had Billy's pearl-handled Colt. "That damned Ras Lewis kid was supposed to be scouting but musta went to sleep. He's got a visitor with him," he snarled.

"Or th' visitor's fetchin' him," Curry grumbled. "As usual," he scowled at the glaring Cully.

It was plain to Billy, as he sat sloshing down rank coffee, this was a regular rattler's den—ready to strike at a stranger or at each other. Aside from Peep, and how could you figure that saddle tramp, the only one in this bunch worth riding the river with was the Lewis kid. No fun in the others. Not like his old bunch—Pickett, Wilson, Bowdrie, O'Folliard, or even rough-and-ready Rudabaugh.

There came the loppity-lop of horses headed toward the cabins. He didn't like being penned up without a firearm—made him feel like a panther with pulled claws. With no gun, he'd have to take his chances to grab one. He kept after the food and caught a jerk of Peep's head, which could mean anything.

Curry shoved back the log bench and stalked to the doorway, followed by the gang, guns in hand.

The riders pulled up. One was young Lewis, his wide face split in a full-moon grin.

". . . horse thief," was all Billy heard—but it was enough.

Peep leaned against the fireplace, watching The Kid with a sleepy stare. "Must be you, Texas Kid," he smiled grimly. "Certain this hombre ain't looking fer me."

Billy walked over, peered between Phoenix and Flat Nose, and saw Bullhead swing heavily down from a thin, tired-looking crow-bait sorrel. The big man's head, under his *sombrero*, was bound in a stained bandage. That shot at Castle's Ranch had done some damage after all.

The long rider stood staring at the crowd of hard faces surrounding him. His right hand stayed near his six-gun in its holster.

"Ain't you kin to Teton Jackson over to Jackson Hole?" Curry drawled.

Billy inching away from the door, heard Flat Nose laugh for the first time.

"Mebbe I am—but that's not here 'ner there,"

Bullhead grunted. "I'm trackin' a little rattler what run off my white mare."

"Just so. I figger you got a better chance to find her over to Teton's. I hear how he's always got a remuda of strayed stock . . . besides you took a mighty big chance ridin' in here. We don't cotton none to visitors."

"Hell, George," young Lewis snorted, "thought this big duffer . . ."

"Hold on a minute, Mister," the flat, cold tones of Cully knifed into the talk. "Call that Texas Kid out to meet company. Reckon he might have seen somethin' resemblin' a lost white hoss."

Billy eased back into the room until his shoulder was punching into a greasy, paper-covered window. Peep lounged nearby, hand on .44.

"Hey Kid! Texas! Out!" Curry bellowed, "git out here, you and O'Day—and pronto."

The Kid looked at Peep, who shrugged and jerked a thumb at the door. There was nothing for it. Billy stepped out.

"All right, Texas," Cully snapped, obviously eating it up, cold-blue eyes blinking in his hatchet face. "Where's that hoss you stoled?"

"Kid!" Bullhead jumped back like a prodded steer, clawing at his holster. His Colt leaped out booming. The shot flew high, hitting the cabin's chimney, outlaws piling in all directions.

"Hell—look out, he ain't heeled," young

216

Lewis yelped from the lee of cottonwood stump.

"He is now," Peep shouted, yanking Billy's pearl-handled Colt from Phoenix's holster. He heaved it underhand to Billy as The Kid made a dive for the doorway.

An instant later, Bullhead's second shot blasted a shower of splinters and bark into The Kid's face—but Billy's .44 echoed the explosion.

Bullhead went over backward, pole-axed by the shot. He was clawing the ground with both hands as Cully ran up to hunker down by him.

The thin outlaw hunched over the Ring gunman as the gang emerged from their various "bomb-proofs."

"All right, Texas Kid." Curry almost smiled, flat nose wrinkling as he snuffed the thin strings of powder smoke.

Billy saw that the gang chief relished death. A real diamond-back if there ever was one.

"All right, it was his play but I don't think Teton Jackson'll like it much," Curry continued. "Here," he held out a dirt-smudged paw. "Let's have that iron . . . gotta git movin', gotta schedule to keep." He glanced over at Cully. "Git away from that stiff. Help fetch th' horses. Guess you all forgot that paymaster waitin' at Deadwood."

The outlaws, their view of Billy blocked by Flat Nose, were holstering their pistols, and failed to see The Kid's gun flip over to point muzzle on at Curry's belly.

"Back off, Flat Nose, I'm gonna decline to go visitin'. I've had one too many visitors." Billy was sweating. Funny thing but, somehow, he felt under-the-weather. But he'd shoot again if this ugly bastard made a move. Why was he always getting pushed into killings? He was sick and fed-up with . . . that damned dirty Ring. They'd have to let go—now. Who else could trail him?

Curry stood stock still—arms raised to the cloudy Wyoming sky. It was so quiet, for a moment, that the clear descending whistles of cañon wrens mingled with the rattling call of kingfishers, circling up into the windy morning from the nearby creek.

"You Phoenix and Peep, go for 'im! He ain't gonna git away with throwin' down on me."

"Yeah, he is," came O'Day's drawl from the cabin door, where he stood with cocked and leveled Winchester.

"Back off, coyotes," Billy ground out. After a quick look at Peep, where he stood with rifle trained on the hesitant gang, The Kid waved the Colt under Curry's nose.

"And you, Cully," Billy clipped, as that hard-case stealthily lowered his hands. "Sure'd take pleasure lettin' you eat some lead. Shot a buzzard back a spell—you remind me of him."

The rigid knot of men watched The Kid approach Bullhead's body and search it. Rising to his feet, Billy motioned to Peep. "I'm on my

218

way. What'd you throw in with me for? Y'know I grudged you for that stick-up."

Peep's rifle banged out, driving a slug into the ground between Phoenix's shifting boots. "Steady up, boys!" The ejected shell spun in a glittering arc, landing in the dark maroon bloom around the dead man's shoulders. "Figured this was a way to square things."

"*Adiós* all! Thanks for th' grub." Billy ran around the cabins and down to the log corral. There was loud noise out in front, but Peep seemed to be holding his own. No one appeared in the two minutes it took The Kid to throw a saddle and bridle on Peep's buckskin gelding and head the animal on a lope off toward the Red Wall.

Billy reached the opening on the fly, hooves throwing a spray of wet sand and gravel. Several rifle slugs cracked against the upthrust red sandstone, but he didn't take time to look back.

Someone had saddled up, or taken Bullhead's horse and followed, but too late. This buckskin was a real flyer, a racer for certain. It was a good joke on Peep!

He pounded out over the sage flats for a long spell before he eased up and stared back at the red walls. There was no sign of any pursuit. He could picture Flat Nose back there turning the crisp morning air blue while his long riders finished saddling up.

Peep would have to ride that crowbait or Bullhead's white mare. And how that gang would take it out of Peep's hide. Well, that was his lookout—*también malo*!

Bullhead, that big, mossy longhorn, lying face up by the cottonwood stumps—what of him—and the Ring? Damn near nothing! For how could the Ring track him now? And they'd tried hard to land him. But two dead men—Jesse and Bullhead was all they'd got for their trouble.

This horse was good. And a good joke on Peep. The kind that he liked. "A race horse," he yelled into the breeze, splitting past his face and pushing back his hat brim. "A race horse for Chisum's beef money—not a bad swap!"

For the next few hours, The Kid alternately loped and trotted the buckskin, while the dull orange-red of the wall dwindled behind, mingling with the luminous peaks beyond. The lowering skies were warming to a sunny-blue. At noontime the sun was bright and burning hot. Without a canteen, he was already dry.

Billy kept on to the southwest, with the Big Horn's blue-haze to his left. He would pass miles to the north of the Castle Ranch, and that suited him—he didn't feel like mixing with any posses that Bullhead might have yarned into riding on the scout. With nothing to eat in the empty saddle bags and no sign of game, he kept on.

One o'clock came as he rode up over a rise

and through a great stretch of buffalo bones. The bone pickers hadn't come this way, yet. He'd heard buffalo bones were fetching a good price back East—for fertilizer.

The wastes of tangled white bones bothered him. The remembrance came sharply of Aunt Kate Bonney reading the bible in the summer twilight, as he, a tyke of ten, sat beside her on the back steps of the pine-board, miner's shack in Silver City: "Bones—the Valley of Dried Bones—And could those bones live again?"

Those bones could never live. They were as dead, the acres of them, as dead as the Indians who'd lived by the beasts, body and soul. Yeah, those dried bones were as dead as Bullhead, miles back in that hazy smear of reddish brown that was Hole In The Wall. Dead as Jesse. And dead as he himself damned well might be if any more of those Ring bastards got on his trail. But how could they—now?

He'd tried it away north here, but it hadn't worked. "Hi-yup! Hi-yup!" He spurred the gelding into a dead run again. He wanted out of this place of old deaths.

The horse could certain bend down and go. A real racer, near as fast as Dandy Dock, his little bay from Tascosa, and faster than Angel, his black mare. He wished he could see both Angels again.

"Hi-yup! Hi-yup!" He belted down a brush-lipped, dry wash and up the other side. The bones lay behind now. A long series of easy hills stretched their waves of sun-yellowed grass before him. All was pretty open country—not much of a chance of a dry-gulch. The badlands were back with the bones.

There was not a sign of water, but there should be a town or a settlement this way, if he was headed for the U.P. tracks.

As he opened his mouth to yell at the horse again, the animal stumbled and slid, nearly pitching The Kid over its head. Billy thought he'd hit a prairie dog town. "Whoa!" He sawed wildly at the reins to keep aboard.

It was a near thing. He dismounted and inspected the quivering mount. The horse had a definitely pulled tendon in its left rear leg. It favored the leg as it hobbled toward a bunch of grass.

"Ain't it nearly hell?" It was all up with riding. The buckskin would have to be turned loose or put up at the nearest ranch or town.

The horse must have strained that tendon when Peep raced him over at that Buffalo burg. And that must have been what he was going to gab about last night, but was squashed when Flat Nose began blowing about his upcoming hold-up plans. Billy had to laugh in spite of his fix.

But what if the gang was following, or a real

posse? A chill twitched his neck, despite the heat. This was a hell of a place!

He pulled the Colt and looked it over. The sun was hotter than ever. No canteen. He kept walking.

As hour after hour burned away, the sun blazed down until Billy felt he must find some real shade or shrivel up in his tracks. The buckskin hobbled along behind, seeming to realize it had to stick with him or up and die.

The Kid staggered along on feet that felt more and more like two lumps of fire. Several times he crouched in the horse's shadow, but when he arose to continue the march, the effort was almost too much.

Five years back, he'd been in a fix like this, losing a horse in the Guadalupe Mountains. Then it was just early summer. But now, it was just plain scorching. *Claro infierno*!

Close on to five o'clock, he limped up a rocky-faced rise in the endless swelling and dipping plain, tugging his "race horse" along, and vaguely saw a road crossing a slight depression fifty yards off.

He lurched through the glare toward the white streak of roadway and pitched down at its side, the tongue in his mouth clogging his heaving lungs.

The reins on his wrist tightened and he dimly realized the buckskin was shying back from something out in the midst of the throbbing light. He staggered back to his feet, blinking at the wavering, black shadow that floated toward him.

"Hi, you cowboy," a voice bellowed in his ear. "You want a lift—or what?"

Pawing the sweat from his stinging eyes, The Kid looked at the dusty-bearded driver of the Concord coach, who was leaning down from the seat, flourishing a whip in his direction.

"Lift?" He unwound the reins from his numb arm. "Yeah—a lift and water." He limped to the stage and tugged open the door. There was only one passenger, and he was sawing wood, slouched down in the far corner, with a fore-and-aft billed hat pulled down over his eyes.

"Only way I could shut him up," the driver grunted. "Had to swap hats. Been up to see his ranch, he has, past Buffalo. One of those dummed Beef Barons from Eeyurrup."

The talkative driver, sporting a tall bowler hat, plastered white with dust, swung down and helped The Kid tie the "race horse" to the back of the stage, a gold watch chain winking from his dusty vest.

"Here," the driver handed down a battered canteen full of warmish water. The Kid swigged a mouthful of sheer heaven and watered the buckskin in the top of his dented *sombrero*. He limped back to the open coach door. It was hot inside and stank rankly—but it was shade.

Its black completeness enveloped him, almost before he could settle back into the scorching, dusty leather seat.

After a while—Billy wasn't aware of how long—someone began pounding him on the shoulder. He was too hot and exhausted to resent the thumping.

"Here we be, cowboy. Casper, pride of th' hull Territory!"

Billy piled out, blinking in the early dusk, brushing at himself. A powerful smell clung to him as tightly as the gritty road dust.

"Yer hoss was hitched behind. Slowed me down but I was ahead of time anyways." The driver beat dust from his hoary beard. "I'd take that hog-laig off'n your person. Least git it under wraps. See thut feller up there at th' oprey block?" He jabbed the butt end of his whip toward the business section of town. "Polices this shebang without packin' a gun, and frowns on firearms."

Billy saw a long-legged, spindly man standing at the end of the next corner, talking to a small group of folks, half-obscured in the swift Wyoming twilight. "Yeah! Where's th' other passenger that was in your coach?"

"That's what I'm talkin' about." The driver turned the reins of the coach over to several young fellows, in overalls, who hustled out of the dusk from the stage office.

"You mean, what?" Billy was feeling a bit

more chipper, but he was powerfully thirsty and his feet were still at least three sizes larger than his boots.

"That's where th' other passenger went." The driver chuckled and spat through his half-cleansed beard at the nimble heels of the baggage smashers. "That jasper was just too fortified against th' trip. Been drinkin' all th' way down from th' Montanny line . . . plumb kicked up hell when he pulled in. Big Ben, that's th' marshal, come on th' run and tossed th' feller into jail. Ben took a look at th' shape you was in, but I tole him you was just a puncher with a lamed hoss."

Billy thanked the obliging coacher, paid his fare to the agent, and led the gelding down past the coach line's office to an adjoining livery barn.

He gave orders to rub the animal down, walk it, give it the finest grain and have a vet take a look at it, as soon as possible.

"We'll do that, for sure, Mister O'Day." The bow-legged livery man pocketed the fat tip The Kid handed him and gratefully directed the man, who'd signed the register as "O'Day," up the street to the nearest hotel.

24   All Aboard

Face down on the rickety, hotel bed, he seemed to be floating in a dusky cloud of uneasy awareness. He dozed and awakened only to doze again. The night breeze growing stronger, tugged the shabby window-blind and rocked a dented tin pitcher on the wash stand.

Billy had tubbed in the ground-floor wash-room at the rear of the hotel and scraped a week's bristles from his face, sparing the mustache. Boots in hand he'd climbed the stairs, too bushed to do more than flop.

He'd thought of going back down to the small dining room for supper, but couldn't get up enough steam to stir. Peep sure had the last laugh—almost, until he, The Kid, had thought of boarding the buckskin in the Casper livery stable, under Peep's name. Grinning, he rolled over to doze again.

The rocking pitcher's clink-clanking filled his sleep, until he gradually had the feeling that riders were galloping out of the dark—and pounding nearer and nearer—while he lay, some-where, sweat-soaked, and chained tight. Like the Santa Fe Jail.

That was it! They had him at last, the Santa Fe bunch. But who was riding? He heard the hooves, nearer and nearer—until the blazing tingle of complete nightmare flared into his mind. He knew! It was Bullhead, and still alive. And Garrett was with him. They'd got him this time for sure.

And they were pounding on the cell door—no, the hotel room's door. He knew where he was—now! Pounding grew until the room rolled with thundering fists.

His reaction was automatic. He yanked the Colt from under his pillow. Pulled the hammer back. Crash! The .44 blew a hole in the door.

Awake in the brittle, shrilling instant, he heard feet running down the stairs. And voices yelling out on the street.

Billy staggered from bed and bent at the low window. The wind still whipped the dirty blind. Behind him, the water pitcher danced its metallic jig.

"Hey John! Hey John! Gitcher gun . . . Frank and John! Hey boys, come a'runnin'." It was the hulking marshal, Big Ben setting up the pandemonium.

For some reason, The Kid wasn't sure why, the marshal had been rapping on the door and damned near took a slug in his unheeled carcass for his trouble. And now he was down there singing out for his pistol-packing deputies.

Billy, cursing nightmares, itchy trigger fingers, that big four-flushing marshal, and Peep's fall-apart horse, tugged his boots on over swollen feet. The racket grew in front of the hotel. He grabbed hat, vest and gunbelt, after another quick look from the front window.

In spite of the noise, no one was in sight. But Big Ben would be back, with his armed followers.

The Kid opened the splintered door a crack and looked into a hall that yawned bare and silent. A kerosene lamp, sooted up to the neck, flickered away on the wall.

Buckling on his gunbelt, he limped down the rear stairs and into the alley shadows.

He didn't know what the law wanted, but he wasn't about to hang around that cracker-box of a hotel to find out. These damned hotels could be death-traps. Look at that one back at Santa Fe!

Slipping down a side-street that led to the U.P. Depot, he passed a few townfolk, but they paid him little attention. Voices, shouting from the direction of the hotel, drifted on the wind, but came no nearer.

"Big Ben's probably cussin' out th' hotel clerk for his brand of customer, and the clerk's bound to be pullin' out his own hair for losin' one," he grinned despite sore feet.

Ahead, a pair of oil lamps, swaying from poles, near the depot, cast their circling amber arcs over the strings of boxcars on the siding. While The Kid hesitated, it began to rain. The downpour was cold and chilling. One shiver chased another

229

down his backbone. If he stayed out in this, he'd be flat on his back—and not from bullets.

The night was filled only with the sound of falling rain. Big Ben and his men must have holed up out of the raw weather. The Kid turned back and stepped under the out-thrust of the depot roof.

The wavering pole-lights touched and retreated from the depot, but cast enough gleam to disclose a half-open door. It proved to be a spare store room. The whole place was dark and uninhabited. But not for long!

Billy rummaging about in the near-pitchy blackness, discovered a baggage wagon, some crates and a large tarpaulin, rolled into a corner. A small, smudged window gave access to the street. He took a long, cautious look, but nothing was moving, only the rain slanting across the darkness under the wind-tossed lamps.

He shed his coat, shook it and batted the water from his *sombrero*. With hat and coat hung from a corner of the baggage wagon, he settled down on the canvas. He found by tugging and hauling at a corner of the tarp, he could cover up snugly. He shivered for a spell, but soon slumbered, gun in hand.

Some time later he opened an eye to find that night was a thing of the past. Something had roused him out of a restless sleep. Sitting up, he rubbed his face with his hands. When he poked the Colt away, his stiffened fingers told him he'd clutched the weapon all through the night.

There came that sound again! The buffalo bellow of a steam whistle. A train was near. Unwinding from the tarp, he arose to find it was earliest dawn. The railroad hands hadn't noticed him—yet.

Brushing himself off as well as he could, he walked to the door of the store room. The rain was over but a chilly wind blustered along the tracks and around the building. The northwest was getting ready for a long, hard winter. He could feel it.

So hungry that he could eat a long yearling, hide and horns, he wandered onto the station platform. No one among the crowd of trainmen and passengers paid him any mind, and he couldn't spot Big Ben or any of his men.

The engine was down the track, twenty yards, with its last two coaches opposite the station agent's office. A half-dozen strangers, apparently cattlemen and drummers, were boarding the yellow, varnished wood coaches.

Billy was walking into the station to buy a ticket—ready to leave before anything else popped—when he spotted Big Ben marching along with two men. They were headed toward the puffing engine, where it spurted up woolly steam beside the water tank.

The Kid ambled back down the platform,

hopped onto the damp cinders and walked to the end of the train.

"Best look out, cowboy. These things buck back sometimes." A greasy-faced man with a tin pot, was poking its long, thin spout at metal boxes over the car's wheels.

"*Bueno*."

"Hey?"

"Just takin' a walk. Stretchin' my legs."

"Oh?" The oily man wiped his hands on his dirty, striped coat and turned back to squat by the wheels. "Well, don't stretch far. This here train's due to pull out."

Billy nodded, walking back around the coach and up the other side. He didn't know where that nosey marshal was. But he'd made up his mind to hop this train, ticket or not.

Swinging up the steps of the second coach, he pushed open the car door. A blast of warmed air, composed of train oil, coal and cigar smoke, sweat, and polished wood, engulfed him.

The car's interior was still dimly lit by overhead lamps, turned down to a dull, butter-yellow. About half the seats were occupied. People dozed open-mouthed, with heads tipped back against the scuffed, green plush or hunched in quiet slumber against the cinder-speckled plate glass windows.

Cattlemen, miners, drummers, some foreign looking folks in dark clothes, and a few women with children, turned and moved restlessly in the growing light.

Billy picked a seat near the door and settled back with his *sombrero* cocked over his eyes. He'd made it. This train was due to pull out, according to the trainman, and he'd ride it—until he could cipher a few things.

He'd worn out his welcome in this part of the country—and just because he thought it was a ring-tail whopper to run off Peep's race horse.

Several figures entered the car. So much coming and going spooked him a bit. He wished the damned train would get moving.

"Mister! Will you please open that there door?" A woman's peevish voice shrilled from the far end of the coach. "Little Jonathan's gotta git in there. He's been poorly half of the night. I'm afeard it could be cholery morbus."

Billy looked over the seat at a large, hefty woman in a red and blue striped dress. She tugged a fat, little boy, with the face of a small moon, along by the hand. A hunched, scowling man in a beard and a gold-braided cap marched ahead of her.

"No, M'am! I told you, this train starts in a minute or so, and we'll unlock the door. Your little man will just have to grin and bear it." The bearded Conductor strove to move around her.

"Mister, he plain can't." She elbowed the Conductor along, and drew the child behind—a train in herself. "He just plain can't! Can you Jonathan? No, you can't."

Passengers were twisting and stirring uneasily, but she never slacked off. "Lookit him! So peaked now, I don't know how he's gonna last the trip."

The Conductor yanked his cap down, fumbled up a big, brass key from his pocket and unlocked the lavatory door. He turned and stalked back down the coach before The Kid could get his attention.

As the muttering official stepped through the door, someone swung up onto the platform, between the cars. Billy saw shadowy smudges shifting beyond the frosted glass. The shapes moved about in the half-gloom, and as one turned, an object hit the door with a clang—a gun barrel!

The Kid raised and looked at both ends of the coach. The striped woman loomed against the far end, her broad back to him while she guarded the small door. Those figures were still in cloudy conference beyond the frosted glass of the car door.

The train whistled twice—shrill in the morning quiet, but remained stationary.

He stuffed his *sombrero* under his car seat and helped himself, quietly, to a long, lightweight topcoat and a plug beaver hat from the rack across the aisle.

Donning the duds, Billy stepped down the aisle to the big woman. "*Señora*? *Pardino*, perhaps I could advise." He kept his head low, and his back bowed.

"Whut?" The big woman lumbered around to face him, glaring.

"Overheard your *molestia*."

"Oh!" She rattled the door knob. "Jonathan—you Jonathan. Let this feller, er Doc, take a look atcher tongue." She tugged the door open and yanked the little boy out by the neck. He was completely dressed in a white, very wrinkled duck suit. Obviously he wasn't feeling very poorly.

"*Gracias*—out in a *minuto*!" Billy brushed past the open-mouthed woman, ignoring her bulging eyes, and slammed the washroom door, as the coach door swung ajar.

The Kid slid the bolt and after a hurried inspection of the narrow, barred, lavatory window, turned with pistol in hand to listen at the thin, wood-paneled door.

Several men had entered the car and were in the aisle, "—can't leave you hold up this train a minute longer." Billy recognized the voice of the Conductor. "Ain't anyone in this section with firearms."

The deep bass rumble of the marshal answered and the party moved down the car.

"Who's in there?" a voice snapped outside the lavatory door.

Billy cocked back the hammer and waited.

"Why's this here door shut? Open up there!" The door creaked as the man beyond heaved against it.

"Hey don't bust'er down!" The Conductor was back. "Ain't no one in there now. Keep'er locked in the stations."

"Yessir they is!" came the high-pitched yelp of a child. "They's an ole man in a high hat."

"That's right. He's a Doc. Doctor Purdum, er some such. A furriner," the woman broke in. "Gonna lookit little Jonathan and see whut's ailin' him."

"Nothin' at th' end car neither," another voice reported.

The train gave three, short and angry hoots.

"Aw right—aw right," Big Ben growled. "Guess that highbinder's still in town. We'll git'm."

The sound of boots moved off. The coach door slammed.

"Whatcha after the feller fer?" the hefty woman inquired of someone still within the car.

"Nothin' much." It was one of the deputies, who lingered. "Took a shot at th' marshal last night when he went up to ask him about a stolen watch. Probably liquored up—but Big Ben's awful touchy about guns."

The door banged again and almost at once, the train gave a metallic shudder, followed by another. It was moving.

So that coach driver had swapped more than hats with the other passenger in that stage coach!

Billy waited a minute and discarding the oversize coat and hat, stuffed them through the lavatory window. The hat disappeared, but the coat, filled with air, flapped off along the right of way like a dying balloon.

He unbuckled his gunbelt and stuck it up under the metal wash bowl and thrust the Colt under his vest in his waist band.

The train was moving at a good clip before he cautiously opened the lavatory door. The woman sat upright in a seat across the aisle with the little fat boy.

"How'd you git in there?" She heaved up from the plush seat. "Whar's th' Doc?"

Billy pointed at his mouth and wagged his head.

"You a deaf and dumber, hey?" She stared at him with bulging green eyes. "What'd you do to th' Doc—that little, hunched up feller?"

The Kid backed down the aisle, grinning and tapping at his ears.

After a suspicious stare, the woman peeked into the barren lavatory, and plumped back down scowling as she grunted about—"furriners!"

Getting his hat from under his former seat, The Kid went on into the end car. The passengers were waking and looking out upon the sun-spangled landscape that rippled past the windows.

It was broad, golden day now and the tracks sliced due east, following the flat, muddy wideness of the Platte—away from Casper—Hole In The Wall—Kate—and The Angel.

25 Tickets Please

The passenger coach was crowded. A drummer "in tin cans," seated by The Kid, reported it jammed all the way from San Francisco. Billy was surrounded by droves of folks. It made him feel odd to be corralled in with so many strangers.

For the first two hours, after leaving Casper, the train had rushed along near the Platte, stopping twice to switch freight and stock cars at Douglas and Fort Laramie. The engine, far ahead, was marked by jetting black puffs of smoke, as it wound over the rolling, dusty sageland.

Several times they crossed tributaries of other rivers. The depressions were thick with brush and cottonwood, but mainly the open range was scarred, here and there, with dry watercourses, fringed by stiff and spindly pines.

He'd intended to ride these rails about a hundred miles and get off at some place large enough to offer horses for sale, then he'd hit down to Cheyenne or Denver—but some hunch murmured "keep east." Maybe *La Fortuna* again?

The ruckus of the past night was a fluke. Who'd have thought he'd be so trigger-fingered as to throw a shot at an unarmed marshal?

The bewhiskered Conductor, after a sideways squint at The Kid, had sold him a ticket to Omaha.

But Billy was still ready for anything. The man's eyes reminded him of Paddy Coghlan's—looking at you, but not really seeing.

Glancing warily around the green plush and varnished interior of the coach, he mentally ticked off the various passengers: traveling men in gaudy, checked suits; well-to-do families off on visits eastward; run-down, seedy "gone-bust" miners; wide-brimmed cattlemen—and even a pair of pig-tailed Chinamen. "But," he thought, "just a bunch of faces. None from my stampin' grounds, and nobody able to cut my trail."

"Yessir, no doubt about it! Like I been sayin', the country's just bustin' wide both east and west." The rotund drummer at The Kid's side had been chattering steadily for hours but Billy had just commenced to listen. "A fountain of Eden, she is!" The man's red fingers twitched in and out of his sideburns—like chipmunks in a weed patch.

"Yet they've taken to dry-gulchin' Presidents again." Billy shifted in his seat, and watched the sun flickering in oblongs, squares and diamonds of bright yellow on the coach floor, as the train rattled over one of the many iron-laced bridges spanning the sprawling, muddy surface of the meandering Platte.

This fellow, beside him, oozed good-will and information. It just bubbled up like a sandy

240

spring, full of hazy lights. Another kind of Easterner. They seemed to come in all shapes and sizes.

The Kid had entered this car early in the morning, but now he wished that he'd gone in the other direction, even if the big circus-tent lady still lingered back there for the doctor.

The drummer eventually was drowned out by the purple-faced Conductor's bellows. "Torrington, Torrington, Torrungtunn!"

The train gradually ground down to a clanking, seat shaking stop. Outside, the station platform soon was a'swarm with passengers and crew.

Billy and the drummer followed the crowd. The air was still sharp with the threat of more northern-bred storms, but seemed to be warming. Up the line, the engine was gulping and puffing as it sucked water from a stocky, pot-bellied water tank, topped with a bean-stalk windmill. There wasn't much to the town, just a tank, the depot and a pair of sun-bleached, wooden store buildings.

But the passengers weren't in a sight-seeing mood. They were plain hungry.

Inside the small, narrow restaurant, beside the tracks, all was uproar. Children shrilled, women shrieked and men yelled. Billy flinched at the noise. The drummer bawled in his ear, "S'matter, ain't ya hungry? They're all tryin' to get their orders took before the train pulls out."

He herded The Kid toward a table in the midst of the echoing din. Before they could tug out their chairs, a thin, frowsy looking girl, in a dirty yellow dress, and patched blue apron, darted at them, slammed down two slopping water glasses and rattled out, "potatoes, bacon, roast beef, boiled beef, salt beef, cabbage and coffee and tea."

The hot smells of overcooked food swirled about the place in steamy clouds—and those clouds were inhabited by flocks of flies.

The drummer and Billy placed their individual orders, but the girl immediately returned, filled their places with small dishes full of the complete menu.

"Don't she hear so well?" The Kid inquired, above the clamor, batting at the inquisitive flies.

The drummer silent for a change, merely muttered, "Hurry up!"

Finishing each of the dishes didn't take long and as Billy drained his rank tasting tea from its thick, chipped mug, he felt someone staring. Looking over, he found the Conductor, seated at the nearest table, picking his teeth.

When he discovered Billy's eyes upon him, the man hurriedly arose and elbowed through the passengers to the cash drawer.

What was up? A moment later The Kid grinned to himself. Probably nothing to get proddy about. A good thing he was on the haul—he needed a change. There's been just too damned much commotion for the past year—getting so he shied at shadows. And the half-healed wounds taken at Fort Sumner didn't help matters any. Half tied up in knots from the things.

When his companion finished, they paid their bill and squeezed through the door. The engine was still slowly huffing away to itself by the windmill water tank while the Conductor stood at the end coach.

A sign on the weather-warped front of the one store to the east of the depot proclaimed it to be a "U.S. Government Postal Office."

The Kid backed away from the drummer, who was working up a debate on railways, and made his entrance into the store. He bought two post-cards, with engravings of an ill-tempered looking Ben Franklin on their respective corners.

The place was empty except for an unshaven clerk who stood at a streaked window, staring like a prisoner at the passengers outside.

Billy borrowed a pencil and scribbled a couple of messages on his cards. By the time he finished the second, the train's whistle echoed through the drowsy, fly-haunted interior of the building. On impulse, he purchased another penny postal and wrote a third note.

With one eye on the rapidly filling coaches, he re-read the cards and pushed them into the black mouth of the mail drop by an oatmeal barrel.

The first missive was addressed to: "Tom O'Day, care Postmaster, Buffalo, Wyoming Territory," and read, "I thank you for the horse. As a racer he'll never raise you much money. I'd never bet a plugged *peso* on him. You can fetch him from the Rush Stable in Casper. I left him under your monniker. Why don't you go back to Texas? Yours, the T.K."

The second card read: "Miss Kate Castle, Dubble K Ranch, Rock Springs, Wyoming Territory. Dear Miss Castle. I hope you know who this is. Things are fine, so far. The *hombre* that called that night won't be back. Hope things come alright for you and ranch. Yours, Respect. W.B."

He wasn't sure why he'd signed the card with those initials—W.B.—most likely just habit.

The last message was short. He didn't have much time, and what could he say, on paper?

"Miss Sandoval, attn. Attny. Juan Ortiz, 233 San Jose, El Paso, Texas. Miss Sandoval. Just a little note. I should be down that way before long. There has been slight mishaps but things are working out. I am very truly yours, Respect. W.B."

Billy boarded the coach, among the last of the passengers, but somehow was not surprised to find the Conductor waiting by the vestibule.

"Ah, there," the man held out his hand to The Kid, "everything coming along as you like?"

Billy leaned against the drumming, vibrating, wooden coach wall to let a couple pass into the second car, while the train jerked and chuffed itself into headlong flight. He let his hands hang loosely at his sides. "Sort of crowded, but I guess that's in th' cards when you travel."

The Conductor bent confidentially toward The Kid, lifting his voice as the engine bellowed balefully ahead. "Ah, what I mean—Cowboy, none got wise to you, hey?" He smiled fox-faced, with a mouthful of sharp, gold-filled teeth glinting through his whiskers. "I been on to you since that blow-hard marshal back at Casper come through the cars lookin' for a feller that raised hob in town."

Billy unbuttoned his vest's top button, ready to grab into his shirt for his gun but kept his mouth shut, studying the grimacing trainman.

"I found the belt where you stuck it in the jakes, but put it up. Like I said, is everything all right, the way you like?" The Conductor leaned back and regarded The Kid.

The rolling, greenish-brown rangeland kept darting away past the windows. The train was hitting it up, rushing along toward the Nebraska line. Too fast to jump. The Kid's hands were sweat damp. This could be *mucho malo*. But he'd play the game out. "Things could be worse."

"Well, I guess so." The foxy smile returned

to the Conductor's whiskey-tinted face. "You wanter keep traveling in style, I guess—and there's only one answer."

"Oh." Billy's jaw set for a moment but relaxed into a tight grin of his own. "I get you, Mister. You're takin' tickets—again." He dug down in his pocket and came up with his roll, or what remained of it after Castle Ranch. "What's your fare?"

"You can stay on to Omaha—first class, for, say a hundred."

"Mister, I thought Jesse James rode a horse!"

"You want to ride this line, you pay . . . or . . ." The Conductor edged away from The Kid's clamped-down look. "No call to rile. I wanter help. I could'a called for the law back at the last stop." He bared his gilded smile again. "Probably pay pretty high fer ya too." He backed up when Billy took a step toward him, both grabbing at the safety railing, as the train commenced to swing in a wide arc, crossing another loop of the wandering Platte.

"All right, you take th' pot." Billy counted out the money and jammed the remaining roll, thinner by a hundred, into his pocket. He was seething with rage, inside, but what could he do? This grafter could take his last *peso*, and still give him the high sign.

"Thanks, Cowboy, you're smartern'n you know." The Conductor counted the money and

246

put it into an inside pocket of his shiny, blue uniform coat. "No hard feelings? I'm a family man. Got a big family, I have. Prices keep going up. We all gotta make it how we can." He sidled to the door, going into the next coach.

Billy found himself a seat as far from the drummer as he could manage, and stared bleakly out the window. The unfazed drummer had already collared another pair of ears.

The Kid was down to a bit over one hundred. That fifty he'd peeled off Bullhead didn't last long. He thought of that big horse choker of a roll he'd tossed back at the Ring Chief in Santa Fe; he'd think twice now again before being so damned honest.

By the time he got down to Texas he wouldn't be able to buy that lawyer a drink, let alone hire him for court. He sure could use that money he lent Kate.

The empty, barren landscape rolled past, its monotony broken by an occasional small herd of cattle, moving eastward, and now and then a settler's cabin.

By the time the train reached Broadwater, Nebraska, The Kid made up his mind to ride the route to Omaha—if the Conductor kept away. He couldn't stand any more shake-down.

When they puffed into Scottsbluff for the supper stop, Billy remained aboard. He watched the crowd milling about a green-fronted restaurant by the tracks but couldn't spot the Conductor in the failing light.

He'd just about made up his mind to get off to eat but was forestalled by the entrance of the little Train Butcher, chanting, "sammitches, pop-corn, pies and dawnuts." The young salesman, about fifteen, his head enveloped in an over roomy, blue infantry cap, minus a button, and wearing patched shirt and pants, halted before The Kid.

"Yessir! Guess you'd rather take your chances on my grub eh, 'stead of that cast-iron stuff out there in that green shanty." He held out a basket half-full of not particularly appetizing victuals. Stuffed in one corner was a bundle of paper-back books, flaming out in gaudy reds and yellows.

The Kid selected a medium-hard meat sandwich and a small, battered peach pie on its paper plate, paying the boy.

"Wanna read some bully books? Just got'm at Scottsbluff. Fresh out. Lookit!" He pushed an orange-drenched publication under The Kid's nose. "Hunky-dory rows down in Arizony and Noo Mexico. You know, where them cowboys and trappers are always shootin' th' air full of blue holes."

He thrust the book under the sagging chin of Billy's fellow passenger, a curly-bearded sheep-man, who'd piled on at Scottsbluff, barely able to navigate. The Kid took the tome, reading the jaw-breaking title: "Billy The Kid, The New Mexican

Outlaw: or The Bold Bandit of The West! A True and Impartial History of the Greatest of American Outlaws—Who Killed a Man For Every Year In His Life."

Billy marveled at the title's out-and-out lie, but paid the young hustler his twenty-five cents. "Got anything by this here Nye? Bill Nye?"

"Nope! He's th' cheese ain't he? But right now all th' go is this Billy The Kid. Plumb outsells Buffalo Bill or Horatio Optic." He glanced brightly at Billy. "Youse a cowboy ain'tcha? You ever been down where such stuff goes on? You bet I'd like to be a real cowboy—a'ridin' and fightin' all day long. Sure would beat travelin' back and forth on this ole mackrel box."

But before Billy could answer, the youngster hurried down the coach aisle to attend to a passenger who'd dozed through the stop. The others were clustering back on board and though The Kid watched their entrance into the growing yellow brilliance of the overhead oil lamps, recently lit by a black man in a white jacket, he saw nothing of the Conductor.

26   Rails Eastward

Billy slept fitfully through the long night. The jerking of the train, slowing for reasons known only to the secret brotherhood of trainmen, at times jolted him from light slumber.

Every other lamp was extinguished, stretching blankets of darkness along the length of the coach. The Kid and the heavily snoring sheepman were on the amber edge of light, fanning down from a half-trimmed lamp.

With the Colt's hard bulk under his shirt, he felt uncomfortable but fairly secure. The Conductor appeared to have bedded down in another coach. There'd been little movement along the aisles since the train stopped at North Platte, at 2:30 in the morning, to take on water and fuel, and change crews.

He saw the tall, sharp lettering on the station slide off into the night as he leaned his head against the rattling smoothness of the window— musing drowsily to himself.

So—North Platte was back there in the darkness, and beyond it Big Springs, where that wild Texan, Sam Bass, struck it rich—for a spell.

And off to the eastward there were more unseen towns and stations with their narrow-wheeled baggage carts, and sleepy station masters in their flat straw hats and their clicking-clicking telegraphs—telegraph poles flitting along the tracksides—unseen in the nights but following, always following. You couldn't run off and leave the telegraph, he drowsily informed that faint, shivering face in the window, no more than you could run off from the Ring. But that was plain foolishness, he argued with himself. How could those sanctimonious buzzards keep a line on him—now?

As Jesse Evans would say, used to say, "Ain't that nearly hell?" To think they'd still try anything—didn't he have the book? Why they'd shrivel up and die to get it—and that was why they'd kept after—trying to get it. Now they'd need better trackers than Bullhead or Garrett—might send that feisty little Charley Siringo—but that—

—"Grand Island—Grand Island. Twenty minutes to eat. Twenty minutes." They'd come over 200 miles in the night and the train was slowing down as it ran clattering over another iron bridge that crossed the unending Platte. The sun was gleaming on muddy water, yellow sandbars, willow clumps and sparkling in windows of red brick and white frame buildings, ranging along the tawny bluffs of the river. The town, itself, sat on an island in the great Platte Valley. An immense sandbar, miles long, held the majority of the town.

While the engine, forever thirsty, took on water from another of the pot-bellied tanks, the usual feverish scramble began at the trackside lunchroom. Billy was successful in ordering some food while dodging the Drummer. The "circus tent" woman and her "ailing" offspring seemed to have vanished back down the line.

His neck felt as though a mustang had kicked it. This sleeping, sitting up and being crowded by a snoring sheepman wasn't calculated to make a fellow feel too chipper.

After a cup of turgid coffee, about the color of the Platte, and a plate of half-cooked griddle cakes, he wriggled back through the jostling mob.

"Better hustle up, Mister Cowboy," a voice piped at his elbow.

He glanced aside to see the little Train Butcher lugging a refilled basket, flat cap tipped over one dingy ear. "She's a' pullin' out fer Omahar. An' if you're lookin' fer ole Elmore," he winked, "he left your package with me."

"Package? Who left a package?"

"Elmore, the Conductor, gits off here. End o' his run. We got a new 'un." And he pointed out a fat, portly man in a blue coat, who stood beside the baggage car, fingering a watch and looking over the milling passengers with a disgusted air. This individual suddenly waved a thick, blue arm and slowly mounted the steps of the first coach.

The train snorted its own loud disgust as it began to creep sulkily off to the east.

"Hurry up! Watcha waitin' fer?"

"I wanted to ask th' old Conductor . . ." Billy stared again through the ticket window where that official stood with his back to the moving train. Inside the office, the Agent was scratching his bald head with a pen and apparently arguing with the Conductor.

The Kid gave one last look and following the trotting youngster, stepped up on the last car's platform. "Where's th' present?" Billy batted off a flying cinder, and held the door open for the overburdened boy. Half his mind was still on the dwindling station. Was it a mistake to stay aboard, with that shifty Conductor back there?

Two items in the Train Butcher's basket decided him to stay put—for a while.

Amid the pies, cakes, sandwiches, bundles of newspapers and colorful splashes that were paper-back novels—he recognized the looping shape of a gunbelt and holster wrapped up in brown paper.

"You bet—Omahar news? Yesterdays. We picked 'em up back at North Platte." The boy took the offered change and dug down in the big wicker basket. "Here's your present. Feels kind o' interestin'." He winked. "Ole Elmore ain't such a bad skate is he?"

"I'll wait and see." Billy took the newspaper

and package, resuming his window seat. He stuffed the gunbelt under the seat and punched open the news sheet.

The item that first caught his eye was short, not more than two paragraphs, but prominently featured on the front page in a black ruled box: "Deadwood, Dakota Territory. Word has just been received that the band of scoundrels who yesterday held up the Shorthills Mine office at Eimgrant Gulch, and seriously wounded a clerk, also created havoc on their way to the robbery. They rode into one of E. W. Brown's camps six miles from town, emptied their six-shooters into a band of sheep and killed 25, while crippling many more. At this time there are three posses in the field, covering the north, east and south areas. Capture seems certain."

By the time the train made its lunch stop at North Bend, much of the swelling, open range-land was giving way to cultivated fields. Corn stalks marched along in thousands of dry, precise rows and at intervals, yellow stubbled wheat fields stretched on either side of the tracks.

The Kid stepped out on the North Bend plat-form, after the rush was past and scanned the depot for signs of trouble. Nothing appeared to be doing. A rotund, sleepy town marshal, in a red shirt and checkered pants, was on the scene, but he sat peacefully on the edge of a baggage truck, spitting tobacco juice at a nervous flock of sparrows and gossiping with the Station Agent.

The sky, crowding over this pleasant, little town, seemed a part of the country. Featherbed clouds, pushed along by warming south winds, rolled flatly over the slanted roof tops. The northern storms were lost in the wide distance westward.

Beyond the depot, two-storied brick buildings—a plough works, a hardware, a court house, and up the street from the tracks, a red tower pushed above the yellowing foliage, with a shiny bell in its peak, and pointed out by a toothless loafer as a "genuine High School."

The East was stampeding in, mile upon mile. It gave him an edgy feel—but also more easy, at that. This was a country where every man didn't stick out like a cactus on a bare plateau. A fellow could fade right into this land of houses and trees, and people—and who'd ever know?

He ate inside the coach as the train sped on toward Omaha. Several seats were now vacant, and The Kid took a spot midway in the car, where he could watch both doors.

After a passable beef sandwich, purchased from Tom Tippet, the young Train Butcher, Billy settled back with his paper-back novel. He was fascinated by tall tales—those outright pipedreams of scribblers who'd put down that stack of wild and woolly tales of an imaginary West—bear hunters, gold miners, stage coach

255

robbers—and especially the book he'd bought about "The Devil of New Mexico." That was himself! He thumbed into the thing and read:

"Where are the prisoners?" asked the Justice.

"I left them," replied The Kid with the grin of a devil.

"You did not arrest them, eh? Well, what return do you make on the writ?"

"I have already made my mark on the writ, you can fill it out," he said coolly, drawing forth the paper, and showing the two crosses made with the blood of his victims.

"Great God," cried the Justice, "you have killed them. Where is McCluskey?"

"Ah, I forgot to make one for him," replied The Kid, with a hideous leer. With the laugh of a demon, Billy The Kid went out to his horse, vaulted into the saddle, and rode away."

This was even worse horse-apples than old Pat's book. Of course that drunk of an Ash Upson really wrote that one—but Pat gave it his name. Billy burned clean through to think that people were reading such *esconbros*—and swallowing it. Why half the folks in the states and territories probably thought that he, The Kid, was a fiend with real horns! He'd better never run into the writer responsible for such tripe.

And there was no doubt that half the kids in the country read such stuff and took it for gospel—but after he got things ironed out in the courts—cleaned up the goddamned Ring whelps—and all this thrashed out, they'd just have to forget such stuff—forget bad, blood-thirsty Billy The Kid. Yeah—they'd have to pick out some other hero—like Buffalo Bill or Jesse James.

He jammed the book beside the seat and glared at the rippling, ever changing landscape that wavered, rose and fell outside the rocking, creaking coaches. There hadn't been any cattle, drifting along with their fur-pants cowpunchers in a hundred miles or more. Rangeland was petering out. Too far east he supposed. He wondered if the whole blamed country back this way was all grown up. The train passed mile upon mile of cornfields and now was cutting between wheatfields—all bare and brown with late September. Crows spun up in lazy black flocks.

The day was clouding over like his thoughts. Back on the horizon, that wide circle of horizon—still sweeping off on all sides of the arrowing train, the sky was dull and hazy brick-red from dust and an overcast sun. Storms came out of the west. And they seemed to be hurrying to stay with the engine and its cars.

He shifted in the grimy, green plush seat and looked up at the scroll-work on the painted ceiling. The passengers were thinning out. Some of the miners had dropped off. The Chinese were gone, maybe to some Nebraska laundry. And most of the visiting families disembarked at the last stop. Even the Drummers were dwindling—but Billy's acquaintance was still up ahead, playing cards with a trio of red-faced fellow salesmen. Billy lazily debated going and cleaning them out. He could use the money, *mucho*! But he hesitated to get within earshot of them.

The little Train Butcher had quit business for a spell and was dividing his time, sitting open-mouthed near the gamblers, and poring over his own copy of the "Bandit of the Border." And probably taking every word for the McCoy. The Kid cursed to himself.

If the two-bit scribbler, who'd corralled that pack of lies, would have traveled along for the past couple of months, he could have written a book to make folks eyes really stick out—but that was life. Everyone said that made-up yarns never touched the real thing.

He placed his hat on the seat beside himself. No use having any more whiskey-soaked bums sitting there. He'd be right glad to get a coat on and rig up a hide-out holster again. That Colt under his vest was commencing to rake a ditch along his ribs. It made his half-healed shoulder wound kick up once in a while as well.

It wasn't that he expected to use a six-gun in the East—for he had now made up his mind to ride 'er out all the way to New York. New York—he recalled telling Pat Garrett, Frank Coe, and even old Governor Lew Wallace that he hailed from New York, told them he'd been born in Brooklyn, though Buffalo Gap, Texas could have the honor. But everyone was telling tales back down there and covering up tracks, for one reason or another. He even doubted Garrett was from where he claimed to hail from.

Now he was going to see that place—New York! He'd see the Elephant and hear the Owl— if he could get ahold of some cash. Maybe Kate would be able to dig up that money her dad had owing. Then he'd get back down to The Angel and try to straighten out things. He could square himself, he was sure. He'd even risk a stretch in the pen, if he knew Angel would be waiting. He hoped she would be getting his postcard soon.

He kept squinting at the folks in the coach. Billy began to drift away—in spite of that shoulder— but he couldn't expect two-and-a-half months to heal him completely. And sitting all day in these coaches was worse than pounding a saddle. How did folks do it all the time?

His scalp wound and the scar on his cheek were tender still, but coming pretty good, pretty good. Those poles outside were running by—fast. The train was making time for Omaha—due to arrive by 3:30—so the grumpy Conductor had growled. Those telegraph poles kept whizzing past—almost like a picket fence—pickets—Tom Picket—where was Tom these days—and Tom O'Folliard—poor Tom O'Folliard—Garrett got that Tom for dirty blood money. Blood on the pickets—at Maxwell's. They got me good at Maxwell's—but I'll get th' whole rotten bunch—all Top Shelvers—but when that book—black book comes out in court—look out Garrett—Catron and company—look out—

27   Change for New York

. . . "Out! Everybody out! Omaha. Get yer baggage. Change fer New York. All passengers detrain . . ."

Half awake, when the beefy, little Conductor began his bawling parade down the car, Billy opened his eyes and tipped his hat back. The aisle was jumbled with passengers as they trampled on each other's feet, wrestling valises and bags out of the wrought-iron baggage above the coach windows.

The Kid watched the large brick warehouse and smoke-dulled factory buildings slide past. One Omaha building was emblazoned from stem to stern with a great, yellow, white and black poster hailing the appearance of a stage play, "The Black Crook." Other smaller banners and posters clamored silently for attention from the passengers—shouting printed messages to the slowing cars—"Arbuckle's Coffee Is Everyone's Friend."—"Chew Star Plug!"—"Wear U.S. Gaiters. Only $2.50 A Pair."

Billy eased onto the platform, and wedged himself into the knots of people. Inside the lofty, echoing depot, he inquired for the next train east. It was the fast Burlington and Missouri Night Express, leaving for Chicago at 9 p.m.

He bought a ticket and was emerging from the station's west entrance when he heard a high-pitched voice calling, "Hi, Cowboy! Mister Cowboy!"

Tippet came hustling up, waving a small, green book. "Here's one fer ya. Thought I might scare one up." He thrust a paper-back copy of Bill Nye's "Boomerang" into The Kid's hand.

"Why, thanks! *Bueno—primorosa*!"

"S'all right. No charge. Just knew there'd be one or two in th' store room. No charge," he repeated as Billy tried to pay him.

Billy whipped "The Noted New Mexico Out-law" from his coat pocket and stuck it into Tippet's hand. "Here, peddle this again. I read enough."

As Billy pushed the book into the boy's hand, he recalled a comment he'd scribbled in pencil across the back: "Take it from me—this is a lot of sheep dip. And I ought to know. But O.K. to pass time with." It didn't matter, Tippet could rub it off with a piece of India rubber. He slapped the boy on the shoulder and stepped into a waiting, side-curtained hack.

The hack, driven by a scraggly-bearded man in a checkered fore-and-aft cap, circled the cinder-packed driveway behind the depot to swing into Capital Avenue.

Billy saw Tippet standing on a corner of the platform. His tray was back on his arm as he conducted business with a round-faced, round-bellied little man.

The Kid, peering back through the rear curtains, carried on a monosyllabic conversation with the driver. This gent seemed determined to cram his fare's head with every piece of information he could summon up, concerning this capital city on the edge of the old Missouri.

". . . Key to Rocky Mountains—and gold of Californy."

What was that little prairie dog of a man staring after the cab for?

"What was that?" Something had got by in the hackman's word stampede. Somehow he resented all this kind of gallus-popping, over such places as this Nebraska city, Santa Fe, or the whole U.S. business boom. Maybe, because he couldn't brag about his neck-of-the-woods. Maybe it was because it was from knocking about from here to there since he wasn't much bigger than that young'un back there. "What'd you say about the Black Crook?"

"Said it wasn't opening at the concert hall fer a week. Said the British Blondes with Lydia Thompson is still in town." He gave a sharp, lecherous yap. "Worth seein'—anyone orta see them gals in 'Robinson Carooso,' if he's time. Plenty to see."

Billy got off at the main district. Though it was only about four o'clock, the sun hung halfway down the sky—a huge, flattened, cherry-red ball. Its fiery light swallowed the black thunder clouds.

"Ya'd best hump yourself. Looks like a duck drownder." With this weather bulletin, the one-man promotion committee for Omaha whipped up his nag, making a turn back to the depot for more trade.

One of the first buildings on the next corner proved to be a clothing store. The tall, scroll-worked, golden letters read: "Phileas M. Babcock's Clothing Emporium." A half-hour within its walls transformed The Kid from a travel-rumpled saddle tramp into a rigged-up dude in a blue-black "cast-iron" suit. His dusted off lid wasn't much wider than many of the hats along the street, so he retained it, but discarded his boots for a pair of those $2.50 gaiters. The boots, wrapped in a bundle, were toted along to a real four-chair barber shop, two blocks down the line. This stop completed his metamorphosis, but the mustache remained.

The pearl-handled Colt was back under his arm in its shoulder holster as he sat down to dine on steak and all the trimmings in the Nebraska Queen. It was a pretty elegant place, with marble-topped tables, and odd, feathery looking bushes in large, green pots. Two fiddlers were slicing away in a corner near the coat rack, playing some sort of foreign dance music.

He emerged from the restaurant and found the late September dusk doubly thick with lowering, wind-grey clouds. He hailed another hack, deciding to kill some time viewing those English Blondes down at the Omaha Concert Hall—and stay out of the weather.

The red-silk curtain was already up and the roomy interior of the theatre was a'dazzle with, what seemed, a thousand gas-lights as it rang and re-echoed with the shouts and laughters of a jam-packed, all-male audience.

The Kid had never been penned in with such a mob, but all seemed bent on having a good time. After a few minutes of wary waiting, he relaxed and stared at the stage. It was certain something to stare about, with all those cavorting, rip-snorting, fancy young females up there in the bright lights.

There may have been only one Robinson Crusoe in the whooping, bouncing layout, but there were at least a dozen Fridays—each filling her smooth, pink tights to the bursting point.

One of the girls reminded him of Celsa, at least from the waist upwards, though all of the fillies were solid-gold-headed blondes, and the leader, Robinson herself, was mighty nigh a ringer for Kate. Omaha was sure shot-full of fancy sights, and he was downright sorry to see the red curtain ripple down on some of the best of them.

Billy thought he recognized a face in the

milling crowd of stiff-collared dudes and bushy-bearded businessmen as they shuffled out into the rainy evening, all humming, like a bunch of locusts, the show's hit song, "Poor Little Friday."

That face back in the crowd was dimly familiar in a round-faced, sly sort of way, rather like Paddy Coghlan minus chin-whiskers. But he abruptly dismissed it when he discovered it was just five minutes until train time.

He'd intended to purchase a valise for his togs, but there wasn't time. He carted his wrapped-up boots under his arm, with his Bill Nye book stuffed in his coat pocket as he hailed a depot-bound hack.

The Kid's train was already at the station, yellow headlight glimmering dimly in the increasing downpour. The storm had arrived fiercely with crashing applause of thunder. The footlights of the lightning glared and ebbed through the descending curtain of rainfall.

A flock of wet hacks were pulled up by the station. Late passengers came running head-down through the rain. Billy piled from his conveyance, ran for and grasped the cold hand-rail of the coach. He swung up the slippery steps of the Silver Palace Car, bearing the name "White Mountains." Odors pungent drifted through the damp night air of Omaha—hot oil and grease, coal smoke, and whiskey fumes from the city's distillery.

The train was already easing from the station. Trains on this line seemed trying to steal out of the towns—as if not wishing to attract attention. Down in the Territory of New Mexico, they made a hell of a racket, ringing bells and shrieking their whistles as if proud to be running on tracks silvered at night by the big Peso Moon.

He wiped the moisture from his face, stepped into the coach, and stared. It was such a fine layout he was glad he had new duds on. Darkly rich rosewood walls, trimmed with oak, shone in warm lamplight. From hand-painted ceiling to red carpet, crunching like dried moss under his gaiters, all was elegance.

"Yessuh!" A black Porter beamed a white-tooth-slashed smile, and bowed him to his bunk—a lower berth on the right side of the car. A smartly uniformed Conductor, face as scarlet as the carpeting, tipped a finger to shining cap bill and punched The Kid's "slim-jim" ticket with a bright brass punch.

Most of the berths were already made up with green velvet curtains masking their comfortable interiors. Scrollwork mirrors at the coach's ends reflected mellow luxury. These Eastern train lines sure knew how to spread their wings. Even the spittoons were high polished.

In a couple of shakes, he was inside the curtain of his berth, and peeled down to his underwear. He cached the Colt under a soft, white pillow, half as big as a water cask. The Black Book was secreted under the mattress before he rolled under the crisp, starchy-smelling covers.

Raising his window shade a crack, he watched the shuttling shadows of the flying girders on the great iron bridge that shouldered the U.P. tracks over the Missouri into Council Bluffs.

He settled into the mattress and pictured those high-stepping *señoritas* back at the theatre— all legs, bosoms and red lips. *Maldito bello*! He wished he were at Castle Ranch again—that Kate was certain an armful—he thought of Celsa, and her warm eyes, and vaguely and disturbingly recalled the dim outline of Esmeralda's face, and felt out of sorts. He couldn't, though he tried, remember her features half as vividly as that wild Kate. But he was headed for his Angel, wasn't he? It might be a round-about trail, but it'd lead back to her. That proved who he really wanted, didn't it?

He rubbed his forehead, thumbing his newly healed scar, and wished it were daylight. He'd get up and read some of Bill Nye's joshings.

The train whistled him out of his thoughts, side-tracking them. Against the window, lights and buildings were receding into churning mist as Council Bluffs dissolved away into the rainy darkness.

28 A Puzzle

A tuneful note threaded itself through a patchwork of sounds composed of voices, wheel-clicking, whistles and the drumming thunder of the engine and cars.

Billy lay staring out at the brightness that was Iowa dawning. A field of corn, its dry leaves waving under the sudden winds of train rush, flew past—followed by an orchard of peach and apple, just fall-turned. There went a white house and two red barns; a tidy looking land.

Out of his berth, he followed the Porter and his brass gong back down the aisle, amongst a half-dozen just roused-out passengers, mostly red-eyed businessmen, boozy-looking and blue-jowled drummers and a pair of chin-whiskered pig farmers, all on their way to Chicago.

Stepping into the next car, he noticed a closed compartment at each end of the coach.

"Latest thing—boss," the Porter gave a chuckle. "Dis is a Mann Kyah, they calls 'um. Privut rooms foh privut folks!"

Billy seated himself by a window in the dining car where he could watch the door. He stared at the woods, hills and farms gliding along as he awaited his meal. This country was just crowded to death. A layout every ten miles or so. How could folks stand such living?

He nodded politely to an elderly farming couple opposite. On the sly he hitched the Colt into a more comfortable position and began to make his way through a hot breakfast of bacon, eggs and really fine light pancakes. He managed his fork gingerly. He'd cracked that thumb good back at the Hole when he grabbed his pistol out of the air as Peep had heaved it to him.

As he walked back up the nearly empty car, he suddenly stopped. It was just a bit of red paper on the floor by the far compartment's closed door. He picked it up and examined a cover from the British Blondes' show. Whether it came from Omaha or not he couldn't tell. Just a torn cover, with the rest of the program missing.

He was about to place an ear to the smooth, dark-wood panel of the compartment when the coach began to fill with passengers returning from their breakfasts.

Up in his own car, he settled back in the seat while cornfields, apple orchards and reaches of Illinois prairie stretched continually back westward. Shifting the Colt in its sling, he pretended to doze as unshaven old farmers commenced to jaw about weather and fall crops.

For the next hundred miles he was vaguely puzzled over the folks behind the door of the closed Mann compartment. He had a feeling, but couldn't put a brand on it.

When the farmers drifted in a body down to the

other end of the coach to swap hog prices, Billy pulled out his Bill Nye book, and read his way through a half-dozen pages concerned with the "Bankrupt Sale of a Circus."

Lunching in the dining car, he'd begun to get up a sweat over that closed door, and was struggling to down a piece of berry pie, when two black waiters came along the aisle, each balancing a covered tray, and heard them commenting on "deh puny gen'men in de nex' kyah."

Later, in his seat, he jauntily traded comments on the weather with a bald-headed veterinarian who was returning from a pow-wow in Sioux City.

Much as The Kid loved horses, he didn't press his acquaintance. And when the elderly man dozed off, Billy watched the country again, as it took on a different, continually shifting appearance hour by hour.

There were more houses and less farms and open stretches—more villages, towns—and here a factory, a plough works, a mill and another mill—more houses—an iron foundry—a bridge over a dull, rock-filled creek—more warehouses—and factories—their smoke lying in horizontal streaks—like a corral fence in early evening. Then Chicago!

Close on to six o'clock, the train chuffed in on one of the countless spiderwebs of steel that the drummer had been so proud about.

Inside the huge, vaulting metal and brick walls of Chicago Station, a rumpus exploded, making the arrival back in Omaha seem like a flash in the pan. Porters dodged each other on the dead run. Mothers shrilled at children. Children squawked at each other. And baggage men did their best to run down everyone with their top-heavy hand trucks.

Billy's train, a through limited, was due to press on eastward in an hour and a half. It hissed leisurely down the tracks onto a siding in time to barely escape a pair of passenger trains that came huffing and pounding in on different lines, filling the station with the roaring fury of steam, and the human freight on the platforms with lungfuls of acrid coal fumes and the odors of hot greases.

The Kid, following a sweating Porter's gasped directions, walked through the droves of business-men in shiny plug hats, and herds of grimy-faced laborers leaving their afternoon work about the great building. The rag-tag crowds of farmers, merchants, and other nondescript passengers, surging about on the wood-block flooring of the echoing, cinder-filled, gloomy cavern, were beginning to look alike—the way trail cattle got turned into hundreds of identical appearing animals.

He was nigh stupified by the brawling uproar. He'd never imagined such a commotion—so many people and such noise! Breathing hard, he escaped from the place into the Chicago night.

Standing on the steps of the Dearborn Street Station, he looked out at Chicago. High on top of the spindly, brownstone tower, spearing up from the building's center, a painted tin angel twisted about in the fitful night breezes, its thin wings glowing moth-like in the moonlight.

All along the way, row upon row of telegraph poles supported whole skeins of wire. Over the streets, invisible in the dark, more wires supported signs, large and small, covered with lettering and images. From the jumble of bobbing colors, dangling over the swarming traffic, it seemed that the city was decorated up for some celebration, but a closer inspection revealed each sign to be hawking some store or product.

Billy walked slowly, in his new gaiters, keeping a wary eye on the stream of vehicles. Constantly-lumbering wagons, loaded with kegs and casks, proclaimed Chicago to be a city with a powerful thirst.

He clambered aboard a lurching, jingling, horse-drawn streetcar at Baker Street, and observing the man ahead, gave a nickel to the red-eyed, glum Conductor. In ten minutes they'd arrived uptown. Everything seemed bright as day, huge store windows gleaming with gaslights.

On the way up, Billy had noticed many lots off the main drag, filled with crumbling, fire-blackened brick piles. But most of the semidarkened streets were trellised with scaffolding on half-completed buildings. The late Chicago fire was being built into a thing of the past.

Descending from the horse-car, he stood before a tremendous place, taller than the Red Wall. It lofted up into the Chicago night, high as a young mountain. Yellow window-light was speckled back and forth across its tremendous bulk. Folks all togged out were pouring through the open, gas-lit doorway. Lettering carved over that doorway read: "Palmer House." He figured it for a whalloping big hotel.

Walking along the building's side, he came upon a barber shop. The interior of the place was the way he imagined the King of Russia's living room to be. Mirrors blazed from all four walls. A dozen gold and silver chairs, with their slicked-up barbers and spotless bootblacks filled the glittering floor. And that floor! It was something to see—all spangled with silver dollars set into the surface of the floor itself. His first impulse was to bend and pick up a handful—but he clambered into the great, leather-backed chair.

"Coat, sir?" A barber was tugging at his collar.

"Nope! Got a chill. I'll keep'er on." He'd almost forgotten his gun.

The barber, a dark man with long mustaches and a spit curl on his low forehead, looked down-in-the-mouth, but got to work, babbling about ball games, politics, prizefighters, the James

274

Boys, and half a dozen things The Kid didn't get, due to the man's peculiar style of speech. Billy figured him for one of those "Eyetalians."

Descending from the chair, smooth-cheeked and trimmed, with his mustache whittled down, and a powerful odor of bay rum clutching at his head and shoulders, he found it was nigh on to train time.

Back at the depot, The Kid settled down in his coach, after checking his valise, and making a careful survey of the coach's interior. Only a few people were aboard for this leg of the trip— mostly quiet men and women with their heads stuck in the Chicago papers.

Sometime in the night, a passing trainman informed someone that the Limited was lying over for a couple of hours at some outlandish place, called Kalamazoo—but perhaps he dreamed, for when morning came, the train was rocketing along the Michigan Central tracks.

The country sparkled crisply in the bright sunlight, retaining much of its summer greenery, though some trees were flaring with rich orange and gold. The land, crossed and patched with fields under cultivation, held more freshly-painted barns and houses then Illinois or Iowa. This Michigan was surely all settled down and tied up with fences, and more crowded by the mile. How could folks live, so elbowed in?

During the nine o'clock breakfast, Billy overheard a bewhiskered dude informing the entire dining car, in mighty poor English, that he hailed from Europe. He was, he said, on a "tour of de vild Amerikund lands."

This Jasper, between huge mouthfuls of potatoes and bacon, compared some of the passing country with a place he called "Poolish Proosha," due to the swarms of lakes, streams and creeks outside the coach windows.

Nearing noon, they pulled into another foreign-sounding town—Ypsilanti, and took on some passengers. An hour later, the train was in Detroit.

The Kid took a stroll up toward the center of the city, during his hour lay-over. Detroit seemed a mighty elegant place. Large, beautiful homes, built like French castles, sat back from the red-brick streets, surrounded by fancy, gilded fences, flower beds and green lawns. A shining, wide river lay to his right and close beyond—Canada. A real foreign country.

He dined on oyster stew in a clean, little restaurant near the brown-and-white station. It was served up by a dark looking man who could have been an Indian from one of the northern tribes, as dignified and polite as the most starchy waiter on a dining car.

The Kid had some uneasy moments at the river's edge as the train pulled out. Like most cowhands, he could swim, but didn't relish it.

That last bout with the river at Castle Ranch was more than enough for him. When his coach was switched onto a huge, flat-bottomed boat, called a car ferry, he thought the water looked mighty deep and wide.

The Detroit River glinted in his eyes, as the ferry steamed toward the Canadian side. Several large vessels, white sails filled with river wind, curved past with the free sweep of prairie hawks. Nearing the other shore, a long, black, hump-backed ore boat, with a red smoke-stack, trailing a long ribbon of smoke, passed them, heading upstream.

It didn't take long to hook up on the Canadian side. A Canadian Central engine, with a big, bright boiler and a shiny, stubby smoke-stack, switched the coaches back and forth in the little Canadian town's freight yard. It wandered along several tracks, as if undecided as to its route, before pulling off for New York State.

The Kid, newspaper in hand, took a walk down the train. He was getting so expert at balancing in the jiggling, swaying aisles that he seldom needed to grab leather at the seat backs. The coaches were now nearly filled, especially the Mann Coach, two cars back. But the closed compartment still stared him in the face.

Looking about, he couldn't notice anyone taking interest in him, and quietly dropped his copy of the Detroit Free Press near the closed door, as the train took a series of sharp, jerking curves.

Crouching on his hands and knees, he shuffled the newsprint, taking his time to fold the pages—and keeping his ear up to the door panel.

While gathering up his last sheet, he heard a voice beyond the door!

That voice, hollow, hooting and bird-like, reminded him of a mesa owl. He didn't catch much of what was said, or make sense out of it, just a word or so: "called me . . . back . . . money in it . . . if you . . ."

"Foot high!" a sharp, yapping voice answered, ". . . surest deal we ever . . ."

A fat Train Butcher, with a face all porky-white like his apron, squeezed along the aisle, with a wicker basket, calling out his wares in a dull, lackadaisical voice, "books, sanwiches, cakes an' cookies." This put an end to The Kid's scouting.

He scrambled up with the folded paper, dusting off his trousers, and went back through the rocking coaches to his own seat.

Well—that was that! Here he'd fussed over that queer compartment, and it had up and held nothing more than a bunch of drummers, holed-up in there, hashing over deals. What he'd expected, he wasn't sure. Maybe old Pat Garrett and Flat Nose George—out to get him until Hell froze over. As for the Ring? Why, they were all back in the dust and cinders somewhere, he was certain. It was all pretty smooth going now. No more shake-down conductors or nosey town marshals away off here.

It was hard to figure he was in a real foreign country. It looked just like Michigan or Illinois, only not so many lakes, rivers and prairies.

He was growing tired of all this bright, fresh, cultivated house and barn-swarming land beyond the coach windows. He yearned for sand and sage. Closing his eyes to put those distant mesas from his mind—he found they stayed.

29 He Hears the Owl

Billy's passenger train pulled into the Canadian Falls station an hour before sundown.

He'd spent the afternoon crossing Queen Victoria's dominions in a doze, or blankly staring at mile upon mile of monotonously similar scenery. Just one farm after another, alternating with acre after acre of prosperous orchards in full fruit. Paddy Coghlan's dinky orchard at Three Rivers Ranch wasn't a drop in the bucket to suchlike, he thought.

Glassy-eyed from the monotony, he'd tried reading his newspaper and book, but eventually they wore on him.

At last when the mutton-chopped, pillbox-hatted Conductor came trudging through the cars to announce Niagara, The Kid perked up and got down his valise for transfer to the New York Central train.

Most of the folks from the five coaches disembarked at a thin, little brownstone and brick station, leaving their baggage in care of porters who bore it away to the American train on the siding. Custom officials would inspect and pass the luggage on the other side of the bridge.

The New York Central engine crept away with its string of cars to the edge of the bridge to await the passengers after a one hour lay-over. Just ahead, the green Niagara River churned along under the mist-draped, iron suspension bridge. Flocks of birds soared like white crosses, hovering and spinning in the cloudy air above the water.

At first The Kid thought another train was nearing, but the rushing sound remained at a steady level, out beyond the station, and he knew it for the roaring, bull-like stampede of great Niagara as it plunged over the brink of its rapids.

"Tree-menjis, chust tree-menjis!" It was the Polander from the dining car. His dark beard was poking forward like the horns of a muley steer, black eyes bulging with admiration. He flipped out a long, white hand and circled it like one of the swooping gulls.

"Yeah, seems to be—and noisy." Billy grinned at the fellow. Likeable but mighty noisy himself. The Kid turned to move after the straggling sightseers.

"Your pardon? I haff been here bee-fore. I could show you de way under de falst—tree-menjis!" He wagged his head from side to side and pulled off a curly-brim pot-hat. "Zienkyvitch." At least it sounded that way to The Kid.

"Pleased to meet you. Mine's, ah—O'Day." It was the first name popping into his head. Well, no use taking chances.

"Gude! Gude! Kom, we go." The man tugged Billy's arm with one hand and his own beard with the other, while a trio of young ladies hustled past. They, in turn, were followed by some honeymooners.

The sun was declining behind The Kid as he approached the booming rush of the foaming torrent. Its nearly vertical rays flamed the mountainous mist to towering orange clouds, where they boiled up from the river surface.

"Kom, Meestair Day—we hurry or too soon ist night." His guide nudged The Kid forward after the crowd, but Billy noticed the fellow was eyeing the two-legged scenery most.

The main group of passengers lined the rapids, separated from the tumbling white foam by a stout, waist-high wooden railing. Beyond the river, the American shore stood out through the swirling foam and misty green patches of trees. Several wide, veranda-fronted hotels testified to the enterprise of those Yankees over the current.

Some of the more daring passengers, mostly the younger husbands, leaned over the railings, tossing half-smoked cigars into the river, and pretending to catch up Niagara in their plug-hats and derbies, while their ladies squealed with fearful admiration.

"Voolish! Voolish!" the Polander scolded as he pointed The Kid toward a row of small, wooden houses, fifty yards back from the river. "Voolish, andt a schlipt und neffer again might dey koom oopt! De river'd grind dem to flinders."

Billy shuddered. Water in such quantities bothered him. It was all right to drink and wash in, but—!

The first building in the row, more cottage than house, held a museum of Niagara curiosities. Several passengers and tourists were strolling about the porch, peering halfheartedly at the squatty, cracked glass cases that lined its floor.

A neighboring cottage housed a restaurant. Painted boldly on its side, a menu offered such riverside specialties as Black Bear, Mallard, Lake Trout and Venison Pie.

This place was better patronized. The Kid saw groups of passengers vigorously working knives, forks and jaws at many small tables. Several absolutely mangy-looking Indians, dressed in cast-off hats, filthy suit coats and shabby moccasins, huddled along the porch. These outcasts grunted as they pushed woven-baskets and small birch-bark canoes under the legs and feet of prospective buyers.

"Zienkyvitch" and The Kid detoured these red bandits, entering a plain, bare room in the end cabin. A Negro, who made a business of guiding sight-seers, helped on their fishskin slickers. He had just finished outfitting the three girls from the train. These fillies stood in front of the cabin, waiting for their guide, and chattering like a flock of mountain jays, and looking rather like a group of Santa Fe Nuns.

When the guide started for the Falls with the young ladies, his wife began to haul out more slickers for another pair of tourists who slowly sauntered toward the cabin.

Tagging along after the first group, Billy and his acquaintance gained the passage under the Falls in an unpainted shed, about two hundred feet from the settlement.

The last in line, Billy looked out at the world, before going down the steep wooden steps in the hut floor. The light still held outside, but the sun was lower and shadows ran long.

As he went downward, the sullen thunder of the Falls filled his ears, nose and even eyes, lifting the hair on his neck. The girls were on ahead, following the Negro, who guided the parties through the uncertain light with shouts.

The Polander tagged on after the girls, offering bellowed bits of half-intelligible commentary about the place, apparently certain the females, and the black guide, accepted him as an expert on waterfalls of the world.

Billy gingerly lowered himself down the steep stairway until he stood on slippery, uneven black rock at the base of the Falls. An incredible curtain, of seemingly motionless water, arched out before him. Footsteps followed down the stairs. More visitors were coming into the greenish glow of the water-filtered dusk.

The Kid recalled another cave, at the Devil's Backbone, where he and Esmeralda waited out a storm, and found each other—for a while. No! Not for a while—he was on his way back, wasn't he?

A pair of hooded figures, wrapped in enveloping slickers, were approaching—walking closely, cautiously together. They appeared to be waiting for their eyes to become adjusted to the fading light.

Casually dismissing them as timid tourists, he turned to follow the guide, whose shouts, muffled by the crashing waters, and distance, echoed and dinned far ahead.

He pulled his hood up tightly to keep the chilling mists from seeping down his neck. Extending his hand, he began to creep forward, cursing that hot-eyed foreigner. "Zienkyvitch" could have waited, instead of panting off on the trail of a pack of females.

An outcropping of rock forced him toward the rippling white inferno seething at his feet, where the tons of water pounded into the broad, river basin. Inching so near the shattering maelstrom, he felt, rather than heard, a sudden movement at his elbow.

Grasping the slick, moss-tufted rock to steady himself, he turned to look back—as a pair of arms flashed by his face. There was the glint of a knife or gun in those sudden hands. Spinning, he slipped to his knees.

A body smashed against his left shoulder, boots giving him a great thump in the ribs. He toppled backward, clutching those legs, to land, half-stunned, on the rocky cave floor.

Grunting from the impact, The Kid rolled over, clutching at the slicker-wrapped stranger. Still seeing the Moon and Little Dipper, he knew he held a man. No girl sported such feet.

Billy saw the other figure charging him through the dim green shadows. He let go his hold on the stranger and rolling over, clawed at his slicker, getting a hand on his gun. It hung-up in a tangle of cloth, but he cocked and pulled the trigger.

The explosion crashed in the echoing reaches of the dank cavern. The bullet ripped through The Kid's slicker, ricocheting off the rocky walls.

Billy leaped up. The man in front was backing away, with hands high. Not hit—but stopped in his tracks. A small, snub-nosed Bull-Dog pistol lay uncocked at his feet.

"Back, you bone-picker," Billy yelled above the roaring. The man pointed one hand in a frantic gesture at The Kid's boots, the other held rigidly toward the vault's roof.

His attacker on the cave floor was rolling headlong into the river. Waving his smoking six-gun at the fellow, Billy reached down to complete a successful grab at a vanishing pair of legs.

The Kid stuffed the Colt into his slicker pocket and kicked the runty pistol into the river. He lugged the stunned hard-case over and dumped him in a heap on the moss-strewn gravel.

What he'd thought, in the fracas, was a knife, turned out to be a pair of nickel-plated handcuffs. Flipping the man over, while keeping a wary eye on the cowering figure in the background, he found a metal badge pinned to the fellow's vest—Law!

"Thanks, Mister! We—we, certainly obleeged to you—pullin' m'friend out before he drowned—decent, yessir, decent . . . I . . ."

"Talk sense, *pronto*!" Billy cursed at the bobbing stranger. He yanked out the .44 and stuck it deep into the man's soft belly, driving half the wind and all the talk from him. "What're you two up to?" he yelled. "Jumpin' a tourist down here? Tryin' to kill somebody or grab his roll?"

"Who . . . who . . . ?" The man's fat face shook like a puffy-headed owl, in his attempt to speak. "Who . . . said anythin' 'bout killin'? We . . . was just a'doin' our duty. You come out from . . . from back to Omaha, or past there, I dunno. But that Dave there follered you . . . tipped me off. And I got aboard at Chicago." He bobbed his chin at his chest, thick glasses jiggling on his round, red nose. "My badge. Both officers. Don't shoot!" he hooted as Billy poked him again.

All at once, The Kid knew—these were the two "drummers" in the closed train compartment. And more than that. He backed up and toeing the unconscious form on the floor into a pale beam of light, saw that it was "the Prairie Dog." The stranger who'd watched him uptown in Omaha, and had taken in the show. That was where the program cover came from.

"If you two rattlers were holed-up in that compartment, how'd you keep an eye on me?"

"Th' porter done our watchin', him an th' waiters."

Without another word, he knelt down for the cuffs, and searching, found their key on a dirty string around "the Prairie Dog's" neck. He locked the groggy sidewinder's hands behind his back.

Driving the other to the bottom of the rustic stairway, he cuffed him with his own bracelets to the wooden railing, while the man puffed and shook—walling out his eyes like a frost-bitten prairie owl.

"Detective, hey?" Billy shouted in the captive's ear. "Why me? Who sent you?" He emphasized the questions with a rap alongside the "Owl's" head.

"Oh, don't, Mister," the man yelped. "We only knew you was probably wanted back sommers, from that wire Dave got."

"From who?"

"From a conductor back to Nebrasky, I guess.

Didn't know who you was, but he said there could be some money for you . . . reward, I mean."

Billy had been filled with a black hatred of such money-sucking skunks since the days of old Buckshot Roberts. It was enough to make a man change his name—from Roberts—but that old devil of a Buckshot was in Hell, and nigh forgot. "You damned, dirty bounty hunters," The Kid yelled, "I oughta scalp you both and toss you to th' fish there . . . and your bones'd be ground to flinders." He almost grinned in the fellow's white face. He was still mad and clean through—but also relieved. These weasels weren't from the Ring after all, just a pair of amateurs.

"Well . . . pleasant dreams. And if you try followin', I'll shoot you both plumb center!" He inspected the "Owl's" cuffs again and holstering his gun, searched for his hat. Finding it, he dusted damp grit and sand from the brim, preparing to go back up the stairs. It was too dark to try to find the Polander and the rest of the party.

The "Owl" was sagging over the railing, hooting something.

"What?" It was getting on and he needed to get moving. The train could pull out, and he didn't fancy being on this side of the Falls with such varmints.

"Said, you'd be sorry enough and soon," the "Owl" hooted with ruffled dignity. "And you

cain't leave us here all night—we'd freeze—
t'aint human."

"I'll be sorry? Why?"

"No matter. Dave there tole me he wanted to
grab you first, 'cause if we missed, there'd be
others with a line on you . . . and they'd git th'
money for sure." The "Owl" clamped his fat jaws
shut, as if he'd hooted too much.

"*Buenos noches, divulgar*!" The Kid bounded
on up the slippery steps and was free of the
damp, watery stench of the cavern. Free—but not
free of a fleeting chill. Did that fat, blundering
Tinhorn mean the Ring? *Quien sabe*?

The train was loading. Billy hurried down the
track to his coach under the red embers of a day
burning out against the rolling river mists. It was
all aboard for New York—and then he'd "see the
Elephant!"

30   New York

The following afternoon, Billy's train was running beside the wide, silvery Hudson under a mellow fall sun. It was a fine, big river, really full of water—not just a muddy trickle like some western streams.

This was the fastest leg of his jaunt, so far. They'd made several stops across the State of New York, with breakfast at Albany, which a porter pointed out as "de boss Capitol of de Umpire State."

About three p.m., the passengers' boredom was lifted by the Conductor's "N'Yawk . . . N'Yawk . . . half hour to N'Yawk!"

Billy, left to himself and his thoughts since the apologetic Polander detrained at Albany, could feature those vinegaroons back at the Falls. The thought of that pair stuck in some cheap hotel, feet steaming in buckets of hot water, trying to thaw out, kept him cheerful.

He didn't think those tin-horns could have wired anyone. Seemed they worked as a free-lance team. But what the "Owl" said about the others, gave Billy a few thought-wrinkles.

The richly rolling acres of the state's farmlands were far behind now, with only isolated glimpses of red barns and heavy orchards. The train rushed along a roadbed, seemingly carved through solid rock, banks towering up until it appeared they traveled on the crest of the Hudson.

Momentary darkness came suddenly—followed by bright day, flooding the coach with sudden gold, as the train plunged through tunnel after tunnel. Acrid, nostril puckering smoke filtered into The Kid's car, vanishing as a porter appeared to open the end door and let in a flood of winey-air and rail-clatter.

With the last tunnel, the engine and coaches began a wide curve, carrying it away from the river, deeper into open, wood-studded country.

"There's the Resevoor," a homeward-bound New Yorker, ahead of Billy, complete with a soft, crush-hat, and tweed suit, nudged a dozing companion. Both pulled themselves up to watch for the approaching city. "And there's the Elevated Station at Harlem."

Billy stared at the long, brown, hulking Reservoir, stretching along the eastern horizon like a low-crowned mountain, and then turned around to peer at a thin, sinuous iron track that swung its long "S" curve a'top beanpole, iron stilts. This fragile-looking contraption straddled a shabby, farming village called Harlem.

A dinky, black locomotive, broad as it was long, pulled a string of miniature green and purple cars over spindly tracks, looking for all the world like a child's whittled-out toy. The distant smoke-stack puffed out tiny strands of cotton-wool smoke as it vanished out of sight. An El. He'd read of them in the Police Gazette, but never thought to view such modern contraptions for himself.

A sign at a darting crossing identified it as "125th Street"—but there was nothing in sight but bare, boulder-studded fields and weeds.

A massive, great brownstone building, more of a castle than a house, drifted past. Someone called it the Dakota Apartments. It lofted towers and intricate chimneys above a cluster of crazy, rickety-looking shacks, spread at its base like chicks about a hen. The Kid was mighty impressed with those fourteen stories out in the middle of nowhere.

Goats and geese scattered in nearby fields as flocks of red-headed, shabbily-dressed children trotted from the little huts near the Dakota's elegance, to halt by the crossroad, waving at the train.

The mingling of such riches and poverty was a puzzle to The Kid, but the others in the coach seemed used to such sights.

He saw a village, called Yorkville, at 86th Street and heard a running commentary on its merits and bad points. The land between there and 50th Street was made up of fields, board-fenced lots and big, hulking brown and red-stone mansions, sitting alone like forts in the autumn-tinted spaces, slanted tin roofs gleaming in the sunlight.

A wide belt of orange and yellow oak, fanning out at 68th Street, was tagged Jones' Woods by one of the New Yorkers. It would have been lost in a minute among the timber-belts of the Capitan Range, but here in all the higgeldy-piggeldy, cluttered buildings, fences and shacks, it was right pleasant to behold as it flashed past.

The same native son, two seats up, also called the passenger's attention to several fine appearing buildings as belonging to the Astors, the Rhinelanders and the Gracies—all familiar handles to The Kid, an avid reader of the Police Gazette, whenever he'd been able to get his hands on a copy at an isolated ranch or cow-town.

This was truly the East he'd mulled over at so many campfires, wondered about and just about dismissed as a land of fable. But in a way, it was partly his neck-of-the-woods. Hadn't he told such fellows as George Coe, Pat Garrett, and others about hailing from Brooklyn—even though he'd first read of the place in a newspaper. And now he was within bare miles of that place.

Streets, more closely built-up, and populated, darted past as the train, like a horse heading for the livery barn, seemed to pick up speed to finish the run.

The hodgepodge of brick, wood and stone

structures thickened. Now the Express clattered over a bridge that spanned a small creek, then leaped another set of tracks. The swing-in of buildings was nearly complete by 40th Street. Here a sun-dappled church spire lifted toward heaven, there a fire station pole sported a breeze-tossed flag, and now and again the black, cornstalk trestle of the "El" crept overhead, small dark cars darting along in their shredded veil of smoke and cinders.

"Grand Central! Grand Central! Grand Central!" The expected call hit The Kid with a jolt like the kick of a mule. Despite its inevitability, it had the rollicking sound of a song in the night—a shout at dawn when things were a'doing. It was a tune humming in his throat. He could feel words in his head.

He wanted to jump out into the aisle and throw a shot through the painting of an old castle on the curved, varnished ceiling. He yanked down his valise, ready for the station. He'd thought of dreading it—again all that hustle and bustle, and the flocks of strangers. But he looked forward to it, as to the meeting with a beautiful woman— like Esmeralda, or Kate.

He felt good. The long, weary ride on the cars was through, for a while. His half-healed wounds were giving him less and less trouble. The surging of his blood told him he could handle anything that might come. The sun outside the cars was flashing with a hundred colors. Everything was *mucho bueno*!

Five minutes later, The Kid wasn't sure he was master of his situation. When the train chuffed through the huge, gaping barn doors of the station, and creaked to a steaming, oily, odorous halt under the lofty glass and iron-beamed ceiling of Grand Central at 42nd Street, the commotion outdinned the maddest confusion of Chicago.

Off the coach and wedged into the midst of a surging, churning mob, Billy was bodily jammed along toward the exit gates in the center of the hollow, echoing gloom.

And when the emerging passengers collided with the frantically milling mob, which was trying to gain any one of the dozen trains on the rail lines, the affair took on the aspects of a war in a madhouse.

Dogs, on leashes, looking like fat sheep and small, squatty, tan and black canines with dark ugly muzzles, and idiotically curling tails, panted and cavorted and snapped and howled, wrapping leashes around the stumbling legs of over-burdened porters. Children, carrying umbrellas, bird-cages and everything from dolls to fishing-tackle, shrilled and whooped and wept as they lost families, or found them.

Sober, mutton-chopped businessmen with bearded compatriots, darted at and struggled through the press—grey toppers or black bowlers tipped over their eyes—with armfuls of portfolios and sample cases, were followed by women—top heavy in unbelievable hats and overbalanced by jutting bustles. And over and above the bedlam of shouts, calls, curses and commands, the Station Master's bellowing rang out in a sing-song chant of train schedules.

Elbowing his way out of the stampede, Billy at last stumbled, sweating, through a door. Stepping from the marble and iron ant-hill into another hurrying world, he began to inquire his way downtown. That he was forced to waylay four separate New Yorkers in a row before he caught a reply, didn't ruffle his growing cheerfulness.

The last man, short-snubbed by the arm, long enough to gain a grudging—"take th' El . . . goes all th' way ter th' foot," broke loose and trotted off with the rest of the stampeding crowds.

There was that ever-present symbol of modern, progressive America—the elevated railway, right across the traffic-filled street. While he stood brushing soot from his travel-scuffed valise, and wondering how he could risk his neck, long enough to make his way through that clanging, thundering, neighing, shouting river of horse-cars, drays, hacks, wains, wagons and coaches—a top-heavy beer wagon lost a wheel. In the momentary half-halting of traffic, caused by rolling barrels, he dared and arrived, sweating, on the other side of the street.

Stumpy, little elevated trains, tooting and clanging overhead, stinking of soft coal and burnt grease, were screeching to a halt two blocks down at a station, and there Billy went on the lope.

The Kid boarded the little cars, after clambering the two-story iron-latticework to the Metropolitan Station at 42nd Avenue and Sixth. The rattling engine sped away, tugging its coaches over the tops of cabs, wagons and people, showering blazing sparks over all until the apprehensive Kid was distracted from speculations of who might be living on those hundreds of second-floor rooms—and what they might be doing. Nothing had taken fire from the fuming smoke by the time they reached the brick and stone corner of Broadway and Bleeker.

On the advice of a short-spoken balloon man, sitting opposite in a cloud of red, green and orange globes, The Kid got off at Bleeker Street Station. He dodged among trams and coaches to enter the side door of the new Grand Central Hotel.

A brass-buttoned, red-coated, little monkey of a Bellboy tugged The Kid's valise away, and retreated like an ancient Irish dwarf with his burden to stand leering near a potted palm tree.

Billy registered in the hotel's yard-wide, yellow-plush guest book as William O'Day of Omaha, Nebraska, while the clerk yawned and polished his nails on a bilious, lemon-tinted vest. That was one thing Peep had done, lent him a name. Well, it was only fair, he'd handed him the moniker of "Peep."

The Kid beheld another wonder of the modern age, when the smirking, button bespangled Bellhop herded him into a gilded, jail-cell of a contraption down the hall. As the ornate cage gave a quiver and slowly rose up past the pink and white marble pillars of the lobby, Billy's legs felt a mite wobbly.

"Ain't'cha been up in one before?" the Bellboy chirped, letting the rubber-kneed Kid out onto rose-red carpeting. "You'll git yer sea-legs back quick. Here we be." He bent his thin back and opened a door, with a large brass key. Turning the valise over to Billy, he held out his hand.

The Kid shook the small, withered paw and shut the door in the man's sober face. "Friendly folks here, at least," he informed the empty room, as he locked the door.

It was certainly a fine, big place, with white-covered, double bed, sitting room furniture, pictures on the blue-striped wallpaper, and three windows overlooking the buzzing clatter of Broadway.

He sat down, pulled off his coat, shed his six-shooter. Yawning, he sank back onto the soft bed.

—When he awoke, it was full night, and the large, honest face of the moon, like an old friend from home, was staring him in the eye. Enough light flowed in to let him see his watch. It was time for grub.

Washing up at a jim-dandy, little, marble washstand in the corner, complete with piped-in water and shiny brass knobs, he stuck the Colt back in his shoulder-rig and put on his coat.

He walked down the stairs, instead of taking that unsafe bird-cage.

After downing a dinner of soup and roast-beef, topped off with coffee and cheese, at the total outlay of seventy-five cents, he went slowly down Broadway. He was so stuffed that he couldn't have moved faster if Pat Garrett was throwing down on him again.

Wandering among endless clusters of people, he gained grit with every block. This many folks took getting used to, but he buckled down to the task. All were hustling along as if there was a fire at their house, or Indians lifting hair two blocks away. It was hard to figure what all the rush was about.

The moon, burning its white fire, high above the cold, blue night, blanched the tops of some absolutely amazing buildings. The Kid counted ten and sometimes twelve floors. The telegraph wires, strung between the structures, had the look of brightly frosted spiderwebs. No one back in Sumner would ever believe it—not that he'd go around that way to tell 'em—if he could help it!

He leaned against a lamp-post and listened to the music a fellow was cranking out of a big box. The man, a dark, long-mustached foreigner in a floppy-brimmed hat, and a threadbare green suit, ground away for a time, but at last surrendered in a torrent, of what Billy took to be, cuss-words, and stumped off into the crowds.

In the morning, Billy sat on the edge of his bed and counted his money. It was melting like snow in the desert. If he figured right, he had enough for another three days at the hotel. They charged high, ten dollars a day, the price of a prime beeve. He'd also just about have passage money to Texas. He wondered how to bump into a Monte game. There were card games going on in this town—the Police Gazette called them "gambling hells."

As he washed up and scraped his chin with the razor, he thought about the Ring. So far they'd not showed hoof or horn—but then, how could they? He shook that trail back at Hole In The Wall. That pair at the Falls had just fallen over his tracks—and were certainly talking through their hats, about anyone getting wise to him now.

He wiped his face and pulled out the little black book, with its list of dirty deals. The Ring was sure plumb over a barrel with this in his hands. Between the black book and his Bill Nye on the dresser there, he had himself a real library. That Ring book gave all the names and shenanigans of every member of that Santa Fe gang—lawyers,

301

bankers and merchants—from 1878 right through the last spring!

Yes, all there in neat little rows. And how he was going to enjoy showing that bunch up in court. A Texas court—where he'd get a fair shake. Esmeralda, and her folks' lawyer would see to that.

He pulled on his other clean shirt, vowing to get to El Paso—and soon. No more *mañana*. He gritted his teeth to think of those cars again—but he couldn't ride a horse all the way down there. It was just too damned far.

After breakfast in the big, barn-like, hotel dining room, he went down the street to a nearby telegraph office. His wire was addressed: "Miss Kate Castle, Rock Springs, Wyoming" and read: "Miss Castle. I would like money I left. Need it today. B. Roberts care Western Union, 15066 Broadway." He hoped the message would reach her *pronto*, but it might be days. He couldn't be sure—or certain her father was able to scare up his own necessary cash.

He'd scarcely returned to the hotel lobby and settled into a big, leather chair, to kill time watching the crowds, when the same little monkey of a Bellboy skipped through a knot of drummers and hailed him.

"Youse Mister O'Day, ain't cha? Seen yer sign th' register."

"Right . . . ?" Billy half-rose, anticipating

302

something out of the way. He wasn't wrong.

"Youse got a call. On da telyfun, over dere." The man pointed to a corner of the lobby past the hotel's oyster bar.

Billy went to the indicated spot, and peering through the underbrush of rubber plants and potted ferns, discovered a long, wooden chest fastened to the wall, studded with several knobs and bells. He was trying to cipher them out when the wizened, yellowish face of the Bellhop poked through the foliage. "Talk inter it, Guv'ner. Pick up de handle an' put'er to yer ear! Talk inter de hole."

The Kid attempted to follow directions as the Bellboy pulled back out of sight, but he just couldn't get the hang of the thing.

"Say hello inter it and listen to de handle." The shriveled face was back, leering wisely.

"Hello?"

"No, Guv! Youse talks inter de hole—not de handle." The head withdrew, but Billy knew it was eavesdropping outside.

"Hello . . . hello?" He'd read about these contraptions in the Gazette. There were supposed to be almost two thousand in New York City, but this was the first he'd ever seen. "Hello?"

". . . you—Roberts . . ." A small, thin sound, almost a voice, and not a voice—more like a bird chirping, or a cricket rubbing its legs. "Can you hear . . . ?"

"Yeah, pretty good. What's . . . who're you callin'?" He hadn't been mistaken in that name—Roberts—though he'd signed the register as O'Day. The voice on the other end of this rig called him by name. That "Owl" knew what he was hooting about—after all. His neck hair prickled.

"Don't interrupt . . . friends would like to . . . you. Come out to Coney . . . tonight. If you don't . . . we'll come to see you . . . better get it over . . . authorized to negotiate . . . thousand . . . deal with you . . . worth your time . . . comply . . . seven at the elephant . . . top of . . ." And a click, like the cocking of a pistol. He listened, but there wasn't any more.

"Musta hung up on youse, Guv'nor." The Bellboy was back. "That's what they do—folks do—hang up they call it, when they's done." Taking the black handle, which he called the "receiver," from The Kid's hand, he placed it back on its hook at the side of the box.

"*Mucho bueno*—thanks."

"That'd be all, sir?" The fellow had his hand out. This time The Kid knew he didn't want to shake.

"T'anks!" The brass-buttoned arm pocketed the half-dollar.

"Where's this here Coney?" Billy inquired, trying to be easy, as if talking over the weather.

304

"Yer wanner go ter Coney? Any place p'tickler? Easy ter git'ter, all right."

"The Elephant?"

"Dat'd be der Elephunt Restrint." He flicked a yellow thumb at the wall near the "telyfun." A framed lithograph hung there in company with a tinted reproduction of Cuban Sweetheart Cigars. "Dat's a pitcher of de Elephunt. Whale of a place. Big landmark. Built 'bout five years back. Hunnerts of folks go ter eat'n raise a little cain. Yer can eat an' have a real top-shelf time."

The Kid stared at the picture. So that was where the Ring wanted to corral him. It must be the Ring. Who else could reach out and lasso him in this tremendous city. And they seemed to be offering a big pile. A thousand for that black notebook. But he wouldn't take one filthy cent from them—unless?

Well, he'd fooled them before. Maybe he'd take the chance. Just once more—*sanamente*!

31   He Sees the Elephant

The streets of New York, though running at right angles, and easy to follow, were full of surprises as the secret paths and canyons of the Outlaw Trail—but not so dangerous—so far.

He minded his own business and hardly rated a second glance from the big, blue-coated New York police, as they strolled along in pairs, swinging thick, brown, locust wood night-sticks.

Billy spent the hours after the "telyfun" call wandering about lower New York. A bit tipsy from craning at the cliffs and plateaus of red-brick and grimy-grey buildings, he pulled up every few blocks to listen to the half-a-hundred lingos and dialects, all jawing at once.

One persistent, scraggly-bearded old man, in a patched coat and flattened derby, tagged along until The Kid bought a packet of needles and thread. He might have some mending to do before he hit Texas.

In an hour's time of sauntering along Fulton, he met and identified, from their calls, burdens or actions—a glass man, with shining, fragile, flat bundle of glass on his back; a scissor-grinder with his little, pale-brown stone wheel; a broom peddler; old clothes men, with their monotonous cries of "cash for cloes." But of all the bent-backed, street merchants, the baker-man with his over-flowing basket of loaves, enveloped in a nearly visible cloud of warmly-wheaty smells, was the most appetizing.

When half-past five arrived, Billy was aboard a Brooklyn short-line railway, and heading for Coney Island.

Light shuttled past, as jumbled street upon street spun away into the early autumn dusk, bearing with them brick tenements with their fringes of iron-dinguses, called "fire-scapes," and gas-lit signboards. The latter, flaring with all the colors of a bilious rainbow, silently screamed from rooftops at the smoky world: "Use Sapolio For Dirty Stoves!"—"Beacham's Pills For Disordered Livers."—"St. Joseph's Oil For Your Lumbago" and "Vinegar Bitters For What Ails You!"

The coaches, minute-by-minute, clattered past a patchwork of thinning blocks of houses, gaunt factories, squat gas-plants, lumber yards, black-smith shops, newly-built "Villas," farms and vacant fields, all stitched together by lines of telegraph poles—and all moon-touched and pale in the misty, cloud-dimmed night. Within the half-hour, they were out in flat, open country and nearing Coney.

Faint lights burned in red and green dots along the eastern edge of the sky, where the ocean washed in a vague white line. Lights burned brighter. Bulky, dark humps and mounds swelled into buildings. First a hotel, followed by a tower, shaggy with wind-ruffled pennants, and piers stretching out grey arms into the black-emptiness of the water. And hulking, with glaring eyes, a hundred feet or more above the sandy flats—the Elephant!

A clock on the wall of the Sea-Beach Railway Station registered ten past seven when The Kid made his way toward the huge, wooden form of the Elephant. That Elephant—it was a sight fit for a nightmare, with its vast, curving, white-painted tusks, and bulking, enormous body, all strung with flags and pennants that flapped and twisted in the damp sea breeze, giving a sort of ominous movement to the beast.

But what gave the animal an awesomeness beyond anything The Kid had ever seen were its huge, baleful, orange eyes—colored glass windows lit by gas-lights within the enormous head.

Those eyes held Billy's attention as he skirted shooting galleries, Punch-and-Judy shows, dime-museums and a balloon ride. This last affair, composed of big hollow balls, rigged up like balloons, dangled baskets underneath its elevated cross-arms, jammed with laughing, waving folks.

He crossed a long boardwalk, past an elaborate skating rink, built in the style of some Oriental Palace, and neared the Elephant, where it loomed with hooked tusks, like the horns of some monstrous, murderous steer. The orange-red stare of its eyes peered out toward the unseen horizon, beyond the lights and laughter.

The Kid walked through a wooden turnstile, guarded by a sleepy-looking gent in a circus-clown's suit. This rouge-faced grotesque sat with red putty-nose stuck in a copy of Beadle's "Old Sleuth at Bay."

"Full up, Mister! Big doin's tonight. Fact, maybe too big. Th' rival politickers got their schedools mixed up." The Clown came unglued from his reading matter, for a moment. "Fact plenty full up. Yep!"

"Got a meetin' with someone in there, myself." Billy barely paused. "*Nombramiento*—appointment!"

"*Nom* ? Oh, I gets yer." The Clown's death-white face cracked in a leer. "Well, g'wan in—but watch out fer her husban'. Them plumbers carries big chunks of pipe, fer luck."

Looping banners and gaudy signs were tacked and lashed about the Elephant's great wooden legs. They marched in unruly parade over the booths and stands in the picket enclosure surrounding the Elephant—"Plumbers Helpers Will Keep Dick Croker"—"Button Hole Makers Union For Mike Morrisy For Our Next Alderman"—"Cloth Spongers Society For Mike Morrisy!"

Mounting several broad, scarred pine steps

at the doorway in the Elephant's leg, The Kid emerged into a room packed from wall to wall with hooting, yelping plumbers and their wild-eyed, long-lipped Irish colleens. These noisy folk were being assailed with the verbal outbursts of a pair of fuming, howling orators—each with his portion of the room in rapt attendance.

The noise was deafening as the air, trapped within the echoing bowels of the great wooden monster, turgid with warm-beer fumes, smoke and cloying waves of perfume, roiled around The Kid.

The sight began to take on the aspect of a feverish dream, with the crowd wavering like imps in a noisy corner of Hades.

He had to move—and collaring a Waiter: "Anyone lookin' for me—O'Day—Roberts?" He'd mighty near said Bonney in his sudden anxiety.

"Louder, Mister! Lookin' fer you? Yeah! They's a couple of gents upstairs in a room by th' Elephant's head. Said someone could be askin'. Thanks, up that way."

Billy handed him a dollar. All these folks with their hands out. And they weren't interested in shaking hands.

He went up a second series of winding, wooden steps. Halfway up, he looked back down. None followed. He slipped the Colt into his hip-pocket, on a hunch.

With the racket covering his footsteps, he

walked down the rough-timbered hall and tried a door marked "Private—Employees Only." It was unlocked, and he entered a room, approximately twenty-feet square, bare and covered with dust. Two large, circular windows, a dozen feet high, flanked the space. Centered in the middle of each window, glowing raw-yellow against the opaque, orange panes of glass, flames flared up from two oversized gas torches—the room of the Elephant's eyes. But empty!

Turning to leave, he discovered the room was no longer empty. The door was closed, and two men stood watching him.

One of the pair, a real swell, was unfastening a red-lined cloak. This gent was togged out like a medicine showman, in dark tie, dark cut-away coat and trousers—with a tall, black plug-hat accenting his height.

The other could have been one of those loud-mouthed plumbers, in flat hat and rumpled, green sack-suit. His face was seamed and ploughed with the scars of a dozen donny-brooks. A twisted cheroot smoldered in a corner of his wide gash of a mouth, half-indistinct under a red, walrus mustache.

Billy backed into the end of the room, placing the flare of the gas-lights in the intruders' faces.

The larger man advanced a pace. "Windy up on the Howdah. Just taking a bit of air before our meeting. Didn't realize it had grown so late. I hope you haven't been detained long?" He had the deep, richly resonant voice of the actor, or orator.

Billy figured him correctly as Croker—the Boss Croker of the signs and flapping banners.

Croker's handsomely-cut face was a bit heavy about the jowls. His smile was warmly winning—but his eyes were cold as a horned toad's. "You couldn't be anyone but our man?" The plug-ugly behind Croker, leaned against the closed door, staring at The Kid, fists jammed in his pockets.

This was a more dangerous pair than any "Owl" and "Prairie Dog."

"I'm myself, all right—and you're th' gent on th' telyfun?" Billy was aware that he was in a real blind canyon. They blocked the door, and here he'd gone and stuck his neck out again—a real *necio*!

He kept his hands at his sides, ready to dive one back under his coat, where the .44 hung heavy in his hip-pocket.

"Yes, I represent mutual friends, or rather business associates, back in the New Mexico Territory. Santa Fe, to be precise." The big man pulled off his cloak, draping it loosely over one arm, like some noble old Roman. "They wired me early this morning, suggesting a mutually advantageous meeting."

"How'd they know where to find me in New York, or even in this neck of the woods?" Billy's glance darted between the "Plumber" and the "Ring-Man." "Who're you, anyways?"

"Ah, just a friend. You might say, in all honesty, that the gentlemen in Santa Fe, and myself are merely businessmen, with overlapping interests. I and certain others present them with bits of advice, tips on the market, and in turn, they include us in on negotiations in land, timber and mines. Most pleasant people to deal with." Croker blandly ignored The Kid's questions. "And now," he nodded to the *hombre* at the door, "we must get along with our negotiations. I'm scheduled to address my supporters downstairs." He thrust out a long, soft hand. "Deliver the book—the one you, ah, found in Santa Fe, and McGlinn here will give you a small reward. A thousand dollars!" He chuckled benignly. "That's not a bad bit of boodle, I'd say."

Billy reached into his inside coat pocket for the notebook, not sure what move to make—playing for time—waiting *La Fortuna*'s next card.

"Hold on, bucko!" the "Plumber" growled, chomping down on his stogie, and pulling a knife from his pocket. "Hold it! No funny stuff!"

"Just reachin' for th' book." Billy opened his coat to display his empty holster. "Let's see that money!"

"Hustle it up, McGlinn," Croker commanded, yellow eyes glittering.

"Hell boss, I'll git that widout spendin' a shin

plaster." The "Plumber" flung down his cigar, and his knife, a blood-red streak in the light, charged straight at The Kid.

The politico threw up white hands, in an attempt to get out of the way, the cloak slipping from his arm.

Billy grabbed the garment and hurled it full into McGlinn's face.

Slashing at The Kid, and clawing at the enveloping folds of the cloak, the man stumbled into a gas torch to rebound backward out through the Elephant's eye in a shattering crash.

With the screams of the "Plumber" shrilling in his ears, Billy pulled the Colt. Menacing the remaining conspirator into a corner, he saw the night sky, beyond the jagged glass, explode with fireworks. Red rockets streaked their looping fire trails, punctuated with gold and green spark-spray.

"Payne's fireworks, down at Manhattan Beach Hotel," gasped Croker, arms trembling over-head—like a noble Roman at bay.

"Good! They can't hear our own brand up here," Billy grated, thwacking his pistol barrel down on that noble brow.

Slamming the door behind him, he stuffed the Colt back into his shoulder holster, and walked down the hallway.

Clattering down the winding stairs, in the Elephant's echoing leg, he came back out onto the main floor in time to bump into the milling crowds who were now shouting: "Dead! Hit th' edge of th' tusk—bounced inter th' beer garding—musta fell out—"

Yelping, sweating plumbers swarmed around, politics forgotten, for the moment, while their females contributed their own variety of shrieks to the increasing hullabaloo.

Billy struggled across the floor. If he didn't get out of the place in a hurry, they'd size him up for a stranger. And when that bunch above found Croker there'd be hell for supper, with Law all over.

A big, strapping Irishman crashed into the slight Kid, and Billy rebounded off the wall. In an effort to keep his balance, he grabbed a pole supporting a banner. The drooping message on the creased fabric hit him right in the eye: "Croker!"

He waved a fist at the high, wood-ribbed ceiling, faking a move toward the stairway. "Croker's up there! Those tailors has got'm! Shoved him into th' Elephant's head. Hey! Help Croker . . . help'm!"

The volatile crowd immediately echoed The Kid's words. "Croker's up there! They got our Dickie! By howly, t'rew his mon out th' windy! Let's go byes! Kick th' tar outa them. C'mon you tarriers!" A hundred strident voices took up the chant, as they rushed at the stairs, in a frenzy

315

to battle the "cowardly Cloth Spongers" and "murtherin' Tailors."

Billy left the Elephant and the mounting rumpus without anyone paying heed. He made his way through the gate and saw, in the bluish half-light of the gas-lamps, the Clown and a knot of people bending over a green bundle by the Elephant's foot.

There was a thousand dollars there on that man, who'd gone out the Elephant's eye—but The Kid couldn't linger.

A train was loading when Billy gained the ticket window. Five minutes later he was rattling along through the darkness. The moon, racing beside the train, was intermittently devoured by wolf-packs of clouds, rushing in from the ocean. Coney, itself, was a collection of distant shadows, touched with flickering shards and pinpoints of fire. It faded and went out with the last sparks.

Looking through the window at the vague countryside, he noticed something wrong with his reflection, the most distinct image to be seen. He put a hand up to his left shoulder. There was a long gash in his coat. The "Plumber" had nearly connected.

The few folk in the car looked at him incuriously as he took off his coat and did a make-shift job of mending the sleeve, with the needle and thread purchased from the little one-eyed street vendor.

By ten o'clock, he was back over the wind-smudged river and opening the fly-specked door of the Western Union office, two blocks from his hotel. The Night-Man squinted up from under a cracked, green eyeshade. "Yair?"

"Roberts. Sent a wire out this mornin'." He wasn't sure there'd be a reply—yet. Kate could be anywhere. When the man pulled out an envelope and a wire from his cash drawer, The Kid could have yelled with relief. *La Fortuna* was sure looking right over his shoulder, and the one with the knife rip, at that.

"Sign here." The Clerk shoved out a ruled book and poked a dirty-nailed finger at a blank line. "An' ya just miss a fella, come lookin' fer ya."

Billy signed his name, saying nothing. What was there to say? No telling when that nosey visitor would return. He accepted the telegram and money, and went out into the beginning of a drizzling fall rain.

Sitting in the musty but secure interior of a Broadway hack, headed downtown, he read the telegram by the passing illumination of the street lamps. It was from Kate, all right, and timed at six p.m. It gave him a strange feeling to think that her words were only four hours old.

"In Rock Springs with Father. Sending what I can. One Hundred. Important to see you. Coming East. Send permanent address. Kate."

He opened the envelope. One hundred was sure

317

a lot less than that five hundred he'd counted on. It wouldn't do much beyond paying travel fare. Why hadn't she sent the whole roll? Her old man must have collected his own money by now. And she was coming to see him. Important? Well, she'd have to stay where she was.

By now the Ring would have flunkies and fly-cops watching all the depots—so it was the water for him. It'd been a long, wide-ranging trail and now it was getting crooked. The thought to take the boat had come to him when he hailed the cab back at the telegraph office. The Ring would be looking for him to go south or back westward—so he'd hit north, far as Boston, and then see what was what—ready to double back.

Billy's ship was the "Doris" of the Neptune Line, a wooden, side-wheeler, old but in service as a night boat. When her paddles thrashed the hazy East River at eleven o'clock, he was on board in Stateroom 20, and lighter by fifteen dollars.

Outside in the steadily pattering rain—and paddle chunking—New York's glow was waning, but The Kid's exhausted slumber precluded darkness and light, as well as life and death.

Again the card was turned—the coin tossed.

32 Boston Boat

Rain squalls beat against The Kid's porthole through the night. About four in the morning, the old steamer commenced a fandango. The motion pitched Billy up against the wooden bulkhead with a thud.

He thought he was in a coach that had lost a wheel, and was tipping over into some deep and bottomless canyon—"Hold on—*estar en vigor*!" Rearing up in his narrow bunk, he cracked his head with a whack that lit the cabin. Stars danced with a collection of the brightest Coney Island fireworks—and he spent a long moment untangling his directions, before he realized he was aboard a ship.

The Night Boat rocked and tossed as it battled an autumnal storm up the Atlantic shoreline toward Boston. It was the craziest jaunt of his whole twisted flight.

Salt air crept into his nose and with it—the fatty-waftings of unattractive food. He rolled over and gritted his teeth, trying to ignore it— the rain and wind lashed the ship with increased strength, and slowly the dark blanket folded down over him again.

A bunk-shaking blast of the ship's horn proclaimed the arrival of the "Doris" in Boston harbor.

319

Out the porthole, diamond-tipped waves, small and brilliant, flecked the bay's surface with a thousand splinters of light. White V's and W's of busy gulls dipped and climbed about the harbor. Several long docks lay to his right, with steam packet-boats berthed at the red-trimmed pilings smoke lazing up from their striped stacks into the bright blue October morning. Boston—the Pilgrim capitol lay off behind those whisping smoke streaks.

Billy washed and gave himself a hurried shave in the small, tin sink in the cabin. The razor came from a steward who'd announced the docking.

He went ashore within the hour in a knot of passengers—some of whom looked less sure of their land legs than The Kid. He was immediately pounced upon by one of the unruly horde of cabmen, who clustered along the docks like the rows of gulls perched upon roofs and peaks of the waterfront buildings.

His cabbie, a wrinkled, red-faced, little Irishman, who could have been a near relative to Punch at the Coney Island puppet shows, drove him toward the center of town, throwing a drumfire of comment at his helpless passenger.

Billy got down at Tremont and Park Streets, giving his driver an extra half-dollar. The blarney and the spicy, clean air, as refreshing as a drink from a mountain stream, cleared his aching head. He'd been dubious about that bump in his bunk, thinking that it might start up his head wound, but he really felt *mucho bueno*.

It was good to plant his gaiters back on solid ground. Boats were mighty unsteady things to ride. How sailors got used to the sea didn't bear thinking about. He'd take a good horse anyday.

He walked along the clean, tidy street. Tremont was in a well built, more modern part of Boston than the narrow, winding old streets that lead up from the docks. Parts of the town back there were almost as pinched as the alleys in Santa Fe.

He couldn't be much farther from Santa Fe if he'd planned on it. But distance hadn't seemed to stop those Ring *serpientes*. And it still puzzled him to imagine how those *lagartos* found his trail. It couldn't have been Esmeralda or Kate, or that Peep, even though he'd written all three, because he hadn't told any of them where he was headed. How could he, when he didn't know himself?

After buying himself a razor and comb at a small notions store on a side street, he breakfasted upon oatmeal and coffee at a restaurant for twenty cents.

A small, well-kept park lay across the street from the restaurant. He crossed to the park, dodging an ambling horse-car, and bought a copy of the Boston Globe from a newsboy for three cents. Half the benches were filled with loafers taking their ease in the fall sunshine.

He picked out an empty bench in the ragged patches of gold and watched the crowds. People still bustled by, but there wasn't the hot-footed, stone-in-boot, hopping along that went in New York. Elevated lines were also here, but not so many cars ran—nor did they seem so belligerently noisy. But the coal they burned was just as sooty. By the time the second train clucked along over on the next street, Billy's paper was speckled.

He rose from the bench and was slapping the paper against his heel, when he noticed an item. It wasn't much, about an inch or so, but it crowded everything off the sheet. Even ads for Orris Cream, Lavendar Salts and Cuban Splits Cigars—the latter, a pretty lady in a lace head-piece, and doing just that—the splits! All were overshadowed by the item: "New York. A tragic accident at a Coney Island political rally last night resulted in the death of Councilman Richard Croker's trusted employee, his Valet, Michael Patrick McGlinn. McGlinn fell from the top of the bizarre Elephant Restaurant, while attempting to subdue a dangerous anarchist who had attacked the Councilman. Police say Croker identified the man as a fugitive who is wanted in several states and territories. An early arrest is imminent."

Well—that was just about hell! Croker would get in Dutch with the Ring for spouting off about The Kid, though he'd only called him a "fugitive." The Ring wouldn't like talk about fugitives.

The sun that had washed trees and browning grass with warm lights was paling with the overcast that had moved in from the bay.

Billy was on the park's edge, watching his chance to cross the street, suddenly busy with near-noon traffic. He casually glanced back at the clattering Elevated across the block. A man had pulled his discarded newspaper from the park waste basket and was peering at The Kid.

He turned away when he noticed Billy watching him. He wore, The Kid saw, a full, brown beard and was round-shouldered and broad as a bull buffalo.

Dismissing it as mere *accidente*, The Kid continued on his way. He was standing in front of a high-toned millinery shop, grinning at the utterly idiotic bonnets—they looked like a bunch of painted birds' nests, when the old "Buffalo" came shuffling along on the opposite side of Tremont. He was scanning the paper, and damned if he wasn't on the same page that held the story of the "Plumber's" death—Billy was sure, he recognized it from the picture of the sassy girl doing the splits on that cigar advertisement. *Accidente*? Maybe. The old duffer couldn't get across the street, for the minute. A whole herd of hacks were streaming out of the side-street, and turning up Tremont—a funeral procession. It began to rain as The Kid dodged between them.

A horse-car came clopping and swaying through the street puddles. He took it toward the depot, without another sight of "the Buffalo." This town didn't look as good as it had. Perhaps it was the weather. Over Copps Hill smoke from a passing El hung above the white, rain-veiled stones in a long curved wreath.

Boston Depot was a large, square building of painted brick, sensible and sober-looking. It wasn't all cluttered with towers and flags like New York's Grand Central Station. Sober and substantial like the city of Boston.

Inquiry produced the fact that two trains were due out within the hour. One ran west across the state and the other down to New York. He settled for the passenger running out toward the interior of Massachusetts—and the Hudson River, and bought a one-way ticket.

Several Boston Police, in grey uniforms and flat, black caps, were ambling down the platform, looking over the passengers and their baggage. They continued on their rounds as The Kid passed them, heading for his car.

Boston might be hard to get into on a ship, in a storm, but the Western Limited flew out of the old city like a cork from a bottle. For a few minutes, freight yards and bridges flashed by, followed by warehouses, grey stone tenements and old, brownish-red brick homes. The next thing The Kid saw was the criss-crossing beams of the bridge over the strip of land anchoring the Island of Boston proper to the built-up suburbs on the landward side.

They rocked along over water-soaked fields and meadows. It appeared to have been raining for some time in the country, from the expanse of fields filled with ponds and shining sheets of water.

At noon, there being no dining car, the train pulled up at a small factory town for a lunch stop. The sun was back out and New England glowed in mellow autumn warmth. Snuffy-nosed little boys in rough tweeds and rubber boots trod the platform with baskets of clams, roasted corn and biscuits, in direct competition to a white-fronted eating house just east of the Depot.

Billy bought two ears of corn, and a half-dozen buttered biscuits, steering clear of the clams. He was sure he couldn't stomach the things. He sat on a chipped, blue bench beside the Depot, along with several other, more daring passengers, who gobbled down vast quantities of clams. The corn was mighty nigh cold and the biscuits inclined to fall apart, but he made out a satisfying meal.

The rolling hills and towering forests of Massachusetts marched past The Kid's window the remainder of the afternoon, interspersed with neat, little towns, buildings painted white and clean as doll houses.

It was plumb relaxing to loll back in the scuffed, yellow plush seat and doze in the westering sun, that came and went with the curve of the gilded rails. It helped him forget where he'd been, or where he was going—just traveling.

The sun was raveling away into pink and green shreds, behind the murky Massachusetts hill when the train chugged into Springfield.

Billy got off with the other passengers for supper. But the sight of a bushy-bearded, round-shouldered man, walking along, head bowed, near the end car, made The Kid forgo plans for a meal. "The Buffalo!"

When the train pulled off, it was minus a passenger. The Kid might be out the price of a ticket, but he wasn't about to stay aboard with a jasper who seemed all-fired curious about his reading habits.

He lingered in the obscurity of the afterglow, watching from the Springfield Depot's corner. The train was two little lights flickering along the blue-grey roadbed.

He was alone, again, in a strange town.

33   Pilgrim's Progress

Springfield, Massachusetts, the town Billy had landed in from the westbound passenger, sat to the east of a good-sized mountain range.

He noticed this on the following morning as he crawled from his bed in the local hotel—the Bates House. From the second story, he could see the hazy-blue of the Berkshire's autumn-edged outlines. They were considerable mountains, for the overcrowded East.

Nature hereabouts was so grown-up and elbowed in on itself, that even the hills and peaks were sort of second rate, he thought. They just couldn't seem to find enough space to spread out. Just too many houses and people.

While those mountains pleased his eye, he also looked toward them with a half-felt unease. He found that he longed, deep-down inside for space, space to move in and space to ride in. Who could peer over your shoulder, when you were horseback?

As far as he was concerned, that settled it. While he was eating in the low, beam-studded dining room, he made up his mind to pick out a horse. He was fed up with snorting, cinder-riddled railway coaches. Damned if he wouldn't be happier back in a saddle. The more he thought of it, the more sold he became.

There was a livery stable four blocks from the downtown part of town, near the poplar-lined Milk River. And there Billy found a bright little, three-year-old roan gelding with one white foot. The asking price was forty dollars, but The Kid, by careful dickering brought the rate down to thirty—and bought a scuffed, black saddle for ten. It was a flat, postage-stamp sort of a rig, but better than bareback.

"That's a good bargain y'made y'self," the chin-whiskered liveryman informed The Kid as they stood in the barn doorway. The man pocketed the money and turned the bill of sale over to Billy. "Course," he squinted slyly, while his tobacco-browned whiskers twitched with goat-like glee, "he's a mite mettlesome. We got'm and a couple more, year back—shipment from N'brasky. Cowpony, I b'leeve. And well—mettlesome."

Billy could see that the man was pleased to be rid of, what he considered, a bad piece of horseflesh.

"Well," The Kid put on a downcast face, timidly patting at the pony. "Well, you might've told me." He tugged his hat down and made sure his coat was buttoned. Wouldn't do to let these Yanks see his hardware. He hesitantly climbed into the rusty saddle, and adjusted the stirrups. And kicked a heel, hard, into the roan's side.

The liveryman and several grinning, shirt-sleeved loafers were, in that moment, treated to a sight they weren't ready for. The mild, young stranger suddenly became a wild man—a wild Indian of a rider, who sat a continuously arching, brown explosion with the aplomb of an angel astride a thunderbolt.

Their hair arose. That barely human shrilling—the sound of faraway wilds jangled in their Puritan ears—the barbarous chant of the Yacqui horsebreakers.

It was over as quickly as it began. The horseman yanked the mount into a rearing, hoof-pawing, high-stand—as the scrambling spectators upset the livery stable goat, which butted the liveryman headfirst.

Billy took the lathered roan up the street at a gallop. Waving his hat, he gave the flabbergasted crowd one last Yacqui war-whoop, and hit along the road in the direction of the mountains.

Slowing his mount, he cantered down one of the tree-lined creeks that cut through the north part of town and shortly after passing the Smith and Wesson Arms Works, stopped at a long, weather-faded, covered bridge to pay his toll.

"This here pike goes north ten mile and then heads off to the westward again," the grizzled tollkeeper replied to The Kid's question, rolling his tobacco quid from one hollow cheek to the other. "Yer hoss seems pretty warm, han't he?"

"Just mettlesome."

Billy rode on across the echoing planks and pulling up in the amber-hued shade of a maple grove, wiped the roan down with a handful of dried grasses. The deep blue of the sky, overhead, was mirrored in the thick clusters of fringed gentians edging the dusty, white macadam roadway.

It was getting on toward eleven, when he mounted the docile horse and trotted along the road. The roan was easy now after its exercise. Several times it turned its handsome head to look at the man on its back.

About noon, The Kid came to a hamlet, consisting of a general store, a couple of houses and barns and a grist-mill; little more than a crossroads, hugging a wooden ridge.

He tied up in front of the rickety store and buying a chunk of good, sharp cheese and a pound of crackers, along with a brown bottle of ginger-beer, the only wet goods on sale, squatted down on the steps and had lunch.

The place was perfectly still, and peaceful. It reminded him of one of the small New Mexican villages—Las Luz, perhaps, but several spindle-shanked, hickory-jeaned natives stalking past, ruined the illusion.

"Goin' far, Mister?" The fat storekeeper ambled out and stood by The Kid, chewing noisily on a pickle. He tried again when Billy, mouth filled with cheese and dry crackers, shrugged. "See you're headin' fer Amherst?"

"Where's—that?"

"Jist up th' pike 'bout nine mile."

"I was goin' west. Man back there said I could strike off to th' westwards on this road."

"Mebbe so, but you got a better route taken'er outa Amherst. Goin' that way?"

Billy nodded and swigged down the rest of the ginger-beer. Back in the Territory such long-nosed gents sometimes got themselves bullets for answers. This must be a part of the, so-called, Eastern progress. Folks had a lot of time to overwork their curiosity bumps.

He mounted and rode off, leaving the storekeeper scratching at his ample bay window. He didn't trust storekeepers much—ever since Paddy Coghlan proved to be a coyote.

The road, he followed, led up among groves of timber, mainly oak, and on down through hollows bright with dogwood berries. It was so still the cheeping of crickets sounded like plucked fiddles. Flocks of crows pitched and dipped in ragged, black strings above The Kid and his horse.

The day arched high and brilliant. Its warmth sank deep into his dark garments, until he began to feel dull and drowsy. Riding off into a stand of maple, he swung down and tied the roan to a spice bush.

On all sides, the woods flamed with quiet frost fire when he lay down to catch his forty winks. The sky was a cloudless blue dome where the sun burnished the world.

He awoke to find the great golden sun burned away into a faded, hazy red star, and sinking fast into a smoky-purple bed in the Berkshires. A pair of jays screeched at him from a nearby tree, and an unseen crow cawed like a creaking windmill in the red light.

The next several miles took him past neat, painted farms, houses and barns clustered on hillsides like flocks of sheep. A farmer or two paused, milk pails in hand, to watch the strange horse and rider loping along in the pale, sunset light. A spotted dog followed for a time, at last sinking down into the dust to bay a farewell.

It was nearly dark before he reined up at a fork in the road, and peering through the gloom at a metal sign, nailed to a tree trunk, read "Home of Amherst College."

Billy traversed the elm-bordered street into the town, which sat upon a plateau, surrounded by half-seen ranges of hills. A pint-sized replica of Santa Fe.

He guided the roan, through the soft darkness, around several surries and hacks, and dismounted at a long, grey building, bearing the painted designation of Amherst House.

A group of well-dressed, young fellows in

tweed and sack suits looked The Kid over as he tied up at the hotel hitching rack. They had been lounging against the wooden pillars of the building, chuckling over some private joke. By the time the stable-boy appeared with his bobbing, yellow lantern, they had gone on up the boardwalk, whistling and gossiping.

Billy looked after them, rubbing his hand along the horse's flank, college students, no doubt. He was only a year or so older, but what a difference in educations! While they had been reaching at life around a stack of books—he'd wrestled his learning with a rope and a branding-iron. And, yes—with shooting irons.

He watched the stable-boy lead the horse toward the alley stables. If the old gambler *Destino* had dealt a different hand, he might have been born here in the East—grown up and gone off to some such school town as this, or even that Harvard. *Si*, he could have studied the law like Mister McSween and then come back to a comfortable marriage with the mayor's daughter—like one of those Oliver Optic heroes. But, he mused, he'd never have known the wild surge of freedom that filled him each time he'd ridden the windy mesas.

Because he knew no one in this peaceful place, and had nothing to do, Billy ate supper and retired early. The night was cool and the bed warm. But for a time he was restless. The old, nearly-healed wounds still troubled him—and he kept wondering about "The Buffalo"—and seeing, again, that man going out the Elephant's Eye.

34   Forbidden Fruit

Rising later than usual, Billy was the sole occupant of Amherst's American House taproom. He browsed through the tavern's copy of the Springfield Republican, now and then slapping a fly away as he munched at his pancakes.

He finished up his breakfast, paid his bill and went out to take a stroll in the bright Indian summer weather. Amherst was, for a fairly small town, active with groups of people, mainly townfolk, milling about the shops and streets, along with the college students. As it was a Saturday, farmers were commencing to arrive in neatly kept, red-wheeled wagons and fringe-topped surreys, filled with scrubbed-up children in clean white collars and topped with yellow straw hats.

The farmers, and they seemed to be a power of them, hitched their rigs to railings lining the grassy town square, and talked crops, politics and weather in voices that seemed to come from the end of their long noses. Farm wives chattered at the edges of the boardwalks, hair pinned up under new black straws and calico bonnets. The farm children romped about within the town square, or stared at the town kids.

Billy went into the stable behind the American House to inspect his horse. He'd decided to call it

Cabra, or Goat, after that Springfield liveryman. That tricky sidewinder, who looked like a goat, tried to make a goat out of The Kid. But Billy had got his goat good when he rode the wild little roan to a fare-thee-well.

He rubbed Cabra's nose, while the wall-eyed stable-hand leaned on a cracked pitchfork and gaped.

"Kin I do anythin' fer yer, Mister?" He cocked his head at The Kid.

"Nope—you're doin' a good job." Billy flipped him a quarter.

"Leavin' today, Mister?"

"Don't know. I'll let you know. Why?"

"They's big doin's at th' college. You heard o' Amherst College? Sorta harvest festival. Nigh big as th' Dairy Show. Speaker's comin' clean from Bahston. Lotsa folk stayin' overnight."

The Kid slapped the roan a farewell. Coming out of the mote-sparkled interior of the barn, he pulled his watch and squinted at it. It was close to ten o'clock and a long way to noon. He was getting dry from those flapjacks. If he were a drinking man, he'd take a couple at the taproom. But water would do for him.

He'd gone a couple of blocks west from the business district and the crowds, and was leaning against a tall, white board fence that enclosed a church-yard, when his attention was taken by a cluster of red flecks, dancing in the breeze—

ruffled trees across the street. It was a sight to make his mouth water for a bit of one of those shining apples.

A woman's voice, crying out in a high Irish brogue, fetched Billy up short. A plump, youngish woman, dark hair skinned back in a knob, dressed in a striped, grey dress, was down on her knees in the dust. Potatoes were scattered about her and a sack of meal had burst open in a stream of dry gold. A dented coal-oil can rolled toward Billy's feet.

"Hold on, Missy. Don't rile yourself." Billy knelt in the road, piling potatoes back into her broken-handled market basket. "We'll have th' vittles rounded up before you can say Howly Moses."

"Oh, no need, sor, to git your honor's pantaloons all be-dustied so!" The woman redoubled her attempts to scoop food from the dirt before the approach of a slowly moving wagonload of country-folks. "There, now—that's got it all, an' a t'ousand blessin's on you, sor!" She was up and clucking at Billy like a fussy little grey hen, endeavoring to balance basket and can.

"Nope, you'll tip over th' kaboodle." Billy caught the basket from her. "Where'd you be goin'?"

"Right acrost there." She pointed toward the apple trees. "It's house-maid I am for thim folk—but," eyes darted from Billy to a tall, brick house, banded by a thick, green hedge to the west of the orchard. "Me ladies will git into a tizzy if you should sot foot there. The darlints have no husban's and all by thimselves, save a brother next door, and him outa town for the week. They just don't niver have company."

"I'm no company." Billy started off for the place. "I'll tote this to th' back door and who's th' wiser?" He'd have himself a couple of those apples on the way back out. He could taste them now.

The servant girl tagged him through the front gate and up a brick walk to the back porch. Nothing stirred but the boughs of a clump of pine trees near the house. An odor of pine needles, sun-warmed brick and old wood hung in the air. It was mighty quiet.

"T'anks agin, sor!" The maid set down the can and took the basket. She stared closely at The Kid, opened her mouth to speak, but turned to the open porch door. When she came back out, Billy was already down among the fruit trees that stretched between the brick house and a large, white, wooden mansion in the next lot toward town.

Feeling as though he was about to raid Chisum's range, Billy looked around. The servant girl was out of sight. Nothing moved in the hushed morning, except a flock of chickens, chasing wind-tumbled leaves around the corner of a small, brown barn at the rear of the brick home. The hedge muffled sounds of road and town. All was peaceful. Pale-gold autumn air was mourning softly among the pines.

He reached up and tugged a big, red-faced beauty from the nearest branch. Ah, that was *bueno*! The skin snapped, tart apple-flesh crinkling under his tongue. The spicy juice slipped down his half-parched throat. He bit off a second delicious chunk—but didn't chew.

A small, red-haired woman, the size of Paddy Coghlan's *Madama*, popped up in front of him—out of the ground—or the trees, he wasn't sure. The apple hung in one hand and his hat in the other. He took a second look and decided she'd come around an angle of the hedge.

She stood for a moment, holding a red-checkered apronful of apples out from her white dress, and looking at Billy with startled doe-like eyes, seemingly about to dart away.

"M'am, I hope you'll pardon the intrusion?"

"Mine, or yours?" Her voice was high, breathless.

"Ah—I was just leavin'—and felt—."

"Like Daniel surrounded by ravenous red lions?" The voice was odd. It shot right up, like an arrow, from the first word to the last.

"No. M'am—Miss? I gave your servin' girl a hand up, and was sort of dry for some apple juice."

"Ah—I think you thirst after a liquor never brewed—besides you have broken one of our Heavenly Father's commandments." Those eyes were still doe-eyes, wary and bright, but now filled with something else, plain devilment. At first sight, she'd seemed a plain, middle-aged, little Yankee lady. An old maid, one might say. Now she sparkled like a girl. "Here, Barabus," she smiled, "take another—your choice."

"*Gracias*. Thanks, Miss." Billy stuffed a couple of the shining, red globes into his coat pockets.

"Don't be ceremonious—or you'll perish away in the midst of plenty. Replace your broadbrim and eat." Without another word, she flitted on up the path toward the pine-ringed brick house.

The Kid looked after the surprising little woman a long minute before pulling on his hat and chomping down on the apple again. He'd heard about *loco* New Englanders—probably the squeezed-up land they lived on.

He finished the apple, hauled out another, and was headed through a gap in the hedge when the little woman came bustling back.

Her red apron, free of apples, whipped about her slim form as she waved to him. "Could you wait?" Dark eyes glowed in her pale face.

"Yes'm?" Billy halted as she glided up. His hat was in his hand.

"Who might you be?" The question was as direct as the gaze from those startling, amber eyes. "I'd not pry into your affairs—but it's possible there could be a difficulty for you in our village." She added, almost under her breath, "Sister thinks I'm more daft than ever. And she might be right. You see, I never speak to any— strangers, least of all . . . but you are no stranger, are you—Peter Rugg?"

Billy saw a medium-sized woman in a dark dress, probably the queer lady's sister, looking toward them from the back steps of the brick house.

"Difficulty, M'am?" The Kid heaved the apple core at a scolding blue jay on the hedge.

"Not from such blue-coats as that." She twisted her apron in her fingers. "But . . ." Her words again climbed up to hang midway, like a misfired gun.

"Y'mean, your sister there would call th' police down on me for trespassin'?"

"We wondered who you might be—but never mind. There's a great many people in town today, they say."

Billy laughed. "No, M'am. I'm not even this here Rugg fellow . . . just, well—a nobody."

Her plain features suddenly were transformed with a smile that darted laughter creases to the corners of brilliant eyes. "You're nobody—and if that's true—why, then we're both nobodies, just we two!" She spoke with an affected, put-on air of an actress. Her arch voice, and upraised hands

341

brought a puzzled look to his face. And then she laughed, he knew, at his wary bewilderment. "Never mind, young Mister Stranger, just a twisted bit of versifying."

"Thought it might be somethin' of the sort," Billy replied. This peculiar Yankee female put him at sixes-and-sevens. He wondered if he wasn't on the grounds of the local loony-bin. But he was, somehow, taken with her, though she must be years older. And something about her prickled his scalp, like an approaching electrical storm on the mesas. "You was sayin'— difficulties, Miss?"

"I'm sorry," she murmured. "We see so few folk, I sometimes forget manners." And she cast her gaze downward at the footpath in a helpless, absent fashion. "Maggie, the hired girl you aided with the elusive groceries, heard talk in the village. There was mention of out-of-town authorities seeking strangers—at livery stables and taverns." She raised her piercing eyes to his and nodded her head toward the brick house, gleaming reddish-hair, neatly gathered at the back, reflecting in the sun. "You might best step into our kitchen. Someone might approach."

Billy was bothered by such talk. The anxiety in the woman's plain, yet oddly attractive face, disturbed him. It was just possible that "The Buffalo" or some other Ring snooper could have cut his trail—again.

"You mean you'd invite in a stranger? Y'know, I just could be some missin' man th' police was trackin'."

"I'm certain you are not, and even if you were, they should not take you." Her mouth tightened. "Captives are not inimical with life."

"Sure th' other lady won't mind?" He indicated the woman who'd returned to the back porch, peering at them from under her hand.

"No, Sister won't mind." She gave a clipped, little laugh. "But she's about ready to take a pitchfork to us—if we don't come up." And she set off up the path, red apron whipping flag-like about her small, erect figure.

The dark-haired woman, holding open the door, snapped, "Em'ly, I swear if you don't beat the Dutch!" Her black eyes glittered with excitement as she closed the door behind them, leaving The Kid to squint about the large, roomy kitchen.

Hazy air swam with wafting ribbons and reefs of spicy, pungently pleasant aromas. A large, iron cookstove loomed out of the dim light, its surface a hodge-podge of pots and kettles. Across the room, a large, wooden work-table was a sparkling mountain of fruit-jars, crammed with golden peaches and clotted with richly-red relishes. It all smelled fine.

Both women drew off to one side, whispering and peering out a window that overlooked the lot

343

opposite the orchard. Billy cleared his throat, and shifted the gun under his arm.

"Sit yourself. Sister wished to have you in for a spell, and . . ." The dark woman shrugged as if to indicate that such a thing was so unheard of to be amusing. Shooing a large, yellow cat from a cane-backed rocker, she pointed to its seat with a dominating forefinger. Billy sat.

"We're certain that you are not the man in question in the papers. But I've sent our Maggie back down the street for some more items and whatever she might be able to hear."

The Kid was taken aback at such hospitality. It could get these ladies into trouble, but they, apparently, couldn't care less. From the looks of the house and grounds, they stood high on the town's ladder as anyone. A real top-shelf old family. Gone to seed some but still quality.

"Maggie should be back shortly," the red-haired sister whispered, while the other woman busied herself around stove and sideboard, slicing bacon and cracking eggs.

Billy was served on a gold-rimmed, chipped plate, and ate at a small zinc-topped table by the back door.

"Hush! Here's our message from Chimbarazo," the little woman in white threw up her hands, pointing toward the window.

"M'am?" Billy answered around a jawful of food. This was an odd house. But nobody'd dragged him in. The eating was good, and it was an easy feeling to sit in the spicy-smelling semi-darkness. "Chimbarazo?"

"She means," the dark sister explained, with the patient air of one used to such things, "that our hired girl is coming and we'll have word on what's doing in our village?"

The back door opened and the broad-faced Maggie entered with several packages. "Oh, yez still have the young gent. That's good. They's gossip down to Cutler's store that a fella's ranging around wid a mouthful of questions."

"Well, Mister, you might as well fess up. If that fellow's looking for you, we'd like to know. You don't seem to fit any description in the paper, but . . ." The dark sister rapped an iron spoon on the edge of a bubbling pot of preserves, like a judge calling court.

"What would that signify, Vin?" The red-haired woman took the packages from Maggie. "Fugitives are notoriously inefficient at self-accusation." She winked a sherry-colored eye at Billy. "That's presupposing our Mister Mystery to be a fugitive. Actually, he's just a nobody."

"*Si*, that'll get me—just a tumbleweed blowin' west." The Kid scraped his plate and stood up. "Might you ladies be able to tell me how to get my horse fetched up, when no one's lookin' sharp?"

The dark sister picked up her yellow cat. "I'll

have our hired-man go down and get it." She raised her voice, "Tom! Tom Kelly."

A broad barrel of a man, in overalls, stepped in, from an adjoining room off the kitchen, with a hefty chunk of stove-wood in his red fist.

"No, Thomas! This gentleman is what our pastor used to term 'sound'—just a visitor from a far away place called out of sight." The little white woman lifted a pale-moth hand, and prompted by The Kid, gave instructions for paying his livery bill. The man took the money from The Kid, bobbed his wide, whisker-fringed face and departed.

While Billy waited, he sat by the window, facing the rear and side doors, turning his hat in his hands. The white lady excused herself, almost inaudibly, and slipped off into the interior of the big house. Miss Vin, the sister, and the hired girl, kept at the preserve making, saying nothing—though Billy noticed Maggie smiling shyly at him, when her mistress had her back turned.

With little to do, save swap grins with the hired girl, Billy looked over a Josh Billing's Farmer's Almanac hanging on the wall, and read the motto for October, over and over: "When a man gits to going downhill, it duz seem as tho everything had been greased for the okashun."

Could that apply to himself? His own life, lately, had been extra full of upsets and downright near disasters. He winked at the yellow cat, who sat staring green-eyed at the rocker. Who'd have thought he'd be riding the grub-line in Massachusetts, or squattin' meek-like in some kitchen, watching Yankee females make sasses?

He kept a sharp eye on the doors and windows. No telling about these folks—obliging but a mite *bizarro*.

A bell jangled on its hook over the pantry door. The hired girl wiped red hands on her apron and went into the front of the house.

Billy unbuttoned his coat—but Maggie returned almost at once. "The neighbor lady's come to play the pianny."

Sounds of music began to drift gently back through the tall, old rooms. It sounded nice to The Kid. He lounged back and listened as song after song rippled in the distance. He couldn't make out any of the tunes, all high-toned but mighty soothing.

"A professor's wife from the college comes in each week and sits in our parlor playing for sister," the dark lady suddenly addressed Billy.

"Right neighborly. Does she want you folks to go listen with her?"

"Oh, no. Sister's in the upstairs hall—says distance rings more sweetly." She bustled around, getting down a silver tray. This she dusted and placed a small glass on. She filled the glass from a dark bottle, with what looked like weak tea. It certainly wasn't whiskey, he decided.

Maggie was about to carry the offering in to the unseen musician, when the red-haired sister floated through the door. Billy was sure a Yacqui Indian couldn't have spooked along any softer.

"This is my thank you." She placed a small, folded note on the tray, and stood to one side with her metallic red head tilted toward the sounds, like a robin listening for rain. Maggie, chin in the air, toted off the peculiar looking liquor and note as if she balanced a stack of twenty-dollar gold pieces on the tray.

"And you, Peter Rugg . . . Ulysses . . . Far-Traveler." The white lady beckoned him toward the pantry door. "I've an eye to see through you—and a point to pierce your cloak of mystery." She held out a needle and a spool of black thread. "Come into the dining room. The light is sharper there."

Billy tagged her into the other room. Covered chairs, so dark they were nearly black, stood about a rich-looking old dining table. Two plain but elegant side-boards holding metal candle sticks, that could have been silver, sat under a pair of paintings of stiffish, old folks in wigs and caps. These painted people looked blankly at The Kid. Faded and thread-bare curtains covered long, deep windows. From the dry, close air, smelling faintly of cloves and old cloth—it was even money that those windows were seldom opened—like the doors of this ancient house.

"Sit there and hand me your coat," she ordered him into a chair by the window, taking another. He sat down, blinking in the light.

"Ah, that must be your charger. We'll have to be nimble." Her voice took that high jump again.

Billy pulled the curtain aside, glancing out the window. The stocky hired man was just rounding the corner toward the barn. The Kid watched, but no one seemed to be following. "Just goin' outa sight."

"Ah, the ideal person—one that is just going out of sight." She held forth a hand, so pale and opaque it seemed he could see sunlight through it. "That's not an ineffable suggestion—rather a fact refined from years of observation."

She waited for his coat, while that music, louder now, but still dream-like, jingled away, and on and on, like breezes coming and going about the eaves of the old home.

He nodded and pulled at his coat. No use stalling. With the garment in his hand, he saw the shoulder was ripped again, where the threads had parted from the "Plumber's" slash.

Her swift glance took in the six-gun, hanging in its cradle, under his arm. She made no comment but placed the coat in her lap and began to mend the tear. The needle in her small, shapely hands handled the material with precision. She finished the last stitch and nipped the thread between white teeth.

"There, young Joseph. Your coat of wonder is complete again. Put it back on, before some alien eye peers too closely." Rising, she handed The Kid the neatly-mended piece of clothing. "It appears to cover a multitude of sins—not all of your own making, I'd hope." She motioned him out toward the kitchen. "It's goodness and mercy that sister Vinnie didn't find out your secret. She'd either have fallen over with a crash, or charged you in battle royal with her rolling pin."

The stocky Irish handyman rose up from a chair when they entered the kitchen to report no difficulty in picking up Cabra at the livery. "Nivir th' flicker of an eyebrow." He also reported that a fugitive escaped convict had been apprehended the day before near Boston. The news was in the Springfield paper, just arrived on the mail wagon.

Billy grinned and said nothing.

The two maiden ladies smiled back, while the servants smiled at each other.

So, there wouldn't be any hue and cry over fugitives, but he didn't know who the nosey stranger up town might be. If it weren't "The Buffalo" it was probably someone like him. It wouldn't pay to linger.

"Here's some provender for your saddle bag," the dark sister held out a neat little bundle of food, wrapped in a Springfield paper, as Maggie smiled bashfully behind her. "Take it and get along with our good wishes. You might be able to reach Ten Mile Tavern by sunset. That's due west. You said you were heading that way?"

"Yes'm, headin' that way, for a spell." He wouldn't let everything out. Who knew what she'd say, after he was gone—he could see the bunch found him sort of different, himself. And the red-haired lady, where was she again? Probably tiptoeing back down the hallways to listen to that visiting lady piano-pounder.

Suddenly the little red-haired woman was back. "Here's a pair of just germinated gratitudes, for your kindness to Maggie." She handed him two folded bits of paper. She'd kept mum about his six-gun, so far.

He didn't quite know what to say, but accepted the notes and stuffed them into a pocket. "*Gracias*, Ladies. I'll remember you in my will, if not my prayers."

Outside, he took the Goat's reins from the handyman, who'd gone to the barn and led the horse up the drive that circled the place. The day was greying up, and wind commencing to shrill through the pines and over the roof of the tall, old home—rain before nightfall.

That phantom piano still echoed through wind-hum and the empty rooms of the house, but no one paid it much attention.

"Straight up the road there, that's the way to

your West." The little white lady smiled at him, while the dark sister and Maggie stood on the porch.

Mounting up, he pulled off his hat, gave them a real Mexican *saludo*, and kicking Cabra in the ribs, went racking away. Turning into the main road past the close-grown hedges, he looked back.

The small woman in white was still standing in the drive, shading her eyes against the fugitive autumnal sun as it slanted through the wind-herded clouds. A shimmering beam, bronzing her gown, encircled her head with a coppery halo.

An odd little Angel—in the westering light. Well, Angels were where you found them. *No es verdad?*

35 Two Rivers

The remaining daylight hours after leaving Amherst, Billy rode across rolling land, flaring with fall shadings and studded every few miles with small hamlets.

At nightfall, the rain, which had hung over the countryside, began to descend, and he was glad to hole up in a rambling, wooden tavern at a place called Deacon's Crossroads—five miles beyond Ten Mile Tavern.

With his horse snug in the tavern barn, Billy clambered into bed right after supper. He pulled a blazing star quilt up to his chin and tried to make head-or-tail out of the little, old maid's messages, or notes—or whatever.

He peered at them through the lemon-tinted glow of the coal-oil lamp for a full hour, but was no nearer to puzzling out the two pieces than when he started. Poems they seemed to be, but what they meant, he'd have to sleep on them.

He lay with the words stampeding around and around in his head, in a sort of pattern wavering with the cold October rain. They could have something to do with him, but blessed if he could exactly see what. He would have to show them to The Angel—Esmeralda. In a couple of weeks or less, he'd be there to hold her and—he turned over again on the lumpy straw-filled mattress and listened to the rain beating—beating in time with those jumbled, irritating scraps—

"A wound that numbs the cloth
"Of cloaks long used to hide
"Shall only be encompassed
"When truth is verified—
"And thread to mend such fact
"Needs inventive seamstress' art
"To drive the needle true
"And bind a wand'ring heart."

The other came to him, all sleepy gibberish, and yet not quite.

"Take this sign to follow
"That you might know—
"Hope oft falls distressed
"Until the best
"By Fate's
"At last compressed."

Next morning was wet and muddy, but The Kid managed to buy a second-hand slicker from the paunchy, wart-faced barkeep, and wearing it, rode at such a steady, slogging gait along the West Hadley Road, that he was in the little burg of Becket, among the cloud-cloaked Berkshires by night.

He traveled through dripping wet forests of fir, cedar, hemlock and spruce in the mountains, and descended through stands of white birch into valleys thick with beech and hornbeam. Occasionally he paused to let Cabra water in some small, fast-flowing, icy rivulet, where trout flitted their way upstream like frost-painted leaves, brilliant under the clear water.

There were farmsteads, even along the mountain edges, corn-shocks dotting the fields like the brown bush hogans of the Apaches. The villages were just the opposite of those untidy, sleepy, dusty hamlets in the Territory, but their neat, spare precision seemed unreal in a picture book way.

The tell-tale church spire, poking its white finger at the low, rolling clouds, signalled each village before Billy could discover the buildings among the trees.

All major streams were spanned by covered, peak-gabled, wooden bridges. Several times he was held up by a toll gate, but the keepers were sober and silent, unlike some Easterners. Billy thought mountain folks generally seemed able to mind their own business.

Three days after leaving Amherst, The Kid rode down the main street of Castleton on the Hudson. He was glad to be out of the mountains, with their wet, bush-lined roads. Bad places for ambushes also.

The Hudson, flowing along, was the same broad, noble river that he'd traveled beside on that Limited—it seemed a year ago. It wasn't as large as the Mississippi, but it could make a dozen Rio Grandes.

He put up for supper at the Nassau House Hotel, giving himself a regular blow-out, after the plain meals in the mountain taverns.

Getting enough out of the roan to pay for passage money, he took the Hudson River Boat down in the evening. Ships were fast and hard to track.

He was sorry to part with the Goat. He'd have to wait a while before getting back into the saddle. But it had been *bueno*, while it lasted. That liveryman who bought the roan, got himself a fine, well-broken piece of horseflesh. The jaunt through the mountains had settled him down O.K.

The Kid wished the trip had settled himself, but he was starting to feel more jumpy with each mile he traveled—again.

The "Mary Powell" was a big, brand-new boat, and sailed the down-river trip in jig-time. Though she smelled of paint and new carpeting, he slept soundly as she made the rocky walls of the Hudson spin past in the misty October night. Out the frost-rimmed port-hole, a clipped and battered fall moon swam along in the river, only to drown in the thickening cloud banks.

Billy was in New York City by mid-morning. The rain had passed and though chill winds whistled along the docks, the sun's warmth grew with the passing hours. New York was the same mob—swarming badlands of brownstone. Its air was sharply pungent with the swirls of ten thousand chimneys, all serenely puffing over a city that was fenced and ringed by the little smoky, zipping Elevateds.

Unsure of who might be on the scout for him in the city, especially since he'd worked over another political boss, he lost himself in the hurrying, faceless crowds of plug-hats and bustles, taking a hack directly to the depot.

The Kid endured the next four days on the rocking, creaking train coaches with the resignation of an old traveler. He ate and slept without calling any more attention to himself than he could. He didn't want any more talkative drummers, or knock-down conductors.

He spent the majority of his time reading through the papers from headlines to obituaries. There was nothing more about the fracas at Coney Island, but plenty about a hydrophia-mad skunk called Guiteau. This loony was due to be tried in mid-November for shooting the President. The man's lawyers claimed him to be insane, and he couldn't be anything else. All assassins were sick or mad or plain black-hearted like those Ring snakes.

The papers told of a gunfight, or massacre, down in Arizona at a town called Tombstone. A bunch called "the Earp Gang" was accused of shooting down some unarmed cowboys. He'd vaguely heard of the Earps, part-time policemen and gamblers.

And they were still having troubles in New Mexico Territory, according to the papers. Some wild-cat named Stockton seemed determined to wipe out everyone concerned with his brother's death. The Kid vaguely knew him, also, as the fellow'd ran a small-time saloon in Lincoln before the Lincoln County troubles.

The Kid knew how this Stockton felt.

Staring at the bare fields and withered woods of Ohio, he thought of the way the Ring had corked him up in their bottle—plain railroaded him. He could still see the Judge who'd done the Ring's dirty legal work at his trial.

Yes, he could still see Bristol's old grey head bobbing over his battered law books, lowering at The Kid like a mossy-horned old steer—old Bristol's nagging, buzzing drawl, hammered and hewed at the all-Mexican jury—and they followed him—didn't dare dispute the old sidewinder, when he as much as told them that Billy was guilty because he was a member of the posse that had fired at the, so-called, Sheriff Brady—though he, The Kid, claimed that he'd fired at another man that day in Lincoln.

Brady was dead, all right, and old Bristol had tried his damndest to nail The Kid's coffin shut with such legal mumbo-jumbo as: "that such fatal wound was inflicted by the defendant from premeditated design to effect Brady's death, or that he was present at the time and place . . . he then and there encouraged, aided, advised or commended such killing . . . he was as guilty as though he fired the fatal shot." And Billy and his men were truly as much officers as that Ring-Toady, Brady, but *infierno*'s *impudente*—that was the way it went.

Si, any lawyer with sand could have secured him a retrial there and then—with just fifty dollars for court costs, but he, The Kid, didn't have even fifty cents, Garrett had seen to that. Shook him down for every *peso*; claimed it was for evidence.

Had the Ring been backing him instead of Major Murphy, Jimmy Dolan, and Jesse Evans and Company, they'd have had him out on "straw bail" in half an hour. But Bristol had won—and old Tom Catron, the Ring Prosecutor, had left the adobe court house at Messila, rubbing his hairy paws. "Well," thought The Kid, "let's see how he rubs them with bracelets on."

Billy was surprised when the train reached St. Louis and he found it was nothing but a big, overgrown country town on the tall banks of the Mississippi. He rode across town from the barn-like station to the steamer docks in a rubber-tired hack with two half-lit drummers. He stopped at a waterfront store just long enough to buy himself some more shirts, underwear and a valise to pack the stuff in.

After purchasing his ticket, he sent two wires—one going to Kate at the Castle Ranch and the other to Esmeralda in Santa Fe.

Kate's telegram read: "Miss Castle, Rock Springs, Wyoming Territory. Can you send rest of money? Need for good reason. Send care St. Charles Hotel, New Orleans."

He'd heard a porter on the St. Louis train extol the St. Charles at Connors and St. Charles streets as a "mighty fine place." But if the money wasn't forthcoming he wouldn't be roosting there for long. Somehow he was betting that Kate would see he got the money.

Angel's wire, in care of the El Paso attorney, was short: "Miss Sandova. In New Orleans soon. On way to El Paso. Hope to have money for law work. Best Respects." He would have liked to have said more—oh, much more—but that would have to wait for a few days.

The Kid's boat, the "Jesse Dean," left the levee docks at St. Louis at high noon. The great, three-spanned St. Louis steel bridge sparkled in the sun as it arched from shore to shore behind the fanning wake, while the jumble of stone and brick buildings along the bluffs dissolved into the

360

smoky-haze from a hundred steamboat stacks.

The big, side-wheeler drummed into the middle of the channel, passing such slower river traffic as flat-boats that floated along among the snorting, busybody tugs and their barges. Other large, two-stacked steamers saluted them with willowy plumes of steam and hollow, bass whistle salutes.

Though Billy had picked his passage at random from the steamship offices on Front Street, his ship was a fast packet and freight steamer, making only half the stops required of most other vessels.

The white and gold-trimmed river queen scornfully trailed her black pennants of smoke past such ordinary, picayune landings as Wilkinson, Commerce and Cottonwood Point—all cluttered with shanty boats and grimy little stern wheelers.

The "Jesse Dean's" imperious blasts summoned up hard-faced roustabouts at landings as seemed worth her time and trouble, such as Natches and Baton Rouge. At these places she took on a few well-dressed passengers, and some freight, but no cotton or timber.

The Kid was bunked in a small, narrow but grandly decorated cabin on what his steward designated as "de poht" side. The encouraging fact that he was located far forward of the boilers was pointed out to him by a hefty, whiskered farmer. This gent, who termed himself a "planter," slept in the cabin across the maroon carpeted hallway, and was on his way to what he called the "Crescent City." He explained to Billy that if one perched above the boilers, it would be a "mahty nigh thing" should they let go.

The purser announced that the following afternoon would find the "Jesse Dean" at New Orleans, as the captain had decided to bypass Port Hudson because of a shifting channel.

The sun seemed to glow with increased strength by the hour—gone was the chill and drizzling fears of the North—and even the alligator-haunted jungles of the upper-river—all burned away in the golden green of Deep South.

Left to himself, The Kid sat on the upper deck, musing on the lazy, uneventful, peacefulness of the trip, sunning himself and listening to the slow, musical voices of the deck hands—listening to the twanking banjos, and taking in the passing curves and sweeps of the ever-widening river.

The blue of the sky, overhead, was a half-heard song—blending, somehow, with all boat and river sounds. Billy tipped his gaiters against the railing and pushed his broad-brimmed hat over his eyes to cut the flashing, water glare—seemed he was in New Orleans—no, it was another place and the tapping sounds rising above the rumbling beat of the paddles was a gavel—a court-room gavel—

. . . "and gentlemen of the jury . . . all things change . . . remember . . . that! The Yanks burned down the place, McSween's place, the Yank soldiers . . . and fired, along with Murphy and Dolan's assassins, at Billy Roberts, alias Bonney, alias Henry Antrim, alias Kid, alias Billy The Kid, alias Texas Kid, alias Far-Traveler . . . but I digress."

He saw the face of Judge Bristol. It was grey with anguish—and a figure, with hidden features, stood behind the Judge with an open book—his book—the black Ring Book, now large as a family bible, and inscribed in letters of twisted fire—each name in the book that of a Ring Man. And as the Judge read the names, those men, hog-tied, with the ropes already around their necks, marched past the bench of the court. "And may God have mercy on your souls . . . on your souls . . . on your souls." And Billy knew these men—all the Ring Men. He saw Garrett trudging past—and Paddy Coghlan—and Rynerson—and Catron. They were going to die. And he was free, at last. Free at last!

The bell rang for the execution—rang again—and a voice called over and over . . . "New Orleans . . . New Orleans 'round the bend. New Orleans."

New Orleans! He rose to his feet, staring with delight. Off there, just a state away—an Angel in El Paso!

36   Basin Street

The St. Charles Hotel, certainly, was "a mighty fine place."

Billy spent ten minutes and five dollars before the thin faced, languid clerk could summon up enough energy to do more than finger at his sparse, blond sideburns. Clearly this fine place had more customers than rooms. New Orleans, the clerk yawned, was in the midst of a boom, with hundreds of winter visitors.

"Last few yeahs we receive many folk here durin' the winter months," he sniffed. "Visitors says this is the comin' thing. Wintering, they call it."

"Be all right if they can stand the gaff." Billy paid up for a day and a night, after the clerk recalled a small, fourth-floor room.

By tomorrow there'd certainly be a wire from Kate with the money. If it didn't come, he'd be bogged to the saddle skirts.

The day ebbed quietly. He took supper in a restaurant on a nearby street. It was completely New Orleans-Creole from its trim, black-eyed waitresses, in their short, puffed scarlet skirts, to the food-steaming, delicious Pompano, with its side-order of red-beans and rice. He turned down the soft-shelled crabs and crayfish—too much like spiders.

He spent the remainder of the evening wandering about the half-lit streets, past pink and yellow houses, where plaster peeled away to disclose ancient, orange-tinted brick. He passed tall, three- and four-storied, wooden buildings all fringed with elaborate, wrought-iron balconies. And wherever he went, he wasn't worried about anyone on the lookout for him. The Ring was out of it—by a thousand miles, and would be—until he called the turn, himself.

In a way it was like Santa Fe, but there was a different look and smell, and feel to the place. The air was vaguely misty with mellow, sour-wine odors of river, trees, shops and the many odd smells that had their genesis in Deep-South cooking. The wind, ambling up from the basin and harbor, puffed fitfully through the evening, rustling and swaying the tropical looking trees and palms.

It was unlike New York or Boston, this New Orleans, and yet also different from towns of the Southwest. In spite of its languid charm, he would be glad to leave the lovely old place and get along toward El Paso. And in the morning he could be on his way.

About eight o'clock, as he wandered along, a mile from his hotel, the air began to lose its balmy warmth, and the chill of the river crept up the narrow streets.

He stepped into a little restaurant-coffee house

off Jackson Square to get on the outside of a hot cup of Arbuckle's.

Seating himself at a blue-checked table, he saw the place was also a barroom—and well stocked. Whiskey-guzzlers were separated from the coffee-sippers by a beaded-curtain, hanging midway down the room.

Customers passed through the jingling barrier from time to time, heading for the bar, or returning to the well-patronized tables.

Before Billy could gulp down the second mouthful of the odd-tasting, chickory-laced beverage, a row at the bar broke out. Peering through the shimmering beadwork, he beheld a smallish man, in a dark suit, topped off with a tremendously wide-brimmed Panama, who was gaining the better of an argument with a large, high-shouldered man—but about to lose out to a fist. That weapon of bone-and-muscle was being juggled under the little man's long, beaky nose by his hulking opponent.

The Kid, along with the rest of the patrons, mostly French-speaking Creoles, watched the sudden eruption and awaited its predictable conclusion. The small man, attempting to duck the descending fist, managed to knock two bottles and a half-dozen glasses from the bar, as he went down—either slipping or hit.

The big fellow, cursing mightily in a mixture of French and English, lifted his gunboat to give the scrambling little rooster a kick in the ribs—and took a coffee cup square in the head.

Billy's heave was a perfect bull's-eye! The unexpected blow distracted the bar-fighter long enough to let the man on the floor hop back to his feet.

"Blithering, blasted, baboon-faced blasphemer!" Here was another mad Irishman, with a brogue thick as Creole coffee. The spitting, little pugilist bored back into his reeling antagonist. "Divil take you—you blue-molded, double-gutted, moronic pot o' tripe! I'll teach you respect for French poetry, or . . ."

Billy cut the little man off in mid-air, as he leaped through the beaded-curtain to haul him out of the way. "Hold it, Mister!" He heaved his burden into a chair. "And you too!" He dodged a bottle. "Try that again—and you'll lose a couple of fingers!" The Colt was out and poked into the big man's whiskey-flushed face.

"Outa here—outa here!" The bartender and manager came running, waving white aprons, as if shooing chickens. "Outa here, you don' need *faire de diable a quatre* 'round here!" They shook their fists at the man in the chair. "Yo', Mister Hearn—we tol' yo', over an' over don' come arguin' aroun'—heh?"

Billy holstered his pistol and dragged the groggy little man toward a side door, clapping the oversize Panama *sombrero* back on his head.

The big battler slumped at a table, rubbing his bump of knowledge, glaring at them.

"Sorry. Here's for th' broken crockery." Billy tossed a dollar on the bar, supporting his limp burden with his left hand.

"An'—Mister Hearn—those two bottles go on yo' bill . . . an' don' forget it . . . ah, *prenez garde!*" The black-mustached manager wiped a sweating face with an apron as the bartender kept his in motion, herding them away.

Once outside, Billy leaned the man, called Hearn, against a damp, peeling side-wall. The fellow was ready for bed. He stared blearily at The Kid, from under that wide, flapping headgear and would have jack-knifed into the watery trickle of the unfragrant gutter—if Billy hadn't grabbed his coat collar.

"Many thanks, young noble sir . . ." he hiccoughed, and turning up the edge of his incredible hat, peered nearsightedly at Billy from an enormous right eye, twice the size of his left. "Many thanks for interjecting China into a discussion on France." He wavered on short, limber legs, clapped Billy on the shoulder and tottered off into the darkness. "C'mon! Avant! That thick-skulled orangutan back there could have whistled up the coppers by now." He hiccoughed again, and waited wavering. "You may have skinned that pig's snout with that cannon you produced out of thin air."

He was right. Drunk or sober, he was right. The Kid knew he'd get in Dutch flashing that Colt. Why was he always so damned ready to stick his nose into trouble? And he thought that the boat ride had settled him down. Getting proddier all the time—when he should be pulling his hole in after himself.

Hearn was still able to blurt his address to a passing cabman, and stumble into his seat with a death-grip on Billy's arm. The hack headed back toward the St. Charles and The Kid rode along. He might as well herd the little scrapper to his layout, seeing he'd rousted him from the bar.

It was a mistake! When the hackie reined in his fat cab-mare before a two-story, red-brick building at the corner of Gasquet and Robinson, Hearn flew into a rage at The Kid's attempt to leave.

Billy paid off the hack-man and helped the muttering Irishman up to his room on the front corner of the second floor. A big, battered, canopied-bed, reaching toward a cracked, yellowish ceiling, with the appearance of a rickety Prairie Schooner, contained enough room to sleep three a'breast. Billy's companion piled into it, gaiters and all, while loudly demanding The Kid spend the night.

He raised such an unholy row, filling the musty room with shanty-Irish, that Billy stretched along the other side of the bed in an effort to quiet him. He was determined to slip away from the curious situation as soon as the little "tarrier" dozed, but—it was The Kid, stuffed with Creole cooking and bone-weary from unaccustomed hiking, that slumbered first.

". . . I said . . . time for me to be off, Mister What's-the-Name." The voice was soft and modulated, with the tone of a gentleman. Billy opened his eyes to see a little gnome of a man, hovering over him. The stranger's face contained a polite, well-bred interest. Its outright handsomeness was partly marred by one, oversized pop-eye.

"I've a job. Newspaper," the stranger continued. "The Times-Democrat. I'm nearly late. Hearn is the name, and very sorry I am for whatever trouble I've put you through. I seem to recall you helping me to navigate homeward." He rubbed two, slimly graceful hands together. "Make yourself at home. I'll be back by three. And if you care to, and have the time, we'll go around to a few spots that might be of interest to you. You are new to town—tourist, I presume."

Billy raised up on one elbow. Before he could frame a serviceable reply, the man clapped that big mushroom hat upon his small head and was out the door.

The Kid got up. His gaiters were standing against the wall, and his coat hung neatly from a wall peg. That was a hell of a note! He felt for his gun—it hung under the coat. His money and the black book were safe and sound in his coat pockets.

He sank back upon the rumpled bed, scratching his head. Well, the St. Charles Hotel hadn't much of his business, yet.

An hour later he had washed and shaved himself with a razor discovered in a drawer. It was time for him to hit back to the hotel for that wire of Kate's.

But—there was nothing at the St. Charles. He went to his room, got his valise and checked out. Money was scarce. If he didn't come up with some, he grinned tightly, he might have to go to work—but at what? He had fare enough to get to El Paso, but nothing for that lawyer. Damn that Kate!

Being a newsman, this Hearn could probably give him tips on where to bunk and eat, until Kate came through with the money. He took a five-cent horse-car back to the little man's rooming house.

When Hearn returned at three-thirty, Billy, shoes off, was sprawled on the bed, pouring through a slim, red copy of "Spanish Gypsy Ballads," reading the Spanish verses and looking over the lively pictures. He'd dug this volume from a large box of books in a corner of the room.

"Still here? Good! Wondered all day about you. Not that I'm too inquisitive. Live and let live, eh? But my nose, it's curious—both curious-

371

appearing and filled with curiosity. Curiosity, that's how I make my living." Hearn tugged off his big hat and sank down in the room's only chair. "You're a bit more than a mere tourist." His eyes, one as big as a door-knob, stared at Billy.

"Well," Billy put down the book, got up and unbuttoned his coat, tossing it onto the bureau. "You're right, more or less. I've come here, to town, just long enough to pick up something, and get along to Texas."

"Thought so. At first I had you figured as one of those tent-show people, out at the Exhibition Grounds at Audubon Park. Out where they've got that wild-west, circus nonsense." His big eye stared like a saucer.

"Right fancy books you got." The Kid tried to change the talk. "Ever read anythin' by Bill Nye? There's a sport I'd give a new saddle to meet." He sat back on the edge of the bed.

"Nye . . . ?" The little man arose and taking a knobby pipe from the bureau, stuffed it full of tobacco from a blue jar. "Nye's a newspaper-man, I think, in Wyoming at one of the county papers. We get his stuff, sometimes. Clip it for fillers. Not bad either."

"That's nearly hell! I came from out that way, a few weeks back. I was there in the same territory . . . *le agrandezco mucho . . . la vida es sueño*!" Billy laughed and slapped his knee.

"Khayyam says, 'the moving finger writes and

having writ, moves on . . . nor all your piety nor wit shall not lure it back to cancel half a line.' " Hearn lit up with many a puff.

"Meaning, what?" Seemed like he'd herded in with another maverick, like that jabbering Polander at the Falls, or that murderous sport on the Elephant—or that odd, little old maid up to Amherst. Well, *su seguro servidor*.

"Meaning," puff-puff, "things are as they will be . . . no matter how we try to change them. Kismet, the old Persians called it. All as changeless as the great luminous Blue Ghost of the sky, hovering forever."

"Ah, *quien sabe*? Who knows, *si*?"

"Who knows, or who, knowing, can alter a moment or a movement?" Hearn sat back down again in the rocker. "You came from the West . . . Wyoming? Then you might be interested in that show I mentioned at the Exhibition Grounds. They had a standing offer, for a week, of a thousand dollars to anyone who could ride Black Beauty—the wildest stallion of the wild, wild West."

"A thousand? Well, maybe. I'd like to see that . . . th' horse, I mean."

"We can get out there all right, but tonight, perhaps, you might like to come along and visit some of our more typical New Orleans spots." Hearn motioned Billy out upon the wrought-iron balcony, pointing out several areas of the city—still brilliant in the yellow light of evening.

There curved the river, a sheet of elongated golden metal, all the way down to the barrel-and-bale-flecked wharves, where hundreds of smoke pillars stained the lemon-tinted air, and sailing ships masts bristled as thick as willow withes along a New Mexican stream.

To the north hulked the massive brick Custom House, lording it over the French Quarter's fragile buildings. And to its right lay Canal Street's acres of two-story buildings. Their delicate iron balconies and white shutters smudged with vines and growing shadows were flung open to the mild evening. Up beyond, rose-red with declining sun, stretched the newer business section.

Hearn pointed out a small building on Dryades Street, nearly indistinct in the last light, where he'd gone bust in the restaurant business.

With the coming of night, Hearn, good as his word, took The Kid upon a winding, curious trek of the haunts of high times and wide smiles. And he appeared to be known to all he met.

They dined upon plain, good steak and potatoes in a little shed-like eatery owned by a large, beefy, good-natured woman, Hearn addressed as a Mrs. Courtney. Later, full as ticks, they wended their way through the mazes of winding alleys and past old buildings festooned with iron-porches and flowerless vines. And in almost every open space, the ancient gnarled-strength of

374

live oaks patiently bore ragged sheets of Spanish Moss like tattered banners.

They visited several concert saloons, including the Conclave, the Buffalo Bill House and the Napoleon, along such streets as St. Charles, Royal and Chartres.

The Kid got Hearn home, without much ruckus, about two in the morning, and they bunked down the remainder of the night.

Billy slept late. These big, soft beds were getting to him. He used to roll out at daybreak, but maybe that was because the damned ground was always so hard.

Hearn had gone off to the newspaper office again, before The Kid had roused up.

The day was cloudy, with great fat, leaden clouds scudding in from the mouth of the Mississippi when he boarded a horse-car for the hotel.

He wasn't sure there'd be anything at the hotel. If there wasn't, he intended to mosey out to that circus grounds affair and take a look at that wild and woolly bronc.

Thinking over his chances for that thousand dollar prize, he entered the gold-and-brown elegance of the St. Charles lobby, and approached the desk.

Before he could open his mouth, a woman's voice called his name.

He turned—and there stood Kate Castle!

37   Spanish Moss

"Billy! Oh, I thought you might be gone . . . maybe that you . . ." Kate's blue eyes were two clear pools darkened with sudden excitement. Her face glowed with high color. Her vivid, scarlet mouth was half-open as she caught her breath and reached out a finely-gloved hand.

The Kid took her hand, despite his confusion at her unexpected appearance. "Kate! Miss Castle—you didn't need to come way down here just to fetch that money." He felt the slim, pliant fingers tense in his grip. "I mean, I'm right sorry to have to ask for any of it. But things have just been breakin' against me . . . and I thought . . ." His words were left in his mouth when she pulled back her hand.

Looking about the busy lobby, she indicated a plain leather and wrought-iron seat behind one of the brown and white marble pillars, near the doors. "Let's sit there. There's no need to stand about and be bumped by all these people."

He looked her over as they crossed the floor to the secluded seat. She was all in blue and white, a striped gown, mighty tight fitting. And her bustle, larger than some and smaller than others. Just right!

"I'm sure certain surprised to see you." He kept

his hands on his knees as they sat on the bench. Her eyes were no longer wary, now they were warm and full—full of what he was afraid of seeing—tenderness. She was pretty as a spotted calf, more so than he'd remembered, but he had to cut this short, and not too sweet. He hadn't asked her to chase him over half of the country. "You got my money—like I said, sorry to ask but right now I need it bad!"

Kate's face was serious. Her blue eyes—how long and dark those lashes were—grew remote. She folded her white-gloved hands in her smooth lap, and glanced around the pillar at a party of well-dressed people just coming into the lobby with a great deal of baggage, and noise.

"Winter people. Papa tells me that New Orleans is getting the name—Venus of the South. More folks coming down each season. We were here three years back."

"I wouldn't be here now, if I had the where-with-all to move on."

"Oh, Billy, I feel so bad about that."

"What'd you mean? Y'got my wires and that there card."

"Yes. The card was from Nebraska, and the telegrams, yes." She placed a hand on his. "But what I'm trying to say, is that there just isn't much money yet. Papa wasn't able to collect the money owing him. And he's so involved with those men in Santa Fe—it's impossible for him to keep his head above water, without them. It was a mistake, that ranch. I guess Uncle Morris gave him too many ideas."

"No money? Well, what'd you spend gittin' down here?" The Kid was getting more riled by the minute. It was all he could do to keep from grabbing this good-looking, chattering female and lambasting her overstuffed rear. No money? What in hell was he to do? *Cornudo infierno*!

"I know it was foolish, but I thought, that maybe, you and I—could, well . . . If we were together . . ." She broke off and pulled at a thread on those white gloves. "I've up and ran off from our ranch . . . I just wouldn't stay there another day. I wanted to see you."

"You picked a mighty poor time to come. You know, or maybe you don't, that I'm tryin' to get enough money to get my name cleared in th' courts . . . at least th' Texas Courts. And maybe in New Mexico too. That probably first." He cleared his dry throat, and shifted his feet. "I was in some trouble, back a year ago—or less."

"Yes." She smiled that warm smile. "I know you had some trouble, the night you left the ranch." Her eyes took quick fire. She seized his hand again, with an almost possessive clasp. "Billy, I've a confession. I can't beat about bushes. I'm not that way. I've a confession . . . I know who you are! And it doesn't matter. That's why I'm here."

"Who I am? Why, Miss . . . ?"

"Kate!"

"Kate, you mean—you know?"

"Pretty much everything. I knew you're the one called The Kid. Billy The Kid! But I don't care. I didn't know what you did to those men in Santa Fe. They're partners, in a way, with Papa—and own part of his ranch. But," she whacked him on the knuckles with her gloved hand, "one of their men came to our place, about a week after you left. A mean looking cowboy. Tall and with a face like spoiled milk."

"Cully!" Billy clamped his jaw shut. Cully, he was certain. So, that tarantula from Hole In The Wall had got through the posses after their Deadwood robbery. What'd he pried out of Bullhead—before that Ring man cashed in? Must have been something, for sure!

"He called himself Crosson, George Crosson," Kate continued, ignoring Billy's scowl. "He hired out but only worked a week for us. Somehow he had a line on you. I was curious about him, and his questions. I trailed him into town a week back, and found that he'd sent off some telegrams. I got the agent to let me read them. And when I did, I got ready and left."

So—that was how they got the word to New York, and how the devils could be on his tracks, again, even down here. It was hard to believe—but it seemed the Ring wasn't going to let up

379

until they had their damned notebook, or he was six feet under—or both!

"Think he's on his way down here?" Billy chose to ignore the fact that this girl knew him—as The Kid—or knew enough to have him turned over to the first lawman who came along.

"He's here now." Her mouth was a firm, red line. And her eyes, two blue watchful pools. "He either followed me, or he was on his way before I started. I saw him two hours ago at the depot."

"Come on." The Kid pulled her up and hustled her through the door. "Where you registered?"

"Back there in this hotel. I already checked in when I saw you come into the lobby."

Billy knew one place where they could be alone, for a while—Hearn's! They went there in a hack that cost a dollar, but he wanted speed. The Kid was getting out of sorts about his lack of money, but a dollar more wouldn't matter.

All the way back to Hearn's, Billy tried to keep on his side of the hack. But Kate's perfume wrapped about him and he couldn't keep from feeling that young, but firmly-rounded thigh against his hip. The girl, herself, sat with eyes straight ahead, chatting about the colorful streets, and the flamboyant people, both white and dark, thronging the sidewalks and doorways.

Arriving at 1565 Gasquet, they went up, Billy having explained his chance acquaintance with the newsman. Before he could open the door, a

380

deep, richly-Irish voice bellowed in their ears from the room beyond, chanting one of those Gombo songs Billy'd heard the night before.

"Mister Hearn," Billy pushed open the door for Kate, "this is a friend of mine from back out home."

Hearn peered up through his good eye, and hopped from the packing box by the west window that was his desk. Paper was scattered about, liberally covered with tiny, closely-written lines.

"Mister Roberts," he bowed until his beaky nose nearly scraped his boots. "I came home early to get some literary work finished and—to see you." His white teeth glinted under his scraggly, pointed mustache, as he turned to smile disarmingly at Kate. "I presume this is the package you were going to pick up on your way out to Texas?" There was no malice in his words.

Billy was surprised to find Kate smiling back at the gnomish, little man, after proper introductions. She was, probably, trying to figure out how such a voice could be jam-packed away in such a small space.

"Nope. We thought maybe you might have some idea where I could make a bit of money, sort of fast . . . but legal." Billy handed Kate to the chair, and winked at Hearn.

"That's what I wanted to see you about. Last night you spoke of needing extra money—any respectable way, you could get it. This morning

I talked to a press agent from the circus out north of town, and their offer just isn't going over. I told him I might have a man to give them a ride for their money."

"How'd you know I could burr onto a bundle of black-blasting powder like, they say, that horse is?"

"Just a feeling."

And Billy, who'd feelings of his own, knew it was a mighty good thing Hearn had been home, or *infierno*! Who knew what his suddenly renewed feelings about Kate could have got them into? Billy went along with Hearn's feelings. "*Si*, you're right. I'd be willing to give it a try!"

Kate, listening to the exchange, sat bolt upright. "Billy! If you go out there, you might be sorry. You know Crosson, or Cully . . . wouldn't he be apt to hang around such a place?"

"We'll just chance that." The Kid rose and pulled on his hat. "What time's th' next show?"

By the time the three arrived at the Grounds, Sells Brothers' Combined Oriental Circus and Great Western Round-Up was in full swing, brass band filling the Louisiana breezes with outlandish sounds.

Hearn had insisted on coming with Kate and The Kid. His old-fashioned bows and great, wavering swoops with his mushroom hat tickled the young girl. Both were chattering of books and poets, noisy as a pair of mountain jays when the horse-car clanked into the circular track, fronting the Exhibition Grounds. Hearn, Billy noticed, had a fine eye, if only one, for the ladies.

Ten minutes later, with the Colt in Kate's handbag, Billy stood with his foot on a rough, wooden tent-peg in the roped-off stockade behind the main tent. Kate and Hearn were seated within.

Inside the canvas arena's ring, the walrus-mustached Ringmaster waved his black slouch hat at the audience, barking to all and sundry that Sells Brothers' Combined Oriental Circus and Great Western Round-Up proudly presented—"an attempt to conquer Black Beauty—the unbeatable, unmanageable, unrideable, bellicose, belligerent bronco of the boundless Brazos . . . never ridden before by man, cowboy, cossak or polack!"

The crowd, shifting on the hard pine slab seats, inside the tent, answered his oration with a medley of hoots, screams, yelps and out-and-out fancy cursing in Creole French and drawling English.

The Kid gathered that such announcements had been going on all week. Boasts were made but the rides never came off, the prospective horsemen all getting second-thoughts after they got a good look at the flashing teeth, frantic heels and flaring wild eyes of the black horse.

Billy, listening to the spiel, heard himself proclaimed as a "sturdy plainsman and rancher from out in the wildest and most woolly part of the Panhandle. An honest to goodness ex-ranger and posseman who can stick to fly-paper, molasses—or his best girl, and who is, unfortunately, about to meet his match with that black streak of four-footed lightning! But give him a rousing send-off and a bully big hand—the Texas Kid!"

Billy had presented the Ringmaster with that moniker—what else could he call himself?

There were volleys of hoots and obscene demands for the ride to get under way. The crowd, mainly levee toughs and dock-pounders, in derbies, pink shirts and checkered pants, out with their painted ladies, for a holiday, were in the majority, but some of the better class of New Orleans' citizenry sat as a minority in the brawling, cheering audience. All were vociferously glad of a break from seedy lions and uninspired clowns. This might be the high spot of the show if the new rider could stick.

With Kate and Hearn among that boisterous, jeering, jostling throng, it was time to see if he could match mouth with action. He kept his coat buttoned, wouldn't do to let that holster show. He stuck the black book in his hip pocket, and buttoned it up. He was ready.

Two roustabouts held the horse, a jug-headed stallion with two white front feet. It had an eye as wicked as Flat Nose Curry's. Billy could tell a real outlaw when he saw one, but he was going to make the ride or bust. It was a horse with plenty of spirit, in spite of the obvious beatings and mistreatments.

The black stood snorting, head down as The Kid adjusted the stirrups of the center-fire saddle. The stallion's barrel seemed mighty large. Billy eased off and punched it one with his fist. The horse stepped sideways, lashing out, barely missing a gawking lion-tamer, who backed away with a white face.

The Kid hauled in the cinch before the brute could blow himself out again, and taking the reins, mounted. One roustabout, held the canvas curtain open as the other poked out a head, waving toward the Ringmaster.

There was sudden, simultaneous motion of Billy's heels, the ape-like Ringmaster's whip, the horse's legs and flying roustabout—kicked ten feet by the richocheting stallion.

A roar exploded from the waiting crowd, as horse and rider burst into ring-center in two bounds.

Billy knew he was on a bad one. So bad, though he'd already discovered the bronco had a tender mouth, he was unable to keep from applying tension to the slashing reins in those first, jarring right-angled bucking jumps.

Hearn and Kate later insisted the ride lasted just over a minute, but those sixty seconds were sixty days on an exploding volcano—shaking him with such ferocious violence that the sunfishing, twisting leaps ripped red-lightning through his shoulder.

By the time he'd sawed the frantic beast back from a head-on crash into the mid-ring bleachers, he felt blood trickling down his back. With each succeeding, smashing bound, that shoulder wound was re-opening.

Horse and rider thudded around and around the roaring ring. At least a dozen times the blurry-eyed Kid sawed back on that pain-tender mouth—but he'd not break his neck if he could help it—pulled up again and again instants before the half-mad bronco could crush them both into the scrambling, shrieking audience.

Those bastards in this show certain knew what they were up to when they laid a thousand-dollar bet that nobody could stick on the black devil for a finish—almost!

Despite each pawing, bounding, swooping, corkscrewing jump—he stuck. With his head nearly yanked off—and shoulder a white-hot misery—he stuck. He stuck until the horse slowed, bounced, jarred and plain quit, to stand heaving and trembling by the center pole of the clamor-filled tent.

When the audience in their swinging, circling seats came back into focus, he made out Kate and Hearn, waving and yelling with the rest.

Hearn, flinging about his big tent of a hat, couldn't see ten feet ahead of his nose, but was kept posted on the performance by Kate.

The Ringmaster, looking as though he'd lost his fourth wife, handed Billy a dirty roll of ten, compressed, hundred dollar bills. "Ladees and Gents—this'll go down in the whole history of circusdom, or any other aggregation under the big top or bright blue sky— the time that the unbeatable, unrideable, fleet-footed King of the Wild Horses was rode! The wild beast met his master!" He cracked his looping whip, puffing as though he'd done the riding.

"Any words to say?" He turned to Billy, who had just picked up his Stetson and was trying to block it out. "Any words to say? Quiet there! Please folks. Let'm talk. Any words, Mister Cowboy?" He backed off, lashing his whip at the New Orleans' riff-raff. "Please to give'm a chanst. The Texas Kid, folks! The rider who today has proved to the hull dummed univers't that he could outride Buffalo Bill, Gen'ral Custer and old Dead-Eye Dick!"

Billy took the wad, waved his hat stiffly at the crowd with his left hand, wondering if they could see blood on his coat. He motioned to Hearn and Kate, and turned back to the grimacing, sweating official. "Yeah, I got a word. *Gracias* for th' cash—but you oughta have that damned bull-whip wrapped around your neck for treatin' horses this way!" He stalked off through the churned-up sawdust of the ring.

He made his way through the bedlam of a crowd that pushed and yanked at him, yelling in French, Gombo-Creole and swamp English. He saw Kate standing up and pointing to a section a dozen rows away. Hearn's weak eye stared in the indicated direction, nose angled like a road-runner's beak.

Billy discovered a tall, skinny man, in a bright green suit and a high-crowned derby—Cully—and headed for him. He stopped. Kate had the gun, and he could see at least five police stationed about the interior of the tent at various passage-ways.

The Kid turned back, and elbowed into the subsiding crowd. Kate rose and followed but so did Cully. So far he hadn't approached any of the New Orleans' lawdogs.

Another racket split the air. The scarlet-uniformed brass-band at the far end of the arena began whaling out a tune as a pair of fat, white horses came lumbering out around the ring, bearing two small, dark, monkey-faced acrobats in orange tights. These performers were flipping from the yard-wide back of one nag to the other. The show went on. The Ride of the Century was over.

Billy saw Kate turn back to Hearn, as he, himself, eased out under the raw-pine bleachers into the back lot. The newsman had his nose straight in the air, like a little, snuffy-nosed coyote. Cully passed within an arm-length of the Irishman and that big, Panama hat swooped up and landed down on the high-roller's head. Hearn crammed it down amid the howls of the crowd, now torn between the acrobats—and this new impromptu side-show.

The girl and Hearn darted down the few steps into the gangway and out of sight as a policeman started over to investigate the extra disturbance.

The Kid waited for them at the edge of the car track. He was leaning against the trunk of a live-oak. Fronds of grey moss hung down into his face, and trailed over his shoulder—blood soaking the tip of a fringe. His face was as grey as the wind-wavered fronds.

"Billy!" Kate reached him just in time. Together, the girl and the hatless Hearn held up the sagging Kid.

"Hell of a way to earn a livin'." Billy grinned and weaved on his feet long enough for them to hoist him into a home-bound car. No one had left the Circus Grounds—yet.

He came to on Hearn's bed. Kate was wringing out a torn shirt that looked like Hearn's. "You'll be all right, now. Mister Hearn's doctor friend, Doctor Matas was here and patched

389

you up. But you have got to lay there and rest."

"Don't mind if I do." He grinned slightly at the pair, as his strangely-heavy eyelids insisted on closing. That Doc sure had spiked his drink.

38 El Paso

The Kid remained corralled in Hearn's big, canopied bed for two full days following his successful but punishing ride of the Circus Bronc.

While Hearn was at work, Kate came over from the St. Charles to keep him company. They talked over the events back at Three Rivers Ranch—the trip to Santa Fe, even laughing about some of the activities at Castle Ranch. Kate colored-up, and nicely The Kid thought, when his last night at her ranch was mentioned.

Billy told the lovely, young blonde as much as he dared of his trip eastward, omitting some of the more lurid details.

Hearn fetched Gombo and other Creole dishes to The Kid from Mrs. Courtney's, all smelling of peppers and odd, sharp onion-like odors, but Kate took her meals out, mainly at the hotel.

The first evening after the girl had returned to the St. Charles, Hearn read The Kid excerpts from one of his favorite books and mulled over the affair at the Circus Grounds. The little man, making no reference to the bullet wound in his guest's shoulder, told him Cully had gone complaining to the authorities.

From the way Hearn spoke, Billy was certain

that Kate had not told him who he, The Kid actually was.

"We received a report at the office this afternoon that someone, perhaps a private detective from out of town, was raising hob at Central Police Headquarters about the way he'd been roughed-up by toughs at the circus—but he didn't say anything, so far as I could discover, about seeking anyone in particular." Hearn's china, darning-egg of an eye inspected The Kid, as Billy lay stretched out upon the bed with his tightly-bandaged shoulder.

"And you're afraid that he'll find out this bucko was you?"

"No. You're the one who should be apprehensive. You know that fellow could make enough inquiries to come up with something on you." Hearn's nose perked out against the fading Louisiana evening.

A flock of birds, like a puff of distant, dissolving smoke, whirled and lengthened into a looping line, for a moment, as they arched over the darkening riverside, arriving in their flight from the North.

The Kid had read in Hearn's paper that there was some snow up in New England. He felt, for an instant, like rolling out, then and there, and moving on to El Paso. El Paso—the very name was a sound, now haunting him. He should be sending Angel another wire, telling her that he'd be there soon, *muy pronto*.

. . . "I said, you're like the fellow in the old Roman legend, who carried a fox in his cloak, and wouldn't flinch when it tore his innards to bits." Hearn had been speaking to him—but The Kid just came back to himself. "A Spartan," Hearn's dusky, birdlike profile, dipped as he bent to light his gurgling, odorous pipe, like a road-runner pecking at grass hoppers. The newspaperman's tobacco smelled worse than wet buffalo chips. "That fellow at the circus, he could be your fox."

"Could be, but he ain't gonna do no bitin'." Billy turned to ease his back. "You saw to it that he didn't get near me, and I sure owe you a hat for that," he grunted. "Don't think I'd be able to find you one outside of usin' a small tent, though."

"It was the very least I could do," Hearn paused and blew out a puff of smoke. "I couldn't allow an obviously cheap blackguard to get at you. It was also worth six months pay to behold you on that black nightmare—what I could make out. You were a veritable Centaur in action. I'd heard Westerners could really ride, but you did more."

"Yeah, busted my back open."

"No. You were a poem in action. Man against wild Nature. It was . . ." puff-puff-gurgle, "it was a recreation of some wild Gothic horseman of ancient times. A Genghis Khan warrior come to life." The dusky, little Shadow in the thinning patch of purple, that was the window, wagged its head.

"You sure can throw words . . . throw and brand 'em." Billy reached over and shoved the coal-oil lamp forward on the bedside table.

Hearn lit the lamp. It was completely dark outside. Off in the distance came the throaty whistling calls of the boats coming in to the levee docks. A wind, springing up with the evening, carried damp, spongy odors of river and swamp. The Kid turned away from the breeze pouring through the windows. He had money now, and tomorrow or the next, he'd be on his way. And Kate? Well—she'd have to take care of herself.

"Speakin' of poems, reach my coat there and you'll find a couple. Lady I met North wrote 'em," he told Hearn. "Look 'em over. Maybe, as you're th' word-herder, you'll tell me what they're about."

Hearn read both. He fiddled with the slips, re-reading them. "Something here, but the rhyme is faulty . . . reminiscent of Japanese Haiku." He nibbled the ends of his scrawny mustache and sucked dubiously on his odorous pipe. His eye protruded with doubt. "Pretty confused stuff. Whoever did these had best stick to baking pies or mending pantaloons."

Hearn replaced them in The Kid's coat, and picked up the book he'd been reading aloud—a French rouser about love among the black natives of North Africa. "The Romance of a Spain," by somebody named Loti. It was all in French, but Hearn read it right along in English with his Irish brogue.

As the book's hero, in brass buttons and fancy red hat, was camping out in the shade of a palm tree with a frizzly headed heroine, Billy drifted off to sleep and never did find out how it finished.

The following night when Hearn arrived back from the office, wearing a small straw hat that looked like a caved flower pot, Kate and The Kid were so out-of-sorts with each other as to be barely speaking.

The argument was always the same—Billy should have to stay put for a week or two, until he was really patched up. And then? Why, Kate would go to Texas with him. She'd travel with him, even though he told her, over and over, politely, very politely—and finally mighty unpolitely that he was making the trip alone!

He was a *cobarde*, and he knew but he couldn't really hurt her. And he could see that it would hurt—if he came right out and told her—told her that Esmeralda and he—that Esmeralda was the only one for him. So it was *mañana*. He kept putting it off, forgetting that *mañana* down at Fort Sumner had damned near killed him—for good.

Mañana of the third day following the circus came, and he did the only thing possible. Rising with the thick, grey, river mist of earliest New Orleans' dawn, he dressed and shaved before Hearn opened his pop eye. He had to get moving, before Kate came clipping up the stairs like a blonde dust-devil.

He shook the newsman completely awake, and stuck a hundred dollar bill in Hearn's shoe—payment for that hat, and then some. The little man opened his eyes, staring up like a ruffled pack-rat. "Whaat . . . ?"

"Shovin' off. *Gracias*, *mucho gracias* for your hospitality. I got to get on over to El Paso . . . can't wait even a day longer."

"You aren't going to notify Miss Castle?" Hearn rubbed his beaky nose.

"No. She agreed, about, anyways, to let me take care of my own affairs."

"Well," Hearn stuck out a thin hand, "you must have a most exceptional prize at the end of your rainbow, to leave such a golden girl." His nose twitched mournfully.

Billy left without more talk. Hearn could be right, as Hearn thought he was. How come all Irishmen were so damned sure of themselves? That was the way it was with Paddy Coghlan, Pat Garrett, Boss Croker, and this likeable, little one-eyed maverick.

The Kid was across the Mississippi on the Texas and Pacific passenger by lunch-time, rocketing along the swampy, green tidelands of

Louisiana, nearing vast Lake Charles before supper.

The six-coach train carried an antiquated dining car. He was finishing a passable meal there when the Gulf Coast dark rolled in like a shadow of Hearn's great Blue Ghost.

Cotton and sugar planters held forth in the coaches but Billy bedded down as soon as the berths were made up. He wondered, as he lay listening to the clattering of wheels over the rushing, dark, roadbed, if Kate had thrown a wingding.

Hearn would see she got on her way to Wyoming or Boston, whichever she wanted. She'd travel money, he knew. He should worry about her, but he'd not asked her to come poking after him. She was a big girl, and could take care of herself.

All next day, The Kid watched distance stretch itself out, transforming the green velvet of the Gulf Coast, with its strings of white, lumpish pelicans and grey-green reaches of live-oak to rolling, broad central Texas plains, thick with pin-oak and threaded along the tracks with weathered, wooden towns. The space he'd been longing for was starting to grow.

They crossed the Pecos, fifty miles east of Fort Stockton sometime in the night. Although The Kid was dozing, the name of Pecos, blurted out by some drunken passenger or loud-mouthed porter, came pealing to him through the dark, like the bells at Las Luz—and he rolled it over and over on his tongue, until it was lost in slumber.

Van Horn, the old Van Horn Wells, a slow-moving cattle and livestock town, deep in the Panhandle, was the stopping point of the railroad. This was as far as present Texas and Pacific tracks ran. The train reached it at nine in the morning.

The place was typical of track-end towns. Though rails were being laid westward, to within twenty miles of the river, at Sierra Blanca, the hook-up wasn't expected before the first of the year—according to a one-armed baggage man at Van Horn's canvas and wood station.

It was now just over one hundred miles north-westward to El Paso. Two stages ran there every day. El Paso, the one-winged baggage-smasher said "was plumb bustin' its britches." At least two other rail lines were turning that border town into a booming city. The Southern Pacific had arrived at El Paso in May and the Santa Fe in July.

So, the spiderweb was still spinning away, tying up the whole U.S.A. with steel ribbon, marked "civilization." Next it could be telyfuns and those smoke-spewing Elevateds. But he and Angel would turn their backs on all such, after his lawyering was over, if she wished. They'd go far enough away and live like real people—not penned-up sheep.

The T.P. tracks made a looping swing to the west of Van Horn, where several switches and good-sized engine shops hulked among a scattering of old, dusty adobes. Off on all sides, the vast reaches of the sub-desert ranged out to the misty-purple haze of the Pecos peaks. Here the stake line picked up passengers.

At last there was enough space to satisfy The Kid, as he stood alone in the cool morning, valise in hand, waiting for the stage to El Paso.

Due at ten o'clock, the stage wheeled in from Austin in a shapeless, arid cloud before the hour was half over. The dust-streaked coach was packed to the windows with ranchers, alfalfa farmers, as well as a bartender and two Sisters of Charity. The latter sat facing forward in black habits and little, round, black straw bonnets, tied under their chins.

After the coach rocked its way up Three Mile Mountain, gaining the crumbling backbone of the Carrizo Range, the two Sisters dozed off, and a wide-faced Mexican farmer slyly produced a tattered deck of cards. The Kid and the sorrowful-looking bartender, who was headed for Socorro, sixteen miles below El Paso, attempted a bob-tailed version of Monte a'top the bartender's small, telescope bag.

Billy, in a completely jovial mood, allowed the

bunch to take ten dollars from him by the time the coach made its noon halt at the rambling village of Sierra Blanca. The way he felt, he could have tossed his hat out the window.

When the Sisters opened their placid gaze upon the sights of the carnal world, all gambling came to a halt, until—full of chili and tortillas—they slumbered again.

"Now! This is the way we play th' game up in th' Territory," Billy grinned and settled down to earnest manipulation of the filthy pasteboards, winking at the ranchers and the rest of the male passengers.

The farmer shrugged, while the melancholy bartender shrewdly tugged away at his black ram's-horn mustache. Shortly all movement ceased, except hands and eyes. When darkness washed in over the mountains and the sleepy Sisters again awoke, Billy was richer by over fifty dollars. Enforced travel hadn't dulled his skills.

"Yu orta stop and give th' boys lessons," the bartender grunted, true sorrow touching his features as he got off at Socorro.

They halted for their last change of horses at Ysleta, ten miles below El Paso. The rough, dry wastelands were back beyond the mountain ramparts of the Quitman Range. All was moonlight and wide sweeping roadway.

Billy and the Sisters stood at the open doorway

of an ancient adobe tavern, waiting for the new team to be harnessed. The remaining passengers, half-asleep on their feet from the battering ride of more than one-hundred miles, huddled in a knot. Billy wasn't sure but what he might not vote for that spiderweb of steel, after all. Progress had some points, mainly soft ones.

Hesitant breezes, drifting from the direction of the nearby Rio Grande, brought with them odors of river gravel, willows, curing hay and dying roses. Summer was going, more slowly here, but surely going.

"*Señor, perdonar*—you have been most fortunate?" The heftier of the two Sisters fingered her plain rosary and smiled shyly at The Kid.

"*Si! Mucho*. I'm a most fortunate *compañero*, in some ways."

"Our Mission is much in need of a new altar cloth, and other things, *Señor*. I thought, perhaps . . ." she paused, while the smaller Sister edged closer to give her support. "Perhaps, you might see fit to share your good fortunes, just a bit?"

"*Si*." Billy peeled off two fifties from his roll. "Why not? And perhaps you might say a *diminuto oración*, when you find time for the sorrowing of the world."

"We shall, and most reverently, with all devout and sorrowful grace, your Honor," the smaller Sister murmured, "and perhaps we could light a candle and say a rosary for a young girl fatally injured, not a hundred paces from here in Ysleta, a few weeks past."

River winds coming out of Old Mexico, just across the dark shallows, blew through the unseen willow thickets, rustling the fading leaves. It had a mighty lonesome sound. Billy gladly mounted the coach for the last leg of the trip.

The stage rolled down El Paso's Overland Street shortly after midnight, crossing half a dozen empty lanes and side-roads, and pulled up at the State Office on the corner of Overland and El Paso streets. The town might be rowdy by day, but it seemed peaceful as a drowsing sheep-camp to Billy. Coney or Bowery could show the so-called "Wild West" aces.

After the Sisters left The Kid, with affectionate smiles, Billy walked over two blocks and took a small room at the Central Hotel.

He pulled off his coat, hung it on a nail on the back of the door and sank down gratefully upon the white, iron bedstead. Taking out the black notebook, he ran his eyes over those names. Soon! *Prontamente*! He lifted the bedding at the foot of the bedstead and cached the book, lowering the blankets again.

After washing and ripping up an old shirt from the valise, he rebandaged his shoulder as well as he could. It was looking pretty good, but no use taking chances. He stuck the Colt under his pillow, shucked his pants and gaiters, and crawled into the creaking bed, aching in every toe and finger.

As he slowly relaxed and rolled over to blow out the lamp on the night-stand, he promised himself Angel would be in his arms come morning. He wondered if she realized he was this close. He could have telegraphed—but he'd surprise her. He tried to picture her face, but couldn't, though he could still see her riding away that day, that last day, at the Devil's Ribs.

He was filled with a hollow feeling. It had been long.

Almost before his eyes closed, all those dark haunts he'd forced away for weeks, all those terrors of the night came swirling about. And he was—alone under the deathly light of the New Mexico moon, with hazy figures of death stalking him. But the gun in his fist was no phantom. It belched fire a yard-long with each thumbing back of the hammer. It kicked like that Circus Bronc while, one by one, those grisly beings fell like bottles in a Coney Island shooting gallery.

"Take it you devils!" Crack! Boom! "Take it— keep off my trail . . ." And they fell, wrapped in blood, shattered, with clothing a'fire and all smoldering from the red-hot slugs. One by one they went down—Garrett, his long legs grasshopper-kicking as he hit the frost-white ground—Bob Ollinger—his face a gaping hole of bloody meat, Joe Grant, Sheriff Brady, Tafala, Jesse Evans, Bullhead, The Ring Chief, The Plumber, Boss Croker, Uncle John Chisum—men he'd killed or who needed killing—and the women—Celsa, Kate, and Esmeralda. They plucked skirts away from the blood-soaked earth, edging nearer, with eyes as red as she-lobos. He could see that they hungered for his death too—all of them. Esmeralda, Celsa, and Kate, all of them.

"Back! Get back. I won't run another yard—from any of you. *Apoyar lupino mujers!*" He fired into the ground in front of the women, just one shot to drive them away. But the bullet rebounded, ricocheted, the same way the ball had killed Long Bell back at Garrett's jail. It took Esmeralda full in the breast. She fell back, calm, placid face turned to the cold, death-pale sky.

And—he reared up—in bed, sopping with sweat and slowly sank back to taste the black nightmare on his tongue. Only bad dreams. He'd had them before, and probably would again—but only dreams—not real. It couldn't have been real.

For a while he lay shaking, attempting to get his thoughts in order. Tomorrow he'd go to that lawyer, and send word to Esmeralda. Then they'd visit some quiet spot—maybe on the outskirts of town, and make plans. He had money. Enough to get his lawyering under way. And after that, well, real freedom. It would be pure freedom, even if he had to do a year or so in the Pen. He'd not deny that it could happen. Men had been killed in those troubles in Lincoln County. But all he'd killed had been shot in fair fights. No one could honestly get around that. Not—if they were sworn to tell the truth, for a change.

Esmeralda would wait, if he had to do that stretch. She'd wait, he knew, like any other woman would wait. Later perhaps, a ranch. It was all he knew—cows and rangeland. And if old Uncle John Chisum and that skunk Coghlan could make a go of it on their range, why he could do the same with his.

39 Silver Harp

—Came a knocking on the door. For a spell, he felt the sound to be part of another cob-webby, half-dream—where he rode along the green bosk of a river-fed valley, with a companion, and the sound he heard was the sound of their horses' hooves. He thought it was Esmeralda upon the black horse, but the other rider kept to the rear of his own mount. Sungleam filled his eyes, wrapping him with hazy light-headed feelings. The sound grew louder—he tried but it wasn't possible, somehow, to get a look at the other rider. The knocking wouldn't let him—that and the light in his eyes. Then he was awake in his hotel bedroom.

"All right! All right, dammit!" he mumbled. With gun in hand, he crossed the bare plank floor and unlocked the door.

It was Kate.

"Kate!" Billy forgot himself and swore. "Hell! What is this? You're damned-well supposed to be in New Orleans—or . . ."

"Anywhere but here," she completed his grumbled phrase, moving past him into the hotel room. "Shut the door, darling." She was all in blue, even her perky chip-hat. Her traveling outfit, blue as her eyes, consisted of a wide, sweeping skirt, and a tight shell-jacket that swelled over her ample young breasts. Her face seemed drawn, tired, yet she still had that same wide, dazzling red-lipped smile. "How is your shoulder? I've worried so. Are you better?" She placed a small, brown grip on the bare floor.

"Well, yeah . . . about." He tossed the weapon onto the rumpled bed, and retreated into his pants. He tucked in his shirt-tail and watched her unbutton her jacket. So far she hadn't spoken another word, acting as if she waited for his temper to cool down.

"Kate!" He couldn't keep still. "This is down-right loco. I'm sorry, certain sorry, runnin' out on you, like I did. But I told you I had business here. Private!" He pulled on his gaiters. "And I got to take care of it right now—this mornin'."

"Billy." Her eyes were large now with something other than excitement. "Billy, you don't have to go anywhere. We're here now . . . just the two of us. You don't need anyone, but me—you're not good for anyone but a person like me. I know you . . . understand you."

"I don't know about that. How'd you get here?" His ire was fading as his anxiety grew to get to his Angel. "You couldn't a' caught th' stage . . . not due in yet." He buttoned his shirt, tied his thin, black cravat, and pulled on his coat. He'd catch a shave on the way up to that lawyer's office.

"I took another line, a rickety old thing, but fast. It ran out of New Orleans to connect with the Southern Pacific above here. And I came down on the Santa Fe this morning from Las Cruces." She smiled. "I'd travel farther than that to keep you from more foolishness. You see, I don't need escorts or *dueñas*. I can take care of myself very well." She turned her back to him, and worked away at a hook on her dress. "There!" It slid down in a perfumed heap.

"Kate!" Billy made a dive to stop her, but she'd peeled out of her slip and corset, and stood in rosy, near-nakedness. "Kate, *deternese*! Stop! Cut th' damned craziness! I told you I had to go—right now." He tugged out his watch. It was near on nine. "Now, you get yourself dressed. What if someone comes up here?"

"Why, we'll tell them we're married." She smiled that radiantly-red, dangerous smile, sitting on the bed in her high-buttoned shoes. Before The Kid could open his mouth, again, the girl slipped out of her long, lace-trimmed drawers, and lay back—completely nude.

"Billy." She raised up on one curved elbow, ripe, full young curves rippling with the movement. "Billy, stay here . . . I'm so tired . . . of traveling . . . following after you—for so long. Don't go. Stay here with me."

Billy reached over, picked up his six-shooter and jammed it into his holster. He was

408

fighting, and fighting mighty hard, to keep from accepting—all she was offering. He'd wanted this blonde filly ever since that night back at Castle Ranch. It had almost happened, again, back in New Orleans, the day she showed up— but now she was here. And right under his hand.

"Kate, I can't. *Infierno*! I told you." He turned away from that bed, shutting away the sight of that shamelessly desiring and desirable, golden girl.

Then—he turned back, suddenly kneeling at the side of the bed, pulling her to him. "Kate, things just didn't break right for us." He kissed her soft, red mouth hard—hard and hot, feeling her fingers on his neck, while his hands touched—roved and clasped—for a moment.

He struggled up and rolling her over, landing a stinging, walloping whack on her bare, velvety behind. "Won't work! Gotta go! Y'need your rest. There's th' bed—but it's *ninguno* for us. Lock up after me."

As he shut the door behind him, a water pitcher, or a lamp, smashed with a shattering thud against the woodwork.

"Billy, damn you! She'll never have you," came Kate's strident voice.

She'd known more than he thought she did!

The Kid hurried through the hall and down the hotel stairs. Outside, he saw an El Paso livened-up by day. Streets were swarming with railroad men, cowboys, traders, Mexicans and plain townfolk, all going about their business in the cool, bright November morning.

He passed half-a-dozen saloons and honky-tonks, already booming full-tilt at this early hour. One of them, Dowell's, was just across the corner from the two-story, brick office building that housed the law firm of Ortiz and Lujon.

He stepped into the crowded barroom to get a glass of whiskey, a mighty rare thing with him. He felt he needed something strong after what had happened at the hotel—and before seeing Esmeralda.

As he worked the drink down—he'd never picked up a taste for the stuff—he heard a loud voice at the end of the room, blustering above the regular bar-buzz—Cully! He couldn't mistake that sidewinder's drawl.

Why hadn't Kate told him the skunk was in town? Maybe she didn't know and the cuss had followed her again, like a judas goat.

Turning casually, he glanced down the mahogany sheen of the bar at the man from Hole In The Wall, where he stood arguing with a couple of railroad men and a rancher. Cully had on the same hand-me-down, green suit he'd worn in New Orleans.

Put him in an evening suit with a plug-hat, thought The Kid, and he'd still look like what he was—a brush-poppin' rattlesnake!

Billy waited, until the group swung back to the bar for another round, before walking slowly back out the door. He didn't want trouble, not now. But he was ready, with his coat unbuttoned.

There was nobody or any commotion behind, so he went on across the littered, dirty street toward the lawyers. No time now for that shave.

Ortiz and Lujon's offices were empty except for a wizened Spanish-American, who sat hunched on a stool over a high desk, under a long-faced, loudly ticking clock. He scratched away with a creaking pen at some legal-looking papers.

Billy had to speak twice before the old man lifted his head from the document to peer nearsightedly at The Kid.

"Said my name was Roberts, W. R. Roberts. I was probably expected." The Kid raised his voice as the clerk stared at him—deaf as well as half blind. "Roberts—I got a case to talk over with *Señor* Ortiz." Now, why was the old man wiping his faded eyes with that bandana? Close eye work?

"*Señor*." The clerk's voice was as creaking as his pen-point. "*Señor*, what can I say? *Señor* Ortiz is gone from the city—but perhaps . . ." He looked dimly at a door, leading into an inner office.

Billy heard someone stir beyond that door. In the silence, the clock ticked, and ticked. He stood looking out the smudged, small-paned window toward the saloon, in an effort to keep an eye on Cully. A good many people were on the wooden sidewalks, and hacks and horsemen moved along the dusty street. But no one he recognized came out of Dowell's.

"*Señor*?" A voice, oddly familiar, heard somewhere before, sometime, made him spin around. For a moment he didn't recognize the thin, dark, young man in the plain business suit. Suddenly, it came back—that night of the *bailé* at Luna's. Esmeralda's brother, Francisco Sandoval, the young *findingo* who'd been dressed-to-the-nines in that *petimetre*, spangled costume.

"*Señor*—Kid," Sandoval spoke quietly, "come back to the office." He led the way, pulling the door partly closed behind them. "Sit down, *Señor*." His face was an expressionless mask.

Billy took the round-backed chair, facing the door, and sat with a thumb hooked on the top button of his coat. Things were starting to smell like trouble. What was all the mystery? And where were those lawyers? Her brother wasn't a part of the firm.

"I had waited for you." The young man rubbed his hands together, absently. Sitting down at the room's flat-top desk, he pulled open a side-drawer, took an object from it. "We, rather I, have been waiting for you for the past weeks . . . since your last wire." He placed the small object from the drawer on the paper-littered surface in front of Billy.

"What's this?" The Kid picked it up with his left hand, keeping his gun hand ready. "Where's Esmeralda? Is she coming down here, or are you gonna try to keep us apart?" He saw the metallic piece in his hand was a comb. The same harp-shaped, silver comb, or mighty-like the one she'd worn in her dark hair. The one she'd fixed her hair up with—back in the cave at the Devil's Ribs. The day they parted.

Sandoval sat with head bowed on his chest, watching The Kid with large dark eyes, his face expressionless. "*Señor* Billy, no one on this earth would keep you apart. You were all she spoke of, until, even I, was an *aliado*, a friend." He sighed. The mask faded and The Kid saw a look of compassion upon Sandoval's aristocratic, olive-tinged features. "Poor friend . . . no. Esmeralda will not be here . . . *jamás*!"

It was so still, so quiet, Billy could hear the clock in the outer office, beyond the half-shut door, ticking, ticking away. He was puzzled, as well as fearful. What was going on? Where was his Angel?

In a stolid daze, Billy heard of her death.

She'd waited for weeks, young Sandoval said, after returning to El Paso—waited to hear from The Kid. And the day his wire finally arrived, she'd taken the black horse, Angel, from the

413

Sandoval stables in celebration, riding it out Montave Street toward the Rio Grande. Reaching the Rio Grande, she'd taken the river road and headed south down the valley.

"She was so happy, *Señor*, that even I felt *contento*," Sandoval whispered. "She was light-hearted and so gay, she must have ridden too far. They told us she'd given the horse a drink in the Rio, and had been returning up the main road from the river bank when she thoughtlessly rode through some willows." He paused and rubbed his face. "Those willows slashed her horse's flank . . . and the wound, barely healed, was re-opened. That animal, you know, normally so intelligent, so gentle—bolted from pain. Esmeralda . . . she tried . . . to hold the mount down, the people said, but she was thrown just outside the little town there—Ysleta."

"Th' horse," Billy heard himself stupidly asking. "What happened to th' horse?" The piece of metal in his hand was hot as fire, cold as ice.

"The horse broke its right leg, and had to be destroyed. I, myself, shot it that afternoon. Esmeralda, she remained in a swoon, dying just at nightfall. We buried her . . . out at our plot in Concordia Cemetery. It is most beautiful, most restful, with its pines. One can stand there and see the mountains—the Franklins . . . holding their proud heads high to the north, like . . ." Sandoval's voice broke apart and he

414

dropped his face into the protection of his palms.

"*Gracias*," Billy got up and went to the door. He opened his coat and placed the little silver comb in his shirt pocket. "*Gracias*, Don Miguel . . . I'll be goin' on."

"You still intend to take up your affair with the law, clearing your indictments . . . and warrants?" Sandoval straightened in his chair. "She spoke much of this."

"Maybe, later." Billy stood with hand on the door-knob, listening to that clock. How many times since—how many times had it ticked—and would tick, and never would she wait for him? "*Nunca, jamás*." He went out the door, out of the office, and away from clocks.

On the street, the continuous bustle of a rowdy El Paso, doing its best to match the hurly-burly of the eastern cities, rang in his ears—filled with horse-clatter, people shouting, arguing and yelling with laughter.

People still laughed. And over on the next street some wild-man was shooting holes in the air.

He hesitated, aimlessly staring at nothing, until he began to move, blindly, across the street, heading for the river. At the end of the first block, he was passing a group of saloons, wide-open gaming parlors and bawdy houses, when someone called his name—once. The real name—jarred him loose from his daze.

Jolted, he heard someone pounding down the

wooden sidewalk. Turning, he saw a man, pistol in hand, coming on the dead run—Cully!

The crowd, mainly Mexican, split apart, ducking into doorways. The Kid didn't have time to see who called. It wasn't a man—he thought. As he faced the approaching sidewinder, Cully fired on the run, his six-gun booming out at The Kid. The bullet smashed through a saloon sign over Billy's head, spraying splinters.

He jumped sideways, pulling at his Colt—but it hung up on his coat.

Cully's second shot took The Kid in the chest, knocking him to his knees onto the dusty planks. Half-stunned and coughing, he rolled over and yanking the gun free—shot the running man—dead center!

Billy staggered to his feet, ripping at his shirt to feel his chest. Cully's shot had punched a big, circular dent in the silver harp—and a terrific welt on his hide. But there was no bullet wound.

The street was bare of humans as Billy stalked, Colt in hand, toward the downed assassin. Cully was still breathing, but done for. His wolf-slit of a mouth opened and closed as he lay on his back in the muck and horse-apples of the gutter.

"What?" Billy knelt at the dying man's side—the way Cully had hunkered down by Bullhead Jackson, when that gunman cashed-in at the Hole. "What?"

". . . too bad . . . tried my . . . damndest . . .

too much luck, you got. Thought you was funny sendin' that card to O'Day . . . follered you to that town . . . and knew who you was then—Kid. That Jackson you plugged . . . he spilled. So went on down to Castle's. Yeah—did a good job cuttin' trail fer that Santa Fe gang." The man raised his head, shuddering, blood pouring from his mouth—choking on bile and hate. "You'll still git yours . . . th' other'll see ya in Hell." He fell back dead.

40   La Mesaje

Billy jogged up an alley, between two gambling saloons, and emerged onto Missouri Street. There was no pursuit, as at Santa Fe. A day ago, he would have stood his ground and proven self-defense, but now he didn't care.

He hailed an open hack, and gave orders to be taken out to the cemetery on Almangordo. There was some shouting behind, and the sound of horses running on the other street, but no one looked at him twice. Several times there came the barking reports of pistol shots from various parts of the town.

"Them railroad mens celebrate another stretch of track done," the roly-poly Mexican hackie grumbled. "Them cowboys they help—always ready to shoot the guns." He sighed and glumly nibbled a red pepper. Clearly he didn't favor railroads and progress.

The Kid, still dazed by his Angel's death—and the recent battle with Cully—sat unmoving in the back, keeping an eye out for pursuit. But the whooping, shooting railroaders and cattlemen seemed to have completely covered his tracks.

The hack pulled up at the tree-enclosed cemetery, and the driver hitched his fat bay mare to a picket of the fence. An enormous cottonwood, completely barren of foliage, cast a faint mass of cross-hatched shade across much of the sandy soil and sparse grass. The day, cool at the start, was now warm and faintly humid. It felt like a change in the weather.

Esmeralda's grave was midway into the enclosure, in a clump of pine. For an instant he thought of another grove, far back, up the trail—where Jesse Evans tried his hand at cutting him down—by Ring orders. But Jesse was the one lying up there in an unmarked grave. And here she lay, the sweetest, most loving human he'd ever known—as far from him as Jesse—gone forever.

He stood, hat in hand, reading her monument, while a spotted ground-squirrel poked its head around the grey stone to inspect him.

"Esmeralda Constancia Sandoval
"Born May 3, 1863
"Died Nov 2, 1881
"Rest Among the Angels"

. . . "For you surely, certain was one," he said, looking at the patch of sandy earth that shut away love.

While he stood there, a grey bird, hopping about the pine boughs, broke into wonderful song. It was like a hymn—a service for his Angel. The liquid notes chimed and rang like heavenly harping, at last dying away as the mocking bird flitted into the cottonwoods.

It was like Hearn had said, "Kismet." Everything was herded and branded in Heaven before it happened.

Rousing the drowsy hack-man, he rode back into town, passing a few, fine, large houses, and one or two actually elegant, two-story wooden frame homes with their white fences, but most of El Paso was still plain, flat adobe.

Probably one of those fancy, tree-bordered places, with its black iron fences was Esmeralda's home, but he didn't want to know—not now.

He piled from the hack, and paying off the driver stood on the wooden sidewalk in front of a hardware store. The red-and-white-striped awning kept off the sun, and it seemed good to just watch a small knot of men, near the clutter of brooms and shovels on the walk, going over the fine points of a pair of clean-limbed, fast-looking horses tied to a nearby hitch-rail.

Billy stepped close enough to hear their talk. The small, quarter-horses had been raced the day before by their owners. One was absent, but the other—a burly butcher, with shaggy eyebrows and hairy arms, stood running a thick hand over the animals' legs and bragging.

Billy hiked up his shoulder holster, on the sly, and was moving off toward the hotel, when he heard the butcher begin to bemoan bad luck at cards. It seemed he'd been off across the river, in Juarez, the previous night, and those Mexican gamblers had left him little but the gold in his teeth.

"I could be in the market for a horse, or two. Know of any for sale?" The Kid inquired of the bunch.

"Well, stranger," the butcher answered, rolling ox-like eyes at him, straightening straw cuffs. "You just might be able to buy th' pair. Great little speeders. That 'un's mine and probably th' best. I got my wings clipped last night at Monte, and I need *araño* enough to go back tonight and take some revenge."

"Ain't needin' t'git out o' town on a fast hoss?" One of the group, a small, ferret-faced man, with barber equipment sticking from his pockets, smirked. "Hear somebody let daylight inter a hard-case over on th' next street this mornin'."

"Hell, when ain't someone gettin' it these days? You wait until Marshal Stoudenmire gets back from out'n th' bresh. Thing'll simmer down then, or Hell will pop sure," growled the big butcher. "Right stranger?"

"Yeah, *mucho emoción* hereabouts," Billy replied, wincing as the big man clapped him on the shoulder.

"May be back." The Kid excused himself and walked down the street toward the Central Hotel. While looking over the horses, he'd formed a decision. That lobo Cully had mentioned the Ring—and that other one! Where was he? What was he up to, right now? The Kid was all done riding the spook-end of a man-hunt. Angel was gone, and there was no hope for him there— *decisivo*! He'd just about give his neck to have her, but she was gone, and with her any positive desire to clear his name for the present—that could come later—but not with that damned Ring book!

If he used that damning book in a court of law, Pat Garrett, Paddy Coghlan, Rynerson, and the rest of that crook-legged crew might go up—but so would Kate's father, and uncle, and God knew who else. He'd have to see it was returned now— as simple as that. And after all the blood, and worry of matching wits and laying his life on the line with that murderous gang. After a doubled and redoubled trail across the whole damned country, he'd have to give it up if he wanted to keep Kate. Before it hadn't mattered enough— but now?

Those crossed and recrossed trails hadn't been traveled for naught, for Kate could still be his. Hadn't she told him so? And didn't those rebus- like jingles of that old maid lady in Amherst mean just about that?

"Hope fell distressed"—that was Esmeralda, his best hope—and she was fallen and gone forever.

"Fate at last, compressed the best"—that could only mean best was last. And the last, the remaining one, was Kate!

He still didn't think she was best, he couldn't really believe that, but Esmeralda was gone and Kate was left. And The Kid was a realist, though he'd never heard the word.

Kate was his last hope, all right. As he climbed the stairs of the Central Hotel, all thought of Esmeralda was, somehow, crowded from his mind by a wild desire to see Kate—see her just as he'd left her. Maybe it had been Kate all along, *quien sabe*?

He rapped on the door, expecting a crash of glass, or the thump of an overturned wash-stand, some wild outburst, but it was quiet—only the racket of his knuckles on the door and his heart, pounding in his ears.

The door was unlocked. He cautiously pushed it open, hand on his gun. It was quiet, and empty.

The place was peaceful as a flapjack. The bed had been made. His valise sat neatly upon the dresser, and even the bits of the water pitcher had been swept up.

"Kate," he whispered, voice loud in the hushed silence. But there was no one. He felt as though he should peek under the bed-like an old maid. Looking at that bed, he pictured Kate sprawling out there in silken abandon, and burned.

The bed suddenly churned into his mind—with a difference. That book of the Ring! Morning had been so packed with Kate's wild, unexpected appearance that he'd walked from the room without the book. He'd stuck it under the mattress last night, never thinking that anyone, least of all Kate, would show up in the morning.

With the visit to the lawyers, word of Angel's death, Cully's shooting—all thought of the book had been completely banished—until now!

He dived for the bed, clawed for the book. It had been there. Its impression was still on the mattress, but it was gone!

He got to his feet. Perhaps it had fallen onto the floor, or the porter had picked it up.

Staring around the room, he, at last, noticed a folded bit of paper on his pillow—white blending with white. It was a message from Kate. He sat down on the rumpled bed and read:

"Billy—if you live to read this. I've already seen you shoot that Cully. I'm the one who called. I got right up and followed you to that lawyers' office, though you didn't see me, too much on your mind, I guess. When you came out, and I saw Cully with his gun, I shouted.

"If you'd loved me enough, things could have been different.

"I'd have helped you clear yourself. Back when you came to our ranch, I suspected you were The Kid. When we got a letter from Santa Fe, I knew

424

it for a certain fact. I steamed the letter open, then resealed it for my father. That was the letter you took that night.

"You see, I knew about this book from the letter, and that Daddy was implicated in Santa Fe matters, and I tried to get that letter back from you when we were alone together in the dark.

"When Cully showed up and bragged to me about the warrant he said he got from Santa Fe, I had to go along with his dirty scheme to try to keep him away from you. I think he got to our ranch house on the sly and read the letter you wrote me. I know he told the Santa Fe people you'd gone East.

"I think he bluffed being a law officer, and bribed the agent at the telegraph office in Rock Springs to read your message, finding out you'd gone to New Orleans. He insisted that he go and the Santa Fe men allowed him to go after you, though I'm not sure they knew he'd gun for you.

"I left two days after he did, having written Daddy a lie about going to stay with people we knew in New Orleans.

"I did all this to get that book back, before you were hurt or killed. When I came here to El Paso, it was for the same reason.

"I was going to tell you Cully was here, he came on the same train though I wouldn't talk to him or stay in the same coach, but I was so crazy mad I let you go, though I did try to hold you, the only way I knew.

"Now, I have the book, from where you'd hidden it. They'll have to let you go. And so do I. Kate."

41   The Other Trail

Billy sat with the note in his hand, rubbing the welt on his chest. So Kate had been the other one. She'd been the last link in the Ring, and the most dangerous to him. But, she was gone.

Locking the hotel-room door, he took out his pearl-handled .44 and cleaned it thoroughly with rags and a brush from his valise. Noticing his razor, he unlocked the door and borrowed a pitcher of water from the empty room across the hall. After washing and shaving, he packed up and went down to pay his bill. He couldn't stay in that room another minute.

An hour later, he'd shed his town duds and was outfitted in a fine pair of soft-leather, red-topped boots, rather like that Santa Fe Ring Man's. He'd admired those boots, if not the owner. The rest of his rig was just as satisfying—low-brimmed grey Stetson with a metal, Indian zig-zag band, a soft, blue, double-flapped Navy shirt with two rows of small pearl buttons and a stout pair of blue Levi's.

He set off the outfit with a buckskin "Ranger" vest. His gun and extra ammunition, as well as a Winchester '73, calibre .38-40 carbine with shells, were wrapped up in three good, army blankets and a slicker.

Carrying this equipment plus a pair of field glasses, a canteen and a small cooking kit, he made his way back over to the loungers on Missouri Street.

The papers for one horse were signed in the nearby meat market. He'd not be wanting two, after all. Billy took the butcher's little mount. He paid out eighty dollars for the horse, but didn't blink. He bought a pack-mule in a nearby corral for twenty dollars to tote his gear.

He'd have himself a nag, that despite its appearance, was hardy and long-winded. And besides, he was counting on making that money, and more back in a couple of races. The horse had the look of his old Dandy Dock, the best little race horse in the whole Southwest. His hand was still good with the pasteboards, and though he still had nigh on to a thousand, why if money ever got tight—he could go back to punching cows, somewhere.

Buying grain at the feed store on the corner, he stocked up on flour, slab bacon and coffee at the grocery across the street. All this he slung aboard the pack-mule. He stowed his blankets and Winchester, in its boot, on "Pat," for he'd silently christened the horse after Garrett. It was long-headed, with a speculative eye, whites showing at times—just like that damned long-legged baboon of a Mick, who'd never know how close he came to biting lead, or for that matter, pounding rocks.

Mounting up, without attempting to find Kate; she'd probably got out of town on a stage already; he rode past the brick and adobe saloons of Franklin Street. His route took him toward the northwest, where ragged, grey clouds were clabbering over the blue-streaked Franklin peaks.

He'd waved a farewell to the ox-faced butcher, while the shifty-eyed, little barber called to ask if he might not be lighting-a-shuck before the marshal got back. Billy had offered to take him up on the mule, betting him that he was wanted somewhere by the Rangers for throat-cutting.

That sort of joshing wouldn't go some places, but back in the Southwest it was all O.K. So even if he was leaving El Paso mighty down-in-the-mouth—pretty near heart-sick—he was still back home.

His last contact with the town of El Paso del Norte ended with the final glimpse of the hulking butcher, spindly barber and assorted hangers-on, watching him from the middle of the dusty street, their shadows running long and black in the westering sun.

He spurred up "Pat" and leading the mule at a lope, hit for the wide-open.

Late in the night, he rolled up in his blanket in the lee of a great rock, near the base of Ranger Peak—halfway to Las Cruces. The steady wind, gaining momentum, roared down from the north—roaring all the way from the bleak, red walls of the Hole—rushing and writhing, an invisible river of cold movement over the creaking, jerry-built ginger-bread of the weather-rotten Castle Ranch House—tugging the false-fronts of a half-thousand, one-street cow-towns, all the way from Rock Springs to the fire-faded adobes of bullet-scarred Lincoln.

The wind continued to grow and spread as it rushed in rippling waves past the crumbling foundations and bare white, flailing cottonwoods of Sumner—all the way down to the peaked hills where he lay.

It poured across him in dark, whistling billows, to flow onward over the nearby loops and curves, of the Rio Grande shallows. Somewhere to the south it would split and splinter from a mighty torrent of air into a hundred creeks and streams of breeze. Eventually defeated and digressing, its zephyrs would warm and wander away into hot motes of emptiness under the golden Mexican sunrise.

Billy drowsily pulled the blankets over his head, after a look at the pack-mule and the snuggly hobbled "Pat."

It was over—*complete!* Kate gone, and good luck to her. Maybe someday? Esmeralda gone— and never, any day! He realized, darkly, in the encompassing but forgiving night that his own actions had caused her death. That raid on Chisum's cattle placed the doom-brand on the black horse. It was that simple, no raid, no wounded animal. With the horse's wound, barely half-healed, Esmeralda rode off on a bombshell. It was *funesto*!

All was over. The wind whispered it, and deepest night agreed. *Sobre*! Over! He'd not now go north into New Mexico to seek out Celsa, or Old Juan, or Fega, or stop by the grave of poor Barlow, "Billy The Kid" under the sand of Port Sumner, according to the gospel of Ash Upson, as told by Garrett.

No! Once away—he'd stay away. No more lighted fuses.

Here it was the shank-end of 1881. In less than a month it would be 1882. He'd grown older with the year. As he drowsed over it, he wished to grow older—*mucho*! No longer to be a kid on the run. No more warring with the world. No more shooting at shadows. He'd been Billy The Kid, and The Texas Kid. What next? Maybe, something better.

South of the Rio there was plenty of country. No telyfuns. No horse-cars or Elevateds. Few railroads, and a lot fewer noisy, smoke-stained cities. Just wild and free land. And time to ride it—with cards to turn and races to run.

He rolled over again, pulling the blanket tighter. The wind was his trail. *Mañana* he'd follow the wind.

431

Center Point Large Print
600 Brooks Road / PO Box 1
Thorndike, ME 04986-0001 USA

(207) 568-3717

US & Canada:
1 800 929-9108
www.centerpointlargeprint.com